"YOU LOVE HIM, TOO, DON'T YOU?"

A tightness squeezed Jessalyn's chest, and tears stung her eyes. She was too soul-weary to lie. "It seems that I have loved him my entire life."

The tide washed against the rocks, again and then again. Emily ripped up a handful of marram grass, sending a tiny avalanche of pebbles splashing into the sea. "I am his wife, but you are his . . . I was going to say heart, but that's not it. His obsession, I suppose."

Jessalyn held herself still, afraid to move, afraid to speak.

Emily twisted around, and her face in the deepening twilight looked brittle as old parchment. "But he is my husband. Caerhays is mine."

Jessalyn's breath stopped in her throat. "I know . . . I know."

Emily's shoulders hunched, and she smothered her mouth with her knuckles. "Oh, *God*, I love him so. He is my night and my day." She pulled down her fists, tilting her face to the night sky. "And he—he is kind to me, but that is all."

Also by Penelope Williamson

KEEPER OF THE DREAM

Penelope Williamson

Once in a Blue Moon

A DELL BOOK

Published by
Dell Publishing
a division of
Bantam Doubleday Dell Publishing Group, Inc.
1540 Broadway
New York, New York 10036

ISBN 0-440-61412-0

Printed in the United States of America

This one is for my father . . .
Because you taught me that if I want to hold the
moon in my hands, all I have to do is reach for it.

PART ONE

1

The blast from the explosion slammed through the air. It rolled across bleak moorlands, bounced against black cliffs, and rumbled out to sea. For a hitch in time all was still again. Then the ground shuddered and heaved like an old man suppressing a cough.

The noise startled a pair of goats that had been eating a prickly dinner of hawthorn. They stood frozen a moment, ears perked, long beards twitching, before bolting up the cliff path. Their hooves sent a tiny avalanche of stones onto the head of the girl who stood motionless on the beach below.

Jessalyn Letty had been scavenging along the edge of the tide. A howling Cornish gale had lashed itself to death on the beach the night before, and the pickings should have been easy. If lucky, she would find something she could use, luckier still something to trade, and luckiest of all something to sell for good, hard coin.

She had been about to pick up a broken spar when at the sharp crack of sound she straightened and whirled, her hand to her mouth. The stones pelted her head, and she twisted around again. She looked up, shading her eyes from the glare of the afternoon sun. A pair of goats flashed their tails at her before disappearing over the lip of the cliff.

A silence fell over the beach. Even the gulls and the choughs had ceased their screeching. A thin column of smoke spiraled upward, barely noticeable against the pale blue of the sky. Jessalyn picked up her skirts and began to run, her bare feet digging troughs in the sticky sand.

She climbed the cliff path as fast and sure as the goats. But at the broken-down stile in the stone hedge she hesitated. It had been years since she'd ventured onto Caerhays land. Not since that summer a gamekeeper had pointed an old blunderbuss at her and threatened to shoot her for trespassing. "With that orange head o' yourn it'd be like shootin' a pumpkin off a post," he'd snarled, his lips peeling back over rotted teeth. "Jist like shootin' a pumpkin off a post. Splat!" He'd laughed, slapping the stock of the gun and sending Jessalyn pelting for home.

She had crawled back over the cliff hedge again the very next day, keeping a wary eye out for the odious gamekeeper and his ancient blunderbuss. Her heart had pounded in time with the beating waves below, but in excitement, not fear. She had been sure she would catch smugglers in the act of hauling brandy casks up the rocks or pirates burying chests full of gold in the sand, for the Trelawnys were notorious for their lawless, wicked ways. But all she'd found were weeds and stagnant ponds and an enormous old manor house crumbling into dust.

But that had been years ago, and the gamekeeper was long gone. The current earl was in London gambling and drinking himself to death, so they said. The house was still closed up; the mines were shut down. There should have been no thing or person to cause such an explosion on Caerhays land.

As Jessalyn clambered over the stile, her skirt caught on a blackthorn vine. She tried to work it loose, then gave an impatient tug. The muslin cloth came free with a loud rip, and she jumped off the stile onto a path choked with gorse. The ground was rough with broken stones that gouged her bare feet as she ran. The column of smoke had long since bled into the sky. The moors lay still and empty.

She topped a rise. In a narrow gill, thick with hawthorn and wind-tortured elms, stood a large brick tower that once housed the pump engine for a tin mine called Wheal Ruthe, long since played out. Tall gorse nearly concealed the arched entrance, but she could see white tendrils curling out the upper windows. An old mule track ran down to the abandoned mine, and Jessalyn took it on the fly.

Sucking in a deep breath and holding it, she plunged through a door choked in a thick white cloud, and . . .

It was like being slapped in the face with a hot, wet cloth. She cried out at the shock of it. And cried out again when a black specter loomed out of the boiling cloud, staggering toward her.

They smacked into each other, foreheads cracking together like a pair of cymbals. The specter fell backward, its head slamming hard on the stone-flagged floor, and Jessalyn, carried along by her momentum, ran right over it. Then she, too, skidded onto the floor, skinning her palms and knees, knocking the breath from her chest.

She knelt on all fours, hunched over, wheezing and gasping. The inside of the enginehouse was smothered with steam. It clogged her nose and throat, and for a moment she was sure she would suffocate. At last she sucked in a soggy breath of air, and then another. She craned her head and peered back through her outstretched arms to see the thing that she had trampled.

A young man lay sprawled on the floor, his arms flung out from his sides like a fallen crucifix. A dark angel cast out of heaven.

She crawled over to him. Pushing herself upright onto her knees, she bent over and patted his cheek. It was rough with beard stubble, yet the skin beneath was startlingly soft and warm. Touching him like that seemed too intimate a thing to be doing, so she picked up his hand and slapped it instead. He didn't stir. She slapped it again, harder.

The stranger's hand was much larger than hers, but lean, with long, scarred fingers and callused palms. Suddenly it seemed improper even to be holding his hand, and she returned it carefully to his side. She sat back on her heels unsure of what to do next.

In the blue books that she often borrowed from the circulating library at Penzance, the hero was always loosening the heroine's clothing when she fell into a swoon. But there was nothing for her to loosen; the stranger wore no collar or cravat, and his shirt was already opened at the neck. Moisture sheened the smooth tawny skin of his throat. As she watched, a drop trickled down to disappear into a light mat of dark hair and twisted white cloth. Jessalyn looked away, drawing in a deep breath. She licked her lips, tasting soot and sulfur.

The air was clammy and so hot. It was like being inside a teakettle as it simmered over a roaring fire. She pushed wet hair out of her face, knocking her bonnet askew. She struggled with the knot of ribbon beneath her chin, then yanked the suffocating hat off, her fingers tangling in its ragged ostrich plume that was now sadly drooping in the damp. She looked back down at the stranger's bare chest, at the place where the drop of water had disappeared. Muscles and sun-darkened skin jerked as he tried to suck in air.

He was having trouble breathing in the thick steam. Jessalyn wondered if she dared leave him to go for Dr. Humphrey. She heard a rustling behind her and jerked around, half expecting to see the doddering and bewigged physician materialize out of the steam. Nothing was there except for a tangled heap of metal and wood—what was left of whatever it was that had exploded. The pile of rubble shifted and settled again, emitting a hiss, as if it were something living that was now slowly dying. Red lumps of smoldering coal lay scattered nearby.

Coal, Jessalyn thought. Coal that was still burning, hot enough to set alight a candle . . . or a feather.

Once Polly Ungellis—the village fish jouster, who made

a bare living gutting pilchards and was prone to fits—had fainted in church, and the Reverend Mrs. Troutbeck had revived the potty old woman by burning a feather beneath her nose. The particular feather responsible for Polly's resuscitation had been part of the plumage of a chicken. But Jessalyn doubted the species of the bird mattered.

She looked down at the bonnet in her lap. It had come from a pawnshop in Penzance and had been in fashion, so Gram had said, the year Napoleon divorced Josephine. Old and shabby though it was, it was still her only hat, and its pride was a long, thick ostrich plume, dyed a primrose yellow, that curled across the front. Since its only other ornament was the frayed blue ribbon that banded the crown, the bonnet would be left sadly bereft without its feather.

Before selfishness could get the better of her, she ripped the plume out from beneath the ribbon trim. After pushing herself to her feet, she ran over and thrust the tip of the ostrich feather beneath a glowing piece of coal. There was a hiss and a sputter as it caught fire suddenly, flames shooting up the quill in a whoosh. Startled, she dropped the burning torch. It floated to the floor, trailing sparks and—

"What in bloody hell are you doing?"

She spun around. The stranger was half sitting up, leaning on one outstretched arm. With his dark hair falling over his forehead and his shirt pulled off one shoulder and gaping open at the throat, he looked more than ever like a fallen angel. His bare chest expanded and subsided with his heavy breathing. She knew she was staring at him stupidly, yet she couldn't seem to move or speak; she couldn't even manage a breath.

Then she felt a fierce heat on her leg.

She looked down and saw a flickering yellow tongue eating a hole in her periwinkle blue muslin skirt. She beat at it with her hands, smothering the flame. "Wait a moment, please," she said. "My skirt's on fire."

Suddenly the whole thing struck her as vastly amusing— here she was calmly announcing to a total stranger that she

was on fire while she frantically tried to put herself out—
and she laughed aloud. But when she heard the sound of
her own laughter, squeaking like a seldom-used pump handle, she cut herself off. She glanced up. The stranger was
staring at her as if he couldn't quite believe what he was
seeing. He groaned and hunched over, burying his face in
his hands.

She went to his side, kneeling in front of his spread
thighs. She tried to keep from laughing again, because he
didn't look like the sort of man who would share her
warped sense of the ridiculous.

"Do forgive me for trampling you like that," she said,
and in spite of her best intentions, a giggle escaped along
with the words. "To barge into a room unannounced is not
quite the thing, of course, but I thought the building was
on fire, and I could hardly leave you to burn to death—not
that I knew *you* were in here, of course, but it stood to
reason somebody was. . . . Are you all right?" Except for
a whitening of the hands pressed against his face he hadn't
moved or made a sound. "How do you feel?"

She began to wonder if the explosion might have damaged his eardrums. Leaning closer, she shouted, "Are you
having trouble hearing me? I said, how do you feel?"

His head jerked up, his eyes winced shut. "My hearing
was quite adequate, thank you, until you took it upon yourself to blast my eardrums." He lowered his face into his
hands again, cradling it as if it were a cracked eggshell.
"And I feel—since you insist upon a bloody report—like a
team of mules has been playing football with my head."

He looked oddly vulnerable, with his shoulders bowed
and his head bent, exposing the bare nape of his neck. His
fingers were thrust through wet dark brown hair. She
touched the back of his hand.

He flung his head up, and she recoiled as if stung. He
stared at her with eyes as black and deep as a mine pit.
There was something strange, something penetrating,

about his eyes; it seemed as he looked at her that he could see right through her, into her heart.

He made her uncomfortable, and she looked away. A silence stretched between them. The old soot-encrusted walls of the enginehouse dripped water. The pile of rubble hissed and settled.

"I was scavenging the beach at Crookneck Cove . . ." she said. She turned her gaze back to him. He was looking at her mouth with those fierce dark eyes. "When I heard this terrible noise," she stumbled on, acutely conscious of the movement of her own lips. "And then I saw the smoke; at least I thought it was smoke. . . ." Again she faltered. She sucked on her lower lip, then realized what she was doing and stopped. "So I came here to investigate and I saw smoke pouring out the windows. That is, it wasn't smoke, of course, but I thought it so at the time. . . ." She waved a hand. "I thought the place was afire."

"Indeed?" He looked at the smoldering remains of the ostrich plume that had once adorned her best and only hat. "And when you discovered it wasn't on fire, you decided to remedy the situation by setting it alight yourself?"

"You were having such trouble breathing, and I only thought to try to resuscitate you. I'll have you know I sacrificed a perfectly good hat on your behalf." Honesty compelled her to add, "Well, it was not precisely new, but it was still serviceable."

His lips curled down slightly at one corner. "Forgive me if I am not overcome with gratitude. But then I wouldn't have needed resuscitating in the first place if you hadn't laid me out cold with your thick head."

She caught the gasp of outrage in her throat. She had never met anyone like him before, so disdainful and ungallant, so blatantly arrogant. She wanted to say something clever and cutting that would put him in his place.

"It would have served you right if I had left you to suffocate to death," she said, which was neither clever nor cutting.

And certainly no match for him. He looked pointedly at the door. "Please," he said, "do not let me detain you further."

She pushed herself to her feet and whirled, heading for the door. It was not one of her better exits. Her heel caught on the hem of her skirt, and she barely kept herself from toppling forward like an axed pole.

His hand lashed out, grabbing her ankle. She tried to tug free, hopping on one foot. "Let . . . go . . . of me."

He let go. She teetered backward, flapped her arms, teetered forward. She stumbled a step, trying to regain her balance, and tripped over his boot as he started to come up. They slammed together like two skittles struck by a ball. She clutched at his shirt, and he fell back, taking her with him.

He lay perfectly still beneath her. Hip to hip, stomach pressing against stomach. One of her thighs wedged between his spread legs. Hot, moist steam drifted over them. She sucked in a deep breath, chest pushing against chest. They were so close her face hovered over his, their lips almost touching.

"Oh," she said.

His lips parted. She felt his breath leave his chest before it caressed her face. She felt the rumble of his voice before she heard the words. "Before this goes any further, hadn't we ought to be introduced?"

There were creases at the corners of his mouth that deepened when he moved his lips. "Uh . . ." she said.

He breathed. "I see. You are now trying to impress me, and someone has told you I prefer my women mysterious and monosyllabic."

There was a thick, rushing sound in her ears, and her head felt heavy and clogged up with the steam. She decided she didn't like his mouth. It was too hard. "Who— who are you?" she said.

His eyes widened slightly. "I believe I asked you first."

His eyes weren't black; they were a dark, dark brown.

With streaks of gold shooting out from the centers, like tiny exploding suns. "What?" she said.

"I really would like to continue this scintillating conversation"—he arched his back, heaving against her—"but you're as bloody heavy as a sack of wet meal."

"Uh!" she grunted as he stood up, dumping her like a sack onto the floor.

Her skirt was rucked up around her thighs, revealing the lacy edge of her pink cotton opendrawers, which had grown so short for her in these last months they no longer covered her bony knees. Hot color flooded her face—not so much because he could see her bare legs as because he would know she was so poor she couldn't even afford nev' underthings.

She yanked her skirt down, glancing sideways at him to see if he watched her. But he had his back to her. He was studying the pile of scrap left by the explosion, his hands fisted on his hips, and she studied him in turn. He wore tight buckskins tucked into top boots. His shirt was made of fine cambric, and as wet as it was, it was nearly transparent. She could see the flesh of his back move as he sucked in a deep breath.

She stood up, and he spun suddenly around, fixing her with those penetrating dark eyes. Caught gaping at him, she flushed and looked away, pretending a sudden and avid interest in her surroundings.

The mine had been closed down long ago. Over the years sand drifts, blown in by the wind, had built up in the corners of the enginehouse. The entrance to the main shaft had been boarded up, but the rotting timbers now sagged in the middle like an old mattress. The Cornish called them bals, these old abandoned mine shafts. All sorts of refuse wound up in the old bals, from sacks of unwanted kittens to unwanted bastards.

But there were also signs of recent occupation. Scraps of paper covered with fine-lined drawings fluttered in the draft of air coming through the open door. A broken kettle lay on its side, leaking tea onto the stones. And scattered throughout the room, the remains of whatever it was that had exploded.

He had squatted onto his haunches to poke with a stick at a flat piece of iron that had a jagged, scorched edge. He picked up a length of twisted copper pipe, frowned at it a moment, then tossed it away. His mouth took on a sulky curve.

"What happened?" she asked, then wished she hadn't. In the dripping silence her voice had sounded much too harsh and loud. And childlike.

He stood up and turned to face her in one quick, graceful motion. "Obviously," he said, drawling the word, "it was a matter of too much pressure per the square inch. It could have been a weakness in the boiler plating. But I suspect the fault lies more with the fire tubes. What do you think?"

"I don't know," she said honestly, for he might as well have been speaking Chinese for all she'd understood of it.

"Then why the bloody hell did you ask?"

"I was only making conversation."

"Well, kindly go make it somewhere else."

She would do that, leave him. It would serve him right; he truly was insufferable and rude. She didn't leave, though. Instead she studied the remains of what she now understood to be some sort of experiment with steam. She did know that steam engines were used to pump water from working tin mines. But such engines were monstrous things, with boilers near the size of a farmer's cart and great beam rods. The boiler he'd been working with couldn't have been any bigger than a brass drum. It appeared to have been built into a wooden framework that had rested upon a pair of wooden trestles. The force of the blast had blown the framework and the trestles into kindling.

Dear life . . . the fool man was fortunate he hadn't been killed.

Her gaze went back to him. There was a taut, arrogant set to his wide mouth and a tension in the way he stood before her, not moving, almost as if he expected her to challenge him. Or to sneer at him.

He hadn't shaved for at least two days; he looked disreputable, like a Gypsy or a vagabond. And he cursed worse than a drover. It was possible, since he was here working in the old enginehouse, that he had something to do with mining. But in spite of all his bloody thises and bloody thats and the scars and calluses on his hands, his clothes were too fine, his speech and manner too polished for him to be a mere tinner or tutworker or even a core captain.

"Have you been hired by the earl to reopen the mine?"

He said nothing. But it was as if her question had released the tension within him, for he uncoiled suddenly like a tripped spring. He swore foully and swung around, making for the door, and she noticed for the first time a definite hitch in his stride.

"You've injured your leg!"

She caught up with him just outside the door. He leaned against the weathered bricks, breathing heavily and rubbing his thigh. A grimace twisted his lips.

"Perhaps I should fetch Dr. Humphrey after all."

His head jerked around, and he impaled her with his fierce dark eyes. "Who appointed you my nursemaid, wench?"

"I am not a wench."

He looked down his long, thin nose at her. "You are a rather gawky, gangly thing. Nevertheless, I think one can safely assume that you are—"

"Of course, I'm a we—female. I only meant that you are not to address me in such a familiar manner. I am *Miss* Letty to the likes of you."

He looked her over again, starting with her scratched and sandy bare feet, and moving with slow insolence up her body to take in the torn, scorched, and soot-stained frock. By the time he got to her hair—which fell about her face in wet, tangled clumps and doubtless looked as ratty as last year's gull's nest—the grimace on his mouth was replaced with a sneer.

She drew herself up. "I do not know who you are . . . *sir*," she said, imbuing this last word with such contempt as to leave him in no doubt she thought the courtesy undeserved. "But one thing you most certainly are *not* is a gentleman. A gentleman would at least thank me for trying to save his life."

"You flatten me like a tin stamp, try to torch me with an ostrich feather. Then you pounce on me and kiss me when I am too weak to defend my virtue—"

"I didn't kiss you!"

"And now you are claiming to have saved my life? Kindly warn me when next you set out upon your errands of mercy, so that I might at least have the providence to duck."

"You, sir, are not only rude, you are as mad as a snake catcher." She thrust her chin in the air, spun on her heel, and stalked up the mule path.

He caught her in two strides, snagging her arm and hauling her back around, slamming her up against his chest. "Just a bloody damned minute. I'm not through with you—"

"I am more than through with you." She spat the words at him, pushing with her forearms against his chest. "And I did *not* kiss you."

"You were thinking about it." His mouth twisted into something that was not quite a smile. "A thought, as they say, is as good as the deed."

"I was not . . . I would never . . . I declare to God, you are the most preening, overweening, puffed-up . . . puffed-up bullfrog! And *that* is an insult to the frog."

She wrenched her wrist free from his grasp with such force her fist went flying. It cracked into his jaw like the snap of a slingshot.

"Christ!" he exclaimed, staggering backward. "Bloody hell, you little—"

Jessalyn didn't hear what he said next. She ran.

She didn't stop running until she had reached the hedge. She leaned against the rough stones, fighting for breath.

Something fluttered in the wind, catching her eyes. A scrap of faded blue muslin snagged on a blackthorn vine. Her chest tightened, and she felt a ridiculous urge to cry. She had too few clothes that she could afford to leave pieces of what she did have scattered around the countryside. Yet she knew it wasn't the ripped frock that had her so close to tears. She was filled with a jumble of strange emotions that tumbled about in her breast like beans in a rattle.

The wind blew her hair into her eyes, and she pushed it back with her hands. It was a worse mess than she'd thought—twisted and tangled like reefer knots. The sun beat down on her upturned face, doubtless bringing out a hundred blasted freckles. She'd left her hat back there . . . with him. But she would rather be spitted like a goose and roasted over a hot fire than go back for it.

Her knuckles ached. She pressed the back of her hand to her hot cheek. Dear life . . . He had a way of talking that made a person feel like an addlepated fool. She'd gotten even, though—landing him a facer and calling him a bullfrog. She laughed aloud, a shaky laugh that cracked at the end. *That* had certainly put the man in his place. Cut to the quick he probably was, wounded in the jaw as well as the heart. Like as not he would never get over it.

She laughed again, and a colony of rooks took flight in a flap of black wings, cawing alarm. She watched them flutter in a row across the sky, like a trailing mourning ribbon.

She looked down at herself. Her dress was a ruin; she was grimy with dried steam and soot. She suddenly wanted very badly to be home, where it was safe and things were familiar, the way they had always been. But she'd left her half boots at the cove. Before anything else she would have to climb back down and fetch them, for they were her only decent pair of shoes.

As she descended the cliff path, she was shocked to see that the tide nearly covered the beach. The sea had taken back the piece of broken spar it had spewed up earlier. Swirling foamy water ate at the white sand and swallowed the granite blocks that tumbled down from the bluff.

She hunted around the salt-encrusted rock where she had sat down earlier to take off her half boots, stockings, and wool garters. She remembered leaving them on the rock before she'd walked the beach, taking such pleasure in the feel of the sand oozing up between her bare toes. The rock, she remembered, had been swathed in dried seaweed. Now the nubbly greenish brown strands glistened wet and slick.

"Blast it!" she shouted, the words getting snatched away by the wind. Just as a greedy, overreaching wave had snatched up the only shoes that still fitted her big, ugly feet. "Blast it . . ." she said again, more softly this time. And then, because he had used the words to such good effect, she added, "Bloody hell."

She sucked in a deep sigh, tasting salt. Clouds were building up in back of the cliffs, turning the sea flat and gray like tarnished pewter, smothering the sun. A gull wheeled overhead, screaming: *please . . . please . . . please . . .* A gust of wind blasted the sand hills, flattening the marram grass, molding her skirt to her thighs. Behind her, a trickle of stones cascaded down the cliff. She looked up, expecting the goats.

And saw him.

She didn't stop to think. She ran into the shadows cast by the cliff face and hid behind a boulder that was hoary with lichen and surrounded by a screen of sea rush. She couldn't stop herself, though, from peering through the stiff-stemmed reedy grass to watch him come.

He went all the way to the edge of the tide, then stopped. He stood with his back to her, and the sea lapped at his boots. The wind made the sleeves of his white shirt luff like sails. He stood still, staring out to sea. But there was a skittishness about him, like a high-strung racehorse awaiting only the snap of the flag to burst into a gallop.

Jessalyn subsided back behind the rock and buried her face in her hands. Dear life, once again she had behaved like an utter nodcock. A one-eyed mole couldn't have missed seeing her standing like a lone fence post in the middle of the beach. She should have waited until he'd come her way, then walked past him, cutting him dead. Instead she had run away to hide like a child. He was probably waiting with glee for her to come out so that he could once again exercise his sardonic tongue at her expense.

She sneaked another look. To her shock she saw that he had thrown off his shirt. He bent over and pulled off his boots. He straightened, and his hands fell to his waist, and the next thing she knew he was peeling his buckskins down over his bare hips. She saw him through a haze thrown up by the breaking waves. He stood facing the sea, his man's naked body hard and dark against the white of the sand and the spumy mist. He moved, startling her. But he was only walking into the surf. She saw where an ugly red scar curled around his upper thigh like a whip lash, before a wave rolled over, crashing against his stomach, covering him.

This was a dangerous place to bathe, even on the best of days. And the day after a storm . . .

He dived into the first breaker. She held her breath until he emerged beyond it. But a second later a new wave engulfed him. It seemed an eternity before his head appeared again, black against the rolling mud gray water. He swam toward the Devil's Jawbone, a jagged rock that thrust up like a shark's tooth from the seabed and had torn the keel out of many a vessel run afoul of it. There were often mysterious currents around the Devil's Jawbone that came from nowhere and sucked swimmers out to sea.

Somebody ought to warn him about the current, she thought. But she didn't want that somebody to be her. She didn't want to have to look into those piercing dark eyes and see within them the knowledge that she had watched him undress. That she had watched him walk naked into the sea.

After the insulting way he had behaved toward her, for the price of a tin penny-mug she ought to let him drown.

He should have been killed in the explosion.

Or at least badly scalded. The blast had gone backward, out the butt end of the boiler, and it had only been sheer, blind, stupid luck that he'd been standing in front. Uncharacteristic luck for a Trelawny, most would say. But although he had been momentarily concussed by the shock of the blast, otherwise he hadn't gotten a blister. He would have emerged from the disaster relatively unscathed if that skinny redheaded wench hadn't come hurtling through the door like shot out of a cannon and trampled him.

The sea tugged at his legs. He pulled against the current, fighting it a moment, then swam free. A sharp pain sizzled in his thigh. He set his teeth and kicked harder.

He had thought the physical exercise would keep at bay the brooding thoughts about his latest failure. But they crowded around him anyway, cawing and flapping their black wings like vultures. He had been so sure he'd had the answer this time, that this time what he'd seen in his head he could build into a reality. He had this idea . . .

That a carriage could be made to run on steam power. Like a locomotive, only on a regular road, not tracks. A horseless carriage . . . But it would require an engine that had yet to be invented, lighter and more compact, yet many times more powerful. The solution, he thought, had to lie in the fire tubes. Not the single-pass and twin flues that existed in the steam engines of today, but a multitubular system of many small flues—twenty or more—that would raise the evaporative power of the boiler enormously. In theory so many fire tubes should have enabled him to increase greatly the steam pressure per square inch within the boiler and, by extrapolation, the power of the engine.

In practice the boiler had blown all to bloody hell.

That was why he had conducted the experiment alone, in the isolated and abandoned enginehouse of Wheal Ruthe, instead of at the foundry in Penzance. That way, if something went wrong, he was the only one at risk.

He'd been living on borrowed time anyway. He should have died at Waterloo a year ago along with everyone else. Waterloo . . . The vultures in his head flapped their wings and shrieked, and suddenly his nostrils were assailed with the rotten-egg stench of exploded gunpowder, the ripe smell of spilled blood, the rancid odor of fear. He ducked his head beneath a wave and kicked hard, gasping at the pain that shot up into his groin, swallowing seawater, and tasting blood. Tasting death. Tasting . . .

Cold.

The water had suddenly turned bitter cold. He tried to change direction, to turn back toward the shore, but the current had him gripped like a fist, sucking and pulling him farther out to sea. He kicked out with his legs and dug into the water with his arms. The current pulled and sucked and tugged, and he might have been a leaf caught in a whirlpool. It was almost as if the water around him had taken life, and the brute, malevolent power of it shocked him. He fought, bending all of his will and strength against the sea, and the sea was winning. He almost laughed. He had always known, even after surviving so much, that when he finally did die, it would be through his own bloody stupidity.

And then, as if it had only been toying with him all along, the sea gave one last tug and let him go.

He rolled over onto his back, his chest heaving. He floated, feeling with relief the tide carry him back toward the shore. Beneath the ragged gasps of his own harsh breathing and the lap of water around his ears, he heard another sound. He thought at first that it was a gull screeching. A sick gull.

He trod water, bobbing like a cork in the troughs of the waves as he looked toward the beach. The skinny red-headed wench had emerged from behind her rock and was now standing up to her knees in the surf, hands cupped around her mouth, hallooing him.

He ignored her, turning over to float on his back. His leg throbbed. Sometimes the pain became so fierce it was like a white heat behind his eyes. At first the bastard butchers who called themselves barber-surgeons had said that he would die unless the leg came off. When he'd proved them bloody liars, they'd said he would never walk again. He had proved them wrong on that count, too, but even he was forced to admit the leg was still weak. And it hurt. Every single waking moment when he wasn't drugged with alcohol, it hurt as if the teeth of hell were gnawing on his flesh.

The redheaded wench was jumping up and down now, flapping her arms like a demented hen. What in bloody hell did she want? He'd have to go back anyway; he hadn't the strength to challenge the sea again. He imagined that the sight of him emerging naked from the surf would probably send her squealing up the cliff path like a scalded pig. He rolled over onto his side, his arm stroking forward, hand knifing into a wave. He spit salt water from his mouth and grinned.

She didn't run. But when he got within a few feet of her and stood up in the breakers, she jerked, scuttling backward like a little sand crab. She stared wide-eyed at him, her face turning the color of crushed mulberries. By the time he stopped in front of her, her gaze was rigidly focused over his shoulder.

He used his drawling gentleman's voice. "Did you want something, Miss Letty?"

"I . . ." She faltered, and he saw her throat work as she swallowed. The wind billowed her hair into a cinnamon cloud around her head. The sea rose and fell around them like a breath.

He sloughed the water off his chest with his hands. Her gaze jerked back to him a moment, then swerved away again. The sea sighed.

She was very young. She had a bony face, with a broad forehead and flaring cheekbones that were dusted with freckles. But it was her mouth that dominated her features. A large, full-lipped mouth, that even drawn in tightly as it was now, seemed on the verge of breaking into a smile or a laugh. It was odd, for she looked like no one else he'd ever seen, yet he felt he knew her.

"You have a punch like a Billingsgate stevedore, Miss Letty."

Her lips pressed tighter together, and her chin shot up, although she continued to look away from him. "In spite of your odious behavior, I never intended to strike you," she said, so prim and proper he had to fight a laugh. "That, at least, was an accident."

"Indeed? Then I shudder to contemplate what mayhem you could commit should you ever be deliberately provoked."

One corner of her mouth trembled slightly, and for a moment he thought it would break into a smile. He caught himself holding his breath, waiting, and the sea moaned.

"I thought to warn you," she said. She still wouldn't look at him. "The undertow is bad in this cove. Especially after a storm. And the current . . ."

He took the two steps necessary to bring himself up next to her, and before she could run off, he cupped her chin with his curled fingers and turned her head to face him. She looked up at him, her gaze wide open and startled. Her eyes were a flat pewter gray, hiding nothing. He saw fear and wonder and a budding sexual excitement. He had forgotten—no, he had never known what it was like to be so innocent.

She licked her puffy lower lip. "The, uh . . . the current is treacherous in this cove."

He stroked the strong bone of her jaw with his thumb. The sea breathed, inhaling . . . exhaling. . . . "Are you playing nursemaid again, Miss Letty?"

A tremor ran through her. She jerked away from him with such violence she swayed backward and sat down in the surf with a splash. Her gaze went up the length of him, eyes wide and lips parted as she took in the blatant change in his body.

"Permit me to assist you, Miss Letty." He leaned over and held out his hand to her as if they were in a drawing room.

She knocked his hand away. She flailed, trying to get to her feet, but her legs kept getting tangled in her wet skirt. At last she made it upright, dripping and shuddering. She pushed her wind-whipped hair back out of her face. Her lips trembled, and her skin was now so pale he could have counted every freckle.

"I see what you mean about the treacherous current," he said.

"You"—her eyes had grown dark, like the belly of a thundercloud—"you can go throw yourself down an old bal for all I care!"

She turned and sloshed with stiff dignity out of the water. She got halfway to the cliff path before she broke into a run. She ran like a little girl, her hair russet as a lateen sail flapping behind her, her arms splayed out from her sides.

He cupped his hands around his mouth and shouted after her, "I remain your most humble and obedient servant, Miss Letty!" He expected her to turn around for a final, parting shot. Or at least to fire one last salvo with those gunmetal eyes.

He was surprised, and a little disappointed, when she did not.

2

"Poor Peaches," Jessalyn said, a gurgle of laughter turning her voice husky. "Is that nasty old bird tormenting you?"

The fat orange cat hissed and cackled, then spit for good measure. The object of her enmity was an ugly black-backed gull. The gull, big as a goose, sat atop the paddock fence, tantalizingly near. Yet cat and bird both knew that bird could take flight long before fat cat could pounce.

The gull squawked and flapped its wings; Peaches hissed. Laughing, Jessalyn stroked the cat's marmalade-and-cream-striped backbone. "You have him thoroughly frightened now, m' love," she cooed. Peaches began to purr beneath Jessalyn's hand, her front paws kneading the weathered wood of the windowsill.

The evening was quiet but for the whisper of the surf and the reedy chirring of a nightjar. The sea caught the last light of a dying sun, shimmering purple like a cup of plum wine. End Cottage was only a hundred yards from the sea, but the cliffs were steeper here than they were at Crook-neck Cove, the beach narrower and usually covered by the tide.

Peaches cast one last baleful look at the gull and then with an air of supreme indifference thumped down from the sill and waddled over to the hearth. Last year Peaches had been a skeletal stray, near death from exposure and starvation. Now she was so fat she could barely make it back and forth between the window and the fire.

Jessalyn took the cat's place at the window. She had been restless all evening, tingly and effervescent inside, like a tub of fermenting cider.

The wind came up again, lifting a corner of loose thatch on the stable. The air smelled heavily of the sea and of the hay that had just been gathered and ricked that week. There was a sweet smell, too, from the primroses and daffodils, splashes of bright and pale yellow, that grew along the paddock where a sorrel-colored colt cavorted around a rubbing post.

Folk around the county called End Cottage a stud farm, although that was being generous. Once, years ago, her grandparents had bred horses to race on the great tracks near London Town. Sir Silas Letty, Jessalyn's grandfather, had been known as a bang-up sporting man who always ran his horses fairly, a man who played deep but covered his bets. In those years the Letty stables had acquired a modest reputation among the other members of the Turf, winning just enough today to support the enormous costs of racing tomorrow.

Jessalyn's grandfather had died long before she had come to live at End Cottage, and in the years since his death the Letty luck had gone tepid and then cold. One by one the prizewinning studs and mares had been sold until only the old and the lame and the losers remained.

Jessalyn had never attended a racing meet, never stood at the finishing post and watched her horse nose out the favorite by a whisker. All she'd had were her grandmother's stories. Stories told in the winter evenings by the fire while a wet and woolly Cornish gale blew outside. Stories told so often that she knew just how it would be: the clang of the starting bell, the jockeys flashing by in a rainbow of colored taffeta, the thunder of a hundred hooves beating at the turf . . . and the sweet, hot taste of winning.

Someday, Lady Letty would say, with the light of the fire
—or perhaps it was the dream—sparkling in her eyes . . .
someday, when the right horse came along, they would go
to Newmarket and Epsom Downs for the season, and they
would race again. Someday, someday . . .

They had high expectations of the sorrel filly in the paddock, foaled just that spring, such expectations that they
had named her Letty's Hope.

A man came out the barn carrying a halter. Jessalyn
waved, but he did not wave back. He carried the halter in
his right hand, and he had to put it in his teeth to open the
paddock gate, for he had only the one arm. The other he
had left on a battlefield in the Peninsula five years ago.
Small, bandy-legged, and dark, he was as Welsh as his
name, Llewellyn Davies. But Jessalyn and her grandmother
called him Sarn't Major, which had been his rank in the
army. The rest of the folk in the county avoided speaking to
him altogether; he was not a friendly man.

A latch lifted with a click behind her, and Jessalyn
turned. Her grandmother entered the parlor with a rustle
of black bombazine skirts. Although she used a cane, Lady
Rosalie Letty was not bent over. A tall woman, she carried
her height with pride, her back and shoulders straight and
stiff as a lance.

"Close the window, gel," Lady Letty said in accents
rough with the burr of Cornwall. "The fire's smeeching."

Jessalyn pulled the old mullioned window shut with a
protest of its rusty hinges, then stooped to poke at a fire of
furze and bits of driftwood, coaxing out a reluctant flame.
Lady Letty lowered herself onto one end of a battered and
patched settee. The settee had once been purple but was
now faded by sun and age to a sickly puce. She lifted a
quizzing glass to her eye, and her sharp gaze honed right in
on the nail of Jessalyn's big toe that was poking through her
jean house slipper. The old woman's lips pulled and
twisted.

Jessalyn noticed the scowl and ducked her head to hide a

smile. "I'm that sorry about losing the boots, Gram," she said. She'd confessed earlier to Lady Letty that the sea had stolen her half boots while she'd been scavenging. She had told her grandmother nothing at all about the explosion. Or the stranger.

Lady Letty thumped her cane on the carpet, snagging the tip in the threadbare nap. "'Tis not the loss of the boots themselves, m' dear. 'Tis the senselessness of it. It's long before time that you stopped behaving like a wild tommy-rigg. Remember who you are—a lady born. Ladies do not walk the beach barefoot."

"Yes, ma'am," Jessalyn said, although she doubted true ladies, even poor ones, went scavenging in the first place. She sat across from her grandmother in a moth-eaten wing chair, folding her hands primly and bringing her holey-shod feet together. She cast a glance up at Lady Letty in time to catch the love softening the old woman's fierce gray eyes, before the wide mouth pressed into a pretended scowl.

The first time Jessalyn sat in this chair her legs had barely been long enough for her feet to touch the ground. That had been a month after her father's funeral, the day her mother had dragged her down to Cornwall and dumped her into her grandmother's care. Dropped her off like a suit of old clothes, no longer fashionable and no longer wanted.

"So the flighty, vain little fool don't want the bother of a daughter now, and she thinks to pawn you off onto me, eh?" Lady Letty had said, peering at Jessalyn through her quizzing glass and not looking as if she had much use either for a skinny six-year-old with fiery red hair and a freckled nose and scabs on her bony knees. But then Lady Letty had laughed and said, "Good God, gel, you're the spitting image of myself at your age." And Jessalyn had thought that perhaps her grandmother thought this a good thing.

"You'll find it ain't easy being a Letty," her grandmother had gone on. She'd flung up a gnarled hand to stop Jessalyn from speaking, although Jessalyn's tongue had been stiff in her mouth, incapable of moving. "No matter that you're *her* daughter, your father was a Letty. You're of Letty blood, and a Letty I shall make of you. A Letty and a lady, by God."

Being a Letty had turned out to be easy. Being a lady was another net of fish entirely.

It wasn't that she set out to be a hoyden. It was that she could never decide upon the correct and proper way to behave—"the done thing," as Lady Letty called it—until the situation had already come and gone. It was a deficiency in her character, which her grandmother insisted with a perverse sort of pride into turning into an accomplishment.

"Never you mind," Lady Letty would say after Jessalyn had succeeded in making a particular fool of herself. "One must always do the done thing, of course, but there is the ordinary way of doing a thing, and there is the Letty way. Sometimes one must do the unexpected thing, the Letty thing, and tell 'em all to go hang."

The trouble was Jessalyn didn't want to tell them all to go hang. Sometimes she wanted to do the done thing the way everyone else did it—to fit in, to belong, to be a proper young lady who would no longer be a bother of a daughter. Sometimes. At other times . . . other times she felt like a kite, blowing only where the wind took her. She wanted to break free, to make of herself what she would be.

Sometimes she didn't care if she ever saw her mother again.

The door opened with a bang, startling Jessalyn back into the present. A serving girl entered, carrying a tea tray. She closed the door behind her with a smart slap of her hip, then set the tray on a gateleg table.

The girl straightened with a groan, rubbing the small of her back. "Me blessed life, what a day she bin. Seems like 'tes nothing but heftin' and tottin' and luggin' I bin doin' since cockcrow. 'Tes a wonder I haven't got spasms in me back, it is. 'Tes a wonder I ain't prostitute with exhaustion."

Lady Letty rapped her cane on the floor. *"Prostrate.* How often must I tell you, you fool gel, that the word is *prostrate."*

The girl's lace cap bobbed in harmony with her head. She had a face plump as a bun with two black currants for eyes. It might have been a pretty face except for the jagged scar that ran from the corner of her left eye nearly to her mouth. When she was twelve, her miner father in a drunken rage had swung a pick at her head, laying open her cheek. Like Peaches and the Sarn't Major, Becka Poole was another of the misfits and castoffs that Lady Letty was always taking in.

Like me, Jessalyn thought.

"Aye, m'lady," Becka said, with a smile so sweet it could almost make one forget about the scar. "That's just what I do say. Prostitute."

Directing another fierce scowl at the girl, Lady Letty took a tortoiseshell snuffbox out of her pocket. She flicked the lid open with one hand in spite of fingers that were bent and gnarled with rheumatism. Raising a pinch of the pungent powder to her nose, she sniffed delicately. Lady Letty's skin was laced with tiny wrinkles like a dried apple, but age had not eroded the bones beneath. Hers was a strong face that conveyed the strength of her will and character.

For as long as Jessalyn had known her, Lady Letty's hair had been dark gray, the color of the tin ore brought up from the Cornish mines. But Jessalyn had heard it said that once her grandmother's hair had been like a flame. Once that formidable old woman had been young with a laughing mouth and a saucy way of walking and talking. She had been a bal-maiden, a girl who worked in the mines.

The story went that Rosalie Potter had been walking home after her shift at Wheal Ruthe when a well-set-up gentleman had come riding by. Silas Letty was of proud and ancient lineage, a son of a landed Cornish gentry family that could trace its name back to the Battle of Hastings. Silas had taken one look at that laughing mouth and all that red hair and had fallen in love. Nothing would do but that he must have his bal-maiden. But being a Letty, he had done the unexpected thing and married her, instead of simply bedding her.

Later Silas had been elected to Parliament and gone to London, where he had done a service for the king, some secret favor that nobody was allowed to speak of, and the king had made him a baronet. Once again Silas had done the unexpected thing: He had accepted the baronetcy to please his king. But Silas had still thought it a trifling thing. Unlike other families, the Lettys did not need a title to increase their consequence.

The title did please Sir Silas in one way. For Rosalie Potter—onetime bal-maiden, who had been born and brought up by the scruff of her neck in a hovel next to the gritty slag heaps of Wheal Ruthe—his Rosalie became a lady.

It was such a wonderful story, more romantic than any tale Jessalyn had ever read in the library bluebooks. Once upon a time a beautiful bal-maiden had captured the heart of a baronet, a man so far above her he might as well have been living on the moon.

Jessalyn's sigh turned into a frown. She wondered what her grandmother would make of a man who had scars and calluses on his hands and swore worse than a costermonger. Who experimented with steam contraptions that blew up and took off all his clothes in front of her to go swimming in the sea. Who had looked at her and touched her—

"Have you fleas, gel?" Lady Letty snapped. "Tain't the done thing to squirm in one's chair like a hooked herring."

"That'd be the exposition what's got her nerves on edge, m'lady." Becka Poole, finished with her arrangement of the tea service in its proper order on the table, straightened with another melodramatic groan. "Look at me own hands. Shakin' they be, like a leaf in a gale."

Lady Letty smothered a snuff sneeze with her handkerchief. "Exposition? What sort of exposition?"

"The gret big sort, m'lady. It happened this afternoon whilst ee was gone up to Mousehole wi' the Sarn't Major. I was just sittin' down to a dish o' tea when, without a breath o' warning—crash! Boom! And the ground she be rumblin' like an old hag's chest when she snores. Gret big exposition it was. 'Tes a wonder I didn't fall away dead on the spot."

Jessalyn got up to poke at the fire, hiding her face from her grandmother's tin gray gaze. She was sure that with one look Lady Letty would see instantly all that had happened today. That she had lain on a man's body—never mind that it was an accident, done in all *innocence* . . . Watched that same man walk naked into and out of the sea. She had *not* kissed him, though . . . Dear life.

"Becka," Jessalyn said, more sharply than she'd intended, "could you cut up some seedcake, please, to take with our tea?"

"Ais, miss. Though how ee can eat so hearty after the scare us had this afternoon, I bain't the one t'say. Threw me off me feed, it did. I had to take some of Dr. Dooley's disgusting restorative, and even then I could only but manage a bite or two of the taties and some leg o' mutton."

Lady Letty watched, her mouth pursed, as Becka Poole sashayed from the room. "That gel! What, pray, is Dr. Dooley's disgusting restorative?"

Jessalyn let out a relieved breath, grateful at the change of subject. "Di*ges*tive restorative, Gram." She laughed suddenly. "Though as it's composed of bat dung, snail water, and ground wood lice, *disgusting* may be a more fitting appellation."

Jessalyn sat down across from her grandmother and poured the tea into a pair of unmatched cups. When times were especially bad, as they had been lately, they tried to make the leaves last three days, and this was the third day. The tea looked like dirty rainwater.

As Jessalyn handed the cup to her grandmother, the old lady's lips twisted into a grimace, which was her version of a smile, and patted Jessalyn's knee. "Don't fret yourself about the boots, gel. We'll scrounge up the ready for a new pair somehow. If worse comes to worst, I can sell one of my boxes."

"Oh, no, Gram, you mustn't!"

Lady Letty had a wonderful collection of eighty-nine snuffboxes, made of every material imaginable—from papier-mâché to japanned copper to cut crystal. All had been acquired during the better times, given to her as gifts by the baronet to mark every race their horses had won or placed in.

"Don't you tell me what I must or mustn't do, gel." Lady Letty dusted a sprinkling of snuff off her bodice. "'Tis a waste when you're as old as I am to have more of a thing than you can use." She took a sip of tea and grimaced. "Bah! This tastes like something that came out of the back end of a cow. Pour me some port, if you will."

Jessalyn got up to pour the port from the decanter that sat on a nail-studded chest beside the window. She poured the thick wine slowly, careful, as she had been taught, not to make bubbles and thus disturb the flavor.

It had grown dark since Becka had brought in the tea. Using a spill of twisted paper, Jessalyn lit the tallow candles on the mantel. As she moved from one to the other, she caught her reflection in the mildew-spotted mirror. Wild color stained her cheeks, and a strange light glimmered in her eyes. Startled, she looked away.

Jessalyn turned to find Lady Letty peering at her through her quizzing glass. "Now tell me about this explosion that seems to have occurred this afternoon?" the old woman said. "Was that when you met the Trelawny boy?"

Jessalyn's mouth fell open. "How—?"

"Simple deduction, m' dear. You've a look about you as if

you've just seen your runner beat the pack to the post by a
furlough and you'd a hundred pounds extra laid by on the
winner. Only one thing besides a fat purse will put that
look into a Letty's eyes. I ask myself who's young and male
and new to the countryside, and only one candidate leaps
to mind."

"But when did he—why is he— He's a Trelawny!" Jessalyn found her chair with the backs of her knees and subsided into it. "Not the earl surely?"

Lady Letty tapped her snuffbox with a blunt-nailed finger. "The late earl had three boys, but I reckon this one
would be the youngest. I remember they went and named
him after a horse at his christening, some Irish nag the earl
had backed in the Newmarket Whip the day he was born.
Mc-something. He was only a little tacker when last I saw
him. That would be at his father's funeral in '01. Fell down
some stairs in a drunken stupor and broke his neck, the late
earl did. He'd be in his twenties now—the younger son,
not the dead earl, of course—and doubtless up to his hocks
in debt and well on the path to perdition. There's bad blood
in that family, bad blood. Dangerous to know are the mad
earls of Caerhays . . . They all die young, violently, and in
disgrace."

Jessalyn had heard the stories. How Charles Trelawny,
the tenth earl of Caerhays, had died fifteen years ago of a
broken neck after falling down a flight of stairs. In his cups
as usual, some said. Though others insisted it wasn't too
much port that had murdered the earl but the jealous husband of one of his many mistresses. He was succeeded by
his eldest son, another Charles, who had died of a ruptured
spleen after falling from his horse during a wild midnight
ride. In his cups, they said again. Though others said his
soul had been fetched to hell by the ghost of a man he had
killed in a duel.

Now the second son, and current earl, was living a life of
dissipation in London and not likely to see his next birthday. The mad earls of Caerhays . . . Jessalyn tried to re-

member what the gossips said about the third son. That he had bought himself a cheap commission in a line regiment and nearly gotten himself killed last year at Waterloo.

"Gram? Do you know what . . ." She tried to remember if she'd ever heard a particular rank mentioned in connection with the youngest Caerhays heir. She settled on captain. "Do you know what Captain Trelawny is doing in Cornwall? Has he left his regiment? Is he here to stay, to manage the estate?"

"What's to manage? Caerhays was bled dry years ago. The Trelawnys have never cared tuppence for their Cornish lands. Would have sold 'em off long ago were they not so heavily entailed. Nay, he's here on recuperative leave, so they say, but he's spent most of his time working at the foundry in Penzance, pursuing some cork-brained, addle-pated experiment having to do with steam locomotion. Disgraceful behavior it is, such that even a Trelawny cannot hope to live down. Just like a common blacksmith, no better than a tutworker really." Lady Letty shuddered. "Getting calluses on his palms and dirt beneath his nails. 'Tain't the done thing at all."

Into Jessalyn's mind flashed an image of long, dark fingers thrust through wet hair. There hadn't been any dirt beneath his nails. But the hand that grabbed her ankle had been rough and had held on to her with a hard, taut strength. . . .

The parlor door flew open, and Becka Poole pranced in, bearing a tray of seedcake in one hand. She put the back of her wrist to her head like a tragedienne traipsing the boards of Covent Garden.

"God's me life, me nerves be frazzled worse'n a hangman's rope. And there's a gret big pain in me chest. Heart pulpy-taties, I be havin'—"

"Palpitations," Lady Letty said with a sigh, and tossed down a hefty swallow of port.

"Aye. Pulpy-taties. I'd better be takin' a double dose of

rhubarb powder afore retirin' this night, else I'll not be gettin' a wink o' sleep."

Becka Poole's hearty snores floated down from the attic, croaking and creaking like a pondful of frogs.

Jessalyn rolled onto her stomach and pulled the pillow over her head. Normally she could sleep through anything. She was famous for it in truth—ever since she had slept through a Cornish *flagh,* a great storm that had uprooted a big elm tree and sent it crashing like a battering ram through her bedroom window. Tonight the air was still, with no sounds to disturb her except for the distant whisper of the surf, the occasional cry of a curlew, and Becka's snores. A small but comforting fire burned in the grate, and a hot brick had been rubbed between the sheets of her old-fashioned box bed. All in her world was as it should be, as it had always been since her first night at End Cottage, and yet . . .

Yet there was an ache in her chest, a muted ache that had been swelling all evening, like a pan of dough set to rise on the windowsill.

"Bloody hell." Jessalyn punched the pillow, then rolled onto her back, staring wide-eyed at the shadow-filled dark. She counted Becka's snores, getting as far as forty-one, before she kicked off the covers and got up.

Lighting a candle, she went over to the cheval looking glass that stood beside her clothespress. She tilted the mirror so that she could look at the full length of herself, frowning at what she saw. The hem of her night rail gaped several inches too short, showing off her thin legs and big feet. The last time she'd gone to Penzance to be fitted for a new dress the mantua-maker had poked her ribs and said she was as skinny as a new-spawned herring. She hadn't grown any curvier in the intervening months, though she had certainly grown taller.

You are a rather gawky, gangly thing. . . .

She picked up the candle and moved closer to the mirror. Gram said her hair was a loamy color, like the last russet leaves of autumn before they were stripped by the winter winds. That was a lot of flummery; red was red. She would have plucked out every single hair from her head if she could have been assured it would grow back blond. Gram also said she had strong, enduring bones, that she would be thankful for such bones when she was forty. But forty was old; of what use would good bones be then? It was her mouth anyway that spoiled her face. It was a clown's mouth, wide and red.

She stuck two fingers into the sides of her mouth and pushed her lips apart, wiggling her tongue and making her eyes bulge out like a cockchafer's. She started to laugh, but the laughter caught in her throat.

She knew she wasn't pretty, but it hadn't seemed to matter before. Well, perhaps it had always mattered a little. . . .

A man like him, though. He was handsome, even in his hard-mouthed way. And an earl's brother, too. He could have any girl he set his fancy for. She could tell that just by the way he talked, that cocky, teasing way he had of talking, that girls, women, always took to him. Anyone he fancied.

He wouldn't look twice at a girl like her.

She turned away from the looking glass. An old walnut bureau with peeling varnish stood next to the window, listing to starboard, for it had lost one of its feet. Jessalyn went to it and took out the journal that Gram had given her for her birthday four months ago. She ran her palm over the tooled Spanish leather, dyed an emerald green. With reverent care she opened the cover, breathing deeply the smell of crisp, new paper. The leaves were slick and smooth like silk, gilded gold on the edges. She had never written in it. She felt an odd reluctance to spoil the pristine whiteness of the pages. It was beautiful and expensive and one of the few gifts anyone had ever given to her.

Yet she yearned suddenly to preserve the memory of today. It would be like pressing the first primrose of the new year between the covers of a book to take out later, during the coldest, darkest day of winter. The petals would be dry and flattened, and the bright gold of spring would have faded to a dull yellow. But the memory would be there still—in the soft whiff of a lingering scent and the shape of the flower, a starburst of petals frozen forever in time.

After a frustrating search through the bureau, she found a pen and standish that still had a bit of wet ink left in it. She gathered this up, along with the journal and candle. Settling onto the bed, she wrapped her arms around her drawn-up legs. She was content just to sit for a moment and watch a blister of grease run down the candle and into the dish. She dipped the pen in the inkwell and scrawled out the date in appalling penmanship.

She brushed the soft quill across her cheek, back and forth. She thought of him walking out of the sea, naked, strong, and beautiful. And she smiled.

The night was still and quiet now, except for the scratch of pen across paper.

I met a man today . . .

3

"I got a pain in one of me motors."

Becka Poole opened her mouth wide and stuck a grimy finger inside. "Rith hereth." Tilting her head, she pulled aside her wren brown hair to show off the roasted turnip parings she had tied behind her ear. "I've tried turnips snips, as ee can see. An' I did rub me feet with bran at bedtime. But them cures bain't workin'. The motor, she still be throbbin' something fierce. I bin prostitute with un for nigh on a month now."

The mountebank stared at Becka, blinking rapidly. His eyes slid over to Jessalyn a moment, and he cleared his throat. "Afflicted with the toothache, are we? I have here a paste of fish eyes that has had miraculous results. Though others prefer a fumigant of rosemary and sage . . ."

The man rummaged among the nostrums and remedies laid out on the tailgate of his gaily painted wagon. He had a lopsided-looking face, for his nose was crooked and his right eye drooped. But he was dressed splendidly, in a laced hat and a gaudily embroidered waistcoat.

While he argued with Becka that fish-eye paste had it all over turnip parings when it came to curing toothaches, Jessalyn studied the mountebank's other offerings. There were corn plasters and cough drops and trusses for any kind of rupture one might experience. Jalap and wormwood for fever, rotten apple water for pox marks, and a perfumed pastille to overcome the stink of tooth decay. A small dark green bottle with a cork stopper claimed her attention. The label said it was a cure for the . . .

Jessalyn peered more closely at the handwritten label. "What is the Secret Disease?" she wondered aloud.

Becka pulled Jessalyn aside, juggling her paper-wrapped medicines. "That ye hadn't ought to be askin', Miss Jessalyn," the girl said in a loud whisper. "'Tesn't proper for a lady to be askin' sich things."

"Why is it that the very things one most wants to know about are the very things one isn't allowed to know?"

"Eh?"

Jessalyn was about to elaborate further on this injustice when Becka shrieked in her ear and pointed behind her. She whirled to see a trio of runaway pigs bearing down on them. The pigs, their little trotters slashing through the sand, their dewlaps swaying in the wind, were being chased by a man in greasy leather leggings, who was bellowing and brandishing a staff. There was only one place for Jessalyn and Becka to go, and that was backward . . . into the mountebank's wagon.

As Jessalyn tried to explain afterward, nothing would have happened if the mountebank had had the foresight to set the wheel brake. She and Becka struck the tailgate hard with their hips, sending cures and nostrums flying and the wagon rolling and swaying like a drunken sailor down the grassy slope and into the south end of the Penzance Midsummer's Eve Fair.

The first thing in the wagon's path was a crockery stall. Teacups, plates, and platters hit the hard-packed sand with a shatter of pottery and a tinkle of glass. A fishmonger's cart was next to fall, followed by a trapper's display and a tent with a gold banner that said HOMEMAKERS' EMPORIUM in tall red letters. The wagon—wearing a set of fish scales, rabbit skins, and shards of broken pottery and trailing skeins of purple yarn—finally came to rest against a rope ring, where a pair of half-naked woman pugilists were fighting for a gold lace cap.

The mountebank, chasing after his wagon, had managed thus far to escape repercussion for the damage done by his wayward vehicle. Everyone was too surprised to do more than shriek and gape. But he stood not a chance against the woman pugilists. They advanced on him, swinging their fists. The crowd around the ring started making bets on which woman could land the most blows.

Jessalyn stared at the pandemonium, her hand over her mouth. Only she wasn't covering up shock or horror, but rather a wicked urge to burst into whoops of laughter.

"God's me life!" Becka exclaimed, her eyes round. "Look at what we've done."

Jessalyn turned, laughter bubbling out of her throat, and saw him.

He stood beside a sheep pen. That Trelawny man. He wasn't laughing. Indeed, he wasn't even smiling; she doubted he was capable of getting his lips to go into anything other than a sneer. He leaned against a wooden post, long legs crossed at the ankles, arms folded over his chest, and a curly brimmed beaver tilted at a rakish angle over one eye. He had on all his clothes for a change.

For a moment she was back on the beach again, the sea breathing and sighing around them, his dark gaze caressing her face, and feeling the roughness of his thumb stroke her jaw. Heat surged up her neck into her cheeks. She turned her back on him.

Becka was still gaping at her. "Cor, Miss Jessalyn. We've gone an' made a proper mess of things again. What m' lady will have t' say about this latest, I'm sure I do not know." She clutched at her chest. "Oooh, I feel me pulpy-taties comin' on."

Jessalyn knew that he still watched her, and her color heightened. "It was hardly our fault. Blame that addlepated fool with the pigs. Look, Gram has given us a whole pound to spend. I think I shall buy myself a new hat." She pushed a lank strand of hair out of Becka's eyes. The girl tended to wear it combed forward, trying to hide the scar on her cheek. "And we can get you a new ribbon for your hair."

A sweet smile broke over Becka's face. "That'd be loverly, miss."

They walked down into the fair, giving a wide berth to its damaged end. Penzance was a seaport, as well as a market and coinage town for tin. On this afternoon, scores of stalls and tents, selling all manner of goods from bootlaces to frying pans, had been set up on the sand hills that bordered the harbor.

They meandered down a path of rough, tufted grass that had been trampled flat by many feet. The air was filled with shouts and drunken laughter, the tatting of a penny trumpet, and the grating shrieks that came from the knife grinder's stall. Pens of bleating sheep, squealing pigs, and bellowing oxen all added to the din. Penzance fairs were rowdy occasions, wrestling, cockfighting, and swilling ale and gin in the taverns they called kiddleys being the favorite ways for Cornishmen to waste an idle afternoon.

They stopped before a booth selling fripperies. Becka agonized over a choice among poppy red, sun yellow, and parrot green ribbons. She finally selected the yellow one because, she said, she found it soothed her poor tired and overworked eyes.

Next door was a stall that sold nothing but secondhand foot apparel. Jessalyn spotted a pair of fawn-colored calf-skin shoes that laced up the front. They were slightly worn down at the heels, but she would rather have had them anyway, instead of the new half boots of stiff black leather that were even now pinching her feet. Two days ago the Sarn't Major had made an unexpected and most propitious sale of a five-year-old saddle horse to Squire Babbage. Because of this windfall, Jessalyn had gotten a new pair of half boots, and they were all still feeling quite flush at End Cottage.

Becka's ribbon had cost a halfpenny, and the rest of Jessalyn's pound was now burning a hole in her reticule. It was a family trait, Gram often said and with more pride than regret, that a Letty held on to money only long enough to wager or spend it.

They passed a spice booth next, and Jessalyn stopped to revel in the exotic scent of cinnamon and cloves and ginger. The smells always stirred something within her: a desire to taste of strange and forbidden things. Her revelry was broken by a one-legged beggar in a tattered army coat, who held a hand beneath her nose. She gave him a shilling.

A roar of raucous laughter burst from the beer tent next door. Turning, Jessalyn caught sight of a dark, sharp-boned profile. That Trelawny man again. She lingered within the shadow cast by the spice booth, where she could watch him unobserved.

He looked very much the gentleman today in a narrow-waisted black coat with gilt buttons, tight beige pantaloons, and tasseled Hessians. But there was a suppressed wildness about him that made a lie out of his refined clothes. He stood with one booted foot braced against a bench, drinking a pint of porter. He was talking to a couple of rough-looking men. As she watched, one spoke to him, and the Trelawny man threw back his head and laughed. A shaft of sunlight streaking through the tent's open door highlighted the tanned sinews of his exposed throat above the starched white neckcloth. She wondered if he knew that the men he was being so free and easy with were gaugers.

Gaugers, preventive men, customs officers—whatever one called them, they were the most hated individuals in Cornwall, more hated even than Catholics. A man known to consort with gaugers wouldn't be welcome for long. Not where every man from the baker to the vicar had been known on occasion to make a run to France to smuggle back a shipload of tax-free brandy, silk, or salt. A man seen drinking in a kiddley with gaugers could end up some dark night in a ditch with a mining pick in his back.

She wasn't about to warn him though—oh, no, not this
time. He could go to perdition without any interference
from her.

Just then he turned his head, and across the length of the
crowded, noisy tent their gazes met—his smoky and lazy
and . . . knowing. He *knew* that she had been standing
there for some minutes, gawking at him like a moonstruck
shopgirl. Her face burning, Jessalyn whipped around and
nearly collided with a perambulating pieman.

"'Ere now! Whyn't ye watch where you's going? Ye
about tipped me pies in the mud!" The man steadied a tray
that was loaded to overflowing with pies, biscuits, and
sweet cakes.

"Gis along wi' ee!" Becka cried, suddenly appearing at
Jessalyn's side. She shook her fist in the pieman's face.
"Pies in the mud, ha! Pies what *taste* like mud, more like."

Jessalyn could feel that Trelawny man watching her. The
commotion was drawing other eyes as well. "I'll take one,"
she said, thrusting a penny at the pieman. "A jam tart, if
you please."

The pieman, mollified by the sale, ceased his complaining. He selected a quince jam tart, wrapped it in paper, and pocketed the coin with a one-handed flourish. Jessalyn dragged Becka out of sight of the kiddley tent, giving
her the tart to stifle her flow of protests over the pieman's
rudeness. Jessalyn strode so fast through the booths and
stalls that Becka had to run to keep up.

They emerged into a clearing where a cockpit had been
scooped out of the sand. Men crowded around the make-
shift ring, shouting and laughing, waving bank notes and
fistfuls of coins. There was a smell in the air around the pit,
almost a stink, of hot breath, human sweat, and the brassy
odor of money.

Within the pit a pair of cocks with shaved necks and
sharpened spurs were circling each other. One of the birds
emitted a low-throated rattle that reminded Jessalyn of the
sound the wind made as it whipped through the gorse.

"Ye ought t' lay a shilling on that red-breasted cock," Becka said, stuffing the last of the pastry into her mouth. "He's got a fire in his eye. Me da always said, bet on the bird what got the fire in his eye."

Gram was the one for betting on cockfights. Jessalyn couldn't even bear to watch them. Just then the cocks flew at each other in a fury of spraying blood and feathers. Jessalyn started to turn aside, but the crowd had closed in around her, pinning her next to the ring.

"Aagh! That pie was some awful," Becka said, licking her fingers. "She be stuck in me throat now. I'll be needing a pint to wash 'er down." Her new hair ribbon swaying, Becka pushed her way through the men, heading toward a tent that sported a banner advertising Bang-Up ginger beer.

Jessalyn had opened her mouth to call after the girl when she saw him again. That Trelawny man. He stood on the other side of the cockpit, the sun at his back. His tall, lean body cast a shadow across the blood-splattered sand. She could not see his face, yet she knew he looked at her. For one suspended moment the bellows and shrieks of the cockfight faded until all Jessalyn could hear was the beat of her pulse, thudding hard and fast in her throat.

Someone jostled her, breaking the spell. She pressed her way through the crush, almost running. Back among the tents and booths again, she looked over her shoulder to see if he followed . . . and slammed into the chest of a dragon.

She barely kept the scream from getting past her lips, before her wits informed her pounding heart that the dragon wasn't real. She had walked into the middle of a group of costumed strolling players who were passing out handbills for that night's performance.

The gilt and spangled dragon clutched at her with his claws. He roared a laugh, breathing gin fumes, not fire. "Eh, girlie, wha's yer hurry? Give us a kiss."

Jessalyn struggled in his scaly embrace. For a dragon he

was a pathetic specimen, missing a wing and two teeth, his green paint chipping. She elbowed him in the belly. He wheezed a fumy breath and let her go. When she looked behind her again, that Trelawny man was nowhere in sight. Obviously he was not the sort, she thought with a sudden smile, to rescue fair damsels from gin-breathing dragons.

Alone now, Jessalyn walked aimlessly past a stall selling ships and whelks in bottles. A caning man offered to reweave a chair seat for her while she waited. Beside him, tied to a stake, was Toby, the learned pig that could guess, so his master claimed, the date of her birth and predict her future. She was tempted to ask the pig whether the man she married would be fair or dark, when her gaze fell on the most beautiful bonnet in the world.

The booth was the most splendid one along the row, for it was covered with a canvas roof, striped and fringed like a Moor's tent. The awning shaded a trestle counter piled high with a colorful profusion of fur and velvet and straw. But one hat stood out above all the others.

Jessalyn picked up the hat and stepped out from beneath the awning to study it better in the fading sunlight. It was tall-crowned, made of midnight blue curled silk and trimmed with enormous rose passionflowers. She smiled at the woman behind the counter. "How much is it?"

"Two pound ten, miss."

"Two pound ten!" Jessalyn didn't need to pretend her shock at the price. "Is this a hat you're selling or the crown jewels?" She laughed, and the sound of her laughter floated over the noise of the fair so that several people turned to stare and then smiled and laughed along with her.

"Don't buy it."

Jessalyn whirled, her fingers gripping the hat's wide brim, crushing the stiff silk. She looked up into a pair of dark, penetrating eyes. "Why are you following me?"

"It's an insanity, you know."

Something swelled inside her chest, making it difficult to breathe. "What?"

"It's an insanity, a mental aberration. Bedlam is full of those who do it."

She wondered why she couldn't make any sense of what he was saying. It was as if she had suddenly sprouted windmills in her head. "Do what?"

"Why, believe that they are constantly being followed by others with evil designs upon their persons. I assure you that I have not been following you, Miss Letty. Nor do I have any sort of design upon your person, evil or otherwise. Fate simply seems to be disgorging you into my path."

"Like Jonah and the whale?"

She had smiled at her own little joke, but he didn't return the smile. He stared at her, and because looking away from him would be the act of a coward, she stared back. His high-boned face held a strange disquiet, and his mouth was set in a thin, hard line.

"My, my," he finally said. "There is a wit beneath all that red hair." He took the bonnet from her nerveless fingers. His hand brushed hers, and a shiver fluttered across her chest, as if a chill wind had come up. Yet the evening had fallen suddenly still. "This hat would not do at all for you," he said. "It is meant for a more mature woman."

Of course, he would think of her as a child. She felt awkward and bedraggled in her speckled dimity frock with its frayed hem and the mended spot on the skirt where she'd caught it on a nail and in her serviceable leather half boots that pinched. She would never be the kind of woman who could wear such a hat and carry it off.

"I thank you for your opinion," she said. "Now if you will excuse me, please, I have business elsewhere."

"Where elsewhere?"

"There." She flung a finger past him, toward the setting sun, and only belatedly noticed where she had pointed. To her horror she saw the Reverend Troutbeck waddling toward her on his fat, bowed legs.

"Miss Letty, here you are at last," the reverend said, panting. "We've been waiting for you." The pastor gestured behind him, where a crowd had started to gather around a gibbet. Suspended from the crossbeam of the gibbet was a row of horse collars. The heads of three widely grinning boys poked out of three of the collars; the fourth was empty.

"A grinning contest!" the Trelawny man exclaimed, shock and laughter in his voice. "You are going to be in a grinning contest."

"No, no," Jessalyn protested. Her cheeks felt so hot she was sure they were on fire. "There has been a mistake. Not a mistake precisely, but a misinterpretation. Of something I said. Or rather, of something I neglected to say . . ."

The Reverend Troutbeck launched into a discourse about the contest, of how it had become a sort of tradition at the last few Midsummer's Eve fairs, as a way of raising money to reslate the church roof. The congregation, he said, made wagers on whose grin was the widest and whose could last the longest.

Jessalyn couldn't bear to look at the man beside her, but she could feel his gaze on her mouth. She quelled a sudden urge to wet her lips.

"Are you certain you are not mistaken, Miss Letty?" he said, drawling the words. "The good reverend here seems to be of the opinion that you've agreed to be in the competition." He waved a languid hand at the horse collars. "Indeed, he has saved you a place."

The reverend's face, florid and fat as a summer pumpkin, beamed above his grease-stained stock. "Our Miss Letty is a past champion."

"Then our Miss Letty has her title to defend, of course." The Trelawny man bowed at her, mockery in every line of his body. "Please, do not let me detain you."

There was nothing for it. She had to go through with it, to put a brave face on it. Or rather, grin on it. Jessalyn followed the reverend toward the gibbet. She mounted the steps slowly, her head high, her back stiff, as if she were Marie Antoinette on her way to the guillotine. She thrust her head through the horse collar, fighting off a cowardly desire to up and hang herself here and now, since she had a gibbet right to hand. So she had a big mouth. But dear life, only a cork-brained, addlepated wet goose would go and make a spectacle out of herself by entering a *grinning* contest.

She had never felt less like smiling.

The hurdy-gurdy ground out its tinny song as around and around they went—the wooden horses with their legs flying high, tails and manes streaming in the wind. Jessalyn had never seen such a wonder before, and she laughed out loud.

The horses had been painted all the bright colors of a peacock's tail and were anchored to a wooden platform by poles through their middles. The platform turned by means of an intricate mesh of chains and gears that were powered by a pair of live donkeys turning a treadmill. A barker dressed in a black checkered coat called out to the passersby to come and ride the merry-go-round.

"It seems we meet again, Miss Letty."

He came toward her out of the falling darkness, limping slightly. He stopped to stand before her, one thumb hooked on his fob pocket, his hip cocked forward. That Trelawny man. She wondered why he kept seeking her out. She wanted him to leave her alone.

"Why are you doing this? What do you want with me?"

He almost smiled. "What do you suppose I want with you?" He paused, and his words hung in the air, full of threat. Or a promise. "I want, as it happens, to chide you for costing me a guinea," he said.

"I cannot imagine what you are talking about."

"The good reverend so bragged of your prowess in flashing your ivories that I laid a guinea on you. He assured me I could not lose."

"That should teach you then, sir—never to bet on a sure thing."

He laughed, and the deep, throaty sound seemed to reso-
nate in her blood. He took a step closer to her. She felt his
nearness like the heat of a candle's flame.

She averted her head, sure that he would be able to read
her feelings in her face. She couldn't understand this
strange effect he seemed to have on her. She disliked him,
in a way he frightened her. Yet her whole body leaped and
came alive at the mere sight of him. It was like being given
one of those electric charges that she'd read about in the
newspaper, which had caused dead frogs to jump across the
room. She smiled at the silly thought.

"I never trust people who smile suddenly for no reason,"
he said.

She looked up at him. He was staring at her with lazy-
lidded eyes. "Oh, they always have a reason," she said.
"You are only angry because you don't know what the reason is, and you suspect that they are secretly laughing at
you."

"All the more reason then not to trust them."

Mesmerized, she watched the creases alongside his
mouth deepen as he spoke. There was a bitter conviction in
his voice and a tautness to his lips, as if he had learned
about trust the hard way.

A silence fell between them. She knew she ought to say
something; otherwise he would think her sadly dull. He
would make his excuses, bow in that mocking way of his,
and depart. A moment ago she had wanted him to leave her
alone. Now, perversely, she didn't. She searched for a topic
of conversation, but her head was suddenly as empty as the
Reverend Troutbeck's collection plate.

The hurdy-gurdy was being cranked to a resounding crescendo, and the spinning horses whirled faster and faster,
until they became blurs of color, like streams of spilled
paint. Chinese lanterns flickered in the dusk, giving the
illusion that the horses were alive.

Jessalyn's breath came out in an unconscious sigh. "That
looks like such fun."

"Shall we find out?"

Before she knew what he was about, he had seized her hand, dragging her along after him. "It's for children!" she cried, but he didn't seem to hear. He dipped two fingers into his fob pocket and fished out a couple coins, which he tossed at the startled man in the checkered coat.

He lifted her onto the spinning platform and leaped up after her. He must have put all his weight onto his wounded leg, for he stumbled slightly and a grimace of pain flashed across his face. She reached out to him, to steady him. But he shook off her hand and, seizing her around the waist, hoisted her sidesaddle onto a blue horse's back. Laughing, she grabbed the pole as the world whirled by. He took the mount behind her. His legs were so long he dwarfed the horse. She laughed again, but not at him.

Their gazes met, and he smiled. The first true smile that she had seen from him. It melted the starkness of his face and turned the creases at the corners of his mouth into boyish dimples. She could still feel the imprint of his hands on her waist, like a lingering warmth. Around they went, riding on the wind and her laughter, and the Chinese lanterns became spinning stars. She wanted it to go on and on and on.

The merry-go-round wound slowly down. The music died, along with his smile. Too soon he was beside her. His hand slid beneath her elbow to help her dismount, then let her go. She had to catch her breath, as if she and not the horses had been galloping around and around. She turned to look at him. The dusk had deepened into darkness. The lanterns cast harsh shadows over the fairground and on his face.

The wind snatched at a lock of her hair, plastering it across her mouth. He plucked it free, the rough seam of his leather glove just brushing her lips. He rubbed the lock of hair between his fingers as if feeling its texture before he tucked it behind her ear, touching her again, and Jessalyn's stomach clenched with a strange hollowness that was close to pain. Or hunger. She wanted something, but what that something was she couldn't name or imagine.

He stepped back, and Jessalyn released the breath she hadn't even known she was holding. "Thank you for your charming company, Miss Letty," he said. "Perhaps someday we shall go riding together on the real thing."

She stared up at his face, at those piercing eyes and hard mouth. *Dangerous to know* . . . He both drew and repelled her. There was something dark and seductive about him; to come within his presence was like walking into a spider web. She knew she ought to tell him that it would be improper to call on her when they had not been formally introduced, but her throat and chest were suddenly so tight she couldn't speak.

"Jessalyn!"

She spun around to see a tall young man striding toward her. He waved his hat in the air, and the lanterns gilded his hair into a golden halo. "Clarence!" she exclaimed, laughing with surprise and delight.

"I thought it just possible that I might find you here," he said as he came up to her. "But I didn't dare to hope. . . ." He seized her hands and looked down at her warmly, with eyes that were bottle green and a winsome smile that revealed the small gap between his two front teeth. Then his gaze slid beyond her, and his eyes narrowed.

Jessalyn turned around just in time to see the Trelawny man's broad back disappearing into the crowd. She felt strangely bereft, like a puppy that has been taken to the crossroads and abandoned.

"Were you with McCady Trelawny?" Clarence said, surprise in his voice.

"What?" She became aware that Clarence was still holding her hands and studying her face. She pulled away from him, forcing out a laugh. "Oh, no, I don't even know Mr. Trelawny. Not at all. Not to speak to, that is. Well, perhaps to speak to, but I don't really *know* him, if you know what I mean . . ."

Clarence was grinning at her. "Jessalyn, you are babbling. You always babble when you're nervous. Or when you have something to hide."

He knew her too well, did Clarence Tiltwell. They had spent so many hours of their childhood together, swimming, fishing, riding. They had shared their dreams and their secrets. But that was long ago; the dreams and the secrets had been those of children. She hadn't seen him much after he had been sent away to Eton and had then gone on to university. She realized suddenly that he was a man now, very much the London buck in his snuff brown coat and fawn-colored ankle button trousers. He had always been fair and slender, like his mother.

Cousins. Clarence and that Trelawny man—they were cousins.

Jessalyn remembered now. . . . His mother's sister had been married to the late earl of Caerhays. They were all dead now—Clarence's mother, the sister, and the earl. There had been some scandal. The kind of scandal that produces a rush of hot whispers that is always cut off when someone young and female enters the room. It meant, of course, that someone had been caught in the marital act with someone one wasn't married to.

"Jessalyn?"

Jessalyn looked up at Clarence's face, searching for a resemblance to his dark cousin. Except for their height, the two young men couldn't have been more different.

He studied her just as intently. "You've changed," he said. "Grown up."

"So have you." They shared a slow smile that was ripe with memories.

"Where is your grandmother?" he said abruptly. "Surely she isn't allowing you to wander the fair alone. Especially now that you're all grown up."

Jessalyn laughed, feeling suddenly carefree again. "Well, I did have a chaperone of a sort. But she was seduced away by ginger beer."

He offered her his bent arm. "They'll be lighting the
bonfire soon. Shall we go watch?"

They left the fair, walking along the top of the seawall.
The bay bristled with masts from all the brigs, cutters, and
ketches, like the spines on a porcupine's back. The smell of
tar and rope and rusted chain was heavy in the air. They
spoke of Lady Letty and the stud farm, of his life at Cam-
bridge, and the party his father was giving at their country
manor house, Larkhaven, on the morrow. Jessalyn smiled
and laughed with the young man who walked beside her,
and all the while a part of her was aware of, was looking for
his dark-haired, dark-eyed cousin.

To take advantage of traffic from the fair, the fishmongers
had set out their wares along the wharf. Shining wet mackerel and bass lay on granite slabs, next to piles of huge
black oyster bags and herring barrels. A fishwife, in her
leather apron and scarlet petticoat, screamed at them as
they walked by: "Ye-oo! Ye-o-o! Buy me fresh cockles an'
whelks-o!"

"Remember that last Midsummer's Eve," Jessalyn said,
"before you were sent away to school." They had discovered, quite unattended, a barrel of freshly tapped ale behind one of the kiddley tents. It had been Jessalyn's idea to
taste of the forbidden fruit. "We both became pickled as
herrings and got caught trying to sneak into one of those
tawdry halfpenny peep shows."

Clarence stooped to retrieve a lobster that had escaped
from a wriggling, smelly brown basket. "And I got a rare
good thrashing for it, too."

She looked down at his bowed shoulders, at the edges of
his blond hair that curled out from beneath his hat. She felt
a rush of fondness for him. "Poor Clarence. I was always
getting you into trouble, wasn't I?"

He looked up at her and smiled. "It was always worth it."

They walked up the center street that climbed to Market
Place. Torches made of old sailcloth dipped in tar had been

set up along the way. Many of the houses had candles burning in their windows and doorsteps.

A great bonfire, made of old pit props, spars, and broken masts, had been heaped into the middle of the cobbled square. They arrived just in time to see the pile of wood doused with pilchard oil and set alight. The bonfire burned brightly and high and was reflected a dozen times over in the bow windows of the houses around the square.

They stood around the fire, drinking noggins of beer laced with rum and waiting to get at the potatoes roasting in the embers. A lemon moon rolled across the sky. The wind came up from the sea, bringing with it the smell of fish and a promise of morning fog.

Clarence had gone quiet beside her. She turned to look at him. He had an odd expression on his face, a kind of tenseness. He dipped his head toward her, and she realized suddenly that he was going to kiss her. She started to turn her head aside and then at the last moment did not. His lips were warm and dry. They brushed her mouth briefly and were gone.

He took her hand, but she pulled it away.

"You should not have done that," she said.

"I beg your pardon," he said, not sounding at all contrite. "I don't know what came over me."

"Nevertheless, you shouldn't have done it."

She shouldn't have allowed it. All of Penzance had seen him kiss her. Her grandmother would hear of it. All of Cornwall would hear of it, and the scandal broth would have them before the altar getting married by the end of the week.

"No. I should not have done it," Clarence said softly, his breath brushing against her cheek. "Yet."

The bonfire collapsed, sending up a fountain of flames and sparks. In the sudden flare of light, Jessalyn caught sight of the Trelawny man standing on the fringes of the crowd. The fire glazed the sharp bones of his cheeks and brows, creating dark hollows beneath. The flames shimmered in his eyes, so that it seemed a hotter fire blazed deep within him. He reminded her more than ever of what she had thought the first time she had seen him . . . a fallen angel.

She wondered how long he had been there, watching her. Watching them. She turned to see if Clarence had noticed him. When she glanced that way again, he was gone.

4

"'Tis not the done thing," Lady Letty pronounced, "to go to a ball in a jingle."

"It was the cheapest conveyance they had," Jessalyn said, for what felt like the hundredth time. "You told me to rent the cheapest they had."

The small two-wheeled pony-drawn cart swayed and jolted down the lane. It carried Jessalyn, her grandmother, and the serving girl, Becka Poole, to Larkhaven for Cornwall's social event of the year—Henry Tiltwell's Midsummer's Day house party.

"One must arrive in style, gel," Lady Letty said, unwilling to let the matter drop. "In style. I cannot for the life of me imagine what you were thinking of to rent a jingle. A jingle! 'Tain't the done thing. Never has been, never will be—"

The cart gave a sudden, violent lurch. Lady Letty grunted, one hand grabbing for the seat, the other clutching her lace cap. She directed a fierce scowl at her granddaughter, who had charge of the ribbons. "Really, gel, must you search out every bump and rut in the road? My teeth are clacking together like a pair of Spanish castanets."

"I'm that sorry, Gram," Jessalyn said, trying hard not to laugh. "I shall endeavor to steer a smoother course."

Poor Becka Poole, who sat in the back with her legs dangling over the tail, was getting the worst of it. She moaned loudly, rubbing her bottom. "God's me life! I'll be sleepin' on me stomach this night, I tell ee. Sich bruises do I have on me dairy-air."

Jessalyn exchanged astonished glances with her grandmother.

"That be an eddicated word, Miss Jessalyn," Becka said, leaning backward to impart this information. "I learnt it from that mountebank what sold me the toothache powder. A furrin word. 'Tes what them Frenchies say when they have a need to speak of their arses, but 'tes more politelike, see? Dairy-air."

Lady Letty snorted loudly and took a pinch of snuff.

Sucking on her cheeks to hide a smile, Jessalyn looked at the passing countryside. Not that she was able to see much over the hedge of herringboned stone, which had moss growing along the top of it like close-cropped hair. She wanted to laugh aloud in her happiness. She was going to her first real house party. There would be music and dancing and . . . maybe him. Her stomach clenched around a strange knot of fear and excitement at the thought.

They turned onto a private road, and immediately the ruts disappeared, as if smoothed by a giant's palm. Through the elms and sycamores that lined the way, Jessalyn caught glimpses of the chimneys and gables of Larkhaven. They joined a serpentine of other carriages and coaches, Lady Letty fussing all the while about jingles, balls, and done things.

A broad green expanse of shaven turf and a neatly raked gravel drive led up to sweeping front steps. Larkhaven was an enormous square granite and slate mansion with columns made of purple stone flanking the entrance and a pavilion at each corner. It looked as though it ought to shelter at least a duke, but the man who owned it was the son of a tutworker. And all the world knew that no matter how much money Henry Tiltwell acquired, no matter how grand a house he built, blood told and birth would always matter.

Still, Henry Tiltwell had such financial power that few in Cornwall felt secure enough, or rich enough, to ignore a summons to Larkhaven. Even if it was couched in the form of an invitation to a party.

Jessalyn and her grandmother were met at the front door by a liveried servant and led up a white marble staircase with gilt-bronze balustrades. The house was said to have more than thirty bedrooms. To underscore Henry Tiltwell's opinion of where the Lettys stood in his social order— which was old name, but no money and even less influence —Jessalyn and her grandmother were given a pair of tiny adjoining rooms just under the eaves. Jessalyn's room smelled of camphor balls, but a velvet curtain had been hung over the door to keep out drafts. A truckle bed and a dressing table with an oval looking glass mounted on brass swivels constituted the only furnishings.

As soon as she was alone, Jessalyn removed a glass jar that she had secreted at the bottom of her reticule. She had purchased it at the apothecary's shop just that morning. The concoction, the man had assured her, was guaranteed to bleach away freckles. Humming a tinner's ditty, she sat at the dressing table and applied the gooey mixture to her face.

The paste, made of barley flour, crushed almonds, and honey, hardened as soon as it was exposed to the air. After a couple of minutes the mask began to itch. Mildly at first. Then almost unbearably. But the apothecary had told her to leave it on at least half an hour.

To take her mind off her itching face, Jessalyn went to the tiny dormer window. She had to get on her knees to look out, so low was the room's slanting ceiling. Through the glazed panes, she could hear the throb of a pump, like a heartbeat. She threw up the sash for a better view. If she leaned out, she could just see the top of the brick en-

ginehouse and the round, smoke-belching chimney of the
tin mine called Wheal Charlotte.

A bell began to clang, signaling the change of cores. A
group of miners, their clothes stained with mud and clay,
straggled over the top of the hill, meeting those going down
for the next shift. Two men walked apart from the rest,
following the rails of the tramroad that led from the mine
down to Penzance Harbor. Clarence Tiltwell and his scapegrace Trelawny cousin. She wondered if they had been doing some sort of rough work, for both were in shirtsleeves
and hatless. Clarence's close-cropped blond curls cupped
his head like a gilded helmet. His cousin's dark brown hair,
unfashionably long, blew in the wind.

They turned toward the house, and as they drew closer,
she could hear the tone of their voices, though not the
words. There was a sense of barely suppressed excitement
between them, as if they shared a secret. Clarence slapped
his cousin on the back, and the man threw back his head
and laughed.

Trying to hear what they were saying, she leaned over as
they passed beneath her. Her elbow nudged loose a slate.
She lunged to catch the slate and fell forward onto her
chest, sliding out the window with a loud rip of corded
muslin. Out the corner of her eye she saw something pro-
jecting from the roof, and she made a wild grab for it.

Several slates landed with a splintering crash on the
brick walk below. Two masculine heads, one fair and one
dark, looked up. Jessalyn lay, half in, half out the window,
clinging for dear life to the snout of a gargoyle.

For a moment they simply stared at her, and Jessalyn
couldn't decide whether she wanted to laugh or to die. She
glanced down, hoping at least that some bosom might be
spilling provocatively out of her modest tucker.

The Trelawny man's face broke into that dimpled, boyish
smile. "I say, cousin," he drawled, "you certainly have big
larks here at Larkhaven."

Jessalyn laughed . . . and felt her face crack.

*   *   *

Downstairs the party had begun. The hum of distant music vibrated the floorboards beneath her feet. Laughing, Jessalyn spun around on her toes, making her skirt bell out.

Her one and only good dress was, the mantua-maker had assured her, quite the latest thing. It had a waist so high it ended just beneath her breasts and tiny puffed sleeves. It was made of the palest green tulle over a slip of jade-colored satin and had lace-trimmed flounces going halfway up the skirt. She twisted her neck, trying to see all of herself in the dressing table's small looking glass. She only hoped so much green didn't make her look like a stalk of asparagus.

The dress had been made for the occasion of her birthday four months ago, and already it was a little short. She sighed. If only she would stop *growing*. Or at least start growing in more appropriate places.

With some of the saddle horse money Jessalyn had, at her grandmother's urging, purchased a pair of white satin slippers that fastened with ribbons around her ankles and evening gloves of soft limerick. In a chest in End Cottage's attic, she had found a fan made of white crepe and a silver beaded reticule. Gram had forbidden her to use carmine powder, so she had rouged her cheeks and lips with red tea leaves instead and had darkened her brows with a bit of burned cork. She brushed her hair until it had a gloss like japanned leather. Now, standing in the middle of her room, she felt almost breathless with anticipation and excitement.

She went next door to fetch her grandmother, only to be told by Becka that Lady Letty had already gone down. Jessalyn took the narrow wooden stairs to the next landing, where the more important guests were sleeping. She glided along the Oriental runner that graced the wide hall, feeling like a countess.

At a jog in the hall she came upon a looking glass above a pier table that supported a tulip-shaped pink and white Wedgwood vase. Caught by her own reflection, she paused.

She unfurled her fan, covering half her face with the white crepe leaves. The effect, she thought, made her look exotic and mysterious.

Lady Letty had told her that there was an etiquette, almost an art, to handling a fan. There was, for instance, the Refusal Look. Jessalyn narrowed her eyes and pursed her lips, screwing her face into the way she imagined such a look would be. Then there was the Lingering Look—calculated to invite but not embolden. She wriggled her brows and blinked her lashes. No, that didn't seem quite right. She opened her eyes wide and tilted her head, first to the left, then to the right.

A harsh face with dark, flaring brows appeared in the looking glass over her shoulder. She let out a tiny shriek and whirled, and her elbow sent the pink and white Wedgwood vase tumbling.

He caught it within inches of its smashing on the floor. He straightened slowly and, his gaze locking with hers, set the vase back on its perch. He looked dashing in his regimentals—a cherry red coat with gold cuffs and collar and full, lacy cravat. Dull gold epaulets enhanced the broadness of his shoulders. His cream-colored pantaloons were so tight she wondered how he sat ahorse in them.

"Are you ill, Miss Letty?"

Jessalyn was still lost in staring at his splendid magnificence "Ill?"

"You were making such horrid faces I thought you might be in pain."

She sucked in a deep breath, recovering her wits. "It was quite rude of you to sneak up on me like that."

He performed a mocking half bow. "I humbly beg your pardon. Next time I'll have a fife and drum announce me."

He looked her over, not bothering to hide the fact that he was judging her as a man was wont to judge a woman. She waited, in spite of herself, for his compliment.

Instead he leaned toward her and sniffed at the air. "What is that smell?"

"What?"

"Almonds." He dipped his head toward her neck. "Almonds and honey."

Her hands flew up to cover her cheeks. "Oh, blast. It's that odious paste I put on my face. Do I stink?"

"On the contrary, Miss Letty. You smell quite edible." Somehow her arm had become linked through his, and he was leading her down the hall toward the white marble staircase. "Although I must confess when I saw you falling out the window earlier, I thought you were a mummer hired to give us entertainment after supper. But tell me, why do you smear almonds and honey on your face—unless it's to attract bees? Aren't you afraid of getting stung?"

There seemed to be a current beneath his words, a deeper meaning she couldn't fathom. He sounded almost angry. "I was trying to rid myself of these wretched freckles," she said.

He pulled her to a stop on one of the steps. Cupping her chin, he tilted her face up. He rubbed his thumb along the length of her cheekbone, stroking, back and forth. "They're still there," he said, his voice low and soft.

She felt his touch all the way down to her toes. Somewhere in another world the band was playing a quadrille; somewhere in another world people were laughing and talking. But in her world there was only the incredible sensation of his silk-gloved thumb caressing her skin.

"Leave them be, Miss Letty. Perfection is boring."

She became lost in the deep wells of darkness that were his eyes. In that moment, if he had asked, she would have given him her heart wrapped with a silver bow. Even if he only meant to break it.

His hand fell from her face. He took her arm, turning her. Together they looked down the stairs to the great hall below, where Henry Tiltwell stood with his hands fisted at his sides and a look of fury on his face.

* * *

"He wasn't invited," Lady Letty said. "But he came anyway. Cheeky devil. The Trelawnys have always been cheeky devils."

She flicked open her snuffbox with a crooked finger and took a pinch of Queen Charlotte's mixture. Tonight she carried one of her favorite boxes, of silver plate with a large piece of cut glass on the lid that twinkled like a ruby.

Jessalyn waited until her grandmother had sneezed into a handkerchief. "Why not?" she asked. "Why wasn't he invited?"

"What a sad crush. We had better park ourselves," Lady Letty announced, "before all the best seats are taken."

Because of the festive occasion, Lady Letty had donned a voluminous white cap decorated with love knots and trailing lappets. In her stiff black bombazine skirts she looked like a coal scuttle under full sail. She set a direct course for one of the few chairs that lined the wall, Jessalyn following in her wake.

"Why wouldn't Mr. Tiltwell invite his own nephew to his party?" Jessalyn said as soon as her grandmother was settled.

"There was a breach between the two families, oh, years ago. But the reasons for the feud are a story too scandalous for your tender ears." Lady Letty frowned and cupped a hand to her own ear. "What's that they're playing, eh? It had better not be a waltz. I shan't let you dance one of those scandalous waltzes."

Jessalyn sighed, but she knew better than to press. For all that she loved to gossip, Gram could be as closemouthed as a clam with lockjaw when she put her mind to it. And as for dancing, well, someone had to ask her first.

Jessalyn flapped her fan in front of her face. The air smelled and felt like a hothouse in July, with so many perfumes and hundreds of beeswax candles burning in the chandeliers. Talk and laughter and the clicking of snuffboxes nearly drowned out the strains of a minuet. Vast pier glasses, set between lofty windows, reflected back the sheen of satin and silk and the sparkle of jewels. The room seemed all mirrors and silvered walls.

That Trelawny man, who hadn't been invited, leaned against a fluted pillar, a thumb hooked on his fob pocket and a sulky look about his mouth. She tried not to stare at him.

She looked for Clarence but didn't see him. Clarence's father, Mr. Henry Tiltwell, moved about the room with ponderous dignity, greeting his guests. He had thick brows that grew like hedgerows across his forehead and a jutting bottom lip. He was a short, thickset man, and in his white breeches and yellow waistcoat he reminded Jessalyn of a boiled egg. He kept casting dagger looks at his nephew, who hadn't been invited. But who had come anyway.

A woman walked by, giving them the sort of smile one presents to strangers one thinks one ought to know. The paint on her face was so thick it looked enameled. A false eyebrow, whose glue had come loose in the heat, was migrating up her forehead.

Lady Letty pointed to the woman. "That fool has a caterpillar crawling about her face. You'd think someone would tell her."

"I believe that is an eyebrow, Gram."

"All the more reason to tell her, eh? If she's losing her eyebrows." Lady Letty raised her cane, and Jessalyn had the horrible thought that her grandmother was going to hail the woman with the wayward brow, but what she did do was even worse. "You there, Trelawny! Quit skulking about and come over here, you rakeshame."

He pushed himself off the pillar and sauntered toward them. Even with his limp he moved, Jessalyn thought, like a lazy cat on a hot day.

He bowed over her grandmother's hand. "Upon my soul, it's Lady Letty. I thought at first that my eyes had alighted on a figure of royalty, at the very least a duchess, so regal did you seem, sitting over here and holding court. All you lack is a tiara and a bit of something trimmed in ermine."

Lady Letty directed a fierce scowl up at him. "Don't talk such fustian with me, boy. I don't like it." She raised her quizzing glass to her eye and looked him slowly up and down as if she were judging the horseflesh at an auction. "The last time I saw you, you were but a sapling. You've grown up. But I tell myself it is a rotted pea that comes from a rotted pod. Are you rotten, boy?"

A tight smile thinned his lips. "All the way through to my black heart."

To Jessalyn's astonishment this answer seemed to please Lady Letty, for she snorted a laugh. "Nevertheless," she said, "in spite of your wicked reputation, I shall permit you to dance with my granddaughter."

After the briefest hesitation he turned slightly and bowed in Jessalyn's direction. As he straightened, his eyes fastened on to her face, and something stirred within their dark depths, like a dragon dwelling deep in a cave just coming awake. Her legs trembled, wanting to flee, but her heart and mind were drawn into that cave to discover for herself the nature of the sleeping beast.

His arm settled around her waist, and Jessalyn's every muscle tensed as she fought off a shudder. She spoke to the brass buttons on his coat. "My grandmother doesn't mean half of what she says. She likes to shock people."

"So do I," he said. His palm pressed into her back, guiding her in a dipping, sweeping circle, and that shivery, hollow feeling gripped her stomach again. "And so, I think, do you. Perhaps we ought to form a club and take subscriptions. We can call ourselves the Dishonorable Society to Alleviate Boredom and Complacency."

She had no hope of matching words with him, so she didn't even try. She was excited just to be dancing. She wondered if Lady Letty had realized the band was playing one of those scandalous waltzes. Jessalyn had often practiced the steps by dancing with a broom. But a broom didn't have legs and feet, and his kept getting in her way.

She stumbled over his boot, causing them to miss a step. "Blast it," she exclaimed beneath her breath.

"They behave better when you aren't watching them."

She couldn't imagine what he meant; then she realized he was talking about her feet. She tried not to look down. But the only other place to look, besides at him, was up. A three-tiered crystal chandelier fringed in gold hung above their heads from a ceiling rose decorated with grapevines and plump, pink-bottomed cherubs. The ceiling was festooned with so many scrolls and rosettes it reminded her of a cheese and raspberry torte. Just looking at it made her dizzy.

Her gaze fell to his face, and she blinked as the room spun around her, momentarily out of control. His expression was politely blank, but his gaze was fastened on to her face again, on her mouth, and it seemed as if he stroked her lips with the heat of his eyes. She looked away.

He was nearly half a head taller than she. Even Clarence, whom she'd always thought of as tall, did not match his height. Although he tried to hide it, she could tell his leg pained him with every step. "That is a terrible wound you bear," she said, and then felt her face grow hot as she remembered the circumstances under which she had seen it.

His arm tightened around her waist, gathering her closer. For a moment his thigh pressed between her legs and she actually felt its hardness and its heat, and then he took another step and they parted. She stumbled again. "How—how did it happen?" she asked.

"I was careless."

"Oh. But I thought it must have happened at Waterloo."

"How perceptive of you."

Another flush spread over her face. His hand burned into her back, and the room was much too hot. Her chest felt tight, as if she couldn't draw a deep enough breath. "I did not mean to pry," she finally managed. "I am sure it is an honorable wound you bear. Your cousin told me last night of how you rallied your men when they were breaking and led them on a renewed charge of the enemy. It was an excessively brave thing to do."

"It was an excessively stupid thing to do. I got them all killed and nearly killed myself while I was about it. Do let us change the subject, Miss Letty."

That wasn't what Clarence had said. Clarence had told her that his cousin's heroic stand had saved the day for his regiment at Waterloo. The king and Parliament had cited him for his bravery.

Her gaze went back to his face. The lace at his throat emphasized the masculine harshness of his features. Shadows stirred again behind the flatness of his dark eyes. She searched for a new topic of conversation. She longed to be able to dazzle him with some witty remark about the weather or the company. What she said was: "Will you be in Cornwall long, Captain Trelawny?"

"I am grateful for the promotion. However, as it is a capital crime to impersonate a superior officer, I am obliged to confess to being a mere lieutenant. Are you disappointed?"

"Devastated. But doubtless you shall be made a captain soon."

"Not unless you have sixteen hundred pounds to lend me so that I might purchase the commission."

She started to laugh, then smothered it with her lips, so that it came out more of a snort. "Don't be a silly goose," she said.

"Do I take it from that profound remark that you are refusing me a loan? Then I fear that I am doomed to remain the oldest lieutenant in His Majesty's army."

"Are you poor?"

His face broke into a dazzling smile. "Wretchedly so."

She floated, lost in the music and the feel of his arm around her waist, lost in his smile. "So am I. Poor, that is."

"What a pity. For I do believe that were you an heiress, silly goose that I am, I just might be inclined to marry you."

He was not being serious. Of course, he wasn't being serious. But even to jest about such a thing sent her heart diving and soaring like the gulls at Crookneck Cove.

He did not ask her to dance again. She stood up only twice more, both times with Clarence Tiltwell. She watched him while she danced and while she drank a glass of effervescent lemon with her grandmother afterward. He spent most of the time talking with the same petite gilt-haired girl. Once he threw back his head and laughed, and Jessalyn felt an odd hollowness in her stomach, as if she'd just been told a sad story. Selina Alcott was the girl's name, and she had curves and she had money. He was not such a silly goose after all.

Lady Letty followed the direction of her granddaughter's gaze. "Good looks, an earldom in his future, and a witty tongue in his head—a thoroughly dangerous combination. I'm thinking I ought to lock you up for the summer."

"He doesn't like me. He teases."

"M'dear, when a man like him teases a gel, 'tis long before time that she should think about running in the other direction." Lady Letty reached for her cane, pushing herself to her feet. "There's got to be a faro bank going somewhere around here. I feel like taking a plunge."

The green baize card tables had been set up in a nearby room. Jessalyn stood beside her grandmother's chair and watched her lose what was left of the saddle horse money, playing a wild game of faro for ruinous stakes. She kept one eye on the open door to the drawing room, where the dancers whirled by to the muted scraping of the band. She did not see Lieutenant Trelawny again.

After a light refreshment of heart cakes and syllabubs, Jessalyn joined several of the other guests who had strolled out into the terraced gardens to watch the sun set. Chinese lanterns lit up graveled paths that meandered through clipped shrubberies and flowers arranged geometrically in beds. Weeping willows shivered in the breeze, and the larks, from which the house got its name, lightened the evening with their song. It all seemed so tidy, so perfect that Jessalyn felt a rebellious desire to sneak over one dark night and plant a gorse bush among the daffodils.

Some sort of commotion was happening on top of the hill before Wheal Charlotte, and Jessalyn walked up to see what it was. What she saw made her laugh aloud with delight.

A locomotive sat huffing and wheezing on the tramway outside the mine house. The cone-shaped boiler, bolted to a frame in the shape of a wagon bed, looked like a big yellow sugar loaf. Its wheels, too, had been gaily painted: a poppy red for the rims, a Prussian blue for the spokes. A tall black funnel, with a lid fluted like a piecrust, burped steam. There was nothing neat and tidy about it. It belched smoke and made rude noises; it had no respect for the proper conventions. Jessalyn thought it the most marvelous thing she'd ever seen.

Henry Tiltwell did not share her enthusiasm. He climbed the hill, huffing worse than the locomotive. He spotted his son standing beside the engine, and he advanced on him, his face mottled with rage. "Clarence! What nonsense is this?"

Clarence paled slightly before his father's anger. "We thought . . . that is, Mack and I thought . . ."

"To do a small demonstration, if you will." Lieutenant Trelawny emerged from behind the locomotive. He was in his shirtsleeves, and he carried an oil can in his hand. His dark, piercing gaze met everyone's eyes in turn, and when he spoke, it was not only to Henry Tiltwell but to all the men there with the power and influence and money to make a reality out of an inventor's dream. Or to kill it through skepticism and ridicule.

"To get your tin ore from the pitheads to the nearest blowing house for smelting," he said, "you mineowners are constantly transporting heavy loads. But pit ponies and mules wear out, and fodder is expensive. What you see here before you is a cheaper and more efficient method. Steam locomotion—an engine capable of generating mechanical power from thermal energy. A single locomotive like this could pull five cartloads of tin from here to Penzance in less than an hour." He had lost the sneering drawl he normally affected. Excitement and a vision shone in his voice and on his face.

Mr. Tiltwell hawked a scornful laugh. "An iron horse, eh? An iron horse!" He looked around at his guests, inviting them to share in his joke. "Didn't I hear of just such a thing up in Wales a few years back? It blew itself to pieces, so they said. Killed four men, it did. They said 'twas like soldering the lid onto a pot of boiling water. It blew so high they heard it nigh up in Chester." Again he laughed.

A muscle ticked once in Lieutenant Trelawny's jaw, but his voice remained steady. "That was an earlier version. The design has been improved since then, including the fitting of two safety valves instead of one." He paused, drawing in a deep breath, and suddenly to Jessalyn's eyes he looked young and vulnerable. He was laying himself open to ridicule and hurt, and he knew, even as he was doing so, that he was likely to get it.

Clarence cleared his throat. "Why can't you at least let him show us, Father?"

Mr. Tiltwell turned on his son. "You shut your clack! I hold you responsible for his being here in the first place." He flung a stiff finger at the locomotive. "And as for this—this belching monster, the only thing it is capable of demonstrating is a singular ability to ruin my crops and scare the livestock. You mark if there will be a cow within miles giving milk in the morning."

He aimed a venomous look at his son that promised trouble later. Clarence flushed and looked away.

As if indifferent to the storm raging around him, Lieutenant Trelawny had jumped onto the steam engine to shovel more coal into the firebox. Henry Tiltwell started forward. Then, as if remembering his own dire predictions, he took a hasty step back. "This is my land, my tramway. I forbid this spectacle. Do you hear me? I forbid it!"

He was shouted down by several of the guests. Having heard about the iron horse that had blown up in Wales, they now hoped to be witness to a similar gruesome exhibition.

Jessalyn was the only one to step up for a closer look at the invention. The frame for the boiler was made of wood strengthened by iron plates. It rested on two large wheels in front and two much smaller wheels in back. To her eyes, the engine seemed a tangled coil of metal tubes and pipes. Hitched to the locomotive, like a cart to a pony, was a tender loaded with wicker baskets of coal and a big water barrel.

The boiler began to sing as it raised more steam. It hissed and breathed as if it were alive, and steam issued from every joint like sweat. It swayed and shuddered on the tramway tracks like a great beast gathering itself to spring. Jessalyn stared at the man who had created the beast, fascinated by the way the sweat stood out on his face and the muscles of his arms and back bunched and flexed beneath his thin lawn shirt as he heaved coal into the glowing red mouth of the firebox. She could not imagine an earl's son engaging in such rough manual labor. Her grandmother, she knew, would be scandalized, yet for some reason the sight excited her.

She called up to him. "I should like to come along with you, Lieutenant Trelawny."

He turned and looked down, and their gazes met. A passionate heat blazed in his eyes, brighter than the fire he stoked. She knew his own excitement had nothing to do with her, but Jessalyn felt weightless suddenly, as if she had just stepped off a cliff and discovered that she could fly.

He slammed the damper shut with a clang and jumped down in front of her. "This is not a merry-go-round."

He had rolled up his sleeves above his elbow, and sweat

glistened on the skin of his forearms. The wind pressed his shirt against his chest and ruffled the lace at his throat. She wanted to touch him, though she wasn't sure in what way. Just touch him.

"You claim that it's safe," she said. "What better way to prove it?"

"Miss Letty, young ladies do not ride on locomotives."

"Why not? Who says so? We ride on horses and drive in carriages. I drove a jingle this afternoon, even though Gram said it wasn't quite the done thing. Please, Lieutenant Trelawny. I would consider it an honor to ride on your splendid machine."

He stared down at her, his mouth hard. He drew in a sudden, sharp breath. "I ought to be kicked from here to London for doing this. You won't thank me for it later, you know." His hands fell around her waist, and he lifted her onto the footplate, coming up after her. "Don't touch the back of the firebox," he warned. "It's hot."

"Jessalyn!" Clarence came striding toward them. "What are you doing? Mack, you can't possibly allow her to—"

Henry Tiltwell slammed a heavy palm into his son's chest. "Let her go with him if she wants. This nonsense was your idea, boy. And it's her neck."

"Jessalyn, come down from there this instant," Clarence commanded, although he had stopped behind the barrier of his father's hand.

Jessalyn pretended not to hear him. The engine vibrated beneath her feet, making her belly tingle. There was life within this monster that breathed and shuddered and trembled, a life that had sprung directly from the heart and mind of the man beside her.

He was studying a pair of dials on the boiler. She leaned over his shoulder, and the wind blew his hair against her neck. "This one is not likely to explode, is it?" she asked, only half teasing.

He glanced sideways at her, bringing their faces closer together. His lips twisted into a wry smile, and she felt her mouth break into a wide grin, heard herself giggle. It was as if she were two Jessalyns: the girl who stood before this strange man, breathless, her heart fluttering with fear and excitement, and the wiser girl, watching from a distance and seeing what a fool she was making of herself, what a child he must think her to be.

"Are you getting cold feet?" he asked.

Actually her feet were becoming quite warm. The metal footplate absorbed heat from the firebox, so that it was like standing on top of a sizzling frypan.

"What you saw that day was an experiment for a steam-powered road carriage," he said. "This is different. This time I know what I'm doing."

"I am relieved to hear it. I wouldn't want to meet my end as little bits and pieces strewn along Mr. Tiltwell's tramway."

He laughed, and she felt the heat of his breath against her cheek. There was not much room on the tiny footplate. Every time one of them moved, their bodies would touch: Hip would rub against hip; her shoulder would brush his arm; his thigh would press against her bottom. She was so very aware of him. Of his smell: grease and soot and male sweat. Of the hard strength of his man's body where it touched hers. Of the fire burning in his dark eyes, revealing the brain behind the power that throbbed and pulsed around them.

She stared up into his face. She couldn't understand why, but the sight of him made her chest hurt. "How does it work?"

"Well, to put it simply—"

"*Very* simply, please," she said, laughing.

"Very simply then. The water in the boiler is heated until it produces steam. The steam from the boiler is admitted into the cylinders." He pointed to one of a matching pair of fat tubes bolted to the boiler. "When the steam enters the cylinder, it expands, pushing the piston—a thick bar, sort of like a hammer—which moves the rod, there"—he pointed at an iron arm that ran from the cylinder to one of the big front wheels—"which turns the driving wheel."

She lifted her smiling mouth and bright eyes up to his. "It's wonderful!"

A dark flush stained his cheekbones. She thought it odd that he would be embarrassed, but perhaps he had received little praise in his life. "The spent steam escapes through the chimney stack into the air," he finished, his gaze averted now from hers.

He reached for a metal lever, and his bare arm pressed against her breast. The monster sucked and breathed around them while Jessalyn stood motionless, unable to breathe at all.

He jerked back as if he'd just brushed against the hot metal of the firebox, and Jessalyn's own flesh burned where he had touched her.

"Perhaps it would be better if you rode in the tender," he said, his voice rough.

Before she could object, he lifted her into the car behind them. She found a place to stand between the baskets of coal and the water butt. He depressed a pedal with his right foot, while pulling on a metal pin and releasing a lever with his left hand. The smokestack huffed and puffed, blowing steam into the air. The pistons slid through the cylinders with hammerlike thuds, and the great beast came truly alive.

The locomotive lurched forward, thumping and hopping like a giant locust. Puffing and grunting and snorting, it clattered along the iron tracks toward a setting sun that cast pink shadows across ripening fields of barley and wheat. The steady thrust, thrust, thrust of the piston seemed to enter Jessalyn's blood until her heart beat along with the pulsing engine. She clutched her hat to keep it from being snatched away by the wind, and she laughed out loud. She knew she had galloped faster many times, but riding a horse had never been like this. This was the only thing man had invented that moved *itself*.

She saw the stone walls of Larkhaven through billows of steam. She thought she spotted her grandmother on the terrace, but they were already past it before she had time to wave. They crested a hill, then lumbered along the down-slope, picking up speed. At the base of the hill the rails cut across a small lane. Straddling the tracks, like a fat brooding hen, was a cart stacked high with hay. A farmer stood beside his balking mule, his mouth open in a perfect O of horror.

Lieutenant Trelawny bellowed at him to move his bloody arse. The farmer remained frozen a moment longer, then brought a stick down hard over the back of the mule. The mule didn't budge.

Jessalyn leaned over and shouted to be heard above the infernal clanking of the engine. "Perhaps we had better stop!"

"We can't!" he shouted back at her.

"What?"

"There aren't any brakes!"

Dear life . . . She covered her face with her hands. But not seeing was worse than seeing. She peeked through her fingers. The mule pricked its ears and took a step. The cart jerked forward. Very slowly. The locomotive tore along the rails, blowing smoke and roaring like a lunatic dragon.

The cart had not quite cleared the tracks when they hit it. The blunt nose of the locomotive clipped the very end of the wagonload of hay, and the world turned into a swirling, dusty yellow cloud.

The collision didn't faze the locomotive; it lurched and chugged along the rails without a pause. Jessalyn looked back over her shoulder, laughing and plucking bits of hay from her hair and eyes.

Suddenly the locomotive gave a wild lurch, bucking like an unbroken colt. A grinding screech ripped through the air. Jessalyn heard him cry "Hang on!" But the warning came too late, for she was already flying through the air.

Blue sky, green fields, and brown earth came at her in a whirl of color, reminding her of the merry-go-round.

Until she slammed hard into the ground and the world went black.

5

"I told you to hang on, dammit." It was Lieutenant Trelawny's voice, and there was a hard edge to it.

Something sharp and spiky poked into her back. Jessalyn
squirmed, trying to find a more comfortable position while
her dazed mind tried to focus on where she was and how
she came to be here, lying on this prickly bed of gorse. She
opened her eyes and saw a pair of black, glossy boots.

Her gaze traveled up the splendid length of him. His
chest and shoulders blocked out the setting sun. She liked
the shape of him, she decided; she liked looking at him. He
did not look at all pleased with her.

She laughed up at him and said in a deep Cornish burr,
"I've thistles stuck in me dairy-air."

For a moment she thought he might laugh along with
her. Instead his lips tightened, and he hunkered down next
to her. "Lie quiet a moment. You've a bump on your head
the size of a gull's egg." He brushed the hair off her brow,
his touch gentle and strangely intimate.

She struggled up onto her elbows. "No, I'm all right.
Truly." But the world tipped sideways, and she swayed.

"Do you ever do what you're told?" His hand gripped
her arm, not at all gently. "Next time I want you to do

something I shall have to remember to ask for its exact opposite."

She pulled free of him, pushing herself to her feet. She walked on unsteady legs over to where the locomotive tilted at an angle, its nose buried in the sod. The steaming, clattering, and clanking monster now stood quiet, a slain beast. Pieces of broken rails lay scattered about, looking as if they had been squashed by the foot of a giant.

She felt him come up beside her. "What happened?" she asked.

"The rails gave way. We were going too fast and the engine is so heavy it knocked the iron plates to pieces."

"What a pity, for now everyone will think your locomotive a failure."

"Everyone would be right." Below his haughty cheekbone a muscle jumped. She ached for him. She wanted to gather his head to her breast, to stroke her fingers though his hair and tell him it didn't matter what others thought.

She touched his arm instead and felt the muscles harden beneath the warmth of his skin. "Oh, no, Lieutenant Trelawny. With power such as this—with power such as this, a man could change the world."

For a moment the shadows in his eyes lifted, and she saw a sort of bewildered hurt mixed with hope. But then he blinked and looked away.

They both turned at the sound of hoofbeats. Clarence bore down upon them on his big sorrel gelding. His father and a few of the other guests, drawn by curiosity, loped along behind him.

"Jessalyn!" Clarence cried, sliding off his horse before them. His eyes widened at the sight of the derailed locomotive. "My God, Jessalyn, are you all right? Mack, what the deuce were you thinking of? You should never have subjected her to the rigors, not to mention the dangers of—"

"God's life, Clarence," Jessalyn snapped. She had forgotten what a prosy old stick he could be at times. "There's no need to enact a tragedy. I'm perfectly all right apart from a slight lump on my head."

"And a few thistles in her pretty arse," Lieutenant Trelawny added.

His drawling remark startled a whoop of loud laughter out of Jessalyn. She tried to stop it with her hand and nearly choked.

"She's hysterical," Clarence said. His color high, he glared at his cousin. "There, you see. The shock has made her hysterical."

Henry Tiltwell and his cronies came trotting up to them. Tiltwell's laughter boomed out over the rolling fields. "Come a cropper, did you, boy? Your iron horse came a cropper, what?" He roared at his joke, and the others joined him.

Lieutenant Trelawny stood rigid before their laughter, his face blank. But Jessalyn had caught the flash of pain in his eyes before he shuttered them, and she couldn't bear it. "You fools!" she shouted, whirling to confront the laughing men. "You are all addlepated, cork-brained fools!"

It stopped their laughter, but only for a moment. "Came a cropper!" Henry Tiltwell bellowed again, slapping his thigh.

Her hands clenched into fists at her sides. She hated them for their ignorance and their cruelty, for mocking the man who had built that wonderful locomotive, simply because it did not fit into their tidy world. Lieutenant Trelawny stood apart, alone, and she felt his aloneness as an empty hole deep within her own self. She had no idea of how her eyes shone as she looked at him, bright as beacons on a black night.

Or that Clarence Tiltwell saw it.

At twenty-two Clarence Francis Tiltwell thought of himself as a man. Yet he could never enter the library at Larkhaven without feeling a sick clenching deep in his gut. As a boy the only times he had ever been summoned to this room was to receive a thrashing. Now, pulling open the heavy wooden doors, he felt all of ten years old again and scared.

Turkey rugs of muted colors covered the floor, and green velvet curtains shrouded the windows. The walls were decorated with hunting paraphernalia—old spurs, whips, horns, and a collection of antique matchlocks and crossbows. Books bound in green and gold-blocked calf filled glass-fronted cases. It was a man's room, but it could not be said that the room reflected the man within it. Henry Tiltwell hated hunting, and as far as Clarence knew, he had never willingly read a book in his life.

The man Clarence called Father was ensconced in a hooded maroon leather chair behind an enormous mahogany pedestal desk. He did not ask Clarence to sit down, but Clarence sat anyway, taking a small satisfaction in this defiance.

"You will kindly explain to me," Henry said in his bull-throated voice, "why you brought McCady Trelawny here to disrupt my party with that belching monster."

"As it happens, he brought himself." Clarence dared a small, taunting smile. "Not that it signifies, for he should hardly need an invitation. He is, after all, your nephew."

"He's an insolent bastard!"

The word *bastard* reverberated like the clap of a church bell in the room's heavy velvet silence. Clarence's smile twisted into one of bitterness.

The green cut-glass lamp on the desk gave an unhealthy tinge to Henry Tiltwell's heavy jowls and pouchy eyes. He could not meet the younger man's gaze but toyed instead with the rings and seals on his fob. He had big, splayed hands. They were a tutworker's hands, though he had never wielded a pick.

In moments like these Clarence was glad the man was not his father.

Except that he *could* be his father. Because his mother had refused to, or couldn't, say which man had fathered him. She had, after all, been sleeping with both men at the same time—her husband and her sister's husband, that lecherous rake the earl of Caerhays. Clarence could never understand why Henry Tiltwell had forgiven her. If she had been his wife, he would have killed her.

"I want you to stay away from the Letty girl," Henry said, and Clarence had to drag his thoughts back with a wrench. "That peculiar friendship was bad enough when you were a boy; it could have disastrous consequences now. I don't want any hole-in-the-corner marriages or paternity suits. I've bigger plans for you than to see you leg-shackled to some provincial chit, who is tarred with peasant blood and has no dowry to speak of."

"I doubt in any event that Lady Letty would look favorably upon the suit of a tutworker's grandson," Clarence said, but mostly to himself. Henry still frightened him and probably always would.

"What? Speak up, curse it."

Clarence lifted his head. "I have no intention of marrying for a number of years yet, sir," he said, which was the truth, though only a part of it. He had every intention of making Jessalyn Letty his wife. But he needed to make a fortune first. His own fortune.

His mother had died last year. There was nothing to prevent his father from marrying again, and rumors had reached him lately that Henry was looking. If another son, an indisputable son, was to blossom suddenly on the Tiltwell family tree, Clarence had no doubt that he would be disinherited as fast as a new will could be drawn.

So in the meantime, as long as Henry held the purse strings, Clarence would dance to the man's tune. It was not in him to starve in any garrets for the sake of pride and principles. Whether he was Henry Tiltwell's true son or not, he would use the man's influence and connections, not to mention the Tiltwell capital, to build his own fortune.

In that way he was very much Henry Tiltwell's son: He was very good at making money.

* * *

McCady Trelawny sprawled in a chair before the fire, his booted feet on a red leather ottoman, a glass of brandy cupped in his palm. It was a sprawl that somehow still managed to convey ancient breeding and sophisticated elegance. It was a sprawl Clarence knew he could never affect if he lived to be a hundred.

Clarence paused in the doorway to his bedroom. McCady looked up at him with heavy-lidded eyes and said in his mocking drawl, "You look as though you could use some brandy to chase away the mulligrubs."

Clarence didn't want any brandy. But he went anyway to the ormolu side table and poured a finger's worth into a toddy glass. He wet his lips, but didn't swallow.

McCady's brooding gaze was on the fire, giving Clarence the opportunity to study his cousin's taut, well-bred face. He could never sort out his feelings when he was with McCady. At times he was sure he loved him like a brother. A *brother*—and he could even see the irony in that. He loved him, but he was not sure he liked him. Perhaps he only wanted to *be* Mack Trelawny. But that wasn't true either because he abhorred the Trelawny vices. He didn't much care for the taste of spirits, so he drank only in moderation. He never gambled; to risk money on the turn of a card or the fall of the dice seemed the height of foolishness to him. He liked girls well enough, but he'd never been moved to bed each one that looked his way. The Trelawny vices, all the vices that McCady had in such abundance.

Perhaps he only wanted to be the man McCady Trelawny had the potential of becoming but never would be. For what was it that they said? The Trelawnys all died young, violently, and in disgrace.

They had never spoken about the possibility that they might be half brothers.

McCady had gotten up to splash more brandy into his glass. He stood before the fire, looking down at it a moment, then threw back his head and tossed most of the brandy down in one swallow. He swung around to brace his shoulders against the mantel, fixing Clarence with his penetrating gaze. The flames were reflected in his eyes, the flames and nothing else. Clarence could rarely tell what thoughts went on behind those dark, shadowed eyes. Sometimes he suspected that McCady was secretly laughing at him, and that hurt.

"I still cannot believe it when I see you in that uniform," Clarence said. "I never had you pegged for a soldier."

McCady's mouth twisted into something that was not quite a smile. "Doubtless my superior officers would agree with you."

"I suppose you'll be off to rejoin your regiment soon, although you'll have little to fight now that old Boney's been breeched. Where are you billeted? I trust it's somewhere close to London."

"The 54th is hardly such a fashionable regiment. We've been sent to the West Indies."

"Good God."

McCady's laugh held a tinge of bitterness. "I doubt God has much to do with the place, so I should be quite at home there. They say there is little to do but play for high stakes and fornicate with the native girls."

And die, Clarence thought, of some exotic tropical disease. For they also said the life expectancy of a man sent for duty to the West Indies was six months. But he tilted his brandy glass in his cousin's direction, as if toasting to his good fortune. "So you'll get yourself a bevy of brown-skinned wenches to frolic with in the tropical sun and forget all about dreary old England and steam locomotion."

A pain so dark it might have been agony flared in McCady's eyes before he veiled it with his lids. He looked down at his glass, but it was empty. "And forget about steam locomotion," he said, but softly, as if to himself.

An intense emotion squeezed Clarence's chest, making him feel light-headed. It might have been dismay. But it might also have been relief. He wasn't sure why, especially since he himself had invested heavily in his cousin's experiments with steam and motion, but Clarence had secretly hoped all along that they would fail. For all that he loved McCady, Clarence preferred him best like this—trapped and slightly desperate. Defeated.

Except that he wondered if it was really possible to defeat his cousin. There had been a story going around the London clubs that after Waterloo, Lieutenant Trelawny had been found on the battlefield, grievously wounded in the thigh and nearly dead from exposure and loss of blood. He had been carried back to one of the hospital tents to have his leg amputated. But when the barber-surgeon leaned over him, to give him a bullet to bite down on, he had grabbed the man's throat with a grip, the surgeon had said later, like a blacksmith's vise. "You saw off my leg," McCady had snarled, "and I'll come for you even if I have to crawl. I'll come for you, butcher, and I'll cut off your balls."

There must be some truth to the story, Clarence thought now with a shudder, for McCady had kept his leg. They also said that the sleeve of his sword arm had been stained black-red up to the armpit. The surgeons had thought it was another wound at first, until they realized it wasn't his blood at all, but the blood of the enemy soldiers he had killed. Clarence shuddered again. McCady had always been a little wild—he was a Trelawny after all—but it was hard to imagine the boy of their school days at Eton being capable of such savage violence. Until one looked into those dark, shadowed eyes.

"Tell me, coz, do you like"—Clarence had been about to say *killing* people, but he changed it at the last moment—"being a soldier?"

McCady lifted his shoulders in a lazy shrug. "What would it signify if I didn't? There are only three paths open to the younger sons of impoverished earls: politics, the army, or the church. I prefer to break laws, not make them, and heaven preserve me from the church."

"Heaven preserve the church from you," Clarence said,

and then flushed, pleased in spite of himself that he had made his worldly cousin laugh.

McCady pushed himself off the mantel and went to the side table for another brandy. Clarence opened his mouth to warn him to go easy on the stuff, then shut it. "Are you still planning to make a run to France this summer?" he said instead.

McCady blessed him with a cocky, devil-be-damned smile. Clarence had never been able to resist that smile. He could understand how Lieutenant Trelawny had managed to lead his men on a charge that had meant almost certain death. In that moment, with McCady looking at him like that, Clarence would have followed him through the gates of hell itself.

"Ever hear of *La Belle Amie?*" McCady said. "She's a three-masted schooner out of St.-Malo, carrying coal and lumber. And a broad-beamed, saucy mademoiselle she is, for hidden beneath a false bottom in her hull will be a hundred tuns of tax-free brandy." His smile turned wicked. "Come a-smuggling with me, Clarey. If you dare."

Clarence forced a laugh. "Maybe I shall."

A log settled in the hearth with a hiss and a crackle. Clarence watched his cousin. McCady stood with one boot braced on the ottoman, his brooding profile turned toward the fire. Another manly pose. With his long, dark hair falling over his forehead like a damned Byronic hero, with his shirt neck opened to the last button and the firelight glinting off the hairy brawn of his chest, he looked dangerous and disreputable. Women would find him fascinating.

A sweet, innocent girl would find him irresistible.

Clarence felt a flutter of unease as he remembered the look of shining hero worship that he had caught in Jessalyn's eyes. She was so young, so innocent. He needed to protect her from rakes like McCady Trelawny, who would seduce her, use her, and discard her without a moment's regret. Just as the old earl had used and discarded his mother. More than anyone, he understood that against the

Trelawny charm even the most virtuous were not immune. Why, even now a part of him pitied his poor cousin, who was only an heir of the legacy he had been born to. Lechery and debauchery—they were in the Trelawny blood, as much as part of their heritage as wild dark eyes and dying young. For a moment Clarence wondered, if he was indeed the earl's son, why he was not similarly afflicted. But then he shrugged off the notion as immaterial. What mattered was Jessalyn. It was his *duty* to protect her.

And as he looked up into his cousin's shadowed face, even then a part of him thought that by saving Jessalyn, they all would be saved.

He cleared his throat. "You should not have taken Miss Letty up with you on the locomotive. She is of an age now where she must have a care for her reputation."

Something flared in McCady's eyes, there and gone before Clarence could divine its meaning. "The irrepressible Miss Letty—all mouth and legs and a laugh like an ill-tuned pianoforte." He took a sip of brandy, staring hard at Clarence over the rim of the glass. "Are you sweet on her, Clarey?"

Clarence felt telltale color flood his face. "She has no one to protect her except that old woman, who is half mad, I swear."

There was a slight curl to McCady's lips that Clarence didn't like. "Clarey, Clarey . . . are you trying to serve me a warning? Are you afraid I'll seduce her? Is she even seducible?" He looked up at the ceiling as if he were giving the question serious consideration. "Yes, I do believe she is, and if she isn't, I can always force her. My father raped a serving wench once. I watched him do it."

"Why are you always saying things like that?" Clarence demanded, his cheeks growing hot. "You might be wild, but I cannot believe you are truly evil."

"Such touching faith. Misguided but touching." A trace of amusement eased the hard lines around McCady's mouth. "Ah, hell. Your precious Miss Letty is safe from my lusty appetites. There are plenty of guinea hens in Penzance to satisfy my base urges, should they"—he widened his eyes in a suggestive manner—"arise . . . But she's a ripe little peach, Clarey, and if you don't pluck her soon, someone else will do it for you."

Clarence looked down into his brandy glass, hiding the anger that flared at his cousin's words. Jessalyn was *his*. She was his, and he would destroy the man who tried to take her from him. Whether that man be friend, cousin . . . or *brother*.

6

Jessalyn and her grandmother arrived at End Cottage the next afternoon to learn of a most shameful tale. It seemed that while the cat Peaches had been increasing all spring and summer, it had not been entirely with fat.

"She had babies!" Jessalyn exclaimed at the sight of the tiny kittens, hardly bigger than mice, suckling at Peaches's white belly. The cat had delivered her litter during the night, and she had chosen the worst possible place to do it —in the corner of a stall occupied by a cinnamon-colored mare called Prudence. Jessalyn had found them when she'd gone to perform her daily chore of mucking out.

"She was pregnant, Gram, and we didn't know it!"

"You watch your tongue, gel," Lady Letty said. "Such a word is never to be uttered in polite society. Use such language within my hearing again, young miss, and you'll be tasting soap for a week."

Jessalyn wanted to point out that they were in a stable, not polite society, but she knew from past experience that her grandmother's threat was not an idle one. "I wonder who the father is," she said instead.

"Father, ha!" Lady Letty shot a killing glance at the unfortunate Peaches. "Let that be a lesson to you, gel. It don't matter what species they are, 'tis always the females who are left to bear the fruit of the sin."

Even Peaches, who was not the most intelligent of cats, soon perceived that her kittens were in danger of being trampled by the mare's big hooves. She decided to move her household into the kitchen. But to do so, she had to negotiate the dangers of the courtyard where lurked her nemesis, the black-backed gull. She had good reason to fear for her babies. The enormous gulls had been known to steal little lambs off to their nests to feed on later.

Hissing all the while between her clenched teeth, Peaches carried her kittens one by one from the stables into the house. Armed with a stout stick, Jessalyn walked along beside her.

Sea-washed sunlight dappled creeper-covered walls and glinted off the diamond panes of the mullioned windows. With its red and yellow patterned brickwork and tall ornamental chimney stacks, End Cottage always looked cheerful, even beneath the gloomiest fog. Jessalyn loved the house. It didn't matter that the rooms were small and dark or that the black oak paneling was wormholed and the paper stained with damp. End Cottage had been her home for all of her life that she cared to remember. It was warmth and security and love.

For a moment her mind was filled with other memories, dark memories, of a house in London with narrow, shrouded windows and thick, tense silences. They had never shouted at each other, had her mother and father, but she had learned all about anger in that dark house. She had learned what love was and what it was not.

But today, here at End Cottage, sunlight shone through the thick windowpanes, painting watery patterns on the kitchen's flagstone floor. It had always been Jessalyn's favorite room, mostly because of the smells, which today came from the bacon and mutton and hams that hung curing from the rafters. Peaches had chosen the wooden seat of a beehive chair that sat before the hearth as a new nest for her babies, and she settled down before the fire to suckle. Jessalyn counted the kittens. Earlier there had been five, now there were only four.

Her heart pounding in her throat, she ran back to the stable. And that was how Lieutenant Trelawny found her—on her hands and knees in a horse stall, trying to rescue the last kitten. For some reason Peaches had abandoned the poor thing, burying it beneath a pile of straw.

When she heard a step on the packed earth floor, Jessalyn thought it was Becka come to help her. "What an unnatural mother that Peaches is, Becka. She's given up on one of her babies just because he's runty."

"A terrible thing to do, I grant you. Especially as we cannot all be such splendid examples of virile manliness."

Jessalyn straightened with a snap. She blinked, looking up at a splendid example of virile manliness through the dusty sun bars that streamed through the stable's open door.

"Hullo, Miss Letty. It is Miss Letty, isn't it? Or have I the honor of addressing her runty brother?"

She lurched to her feet, brushing the straw off her knees. Her hands fluttered over the front of her clothes, as if she could magically whisk away the boy's shabby blue fustian jerkin and whipcord trousers that she was wearing and replace them with the latest fashion in sprigged muslin. She settled for brushing back her hair, which had fallen out of the binds of a frayed pink ribbon.

"What are you doing here?" she demanded, her voice made sharp by nervousness and excitement.

Her hair fell into her face again. She reached up, but he pushed her hand aside. He tucked the wayward curl behind her ear, then trailed his fingers down the side of her neck, as his piercing gaze moved slowly over her face. She quelled an impulse to shiver. She had never known anyone, man or woman, to touch so often as he did. Somehow he even managed to touch with his eyes. She wondered if he did it with everyone and what he meant by it.

"I thought to see if you might wish to go riding," he said. "And to give you this."

"What is it?"

He pretended to contemplate the object in his hand with utmost seriousness. "It could be a hat. That is, it has the look and shape of a hat. Although it might be a pair of breeches in disguise."

Jessalyn seized the bonnet, flapping its brim in his face like a fan and laughing. "Don't be a silly goose. I mean, why have you brought me a hat?"

"It is to replace the one you so gallantly sacrificed on my behalf."

It was not the one that she had so admired at the fair, the one he had insisted did not suit her. It was an adorable little cottage bonnet made of chip straw and decorated with a posy of primroses the exact pale yellow shade, like whipped lemon custard, of the primroses that grew around the paddock fence.

She tied the wide satin ribbon beneath her chin. Tilting her head, she smiled at him. "How do I look?"

"Stay away from the goats. They might mistake you for lunch."

She knew he hadn't meant to hurt; it was his way to be flippant. Yet she had wanted him to tell her she looked pretty. Even if it wasn't true.

Her fingers trembled as she tugged at the bow, and her chest felt tight. "I shan't wear it riding, though. It will only get soiled."

"Miss Jessalyn!" Becka Poole burst through the stable door, wringing her apron. "That Peaches, she don't know what she be about, esquiring them poor kits onto that chair. One of them nearly tumbled right off and into the fire—" She skidded to a halt when she caught sight of the lieutenant. Quickly turning her head, she pulled her hair over her cheek to hide the scar.

But she still managed somehow to gawk at him out the corner of her eye. "You be the gennelman what nearly killed Miss Jessalyn with his iron horse. 'Tes a wonder I didn't fall away dead on the spot when I heard tell of it. I was prostitute all of last night, I was, with me scattered nerves."

"She means shattered nerves," Jessalyn said. Lieutenant Trelawny was getting that cross-eyed look most men got when they listened to Becka talk.

"Aye, me scattered nerves. Miss Jessalyn will tell ee, sur. The least little thing overturns me poor nerves."

"Becka suffers from indifferent health." Jessalyn's voice was muffled, for she had dropped down on her hands and knees again to crawl beneath a pile of hay. She emerged with straw sticking out all over her head like pins from a cushion and the kitten cradled in her hands.

"Poor hungry little spud," she crooned as she put the mewling piece of orange fluff into Becka's open palms. "We might have to feed him with a sugar tit. I don't trust that wretched Peaches to be a proper mother."

"No, nor me neither, miss. I tell ee, already one nearly fell into the fire. Nearly emasculated, it was."

Becka Poole sauntered from the stable with the kitten just as the Sarn't Major entered. He, too, came to an abrupt halt when he caught sight of the lieutenant. His thick lips pouched out, and his head sank into his shoulders like a toad's. Black eyes the color of old ink stared unblinking. Then he spit through his teeth, spun around on his heel, and left.

Jessalyn waved her hand at his disappearing back. "Don't mind the Sarn't Major; he's always sour enough to pickle cucumbers. He doesn't like people, only horses."

Lieutenant Trelawny was staring at the now-empty door, a bemused look on his face. "What an odd household you have," he said.

"It's Gram. She collects misfits and strays the way other people collect butterflies."

"She pins them to a board?"

Her head fell back, and her laughter filled the stable

until the sound of it, rusty and grating like an old gate, echoed back at her. She caught the last of it by sucking hard on her lower lip. She could feel his eyes on her, on her mouth.

He had started to say something else when behind him Letty's Hope let out a sharp whinny. Turning, he leaned his forearms on the stall door to take a better look at the filly. Jessalyn stared at him openly. He wore a snuff-colored riding coat and fitted doeskin breeches tucked into spurred long boots. The sight of him this morning left her feeling slightly breathless.

"She's a fine-looking filly," he said. He was smiling at the horse, the creases deep at the corners of his mouth, his eyes a little sleepy-looking. *He should do it more often,* Jessalyn thought, *smile more often.*

She joined him by the stall. "Her dam, Prudence, was out of Flying Betty, who won the Newmarket Whip twelve years ago. The sire was out of Silver Blaze. He won over twenty thousand pounds in stakes and four hundred hogsheads of claret in his prime." The filly bumped her arm, seeking a pat. Jessalyn rubbed the blaze on her forehead. She told him about her grandmother's dream to race in one last Derby. "That is why we've named her Letty's Hope."

"And what of your parents?" he asked after a moment.

"My father died when I was six. My mother lives in London." She had not seen her mother since that day she had been left here at End Cottage. At first she had lain awake at night, her throat tight and aching with unshed tears, wondering if her mother would ever come back for her. But her mother hadn't come, and now Jessalyn no longer wanted her to. *I rarely think of my mother anymore,* she told herself, and most of the time it was true.

The lieutenant watched her saddle Prudence, not offering to help, as if he sensed that she was enough of a horsewoman to want to handle her own tack. She owned a sidesaddle, but she preferred to ride astride, and he made no comment on her choice. His own horse, a big bay with a black mane and tail, was tied up to the paddock rail. The courtyard was otherwise empty except for the gull, which had not yet given up on the idea of kittens for dinner.

"Where is your groom?" he asked as they prepared to mount.

Jessalyn glanced up uneasily at the shuttered windows of the room where her grandmother lay napping. Lady Letty would never countenance her riding unescorted with the lieutenant.

She put her foot in the stirrup, and he gave her a boost up, his hands gripping her hips. "We have no groom," she said, settling into the saddle. And feeling the lingering imprint of his man's hard hands on her body, which was disturbing and frightening, and in some mysterious way, wonderful. "There's only the Sarn't Major, and he's busy."

One of his hands still cupped her calf. She shouldn't have been able to feel the heat of it through the stiff leather of her boot, but she did.

"We can't go riding unchaperoned," he said. "People will talk."

Even if they only met brown rabbits and grouse chicks on their way, by tomorrow everyone breathing within twenty miles would know that Lieutenant Trelawny and Lady Letty's hoyden granddaughter had been seen riding alone together across the moors. "Let them talk," she said, waving an airy hand. "Why should we care a rap for a bunch of useless, clacking prattle-bags?"

"You'll care. Once they start crucifying you for it."

She didn't like the set of his mouth, so brooding and serious. She wondered what had been done to him to make him this way, so bitter against the world.

"I hardly know whether to believe my ears," she said. "All this talk about propriety coming straight from the mouth of a founding member of the Dishonorable Society to Alleviate Boredom and Complacency. You are letting the club down, Lieutenant."

His hand fell, and he stepped back. "Don't say later that I didn't warn you."

She watched him mount his horse. There was a look of infinite weariness on his face now, and the eyes that stared back at her held black secrets. They had seen too much, had those eyes. He was a Trelawny, and he had done things, wicked things, that would make her shudder if she knew of them. He had warned her, and she ought to take heed. But it wasn't gossiping tongues she had to fear. It was he.

They rode side by side through the back gate, toward the cliffs and the sea. A stiff silence came between them that was broken only by the click of hooves upon stone and the creak of saddle leather.

"That is a bang-up mount you have, Lieutenant," she finally said for lack of a better topic, though in truth she thought the bay too shallow through the chest, his tail too high-set. He was likely to become winded in the stretch.

He gave her a look with those piercing dark eyes that made her think he had divined her unspoken aspersions against his horse. "The nag serves my purposes, and he had the advantage of having been cheap off the block."

More lengthy silence followed this statement. She was beginning to wonder if the black-backed gull had stolen his tongue. "You never told me how long you will remain in Cornwall."

"I must take ship to rejoin my regiment in the West Indies in three weeks."

The sun was tin bright, and it cast harsh shadows over the barren moors, made cruel with granite boulders and broken stones. The wind had a salty taste to it, like tears, and though the sun was warm, Jessalyn shivered. Three weeks . . . The silence drew long between them again, tense like his face.

"Do you know where Claret Pond is?" she asked.

"Of course. A good soldier always scouts the countryside.

One never knows what man-traps might be lying in wait for the unwary."

Jessalyn suspected that there was more than one meaning in what he said. She wondered if he thought of her as a man-trap. The idea brought a swift-flushing color to her cheeks . . . as if he had read the words that she had written in the green leather journal.

She squeezed her mare into a trot, pulling ahead, then wheeled around to face him. "I'll race you from here to the pond."

He walked his horse up to hers. There was a tautness to his face, and his eyes were hard and glittering, like chips of onyx. "We must have a wager on the outcome," he said. "And no chicken stakes either."

"But I've only a few shillings left. Gram and I lost all the rest at the Tiltwell faro tables." He had brought his horse so close her knee rubbed against his thigh. He leaned into her, and her belly began to flutter with a strange anticipation as his gloved finger came up to touch her mouth.

"Then you must stake something that you have a lot of." He ran his finger along her lower lip. The leather felt as soft as butter. "Such as a kiss."

She could feel the beat of her heart in her lip. "And— and if I win? What will you give me?"

"What would you like?"

What she wanted she could not even formulate as a thought, let alone put into words. His finger had stopped its stroking, leaving her mouth feeling naked. "I can't think," she said.

"Allow me to think for you then. Should you lose, you must grant me a kiss. Should you win, you may name my forfeit after the fact."

"What if I demand more than you can pay?"

"Why concern yourself with impossibilities?" He took the riding crop from his boot. His mouth twisted, looking a little mean. "I've never lost a bet with a woman yet."

"There is always a first time, Lieutenant." She wanted to

beat him. She would beat him hollow. She thrust herself forward in the saddle and loosened the reins. She cast a quick glance in his direction, then dug her heels into Prudence's sides. "Go!" she shouted.

Prudence, who had galloped neck or nothing on this path many times before, was surefooted among the scrub and loose stones. She was bred to race and would have made a fine runner in her prime, except that she had a weakness in her blood vessels, which had a tendency to break under rigorous training. She was as honest as they came, though, and she ran to win.

Jessalyn could tell that he, too, was riding all out to win. His bay had the advantage in height and stride. But her reservations about the gelding were proving true. He had no bottom.

They dipped down into a small, weed-choked gill. Brambles and briars clutched at her legs, but she barely felt them. On the upward slope she and Prudence nudged ahead. They had perhaps two hundred yards to go to reach the pond; she could already see the wind-tortured elms and mallow grass that encircled its banks. There was a crumbling stone hedge, about three feet high, that would have to be jumped first, but Prudence was a champion fencer. The hedge rose up before them. It had primroses blooming on the top of it, and their yellow petals fluttered in the wind like butterflies. She was going to win . . . and suddenly that was the last thing Jessalyn really wanted.

What she wanted was that kiss, and the only way she would get it would be if he had the right to claim it of her.

It wasn't that hard to throw a race; jockeys did so all the time. She did it just before the hedge, a subtle check on the reins so that Prudence felt a pull in her mouth and couldn't stretch out her head. Instead of taking the jump cleanly, the mare popped over, going up in the air and landing on all four feet with a hard and jerky jolt that rattled Jessalyn's teeth. The bay sailed over the hedge, gaining at least three strides. It was all he needed.

Lieutenant Trelawny had already dismounted and was waiting for her, standing beneath the biggest of the elms. Jessalyn pulled up Prudence at the edge of the pond. Knotting off her reins, she slid from the saddle.

He slapped his riding crop against his boot. The loud thwacking sound sent a jackdaw bursting out of the reeds with a frightened squawk, and Jessalyn jumped. The tree's broad, cone-shaped leaves cast harsh shadows on his face. She couldn't meet his eyes.

She started for the pond, but he snagged her arm as she went by. Throwing the crop aside, he spun her around, slamming against her and pinning her to the trunk of the tree. He brought his face within inches of hers. She could see the flaring of his thin nostrils as he breathed, the creases at the corners of his mouth, the sunbursts of gold within the dark night of his eyes. He smelled of horse and leather and hot anger.

"You little cheat," he said.

She made a movement to get away from him, but his hard weight held her fast. His chest flattened her breasts; his stomach pressed against hers. One of his thighs was braced between her legs.

She drew in a breath of pure fear. "What a nasty, spiteful thing to say. I cannot imagine what you mean by it."

"You know damn well what I mean by it. You threw the race, and we both know why. So now, Miss Letty . . ." He brought his face even closer, so close that if either of them so much as breathed, their lips would touch. "Now you are going to get precisely what you deserve, and you are not going to like it."

She thought: *He is going to kiss me.*

"I might like it," she started to say, but she never quite got the words out.

Because by then he was kissing her.

His mouth crushed down on hers, forcing her lips open, and panic slammed into her chest. She made a little gasping, mewling sound in the back of her throat and tried to twist her head away. His hand closed around her scalp, pulling her head back so that he could kiss her harder. His mouth plundered hers, and she gripped the front of his coat to keep from falling, for it felt as if all the bones had been sucked out of her legs. Her nostrils flared wide as she drew in a desperate breath, and her senses reeled from the hot, tangy smell of him. She heard nothing but the fierce rushing of her blood, knew nothing but that he was devouring her with his mouth.

He ended the kiss abruptly, tearing his lips from hers. His fist tightened in her hair, hurting her. His face was so close the moist heat of his harsh breaths was like steam against her skin. Her lips felt thick and hot. She touched them with her tongue and tasted him.

"Y-you are not a very nice person."

"I have never pretended to be a nice person." He let go of her hair, and his hand slid down around her neck to span her chin. His thumb rubbed her throbbing lips. "And you, Miss Letty, kiss like you have never done it before."

"I have so done it before."

He laughed. Jessalyn thought she probably hated him. "What you did with Clarence Tiltwell on Midsummer's Eve was not a kiss."

He was right; that brief brush of lips had not been a kiss. A kiss was a taking and a mating of mouths. A kiss tore through your belly and left your throat aching and your knees weak. A kiss sent your heart hovering somewhere between terror and bliss.

She jerked her head out of his grasp, and he stepped back, letting her go. She walked on shaky legs toward Prudence, barely aware of what she was doing. Her mouth hurt, and she felt strange inside, sort of hungry and empty.

She tried to make her voice sound nonchalant and thought she succeeded rather well. "If you are done with teaching me a lesson, we should cool down the horses. They're sweating."

They walked side by side along the tree-shaded bank,

leading the horses. It was called Claret Pond because the streams that fed it had once run red from the waste water that came from washing tin ore. But the mines were all shut down now, and the pond lay gray and dull, like a tarnished pewter bowl. Clouds billowed like tossed sheets above their heads, but the wind was warm. It smelled of summer: of dust and dry grass and long, sunbaked days.

Jessalyn could feel the lingering heat of a blush on her cheeks, and she wished that he would say something. She thought that perhaps he had kissed her the way a man would kiss a woman he wanted—hard, rough, hungry. She thought of him kissing her in that way, and the memory of it was a burn on her lips.

"You know what I think?" she said, to end a quiet that had become too hot and heavy. "I think you are only angry because you know that I, a mere female, could have beaten you. Doubtless even the thought of such an odious possibility is a sore blow to your manly pride."

One corner of his mouth creased, a flash of a smile that was there and then gone. "So that is why my manly pride has been feeling tender of late. And here I was about to do it further damage by conceding that you sit ahorse rather well. For a mere female."

He was talking flummery again, but she also suspected that he was offering her a compliment in his own backhanded fashion. She did ride well; it was her singular talent. "And I concede that on a worthy mount you would be a most formidable opponent, Lieutenant"—she whirled, flashing a sudden and brilliant smile—"but I'll wager you can't do this."

"More wagers? I wonder that you dare."

She only laughed, for a devil had seized her. Leaning against a tree trunk, she pulled off her boots, then gave a tug on Prudence's reins. The mare came reluctantly, for she'd been enjoying a snack of reed grass. Jessalyn removed the saddle and bridle and, with a smart slap on the rump, sent the mare cantering away from the pond and into a field of greensward and scrub. She caught hold of her mane and ran alongside for a few strides. Springing forward and up on both stocking feet, she raised her right leg high over the horse's back, landing smoothly astride.

He applauded, but she shook her head and laughed again, for that was only the beginning of the trick. She cantered in a circle, legs hanging straight along the mare's sides, her seat sure and graceful. She took a deep breath now, centering herself, becoming part of the fluid, rocking motion of the horse. She tried to ignore the man who watched, for she would impress him only if she succeeded. Yet he was there, at the edge of her vision. Seeing him, dark and tall against the vivid green of the trees and the sward, reminded her of the Gypsy boy who had filled her days last summer.

It had been the Gypsy boy who had taught her a whole repertoire of circus equestrian feats. His band had camped in the shelter of a coppice of pines near the little fishing village of Mousehole, and she had met him almost every morning for lessons. One day, while showing her a trick called the Mill, he had accidentally touched her breast. Then he touched her there again, deliberately, and she had let him. She had spent that night praying on her knees, sure that her soul was going to burn in hell's all-consuming fire, and even more terrified that Gram would learn of her sin and give her mortal flesh a well-deserved birching. But the next morning she had hurried out to the pines, eager for more lessons in trick riding, and other things, only to find the Gypsy camp deserted.

One of the most spectacular tricks the Gypsy boy had taught her was the Standing Somersault. Jessalyn wondered if she dared do it now, because it had been weeks since she'd practiced. But then, as Lady Letty always said, it was better to die game than to die chicken.

Pushing on the horse's withers, she swung her legs forward and lifted her knees onto its back. She straightened into a kneeling position, stretching her arms out from her sides. Then, before she could lose her nerve, she thrust upward with her thighs and jumped to her feet. Consciously she relaxed her knees, to absorb the shock of the mare's pounding hooves. She was standing upright on the horse's back now, a mile in the air or so it seemed. The wind rushed in her ears and flattened her hair. The world whirled, images flickering before her eyes: gray water, green trees, blue sky and him . . . him . . . him. . . .

Sucking in a deep breath and releasing it, she flexed her legs, leaped high, and turned a complete somersault in the air to land on the mare's broad back, standing and with her arms raised above her head in triumph.

Short-lived triumph.

As she tried to explain afterward, it was the wretched rabbit's fault for digging a hole in the precise spot where Prudence planted her left forefoot. Prudence stumbled, and Jessalyn lost her precarious balance, flipping cat in the pan over the mare's tail.

But that was not the worst of it. For Prudence had been running close to the pond, which was in a deep bowl scoured out of the earth. Jessalyn hit the lip of the steep bank and rolled over the edge of it. She slid down the sharp incline, her grasping hands pulling up reeds and mallow and ferns by the roots, and continued on her inevitable course into the placidly waiting water.

She didn't scream—but only because the water was so cold it snatched the breath from her lungs. Her head went under for a brief second, then bobbed back up. Her jerkin buoyed out around her like a fishing float, helping to counteract the dragging weight on her legs from her heavy whipcord trousers. Water swirled and bubbled up around her. It came from an underground spring, which kept the pond perishingly cold even in the middle of summer.

She pushed her streaming wet hair out of her face and spit the taste of the pond from her mouth, which was bitter and metallic, like biting down on a tin cup. She trod water and looked up. He sat on a rock, his forearms resting on his drawn-up knees, totally at his ease and not the least bit concerned that she could momentarily drown or die of frostbite. She thought that if he laughed, she would never forgive him.

He didn't laugh. But then he didn't have the sense to keep his mouth shut either. "You have won your wager handily, Miss Letty," he said. "I could not duplicate that feat should I live to be as old as Methuselah." He plucked a reed and stuck it between his teeth. "You look wet, Miss Letty. And cold."

"Oh, no, I assure you, Lieutenant, it is most invigorating." She floated on her back, making a lazy circle. The water was so blasted cold it burned. She forced herself to make one turn around the pool, although she had to set her jaws to keep her teeth from chattering.

She swam over to him. The pond was deep, even up to the very edge of the bank. It would be difficult for anyone to make it up the steep escarpment without help. He grinned down at her—one of those superior smirks that only men seemed able to manage. "Are you having a pleasant bath, Miss Letty?"

She produced a helpless little smile. "Give me a hand up, please."

He stood and bent over, stretching out his arm. She deliberately kept back so that he would have to lean way forward as he reached out to her. His hand closed around hers; she felt his strength in his grip. But she had a strength, too, in her arms and wrists made wiry by years of riding. He tensed to pull her out of the water, and she gave a hard tug.

He hit the pond with a grunt and a giant, fanlike splash that wet the topmost leaves of the elm trees.

She tried to scramble up the steep slope of the bank, but her heavy, soaked clothes dragged her back like an anchor. Behind her, she heard his head break the surface and his mouth swearing worse than any drunk tinner outside a kiddley on a Saturday night. At last she got a foothold, and then she was on her hands and knees on the slippery grass. She stayed that way a moment, hunched over and breathing hard.

Water splashed and lapped against the bank. His voice changed, became soft and rather nasty. "My dear, sweet, gentle Miss Letty . . . you are going to repent the day you were ever born."

She dared a glance over her shoulder—and screamed. He slammed into her, rolled her onto her back, covered her with his body. She went quiet beneath him, breathing quickly like a cornered animal that knows it has been caught.

The water ran in rivulets from his hair down over the sharp bones of his face. He lowered his head until they were nose to nose. His eyes were blacker than the devil's sea. His lids drifted closed; his mouth softened. He was going to kiss her. . . .

Jessalyn's breath caught, and her heartbeat skittered. His lips lowered another inch, and her mouth parted on an expulsion of breath that was more of a sigh.

"How old are you?" he said against her open mouth.

She could barely push the word out her tight throat. "Eighteen."

"Not only a cheat but a liar as well." He wrapped his hands around her neck, pressing his thumbs into the hollows of her throat, pushing her head back. Her blood quickened, drumming against his fingers. "How old are you, Miss Letty? And don't you *ever* lie to me again."

Her pulse plunged and dipped. She swallowed, hard. "Sixteen."

"Good Christ!"

He shoved off her, sitting up. She lay on her back a moment, watching the procession of clouds across the sky. She turned her head; he sat next to her, his wrist resting on one bent knee. It was a relaxed pose, but she could feel the tenseness in him as if he were giving off heat. She sighed, at the mystery of him, of what she felt for him, that strange mixture of fear and longing. He was the handsomest man she had ever seen, even with his mouth set the way it was now—hard and just a little cruel. Being with him was like drinking wine that came from a cold cellar. Tangy, exhilarating. Intoxicating.

She pushed herself up to lean back on her elbows. "Sixteen is not so young," she said.

His mouth tightened even more. "Oh yes it is."

"Many girls are married at sixteen."

His head swung around, and he pinned her with his hot gaze. "Many girls are whores at sixteen. Just because you have an itch does not mean you have to scratch it." In a movement so quick she didn't see it until too late, he seized her wrist and hauled her up with such force her neck snapped. His voice, harsh with fury, lashed at her. "I have no reason to guard your virtue, *little girl,* and every reason to take it. So use the wit beneath all that red hair and stay the bloody hell away from me." His fingers tightened around her wrist, and he jerked her hand up to her face. "And the next time a man tries to kiss you, use your claws on his eyes."

She stared into dark eyes that were wild and dangerous. She felt helpless with fear and a strange sort of excitement. He acknowledged no rules, did McCady Trelawny. He was capable of doing anything at any time, and a part of her understood that it was his very unpredictability that made him so attractive.

A cloud smothered the sun, and the wind kicked up, flattening the sward and sending ripples scurrying across the pond. A shudder racked her.

He dropped her wrist and leaned back. Unconsciously she rubbed her arms. His gaze followed the movement of her hands, then came up, settling on her mouth. The dangerous glint in his eyes flared like a fire fanned by a draft.

"We—we had better go back," she said, suddenly frightened by what she saw in his face.

She kept up a stream of constant chatter on the way to

End Cottage. He contributed little, but she no longer minded his silences. For when he did talk, it was to use words like hedges. Cornish-type hedges, made of rough, hard stone and covered with prickly bracken, that he threw up to force others to keep their distance. She suspected that if he ever felt deeply about something, he would not speak of it at all, not even to himself.

He left her at the gate to End Cottage without even telling her good-bye.

Jessalyn rubbed Prudence down and gave her some oats, but once this chore was done, she felt too restless to go inside. Instead she walked out to the cliffs. She looked around her as if she'd never seen it all before, never seen the sea lashing the black rocks or the white flash of a gull's wings riding the wind. Surely the surf boomed louder than it ever had before, and the air, thick with salty sea spume, had never felt so soft. She thought that after today nothing in her world would ever be the same again.

That night she took the journal out from beneath her mattress and wrote: *Today he kissed me. . . .*

7

She waited for three days, and then she went to him.

She had taken pains with her appearance. She wore the hat he'd given her and a fancy pair of green leather gauntlet gloves. Her riding habit was old and outdated, but the only one she owned. It had black frog buttons and bugle trimming and was fashioned of a dusty rose kerseymere that Gram assured her was flattering to her complexion.

She approached Caerhays Hall from the coast road. Its gray chimneys and gables could barely be seen through a thick curtain of elm and sycamore and wild nut trees, yet the castellated manor house was massive, built of gray stonework discolored by salt and wind. No panes were left in any of the salt-encrusted windows, and many of the shutters were missing or dangling by one hinge. The wind stirred the dead leaves and grass piled in drifts on the front steps. It was as if no one living had set foot here in years.

A door slammed shut behind her, and she twisted around in the saddle. A tall, lean figure emerged from the gatehouse, and the bottom seemed to drop out of her stomach at the sight of him.

"Good afternoon, Lieutenant," she called, smiling.

His head snapped up. He paused a moment, then strode

toward her. "What the devil are you doing here?" he said, practically snarling the words.

Her smile faltered. "I was wondering . . . if you wanted to go for a ride."

"My horse is lame, and I'm busy."

He was dressed rough, in a miner's blue wool coat and old drill trousers. He carried a haversack slung over his shoulder and a small pick stuck through his belt. He swung away from her and walked down the lane, using long, limping strides.

She brought Prudence into a trot to catch up, then eased her down into a walk beside him. He hadn't shaved this morning. The lines were drawn white around his mouth, and his eyes were bloodshot. He held his head as if it hurt even to breathe. She knew what was wrong with him. He looked like the Sarn't Major after he'd spent all night in a kiddley getting good and pickled on blue ruin.

She decided to behave with him just as she did with the Sarn't Major—which was to ignore his surly temper. "Where are you going?" she asked brightly.

She thought he wasn't going to answer, but then he said, "Wheal Patience."

Wheal Patience was an exhausted copper mine on the south coast, at the very edge of the Caerhays estate. "That's a bit of a ways to walk—"

His head swiveled around, and he impaled her with his dark gaze. "For a crookshank."

"For anyone. Really, Lieutenant. I can't imagine why you are throwing your unfortunate injury up in my face, unless it is an attempt to give me cause to pity you. In which case you are far off the mark, sir, for I'm much more likely to think ill of your sulky ways."

"My *what?*" He had stopped and was staring at her as if he couldn't believe her temerity.

"You are sulking. Like a little boy who has been whipped and then sent to bed without his supper. Who's the wicked

ogre who has been mean to you and made you so un-
happy?"

"It just so happens that I'm as happy as a weevil in a
biscuit. As happy as a flea on a mule. As happy, dammit, as
a randy tom in a cathouse. Now, if you will grant me leave,
I have business to attend to." He started down the lane
again, walking stiffly in a poor effort to disguise his limp.

Jessalyn sent Prudence ahead of him, then wheeled the
mare around, blocking his path. Smiling broadly to take the
sourness out of his temper, she slipped her foot from the
stirrup so that he could use it. She leaned over and held out
her hand. "Come, Lieutenant. Prudence doesn't mind carrying double."

"I told you to stay away from me."

The blunt cruelty of his words so stunned her she simply
sat there saying nothing, doing nothing. Tears pressed behind her eyes. She blinked hard to hold them back.

She fumbled with the reins to turn Prudence's head, but
he grabbed the shank of the bit, stilling the mare. "You
think that simply because you are gently bred and so
bloody young that I will have a care for you, that I will
suddenly develop a conscience where I've never had one
before. You couldn't be more wrong. I am fire, and if you
play with me, little girl, you are going to get burned."

She looked down into his upturned face, a face as impenetrable as the cliffs at their backs. She couldn't make herself believe that he would ever really hurt her. She didn't
want to believe it.

She held out her hand again. "I trust you."

His mouth twisted into a mean smile. "Don't. Oh, don't,
Miss Letty. Don't ever trust me." Yet he reached up and
put his hand into hers.

They rode in silence, his chest pressed against her back,
his hands resting lightly on her waist. She could feel his
breath on the back of her neck, feel it fluttering and brushing all over her skin like the wings of a thousand butterflies.

She felt caught and helpless—as if the currents of Crook-neck Cove had gotten her.

The land around Wheal Patience was wild and bare, falling sharply to the sea. No coves and beaches marked the coastline. Only stark cliffs, seamed by the wind and weather like a fisherman's face, and an occasional narrow neck of pebbly sand strung with garlands of seaweed.

The enginehouse stood on a promontory of rock with the sea frothing at its base. The tall brick tower rose like a ruined cathedral against the cloud-shredded sky. No smoke curled from the chimney stack. The wind blew through empty windows, carrying ghostly echoes from when the mine was alive: the clang of the core bell; the throbbing beat of the pump engine; the shouts and laughter of men coming up to the bright sunlight after ten hours in the dark belly of the earth.

Wheal Patience was unusual in that much of its subterraneous workings extended below the seabed several fathoms deep. The enginehouse was accessible only by foot at the end of a narrow, dangerous path. Even Jessalyn, who was used to the Cornish cliffs, found the way rough going. She imagined how it must have been for the men coming up from the night core in pitch-darkness and with a winter gale blowing.

The pump engine had long ago been dismantled and sold for scrap; the house was empty now except for a rust-pitted shovel and an old barrow leaning drunkenly on one wheel. Lieutenant Trelawny went immediately to work, prying loose the rotting boards that covered the main shaft. They came free with a squeal of rage and a flying of splinters. Cold, stale air wafted up from the open bal at her feet, and Jessalyn repressed a shudder. The thought of going down deep into the earth had always frightened her.

"What do you hope to find here?" she asked, the first words spoken since they had left Caerhays Hall.

He took his time answering. The veins and sinews on the

backs of his hands stood out as he pressed down on the iron crowbar. She stared at his hands, mesmerized by the power of them, hands that could both caress . . . and hurt.

"Wheal Patience was mined only for copper in her day," he finally said. "I've been talking to some of the old tributers who worked her. They all claim to have seen evidence of tin-bearing lodes."

There was a tightness in her chest. She realized that for some strange reason she'd been holding her breath. "And if you find tin, will you and your brother the earl reopen her?"

"Not bloody likely. Starting up a venture takes a hell of a lot of capital."

She wanted to ask him why they were here then. Perhaps mining was simply in his Cornish blood, for this was a land whose fortunes ebbed and flowed by what was brought out of the earth and the sea. A bal could bring untold riches for years and then suddenly run dry. Or the price of ore could drop beyond the cost of bringing it up from the ground. That was why the shareholders of a mine were called adventurers.

"My grandmother held some shares in this mine," she said. She remembered when the mine had closed down, the winter she was ten. It had been a bad winter that year, days full of bitter frost and snow unusual for Cornwall. "So many men lost their livelihood when she shut down, and there was famine that year," she said, reminiscing aloud. "Many families wound up on the parish. A few even had to go into the workhouse. . . ."

He had gone still beside her. He stared down into the gaping black maw of the pit, and a strange light, the same passionate heat that she had seen on the day they had ridden the locomotive, shone in his eyes. She knew suddenly that he had been lying. He was a gaming man; if he found tin, he wouldn't rest until he'd also found the means to start up the new venture.

She touched his cheek, rough with beard stubble. She

had wanted to do it a hundred times before; this time she did it without thinking. "You care, don't you? You would open the mine if you could, for Cornwall, so that the men here would have work. . . ."

His hand closed over hers. He raised his gaze to hers, and something flashed in his eyes. She had seen it before, when she had told him his locomotive could change the world: that look of bewildered hurt mixed with hope.

She felt his jaw clench before he jerked her hand away. "I don't care about a bloody damn thing," he said.

He bent over and removed an Instantaneous Light Box from his pack. He dipped the chlorate match into the bottle of vitriol, and it burst into flame. He lit a hempen candle, then fixed it to the front of a hard-brimmed hat with a lump of china clay.

"You shouldn't go down alone," she said. "It isn't safe."

"One of the tributers drew me a map."

"But . . ." It was a cardinal rule, given to Cornishmen along with their mothers' milk: Never go down into a mine alone. Jessalyn chewed her lower lip. She knew she should offer to go with him, but just the thought of all those tons of rock and water bearing down on her head made her hands shake and cold sweat start out on her scalp. "I should come along with you," she said.

He was bent over, taking more candles from the pack and stuffing them into his coat pocket. "No," he said, not even bothering to glance up at her.

"But it isn't safe."

He straightened and swung around to glare at her. "You are playing nursemaid again, Miss Letty, and frankly I am beginning to find it tedious."

She glared back. "Fine then. But if you get lost, or a pit prop collapses and cracks open your stubborn head, don't expect me to come along and rescue you."

His mouth curled into that expression that was meant to be a smile and wasn't at all. "I never expect anything from anyone. That way I am never disappointed."

He bent over again to stuff more excavating tools into his belt: a heavy iron jumper and a rock drill. She stared down at his broad back, hating him. He had none of the qualities she had been taught to admire in a gentleman, no gallantry, no compassion, no kindness. There was no softness in him, none at all.

The last thing he picked up was a coil of rope, and in spite of her anger Jessalyn had a sudden thought that she wanted to take that rope and bind him to her. Not just to stop him from going down into the mine but to keep him with her always.

He swung onto the pit ladder. "I should be back up in an hour or so," he said, and the next thing she knew he was gone, swallowed up by the black hole in the ground.

For a moment longer the light from his candle winked at her like a yellow eye before it, too, disappeared.

Jessalyn sat on the cliff path, her feet dangling over the side. Below her the sea lay drab and sullen. High, flat clouds made the air seem hard and metallic, and the wind sighed mournfully among the rocks and bracken.

It had to have been at least an hour since he had gone down into the mine. But he had said an hour *or so.* She cursed him for not being more specific and for being a stubborn, know-it-all cabbagehead to go alone in the first place. Then cursed herself for being such a pudding heart that she hadn't made him take her with him.

She thought of all the evils that could have befallen him. It was an old mine. The pit props were doubtless rotted. Perhaps one had given way, letting loose tons of rock and sea and burying him alive. One of the tributers had drawn him a map of the workings, but what if it was inaccurate? Mines were a spider web of shafts and tunnels. It was easy to become lost and disoriented in the smooth, thick blackness of the earth.

Waves thumped heavily against the cliff; the tide was coming in. Without a pump, the mine's lower levels would fill with water at flood tide, and when they filled, they filled fast. More miners had been drowned than had ever died from cave-ins. She saw him helpless, pinned beneath a collapsed pit prop, the cold black water rising up around him, filling his mouth, smothering his cries, drowning him. . . .

She went back inside the enginehouse. She removed her primrose bonnet, set it out of the way on a windowsill where it would not get soiled, then peered down into the gaping shaft. Black and empty, like the dead part of the night. She couldn't do it. She just couldn't do it.

She had to.

He had taken the Instantaneous Light Box with him, but she found a tinderbox in the pack and plenty of extra candles. She didn't allow herself time to think. She slung the haversack over her shoulder and, clutching a burning candle tightly in one hand, descended the rickety wooden ladder that was nailed to the side of the vertical shaft. Her legs felt as soggy and mushy as day-old pudding.

The ladder seemed to go down forever. Finally she reached the first level. She took a deep breath of air that was old and stale, like the crypt beneath a stone church. Her smoky, flickering candle cast shadows on water-slimed walls, but the supporting timbers above her head seemed sound enough. She called his name several times but got no answer.

Now that she was down here, she realized there was actually little she could accomplish. She dared not go more than a few steps beyond the main shaft without risk of getting lost herself. This was not an adventure out of the pages of a blue book, and rather than save the day, she was more apt to make it worse. Although it wouldn't be very heroic of her, she knew the sensible thing to do would be to ride to Mousehole and fetch a couple of the old tinners to do the rescuing.

She had her foot on the ladder, prepared to climb back out of the shaft, when she heard it—a faint, mewling cry. She froze, her breath trapped in her throat, ears straining, and just when she had herself convinced that she had imagined the whole thing, she heard it again. Louder this time, almost a scream, like someone in pain.

Three tunnels led off from the main shaft. She thought the cry had come from the widest one, and she took it, climbing and slipping over piles of attle and other mining refuse. She paused a couple of times, trying to listen for the cry above the loud thumping of her own heart, but she didn't hear it again. Before long the way began to narrow, and soon she was walking bow-backed like an old crone. The tunnel sloped downward and was intersected by numerous crosscuts and winzes. But these were much smaller —just big enough to allow the passage of a man bent double, wheeling a barrow.

She had expected it to be cold underground, but it was hot, and before long she was sweating. Under the ground . . . Tons of earth and rock and seawater pressing down, putting a strain on the prop timbers, old wood, weak and probably rotting—

Stop it, she told herself sharply. "Lieutenant!" she shouted, and her voice echoed back at her, *tenant . . . ant . . .*

She was beginning to think that she ought to return to the surface after all and ride for help, when the way ahead of her widened, spilling into a big cavern.

Holding the candle above her head, she turned in a slow circle. The candle drew smoky patterns in the air, its feeble flame revealing the marks of old excavations and dark mottled veins in the rock. The place smelled rotten, of stagnant air and dead things. A crack in the stone seeped water in a small pool that was dark and smooth as bottle glass.

She heard the cry again. So faint this time that she was not quite sure she *had* heard it. She waited, holding her breath. . . . There it was again.

"Lieutenant!" she shouted, starting toward the direction of the cry.

And stepped into a black hole.

8

She twisted sharply, her flailing hands grasping at air. Her hips and knees banged into rough rock, and then her feet hit something wooden, a ladder, skidded along the rungs of a ladder. One of her scrabbling, clutching hands found the side rail, and she grabbed it, halting her fall with a hard jerk that wrenched her arm and tore a harsh cry from her throat. Pebbles and dirt rained down around her, falling into emptiness.

She hung, swinging by one arm, gasping and sobbing with terror. The candle had gone out, dropped when she fell, and the darkness was absolute. She had fallen into a shaft that led down to a new level, and the ladder, nailed into the rock, had saved her life.

Slowly she searched with one foot, found a rung. She put her weight on it, and the wood gave way with a splintering crack. She slid down the ladder several more feet, ripping her glove and tearing the skin off her palm. Her scream echoed back at her.

She hung, sucking at the foul, hot air and trying not to cry. Her arm shrieked with pain.

She shouted for help, her voice bouncing up into the cavern and down, down, down. . . . Shouted until her throat was raw and she couldn't breathe. It felt as if there were a vise around her rib cage, pressing against her lungs, slowly strangling her. The pain in her arm and across her shoulders became so intense it was a scream in her mind. But the fingers of the hand that grasped the ladder were growing numb. She could not hang like this much longer. She was suffocating, and it was so hot . . . so hot . . . like hell.

She would have to help herself, or she would die down here. Throwing her weight sideways, she swung like a pendulum, grabbing for the other side rail. Missed. Swung around again. Missed. Swung. Had it.

The relief of taking some of the weight off her right arm was so exquisite she sobbed. But she allowed herself the luxury of only a few moments' rest. She pulled her leg up and put the toe of her boot on the first rung she could find. She applied the barest pressure, heard it crack. All the rungs were completely rotten.

But the side rails seemed sturdy enough. She made sure she had a good grip with her left hand. Sucking in a deep breath of the hot, stagnant air, she let go with her right hand and slid it up the rail as far as she could reach, gripped, and pulled. Let go with her left hand, reached up, and pulled. Inch by painful inch she crabbed her way up the side of the shaft. It took an eternity. Sometimes she had to stop and rest. And test the rungs again, which were always rotten. She cried the whole time because it hurt so much. She told herself it didn't matter that she cried, because there was no one to see it.

A hysterical giggle burst from her throat. As if anyone could see anything in this black hole. In a way that was the worst part. The utter impenetrable darkness. Until now she hadn't known what darkness was. Always before, even on a moonless night in a shuttered room, there had been *some* light. She hadn't known that darkness could be felt. She thought that if she were ever to be touched by Satan, he would feel like this darkness—hot, thick, utterly lonely.

She giggled again, reached up with her right hand . . . and felt air.

Startled, she jerked her hand back, scraping her knuckles on the floor of the cavern. Relief flooded through her, so strong it left her dizzy and shaking.

But it was much harder hauling herself over the lip of the shaft than it had been to pull herself up the rungless ladder. Once she lost her purchase and slid back down several feet—agonizing feet that she had to pull herself back up again. She cursed then. She cursed God and herself and McCady Trelawny, oh, especially Lieutenant Trelawny, whose fault it all was and who should have *been* here by now to rescue her.

But then at last, at last, she was safe, lying on the cavern floor, her chest heaving, breaths coming in stertorous gasps, her muscles burning and cramping, and sweat running into her eyes and stinging all her scrapes and scratches. Lying still . . . until she began to think again, to understand that the danger wasn't over, not over at all. Somehow she had to find her way out of a mine honeycombed with tunnels and crosscuts and winzes, in the pitch-darkness.

She heard it again, that faint cry.

She sat up, feeling the darkness with her outstretched hands. She didn't have a light or hope of one. The haversack with the tinderbox and extra candles was at the bottom of the shaft. She would have to feel her way, crawling carefully on her hands and knees, so that she wouldn't step off into any more holes.

She crawled. She made sure her shoulder brushed against rough stone at all times, and she felt the way ahead of her with her outstretched hands. The mewling cry, growing ever louder, pulled her on. Eventually she decided it could not be a man making that sound. An animal, perhaps. A small animal.

She thought at first that she was imagining things, her eyes after so much darkness playing tricks on her. Water glinting on stone, the round shape of a pit prop. Then she realized she *was* seeing things: the walls and roof of the tunnel, the rock and attle, even the rusted head of an old pick. She stood up and stumbled forward, toward the source of the light.

It was an adit—a narrow hole cut through earth and rock to the outside world to let in air or, more often, to drain out water. This adit ran upward at a sloping incline like a laundry chute. Jessalyn peered up the chute, at a small circle of light, at gray scudding clouds . . . and a grist sack, caught on a finger of rock, swinging like a hammock. The grist sack squirmed and emitted a squeaky, mewling cry.

There were steplike indentations cut into the rock that miners called stopes, which resulted from the removal of the ore. She was able to climb up the stopes far enough to reach the sack. She thought that someone had tried to dispose of a litter of kittens by throwing them into the adit, and the sack had gotten caught on the finger of rock on its way down.

Until she touched it . . . Then she saw that it was a baby, a human baby.

She had a harder time making it back down the stopes with the grist sack and its fragile contents in her arms, but at last she was on firm ground again. The ragged bundle cried and wriggled as Jessalyn gently unwrapped it. The baby, a girl, was extremely tiny, hardly more than a day old. She was covered with dried blood and mucus from the birth, and her cry was weak. But she was alive.

Jessalyn wrapped the baby back up in the sack. She leaned against the rough tunnel wall, drawing deeply of the fresh, salt-laden air.

A harsh shout floated down to her. "Miss Letty, damn your eyes! Answer me!"

She cupped a hand around her mouth. "Hellooo! Lieutenant!"

A hail of stones fell past the hole in the rock. His upside-down face took the place of the sky, cutting off most of the light. The adit, she realized, must open out right beneath the cliff path. She was so relieved to see him she laughed out loud. "There you are," she said. "Where have you been?"

"There has never been any doubt where I have been, damnation. The question is, Where the bloody hell have you been?"

She laughed again. "You have not been properly brought up, Lieutenant Trelawny. Your speech has far too much of the attle gutter in it. I've been meaning to bring it to your attention for some time now."

"Hellfire, rape, and sodomy."

She nearly choked on another gurgle of laughter.

"What the devil are you doing down there and quit giggling. I cannot abide giggling females."

Perhaps it was the sudden relief after being frightened near half to death, but she felt slightly giddy. She looked at his hard mouth and wanted to kiss it. It also seemed too much of an effort to explain the whole story to him, so she edited out all the interesting bits, the way the Reverend Troutbeck was always doing to the stories in the Bible.

"You were gone so long I thought something had happened," she said. "I came down to look for you, and I got a trifle lost."

"No one can be a *trifle* lost." He was getting quite red in the face. Doubtless because he was hanging upside down. "You are either completely lost or you aren't lost at all. Is this an innate talent you have for turning the simplest expeditions into unmitigated catastrophes, or do you have to practice at it?"

"Don't be beastly. It isn't nice."

His head disappeared from the hole.

"Lieutenant!"

"Don't move—don't you move a bloody inch. I'm coming to get you."

"Thank you, but—"

"Think nothing of it. An afternoon spent crawling

through dark and slimy tunnels and hollering myself hoarse has always seemed the epitome of entertainment to me."

"Lieutenant. I have a baby."

His head reappeared. "How in the bloody hell can a virgin have a baby? And don't tell me it was an immaculate conception; that story just won't wash a second time."

"I didn't *have* her, you silly goose. I found her. Here. Just now."

"Of course. It stands to reason that you would go looking for trouble and find a baby."

She laughed again and sat down on a stope, clutching the baby to her breast. It wasn't long before she heard the hollow echo of his footsteps and saw the glow of his candle on the stone walls.

He set the candle down on the stope and with gentle fingers peeled back the sack from the baby's head. "Is he all right?"

"It is a she, Lieutenant. Can't you tell the difference?"

The corners of his mouth creased in a quick smile. "Not from this end." Then he did the most unexpected thing. He traced the curve of Jessalyn's jaw with his knuckles, and even in the dim light she could tell that his hand was shaking. "You've scratched your face," he said.

Their gazes held for a moment; then his dropped to her mouth. She ran her tongue over her lower lip, swallowed. "I—I think the baby's cold," she said. "All she's wearing is a sack."

She wasn't sure he'd heard her. The flame of the candle was reflected in the flat darkness of his eyes; his face had turned hard.

He broke abruptly away from her, shrugging out of his coat. He took the baby in his hands, wrapping her up in the warm woolen material. Although she had been crying steadily, a thin, pathetic mewl, since Jessalyn found her, now she quieted.

"She likes you," Jessalyn said.

"The sentiment isn't mutual. The brat just piddled all

over my coat." At the sound of his voice, which had been deep and slightly rough, the baby started to cry again.

"She's probably hungry," Jessalyn said. "The poor little spud."

"Well, don't look at me. I haven't the right equipment."

She looked at him. He held the baby cupped in his scarred, fine-boned hands. It didn't seem possible that a man's hands could be at once so frighteningly strong, and yet so gentle. Tender and violent.

"I hate it when you do that," he said.

She looked up to find his eyes on her. "Do what?"

"Smile at me as if you know something I don't know."

"I was thinking that most men turn pale with fear when they are handed a baby, yet you hold her as if you've had plenty of practice. . . ." Her voice trailed off. His father was said to have sired bastards all over Cornwall, and he was a Trelawny, his father's son.

He was looking at the baby not at her, and he spoke in his teasing drawl. "But I am terrified, can't you tell? Babies and winsome virgins always put a quiver in my knees and a quake in my heart."

She started to smile, and something cracked within her chest. A piece of her cracked and tore loose and fell away from her, fell into a black hole more terrifying than a mine shaft. His face was nothing but shadows; she couldn't see him, she didn't know him. Yet she felt within her very soul a need for him in her life, the way the earth and the sun and the air were needed in her life—elemental, essential, eternal. And she felt, too, a terrible fear that this need might never go away.

He kept the baby, and she followed him in a daze. Her skin felt tight all over, too small for her body. She thought that if he touched her, if he so much as looked at her or spoke to her, she would fly all apart like an exploding steam boiler. Her chest hurt, and her eyes burned, as if she had to cry. Or had already cried too much.

He climbed the ladder first. Kneeling at the edge of the

pit, with the baby tucked into the crook of his arm, he held out his hand to her. Jessalyn looked up at him, her eyes narrowed against the harsh light. She took his hand, and as she came up out of the dark hole, his gaze raked the length of her.

She knew tear tracks had streaked the grime on her cheeks. Her hair was tangled and wet with sweat, her riding habit in shreds at the knees and elbows and gaping open at the bodice where she'd lost several buttons. Her hands showed raw and bloody through the rips in her gloves.

"I fell down," she said when she could no longer bear his silence. Her smile trembled at the edges. "I feel a bit wonky, but I'm really quite all right."

He made an impatient movement. "Down what, for God's sake—a shaft?"

"Yes." She couldn't meet his eyes. She didn't know why she should feel so ashamed. Except that things were always happening to her around him, and she always felt like such a beetlehead afterward. He was staring at her, saying nothing, and she knew how childish she appeared in his eyes.

They had left Prudence, hobbled, to graze among the moor heather. Jessalyn had her foot in the stirrup and was about to haul herself up into the saddle when she suddenly hopped down and took off running back to the mine.

The primrose bonnet lay on the windowsill where she had left it, a splash of yellow on the gray stone. The sight of it did something to her chest, and she felt it again—that cracking and tearing away within her, as if pieces of her heart were breaking off. *What happens to you,* she wondered, *when you need someone and they need you not at all?* She snatched up the hat and ran from the enginehouse as if she were fleeing it and not the fear within herself.

She ran toward him, trying to tie the bonnet on her head at the same time. But its big brim kept falling over her eyes, and she was laughing by the time she came up to him.

Her laughter trailed off like a squeaky wheel when her gaze settled on his taut mouth. "What's the matter?"

"Just get on the bloody horse."

She got on the horse. He handed the baby up to her, then mounted behind her. His arms came around her to take the reins. She breathed, and her breast pressed against his arm. So she stopped breathing altogether, then sucked in a draft of air with a sharp gasp. He urged Prudence into a trot, and her breast bounced against him, and she went rigid.

"Where are we going with the brat?" he asked, the words warm and moist against her ear.

She breathed. She could feel the heat of his arm now through her clothes and his. "We're taking her to Mousehole, back to her mother," she said.

"Won't her mother just throw her away again?"

She breathed. And her nipples hardened, rubbing almost painfully against her cotton shift. Her breasts had never felt this way before. Not even when the Gypsy boy had touched her. There was such a squeezing tightness in her chest that suddenly she couldn't bear it. She squirmed, and he shifted, breaking the contact, and she was sorry afterward that she had moved.

"I think it was probably her father, Salome Stout's father, who threw the baby away," she said. "She has to be Salome's baby, you see, because Salome is the only one in these parts who's been preg—in a delicate condition. They say the man who did it to her, who gave her the baby, was a sailor out of Falmouth, and he couldn't marry her because he has a wife already. I suppose Jacky Stout tried to get rid of the baby because he didn't want another mouth to feed. It couldn't have been shame that drove him to it. Jacky Stout knows no shame."

Jessalyn had always held a particular aversion for the fisherman ever since she had caught him tying a tin plate to a dog's tail. Her jaw clenched with anger as she thought of this man who would dump his own grandchild, by-blow or

not, down a bal. "Just wait until I get my hands on that
Jacky Stout. He won't be abandoning any more babies. I
will put the fear of God into him, and I heard that dubious
snort, Lieutenant."

She felt him smile against her neck, and she shivered. "I
assure you, Miss Letty, that I have never uttered such an
uncivilized sound as a snort, dubious or otherwise, in my
entire life."

"Hunh."

"Now hear who's snorting."

The sun was setting by the time they arrived in
Mousehole. Granite and slate cottages tumbled like a
child's spilled blocks down a hillside and into a horseshoe-
shaped harbor. But it was picturesque only from a distance.
Rotting lobster baskets, tangled coils of rope, and pieces of
broken spar littered the uneven stones of the old quay. The
place stank of decaying fish, and the steady thump and
clatter of the tin stamp battered their ears.

They passed no one along the way, except for an old man
who sat on his front stoop, mending a sail. He lifted his
head and stared at them, his toothless mouth falling open as
if his jaw had come unhinged. Jessalyn pointed out the
broken-down cottage where Jacky Stout lived with his two
grown daughters, Bathsheba and Salome. There had been a
Magdalene, but she had died two years ago of the spotted
fever.

Like the rest of the Mousehole cottages, the Stout home
had steep stone steps that led to an upper floor where the
family lived. Below was the fish cellar, where every year
pilchards were packed in rows and left for a month or so to
allow the blood and oil to drain. Although the season was
still a couple weeks away, the reek of rotting pilchards was
so strong Jessalyn had to breathe through her mouth to
keep from gagging.

Lieutenant Trelawny kicked aside a pile of sacks and
smelly fishing tackle that blocked the front door. Waving a
gust of gnats away from her face, Jessalyn knocked.

The man who flung open the door had a thick face badly pitted by the pox, like a frostbitten leaf. His belly, stout as an ale barrel, was covered by a smock frock that was smeared with fish scales and reached as far as a pair of leather gaiters and hobnailed boots. He was unshaven and slightly drunk.

"What d' ye want . . ." Jacky Stout began. Then his snake gray eyes caught sight of the lieutenant, and he tried on an obsequious smile. "Sur."

"We want to see Salome," Jessalyn said.

"That ye can't, Miss Letty. Proper sick, she be."

He started to shut the door, but Jessalyn put her foot across the threshold. "Don't you try to gammon me, Jacky Stout. Salome isn't sick. She's just had a baby. This baby."

Jacky's gaze, which had wandered everywhere else, had yet to alight upon the bundle in Jessalyn's arms. He licked his lips. "That can't be hers. Salome's baby died. Died last night. Born dead, she be. He be. 'Twere a boy. Born dead."

Jessalyn raised her brows in mock surprise. "Why, what a strange coincidence. Salome's baby born dead last night, and here this afternoon I find another baby tossed down an adit at Wheal Patience like so much unwanted rubbish. They say coincidences come in bunches, did you know that, Mr. Stout? I'm wondering what the magistrates would say if they knew the bird in your Sunday pot isn't always chicken, but one of Squire Babbage's prime pheasants. What do you suppose the magistrates would make of that coincidence, Mr. Stout? A man could get transported for poaching, so they say. A man could even hang. Just like a man could hang for trying to murder a helpless baby—"

The door was snatched from Jacky's hands, and a girl with a mane of wild, tangled black hair stood, swaying, on the threshold. She wore only a thin, tattered shift, and her eyes were like two bruises on her bleached face.

"Me baby!" she cried, holding out pale, trembling arms. "Ye've brought back me baby. Oh, please, give 'er to me."

The look of tear-filled joy on the girl's face more than

convinced Jessalyn that she'd had nothing to do with the abandonment of her child. Jessalyn gave the baby to her mother, helping her inside. The girl stumbled over to a sagging, straw-filled pallet and collapsed upon the edge of it, moaning and weeping and stroking the baby's face again and again.

She lifted eyes full of horror and hatred and searched the room until she found her father. "Ye told me she had died."

"'Tes what ye get, ye slut, for gettin' yer belly knocked up. An' who's got t' feed it now, eh?" Jacky Stout threw a baleful look at Jessalyn, then turned his back on her and poured gin down his throat from a stone jug.

The cottage smelled of fish and moldering roof thatch. Besides the single pallet, the only other furniture was a rough table tacked together from flotsam washed up from the sea and several mismatched stools. The single window was stuffed with rags, the only light coming from a tallow candle stuck in a turnip and a smoky dung fire.

A humped shadow by the fire stirred and became a girl sitting on a stool. She got up and came toward them, walking as if her hips were connected to swivels. Bathsheba Stout had a pointed, fey face, soot black hair, and slanted tawny eyes. Of the two sisters, Jessalyn would have thought Bathsheba more likely to be the one to bear a child out of wedlock. But then perhaps she was too experienced to get caught.

The baby was suckling at her mother's breast now, and Jessalyn couldn't help staring. Salome's breast was large and veined, like a cantaloupe. The baby's mouth pulled hard at the brown, distended nipple; Jessalyn wondered what it felt like, if it hurt. Her gaze moved up to the girl's white face, which wore a mixture of fear, anguish, and a stubborn pride.

"Ye won't peach to the magistrates, will ee, about what me da tried t' do? Please, miss, he won't do nothin' else t' harm the babe now that ye're on to him. Sheba and us, we'd starve without Da, without what he brings in from the fishin'. There bain't any work for the likes of us."

Jessalyn's hand fell on the girl's shoulder. She could feel the sharpness of bone beneath the thin shift. "I overheard the Reverend Mrs. Troutbeck mentioning last Sunday after evensong that she has need of a new scullery girl. I could put in a word for you."

"Oh, miss, ee are ever so kind," Salome said, but the fear did not leave her eyes. She pulled the baby tighter to her breast. "But what about me da?"

"I won't go to the magistrates," Jessalyn said. If the Stout daughters closed ranks to protect their father, there would be little proof anyway. "But if he ever threatens you or the child again, you must promise to come to me."

Bathsheba, taking advantage of Jessalyn's preoccupation with her sister, had sidled up to Lieutenant Trelawny. Her amber gaze traveled the length of him before settling on his face. "I hope ee don't think I'd nothin' do with dumpin' the poor l'il un down an old bal. I thought she'd died, same as Salome."

The lieutenant looked her over, slow and easy. "You seem to have borne up well under the tragedy, Miss Stout."

Jessalyn snorted.

Bathsheba gave Jessalyn a baleful look that was a mirror of her father's, then turned back to the lieutenant wearing a butter-wouldn't-melt smile. "I think of ye livin' up there in that gret big house, all by yerself, wit'out no one t' turn a hand. I could come do fer ee, sur. From time t' time, like. Mebbe bring ee some fresh mackerel when me da gets hisself a netload."

The lieutenant produced one of his rare and dazzling smiles. "I have always been partial to fish."

Jessalyn snorted again, louder. *Do for him.* Oh, Sheba Stout would *do* for him all right. And nine months hence there would be more fodder for the bals.

He could stay and flirt with Bathsheba the rest of the day; Jessalyn had better things to do. She issued a final warning to Jacky Stout, who kept his pride by ignoring her, then started for the door.

But the lieutenant's hand fell on her arm, holding her back. "Stout," he said, and there was the sharp crack of command from the parade field in his voice, "you will acknowledge Miss Letty when she speaks to you."

Jacky Stout's back jerked. He turned slowly, wiping his mouth with his wrist. "Sur?" The surliness was gone from his face, leaving fear.

"Henceforth, when Miss Letty addresses you, you will doff your cap in respect. And you will remember, too, that what is found on Caerhays land belongs to the Trelawnys and what is ours, we protect. I would pray, were I you, that the babe has a long and healthy life."

A warmth suffused Jessalyn at his words. No one had ever done that for her before; no one had ever stood as her champion. For a moment she allowed herself to wonder what it would be like to have him there always. At her side.

But once outside, when she was about to mount Prudence and she felt his hands, warm and strong, pressing into her flesh, she said, "You will kindly remove your hands from around my waist, Lieutenant."

He lifted her into the saddle and stood grinning up at her. "This sudden and totally female behavior on your part wouldn't by chance have anything to do with Miss Bathsheba Stout?"

"You preened and ruffled your tail feathers like a strutting turkey cock. While she looked at you as if she were a hungry black-backed gull all set to pounce."

His grin deepened. "Actually she puts me more in mind of a plump and succulent little pouter pigeon."

Jessalyn jerked Prudence's head around and drove the mare into a trot. If he was going to be that way, he could walk home. His laugh followed her into the dusk, a laugh that was almost all breath, low and husky.

She heard the clatter of boots on stone. She turned

around and nearly screamed as he vaulted up behind her onto the mare's back in a trick worthy of the Gypsy boy. His arms clutched her waist and his breath stirred the hair at her neck. "Don't be a silly goose, Miss Letty."

9

Jessalyn opened her eyes and nearly screamed.

Becka Poole's round muffin face stared at her from above a flickering candle flame and beneath a droopy red bed cap, so that her head seemed to be floating, disembodied, in the darkness. "Are ee awake, Miss Jessalyn?"

Jessalyn flopped onto her stomach and pulled a pillow over her ears. "No, Becka. It is the middle of the night, and I am sound asleep."

"'Tes no time for jesting, miss. There be ghosts out on Crookneck Cove this night. Ghosts, I tell ee. I near died of heart stroke. 'Tes a wonder I ain't laid out cold in me coffer, the immoral scare I did have."

Jessalyn threw off the pillow, sitting up. "Are you sure you didn't just have a nightmare, a hilla?"

"That's what I, too, thinks at first, miss. That I be hilla-ridden 'cause of them dough cakes what I ate for supper last night, which sat like stones in me belly afterward and gave me indignity something fierce. I thought maybe I was only dreamin' that I got up to look out the window. But then I says to meself: *Cor, Becka girl, yer eyes be open. 'Tesn't no hilla ye be havin'. 'Tes ghosts ye see. Real live ghosts!*"

Jessalyn got up to see the ghosts. It was a foggy night—

thick as lamb's wool in some places; in others, thin as a lace veil. Through the drifting curtains of white mist, she saw a light flicker on top of the cliffs that overlooked Crookneck Cove.

"See, miss. They be corpse lights, ee mark my words." Becka spit on her right index finger and drew a cross between her eyes. "Listen. Ee can hear their dead voices a hailing their own names."

"That's the wind you are hearing." Sometimes the bodies of dead sailors would be washed onto the beach by the tide, and they were often buried where they were found. But Jessalyn didn't believe in ghosts or corpse lights. "It's a wicked night," she said. "Perhaps a ship got caught on the Devil's Jawbone."

Her Cornish blood quickened at the thought that there might be a wreck. When times were bad, folk often prayed for treacherous weather, for a wreck was a gift of God, a spoil of the sea, as surely as a shoal of fish. The survivors would be seen to first, of course. But a vessel cast upon the shore was as good as a harvest, there for the gleaning.

Moving quickly, she thrust her feet into a pair of pattens and threw her red wool cloak over her night rail. All the while Becka bewailed the fate that was sure to be hers if she ventured out in the dark of a foggy night to tangle with ghosts.

To light her way, Jessalyn took a chill—a thin earthenware lamp that burned pilchard oil. At the door Becka stopped her to press a hagstone into her hand. It was a flint with a hole in it that had been threaded through with a leather thong and was supposed to be a safeguard against ghosts and witches. It was one of the girl's most prized possessions.

Smiling, Jessalyn slipped the hagstone over her head. "Thank you, Becka. I shall only be borrowing it, just in case. And please, while I'm gone, get out the extra blankets and heat up some hot water—and try not to wake Gram."

Becka flapped her hand and giggled. "Gis along wi' ee,

miss. Ghosts ain't got no corpus bodies. For what would they be wantin' blankets and hot water?"

Jessalyn's rusty laughter floated off into the thick night. "Not for the ghosts, Becka. For the survivors, in case it's a wreck."

The Sarn't Major was not in his room above the stables, and Jessalyn hoped he wasn't spending the night in a kiddley again. All was quiet, too quiet. If there had been a wreck, she would have heard shouts by now and feet pounding down the cliff path. A bonfire would be blazing as a warning to other ships and to warm up those survivors dragged in from the sea. But even the small flickering light she'd seen earlier had vanished.

She wondered then if the mysterious light had something to do with Lieutenant Trelawny. She hadn't seen him for over a week, since that day they had found Salome Stout's baby. It hurt that he could so easily stay away from her, because she could hardly bear to be apart from him.

She couldn't understand this obsession she seemed to have developed for a man she was not sure she even liked. Yet she felt driven to be with him every waking moment, and when they were apart, she spent all her hours remembering the times they were together and planning the moments when they would be together again. Worse, she had allowed him to steal her pride. For when he did not come to call, she had haunted the beach and the moors in the hope that she would cross his path. One day she had even ventured as far as the gatehouse. She had tried to peer through the grimy windows, even tested the door latch, but it was locked. Her blood had been pumping hard and fast in her throat, with fear that he would discover her, with even more fear that he would not. A terrible sickness had squeezed her chest, an actual ache in her heart, that if she did not see him, see him that very day, that very next minute, she wouldn't be able to bear it, she would surely die from it.

But she hadn't seen him and she hadn't died, and she

had thought perhaps this sickness, this obsession would pass. Yet now she found herself running toward the sea cliffs, her heart and breath once again suspended in that otherworld of joy and terror at the thought that he would be there, that she would see him again.

Tonight the fog was as thick as pease porridge along the beach. Foamy fingers of seawater clawed at the sand, then disappeared. The air was wet and heavy, smelling of decaying seaweed and something else, something suspiciously like . . .

A scream started to rise in her throat just as an arm encased in wool wrapped around her neck, a rough hand clamping down hard over her mouth. The chill fell from her fingers and rolled across the sand, but did not go out. It cast light in a small arc through the shrouding mist onto the bottom of her red cloak and the booted legs of her attacker. His other arm wrapped around her in a bear hug, squeezing all the air out her lungs. The palm that smothered her mouth reeked so strongly of brandy the fumes made her head reel. She rammed her elbow backward into his belly and heard such a satisfactory grunt that she did it again.

Hot breath blew against her ear. "Christ, have you got spikes for elbows? I'm not going to ravish you, except in your dreams."

Jessalyn's heart turned over, and she went still in his arms. He kicked sand over the chill, dousing the flame and plunging them into darkness. "Will you scream?" he growled in her ear. "Have a fit of the vapors? Lose your scattered nerves?" Jessalyn shook her head and gasped muffled words against his hand. "Peach on us to the gaugers, collect the reward, and dance beneath the gibbet when we hang?" She started choking on her laughter, and at last he let go of her mouth.

"Lieutenant!" she exclaimed on a deep intake of breath. She nearly threw herself into his arms, only stopping herself just in time. He bent over and picked up something from beside him in the sand. It was too dark to see his face.

"Why, if it isn't Miss Letty—regular as a cuckoo out of a clock," he said. "I might have known you'd make an appearance. A perilous occasion such as this, when the least little thing is apt to go wrong at any moment, would hardly be complete without your presence."

Metal scraped against metal, and suddenly a narrow beam of light shot through the fog from the bull's-eye lantern in his hands. He closed the shutter, then opened it again. For a moment there was a break in the white clouds, like a rip in a curtain, and Jessalyn thought she saw a flotilla of longboats and the four-cornered sails of a lugger rounding the point.

"You've been smuggling!"

"And here I thought we were merely having a midnight picnic on the beach." He laughed and took her arm, pulling her with him back toward the underside of the cliffs.

There was a wild excitement about him tonight that was infectious. Her heart tripped in a light, quick dance. "Why didn't you tell me you were going smuggling?"

"For the same reason that I didn't take out a notice in the *Times*. And I prefer to call it free trading. Smuggling has such nasty, illegal connotations that make one think of magistrates and gaol and penal colonies."

As they drew closer to the cliffs, Jessalyn heard the crunch of footsteps on stone and a low murmur of voices. Again the fog parted for a moment, and she was shocked to see a gaping hole in the ragged face of the rock where there had never been a hole before. A large boulder had been pushed to one side. All the days she had walked this beach and she hadn't known of the cave's existence.

He let go of her hand, and his voice floated out of the darkness. "Wait here, and please try, no matter what the temptation, not to make any trouble."

Jessalyn resented his remark and would have told him so, but his footsteps had already receded. She tilted her head, trying to peer upward through the fog. This part of the bluff was not sheer but rather tumbled down to the beach in rocky steps, like a child's blocks. He had told her to wait; he'd said nothing about not looking inside the cave.

Gathering up the trailing folds of her cloak, she climbed up the rocks until the entrance was at eye level. The cave was about the size of a small parlor and dimly lit by a tarred lantern. Two men carrying ankers of brandy beneath each arm disappeared down a narrow passage that no doubt led to the fish cellars of Mousehole or more likely the wine cellars of Caerhays Hall. Two other men hovered closer to the entrance. One turned toward her, and Jessalyn got a glimpse of the pitted face of Jacky Stout.

"Fetch the glim o'er here," he growled. "'Tes dark as a bloody sack."

The other man passed the lantern forward. Then he, too, turned, and his hair glinted like a gold sovereign in the dim light. "Jessalyn!" he exclaimed. "What the deuce are you doing here?"

Jessalyn stepped back, more shocked at finding Clarence Tiltwell here than at the chill of his welcome. It was understandable why Lieutenant Trelawny would engage in smuggling—for the money and love of the game. But Clarence always had to be prodded into taking risks, and the reward of such a venture would hardly be worth it to him. The share-out of a run to France couldn't be more than a month's or two's worth of the allowance he got from his father.

Clarence jumped down beside her. Seizing her arm, he jerked her away from the cave, practically dragging her down the rocks and back onto the beach. His lips were drawn tight against his teeth, and a tic pulsed beneath his right eye. It suddenly occurred to her that if she could see his face so well, the fog must be lifting.

His fingers clenched, digging into her flesh and hurting her. "You've got to get back to End Cottage this instant—"

"Gaugers, sur! Coming this way!"

A man pelted full speed down the cliff path, a tarred lantern swinging from one hand, an empty coat sleeve flapping where the other hand should be. Lieutenant Trelawny appeared from behind some dunes, intercepting him. Jessalyn was shocked to see that the man with the lantern was the Sarn't Major, *her* Sarn't Major, who had never wanted anything to do with anything before, except horses. She stared openmouthed as Lieutenant Trelawny had a quick, low-voiced conversation with the Welshman that consisted of an exchange of several long and convoluted sentences.

Clarence stirred beside her. His face was pale as a wraith's in the disintegrating mist. "What rotten luck that they would be patrolling this stretch of coast tonight of all nights," he said, his voice sounding queer and tight.

"Luck had nothing to do with it," Lieutenant Trelawny said, striding up to them. "Clarey, you see the last of our cargo through the tunnel and get it sealed up. I'll try to delay the preventive men long enough for you to get it all safely stowed."

He took Jessalyn's arm, hauling her after him down the beach. She was beginning to feel like a dog on a leash, tugged this way and that, and she would likely have a score of bruises come morning. "That was the Sarn't Major," she said, panting slightly, for he was walking fast, though limping badly. "You were talking to the Sarn't Major."

"The man's not deaf."

"I know, but you were *talking* with him." He stopped before a pile of driftwood, a fire that had been laid into the lee shelter of a heap of rocks and marram-covered dunes. He took a flask out the pocket of his greatcoat, which he wore carelessly unbuttoned to the cold, and splashed liquid onto the wood. Her nostrils pinched at the sudden pungent odor of spilled brandy. "What . . ." she began as he pushed her down onto a shelf of sand and grass. He yanked the hood of her cloak so far over her head it covered her eyes. She pushed it back a bit. "What are you doing?"

"Just sit there, and no matter what happens, keep your hood pulled close around your face."

Jessalyn heard the scrape of a flint, and the driftwood

burst into blue flames. She shut her eyes against the sudden blaze of light. He dropped down onto a rock beside her. She leaned toward the fire, wrapping her arms around her bent knees. "Do you think there was an informer?" She would have put her money on Jacky Stout.

"Hold your clack, girl."

"Who do you think it is—the informer, I mean?"

"If you don't shut your mouth, I will shut it for you."

She shut her mouth. The fire spit and hissed like a cat, and the sea whispered across the sand. She stole a glance at him. The flames glinted red in his damp hair and glazed the flaring bones of his cheeks, casting deep shadows in the hollows beneath. He looked like the devil come straight up from hell.

Shouts bounced against the rocks, and lantern lights bobbed like fireflies above their heads. Stones clattered and rolled down the cliff path.

"Here they come," he said, his voice low and breathy. "We are two lovers enjoying the night and each other. No matter what I do, keep your face hidden and your mouth shut."

The gaugers were getting closer. She could hear their boots crunching across the sand, and their lanterns threw shafts of light through the decaying fog. "Why can't you tell me your plan?" she whispered. "Surely it would help—"

He turned toward her. She caught the flare of twin fires reflected in his dark eyes before he rolled over on top of her and his mouth slammed down on hers.

He molded his mouth to hers, sucking and pulling on her lips, filling her with his breath and the taste of brandy. Her fingers dug into the muscles of his back, to hold on to him, hold on. . . . His tongue slid past her parted lips, filling her mouth. Dear life, his tongue was in her mouth, and the thought of it, the pure, piercing intimacy of it, ignited a hunger deep within her that exploded, blazing up hot and fast as if she, like the driftwood, had been doused with alcohol and set alight. Moaning, she arched into him, press-

ing, trying to fuse their two bodies and assuage this burning, burning place in her belly. His tongue moved, stroking
the inside of her mouth as if he were tasting of her, and the
burning place grew hotter, melting her from the inside
out. . . .

"Stand up there, and do it nice an' easylike."

His mouth released hers, but slowly, coming back to
brush her lips with his, once, twice more. The color was
high on his cheekbones, and she could see the pulse beating wildly in his neck before he rolled off her. He stood,
pulling her up with him and thrusting her behind his back.
Her muscles were heavy and aching, and her chest heaved
so hard she unconsciously put her clasped hands up to her
breast to keep her heart from bursting right out of her.

A group of men stood before them, bundled up against
the fog in oilskins and seaboots. One disengaged himself
from the rest and stepped forward. He had a brace of pistols tucked into his belt and a battered face with a nose like
a grubbing hoe. He was one of the men Lieutenant Trelawny had been drinking with at the Midsummer's Eve fair.

"Lieutenant, sur!" the customs officer said, surprise in
his voice. "What are ee doing out on a night such as this?"

"I'm spending an hour or two with my girl," he answered, but there was a rusty catch to the words, as if he
were having a hard time finding his breath.

"Bain't the weather for it, if ee don't mind me sayin' so,
sur. 'Tes weather for staying close at home by the fire."

"This fire does us well enough. Her father doesn't like
me. And she has lots of brothers." He shuddered dramatically. "Big brutes, they are. With lots of muscles and fists."

The customs man tried to get a look at Jessalyn, but
Lieutenant Trelawny shifted his weight, shielding her. She
pulled the hood closer about her face.

"Ye wouldn't happened to have seen a lugger, would ee,
sur?"

"Well, I've been a bit preoccupied, you understand." He
flashed a just-between-us-men smile that the gauger an-

swered with a leer. "But I doubt I could have missed seeing a ship come into the cove, even in this fog."

The gauger scrubbed a big paw across his chin. "Ais, no doubt, sur. No doubt. A score of longboats unloading tuns of brandy on this beach would have been hard to miss."

"The only brandy I've seen is this which I've brought along with me to keep the chill away." He produced the small flask from his coat pocket, flashing his sudden, charming smile. "Though I could not swear any tax was paid on it, coming as it did from my brother's cellar."

"You wouldn't mind us searching them cellars, would ee . . . sur."

He hesitated for the briefest moment. Then he lifted his shoulders in a lazy shrug. "If you think it necessary. But I must see the lady home first. You may wait for me at the entrance to Caerhays Hall."

"Oh, we'll do that, sur. You can be sure we'll wait for ee, sur. Right there on the front steps o' Caerhays Hall."

"Dear life, what can you be thinking of?" Jessalyn said in a loud whisper as soon as the preventive men had disappeared up the cliff path. "You can't let them search the hall. Won't they find—"

His fingers brushed her lips, still swollen and tender from his kiss. "Shhh. They won't find much. All the good stuff was drunk long ago."

"Then they'll search all the fish cellars in Mousehole and—"

"And they won't find anything but fish." He reached for her at the same time that she took a step toward him. The hem of her cloak caught on one of the rocks, gaping open. He had meant to take her arm, but his hand closed over her breast instead.

She wore only a night rail of loosely woven linen. The thin material, damp from the fog, clung to her skin. Her breast tightened and swelled, her nipple hardening and pushing up between his fingers.

He went utterly still.

The fire blazed hot at her back, and the wet sea air caressed her face. Her breast where he touched her burned, burned. . . . He stared at her breast, at her taut nipple pushing against his fingers, and his eyes were two black pools, reflecting nothing but the flames. He looked feverish, as if the skin had been pulled too tightly over the sharp bones of his face. His nostrils flared wide, the way a stallion's does when it is frightened. Or excited.

She leaned into him, to feel his heat, to fill her senses with the hot smell of him. His fingers moved, closing around her nipple. She gasped at a feeling so piercing it was on the edge between ecstasy and pain. The words came out of her without thought. "Kiss me again."

"No," he said, on a rough expulsion of breath. He jerked his hand back, as if he had just now felt the searing fire.

Her heart swelled, pushing against her chest, making it difficult to breathe. "Why not?"

"Because you are too young," he said, his chest expanding in a deep sigh.

"You kissed me a moment ago to fool the gaugers." Her lips trembled into a smile. "I am a whole five minutes older now."

"I don't want to kiss you, dammit!"

Something broke inside her in a terrible gush of pain. She whirled and took two stumbling steps through the deep sand.

"Oh, bloody hell!" He snagged her cloak with one hand, the other grabbing her waist, twisting her around and hauling her up against his chest. Seizing her hand by the wrist, he pressed it against the front of his buckskin breeches. "Feel that, damn you. Feel it! You might be a virgin, but you live on a stud farm, for the love of God. You've watched a stallion cover a mare. You know bloody well what it means when a man gets hard like this for a woman. If I kissed you, feeling the way I do now, I'd soon have you flat on your back on the sand with that bloody, useless thing you're wearing ripped right down the middle. And then, by God, there would be hell to pay. For the both of us."

He was stiff and hard beneath her hand. And alive—a swelling, pulsating heat. Her fingers closed around him.

"Jesus Christ!" He flung her off him so violently she nearly stumbled.

"If I wasn't a virgin, would you want to kiss me then?"

He thrust his fingers through his hair. His head fell back, and his eyes squeezed shut. Tremors racked his body as if he had a chill. "Don't ask such improper questions."

She didn't care. She needed to get close to him, to be held by him. It took only one step to bring her body up next to his again, and she took it. She laid her open palms on his collarbone, pushing aside the lapels of his coat. He was breathing fast, his chest rising and falling. "Please," she said. "Don't treat me like a child. I—"

"You *are* a child!" He thrust her off him. But then a harsh, racking sound burst from her, and he pulled her back against him, gathering her in his arms. "Ah, dammit, come here, baggage."

Tears clogged her throat, building and building, until it felt as if she were choking. Then they exploded out of her in shuddering heaves. "I only asked you to kiss me. I never meant, I never wanted, I didn't—"

"I know. It's all right." He held her while she cried, and though she didn't feel it, he buried his mouth in her hair. Finally she subsided into shudders and little hiccuping breaths. "Are you done blubbering all over my chest?" he said.

She nodded, her forehead rubbing against his shoulder. Her throat was sore, and her eyes burned. She couldn't lift her head and face him. The pain had drained out of her, leaving her sick with shame. Keeping her head down, she sniffled in a deep breath, rubbing her eyes with the tatted lace cuff of her night rail.

"Don't use your sleeve, for God's sake. Have you no idea

at all of correct behavior?" He thrust a handkerchief of fine
Indian cotton into her hands. "Here. Use this."

She pressed the bunched-up handkerchief to her mouth
to hold back another welling sob. Her head fell against him,
her forehead nuzzling into his neck. He was still holding
her, one hand tangled in her hair, the other pressing into
the small of her back, and, oh, the way it felt to be in his
arms, to be surrounded by his wonderful heat and strength.
. . . She nestled into him, breathed against the warm skin
of his neck, smelling sea salt and woodsmoke and brandy.
And that male smell that was uniquely his. She wanted to
burrow deep into him and breathe in the smell of him
through every pore of her body.

Her lips brushed against the pulse in his throat. It leaped
and throbbed against her open mouth, pumping to the hard
rush of her own blood. His fingers tightened in her hair,
pulling her head up. His eyes flared like exploding suns as
his gaze fastened on her mouth. She leaned into him,
melted into him. His head dipped, and his breath trailed
across her lips—

"Jessalyn!"

They separated slowly, as if drugged. Clarence Tiltwell
stood at the very edge of the light cast by the fire, his eyes
wide with shock. He jerked into movement, striding across
the sand to grasp Jessalyn's arm, pulling her away from
Lieutenant Trelawny's side. His gaze stabbed at his cousin,
and his jaw muscles tightened. "You bastard."

One corner of Lieutenant Trelawny's mouth twisted with
something that might have been regret. "I know. You think
I ought to be buried at the crossroads with a stake through
my heart."

"You bloody bastard," Clarence said.

Lieutenant Trelawny met Jessalyn's eyes, but his
thoughts, his feelings were shuttered against her. She
didn't know what he wanted, what to do to make him want
her.

"I'm taking her home," Clarence said.

"Please do," Lieutenant Trelawny answered, and to Jessalyn's horror he sounded utterly bored with the whole tawdry scene. Fresh tears welled in her eyes as she turned away from him.

McCady Trelawny stood still, his hands hanging loosely at his sides, until Jessalyn and his cousin disappeared beyond the reach of the firelight, into the darkness and the mist. He groped behind him, felt rock and grass, and subsided onto the dune. His long fingers pressed hard against the bones of his face, stopping the ragged noise of his breathing.

But it was a long time before he stopped shaking.

"We thought ee had forgotten us, sur," the gauger said.

"On the contrary." McCady's voice was full of sophisticated ennui. "I had, however, unfinished business to attend to first, you understand. A gentleman should never leave a lady unfinished."

The gauger's thick lips twisted into a leer. "I told the others, sur." He looked to his cohorts for confirmation. "Didn't I tell ee the randy young buck would probably take his sweet time a-rogering the wench, whilst our own cocks and bobbles rotted in this frigging damp?"

McCady laughed, for even in his present mood he could appreciate the irony. The one time in his sorry, misbegotten life he'd actually done the honorable thing, and here he'd had to disguise it with a cloak of indecency. He couldn't understand anyway what it was about sweet, innocent Miss Letty that made him behave so outside his reprehensible character, that inspired strange protective feelings within him he didn't want and didn't know what to do with.

Young Miss Letty. Too bloody young, but not so young that she didn't know what she was offering. Yet when he was with her, when she looked at him with those gray eyes that saw everything and hid nothing . . . She almost had him believing that he could do anything, even change the man that he was. She had him feeling that he'd been put on

this earth to protect her from the world. And God, what a
bloody jest that was, because it wasn't the world she
needed protecting from; it was himself.

His mouth twisted into a bitter smile as he led the gaugers up the steps and into Caerhays Hall. The front door was
unlocked, for there was nothing inside to steal. His brothers had pawned or sold everything down to the wood paneling to feed their gambling and opium habits.

He had been inside the house only once since he'd returned to Cornwall, and now, while the gaugers searched
the cellars, he roamed the rooms. He climbed rickety,
worm-eaten stairs to bedchambers that were sour-smelling
from the damp and full of mouse droppings. His footsteps
rang on the stone-flagged floor of the great hall. He looked
at the empty niches that had been cut into the walls for
statues long gone, and he felt sad. No, sorrow was too
strong an emotion. He felt regret. He wondered, in the
same idle way one would wonder what it would be like to
be the prince of Wales, how much it would cost to restore
the house to its former glory, if it had ever had a former
glory. As far as he knew, every Trelawny ever born had
died in debt and disgrace, and he wasn't likely to break
with the tradition.

The gaugers rejoined him with a rattle of lanterns and
scuffling of boots. McCady Trelawny looked down his patri-
cian nose at their leader and said in a voice underlaid by
generations of inbred arrogance, "I trust you gentlemen are
satisfied."

The customs man scraped his beard-stubbled chin.
"Well, as to satisfied, that I couldn't say, sur. There be no
contraband in these cellars, that much we do know. But as
to what might be stashed elsewhere, well . . ."

McCady ushered them down the length of the great hall.
"Nevertheless, I'm sure you'll forgive me if I do not share
your enthusiasm for apprehending the malefactors at this
very moment," he said, producing a huge, jaw-cracking
yawn. "It has been a rather exhausting night. The lady was

a bit of a stickler at the starting post—most of 'em are, don't you know—but Christ, once going, there was no stopping the wench. I rode her hard and fast down the stretch to a bang-up finish that has left me quite wrung out. . . ." He had to yawn again to keep from laughing at the drooling looks on the gaugers' faces.

He saw them to the front gates, and they set off down the lane to search the cellars of Mousehole, where he hoped they really would find nothing but fish.

He had not lied to the gaugers about one thing: He was tired. Pain cut deep like a sword thrust into his thigh with every step.

A discordant scream startled him for a moment, until he realized it came from the night owl that lived in the wild nut trees growing next to the gatehouse. He set his lantern down on the mounting block and stepped up to the gatehouse door . . .

And into a swinging, balled-up fist.

Clarence Tiltwell stood over the man he had felled, his breath sawing in his throat, his fists clenched. "You bastard. You bloody bastard," he said. He knew he was repeating himself, but then he had never been clever with words. Not like his cousin. His clever, degenerate Trelawny cousin.

McCady got up slowly. He tossed the hair out of his eyes and backhanded a trickle of blood off his mouth. "I'm willing, out of a fondness for you, dear cousin, to allow you a few liberties. But not at the expense of my good looks."

It was the voice of a man who had stood on a knoll in Belgium and slashed and slashed with his sword until the bodies piled up waist deep around him. Clarence tasted fear.

Yet hatred was there, too, burning the back of his throat, and the hatred was stronger than the fear. He had to swallow several times, nearly choking, before he could speak. "You were kissing her!"

McCady laughed, he actually laughed, and Clarence

wanted to kill him. "I suppose it hasn't occurred to you that you might have misinterpreted what you saw," McCady said.

Clarence knew what he had seen. McCady had been about to kiss her, had already kissed her, and the look in those dark eyes . . . the raw sexual hunger blazing in those eyes. McCady Trelawny wanted Jessalyn, and he had been about to take her. "I saw your face."

McCady's head fell back against the door. "Ah," he said, almost as a sigh.

Hurt and an awful sense of betrayal squeezed Clarence's chest. To his utter horror he felt on the verge of tears. "Do you intend to marry her?"

"Don't be absurd. I couldn't support a wife, even presuming that I wanted one."

"Yet you've made her fall in love with you. Damn your rotten Trelawny soul to hell."

"You can't damn the already damned. And she isn't in love with me; she's in lust. If you were acting your age instead of hers, you would know that all you have to do is wait long enough, and she will eventually see me for what I am and share, I am sure, in your righteous disgust."

Fear, anger, and despair all raged through Clarence's head. He could barely hear what his cousin was saying. McCady started to turn aside, but Clarence seized his arm. "If you've ruined her, I'll kill you."

He peeled Clarence's fingers off his sleeve. "For Christ's sake, Clarey. If I wanted a child virgin, there's a house I know of in London where one can buy them at ten."

"My God, you are depraved!"

McCady's head fell back as he drew in a deep breath, his lids drifting closed. "I said I knew of it; I didn't say I frequented the place." He opened his eyes, his gaze fastening on to Clarence's face. For a moment Clarence thought he saw pain flash raw and deep within the dark wells of his cousin's eyes, but then they turned flat and empty again. "I have already given you my word," McCady said, his voice flat and empty as well. "I will not take Miss Letty to my bed—"

Clarence barked a harsh laugh. "Your word! What is that worth?"

For a moment a taut silence filled the night. Then Mc-Cady said, his voice rough, "It is worth everything to me since my word is all that I have."

Clarence stared at that handsome, worldly face. "Why should I believe you? I don't believe you."

McCady leaned forward and light from the lantern shone on the bitter slant of his mouth. "Then stick it up your arse, *cousin.*"

Clarence felt a wetness on his cheeks and knew to his bitter shame that he was weeping. He wanted to smash his fist into his cousin's mouth again, but he didn't have the courage. His hands, hanging loosely at his sides, clenched and unclenched in helpless hurt and fury. "If you harm her in any way, I promise you this, Trelawny: I will make you pay."

He pivoted on his heel and walked off with jerky strides. Even then a part of him hoped that Mack would come after him, make it better between them, and he held his breath, straining to hear Mack's voice calling his name, long after it was too late.

McCady Trelawny leaned back against the gatehouse door and watched his cousin go, his face blank except for an occasional twitch at the corner of his mouth. He stayed that way, propped up by the door, until the wind chilled the sweat on his forehead and the owl screamed again.

He went inside the gatehouse, which had been his home for the last month. He had furnished it with bits and pieces of things that he had found in the hall, things not worth pawning or selling. A green-faced clock missing its minute hand, a wobbly table, a chair with only one slat. In a corner, a faded Chinese screen hid a cracked yellow tin bathtub. A kettle sat on a trivet beside a dead fire.

It was hardly the lap of luxury, but then he'd lived much

more roughly during the war. Along one wall stood a pair of nail-studded leather trunks, filled with books on engineering and science and his expensive clothes. At least no matter how poor he was at any given time, he always managed to dress like a gentleman, even if he probably wouldn't live long enough to pay off his rags and tatters bills. But then London tailors and bootmakers understood these things. His lips curled into a self-deprecating smile at the thought. Appearances should always be deceiving.

He looked around the room with distaste. There was nothing to keep him here now. A week at the most to arrange for the sale of the brandy, and he would clear maybe a hundred pounds' profit on the deal. It would all have to go toward repaying the money that Clarey had lent him for the locomotion experiments. Then he could kick the mud of Cornwall off his boots and debauch the rest of his life away at the expense of His Majesty's army.

He threw himself down onto a rope bed that squealed in protest. He kneaded his eyes with the heels of his hands. God, the look of horror and disgust on Clarey's face . . . McCady thought of what he himself had never had, of youth and innocence. Of a belief that somewhere in this corrupt and corruptible world there existed a tiny, shining scrap of decency and honor and— Damn her! She'd all but been begging for it, and he sure as bloody hell had wanted to give it to her. He should have borne her down onto the sand right then and taken her.

And he would have ruined her life.

He stretched his arms above his head, his fingers grasping the wooden slats of the bedstead. He stared at the roughhewn beams above and saw . . .

Saw her eyes, dark gray and turbulent as the sea before a storm, and her hair, russet and loamy, the color of autumn leaves strewn in wild abandon on his pillow. Saw himself burying his face in that hair, drowning in her smell. She would have freckles on her breasts, and he saw himself tasting them with his tongue. Saw himself spreading those long, long legs wide, kissing that laughing mouth senseless . . . Her mouth. God, the things he could teach her to do with that mouth.

He sat up abruptly, cutting off the thought with a ruthless effort of will. He could not as easily control his sex, which had stretched and grown hard, pressing painfully against his tight buckskin breeches.

He stood and limped over to the table. He picked up an old trapping knife, cut three rashers off a slab of bacon and put them into a frypan. The fire had gone out. He took the tinderbox off the mantel and tried to light it, but his fingers shook so badly he couldn't get a spark.

"Bloody hell!" He threw the tinderbox against the wall.

He stared at the piece of tarred sacking that served as a rug beside his bed. It also served to cover the trapdoor that led into a cellar that just happened to be filled at the moment with a hundred tuns of tax-free brandy. It was a foolish smuggler who consumed his own profits, but the only way he was going to get through what was left of the night was to drink himself insensible.

Yet he did not kick aside the sacking and lift the trapdoor. He crossed over to the bed and sat. His hands gripped his thighs so hard the tendons stood out like ropes. He felt as if every muscle in his body were straining against his skin.

His head fell back, and he swallowed hard. "Jessalyn," he said into the cold and empty room.

10

Three days later, on an evening of summer wind and lavender twilight, a lookout on the cliffs above Crookneck Cove spotted a dark red tinge far out to sea.

He waited a few breathless moments to be sure it wasn't a trick of light on water, a part of the sunset. But the red tinge grew darker and spread like a pool of blood, and soon there was no doubt. He shouted and did a fancy leap in the air. Throwing back his head, he blew a blast on his tin trumpet and followed it up with a cry, *"Hevva, hevva!"*

Becka Poole burst into the dining room where Jessalyn and her grandmother were having supper. "The pilchards are in!" she cried, hopping up and down in her excitement. "The pilchards are in!"

Jessalyn looked at her grandmother. Color bloomed on her cheeks that for three days had been as pale as old parchment. "Gram, may I? Please."

Lady Letty's lips pursed. "'Tisn't the done thing . . . oh, very well."

Jessalyn dashed from the room before her grandmother could change her mind. She stopped only long enough to tie a man's blue kerchief over her hair, then burst from the house like a frisky colt let loose into a field of clover.

Schools of pilchards had turned the sea red. Jessalyn ran

hand in hand with Becka along the top of the cliffs. They were joined by others, all racing toward the village of Mousehole. Everyone took up the huer's cry, *"Hevva, hevva!,"* the old Cornish word for *shoal.*

Barrels of burning oil threw streams of light onto a harbor packed with fishing vessels. The huer who had first spotted the shoal now stood atop the cliff, signaling with a burning torch the direction the fish were heading. The men in the boats below dropped the seine net into the water, then attached a tucking net to the enormous sheet of mesh, forming a circle.

The boats began to haul on the tucking net. Shouts cut off abruptly; laughter died away. All waited to see if the catch would be a good one, if the bellies of Mousehole would be full that coming winter, or empty. Oh, there were sounds—the screaming gulls, the lap and gurgle of water against the shale, the slap of oars, and the grunts of the men as they hauled on the net—yet it seemed to Jessalyn as if all the world had grown silent, watching, waiting.

Suddenly the water erupted into a seething mass of leaping, writhing fish. People in boats and onshore, people knee-deep in water that boiled like a caldron of hot soup scooped up the pilchards in baskets and buckets, laughing and shouting, while overhead the sea gulls cried.

Jessalyn pulled off shoes and stockings and kirtled her skirt above her knees like the other village women. She took up a wicker basket and waded into the bay. Pilchards flashed like silver coins in the water, tickling her bare legs, and she laughed aloud. Leaning over, she scooped up a basketful of fish and tossed the wriggling load into the well of a nearby boat. Suddenly a stream of pilchards sailed through the air into the boat, barely missing her head. Jumping back out of the way, she spun around, more laughter gurgling up in her throat . . . and dying.

Lieutenant Trelawny stood before her, an empty basket in his hands, an empty look in his shadowed eyes.

Their gazes clashed and locked, and the world went utterly still as if every living creature held its breath. Memories of that terrible night on the beach lashed through her mind, memories of how she had thrown herself at him, begging him to kiss her, and he had rejected her. Hot embarrassment washed over her, and her legs trembled, wanting to run away. Yet she stood unmoving while around them the water churned and the gulls screamed.

The words poured out of her throat unbidden, welling up from within her heart. "Why can't you leave me alone?"

He lifted his hand. She flinched, and so he let it fall without touching her. "I cannot," he said, or might have said. For she couldn't hear over the gulls and the shouts of the fishermen and the splashing water.

He stared at her forever, and she actually felt his gaze—the way she could feel the sea breeze on her hot cheeks and the current wrapping like seducing hands around her bare legs. His gaze touched her, his lids growing heavy, something moving now behind the darkness in his eyes, like wafting smoke. A tightness squeezed her chest, squeezing, squeezing until she wanted to scream. Just when she thought she could bear it no longer, he dropped his gaze, and she expelled her breath in a sharp sigh.

He bent over, filling the basket. He wore only a shirt, unfastened at the neck. It gaped open at the throat, exposing the beginning swell of hair-covered muscle. His collarbone rose and fell with each breath. She stared at him, at that tawny brown skin, and the tightness began to build in her chest again, cutting off her breath and pushing her heart up into her throat.

She was never sure afterward what led her to do it. She only knew she could no longer bear the tension that twanged between them like a taut wire. Perhaps she simply wanted to make herself laugh because in another moment she would have been crying. She did it without thought. She scooped a pilchard out of the water with her bare hand and tossed it down the front of his shirt.

He straightened with a snap and a hiss of indrawn

breath. He stared at her in shock while the pilchard thrashed like a trapped dove within the confines of the white cambric. Jessalyn laughed.

He reached down his shirt and came up with the wriggling fish. He looked at it a moment, and a strange light came into his eyes. He advanced on her, evil intent writ on his face.

She backed up, her arms flapping like a nestling trying to fly. "Lieutenant!" she shrieked, laughing still. "Don't!"

"Where shall I put it? Down your back, in your ear?" He opened his eyes wide, pretending to be struck with sudden inspiration. "Your mouth. That big, gaping mouth of yours warrants stuffing."

He made a grab for her, and the pilchard squirted out of his hand, diving back into the roiling water. He swore and then began to laugh, so that the sounds of their laughter—hers wild and squeaking like an unoiled hinge; his deep and husky—were carried out to sea, entwined together on the warm summer wind.

His laughter died first. He was staring at her mouth, and a strange tautness had come over his face. She wondered what he saw when he looked at her. He kept insisting that to him she was just a child, but at times she caught a white heat in his eyes that said he lied.

They didn't laugh again; they didn't even speak. But they worked side by side together well into the night, dumping basket after basket into boats that soon became loaded up to the gunwales with pilchards. At midnight Jessalyn waded out of the water without a word to him. She stopped to wring out her skirt, and when she looked up, he was beside her, staring at her bare legs. She felt nearly breathless with a growing excitement. For the first time she began to understand the power she held over him, that she could make him want to touch her, to kiss her, in spite of himself.

They walked along the stone hedge that followed the cliffs, and soon the sounds of the pilchard catch faded until they were wrapped in the soft silence of the night.

She pulled off the blue kerchief and threw back her head. She gathered her hair in her hands and lifted it off her neck, then slowly let it all tumble down her back. She felt the heat of his eyes on her, and she smiled.

The sky was black, sprinkled with stars that were faint and withdrawn. But the moon was round and full and golden, like a fat orange heavy with juice. The wind, restless and warm and smelling strongly of the sea and the earth, stirred her hair. She felt so glad to be alive it was a song in her heart, in her blood. She wanted to shout with the wonder of it.

She skipped a few steps ahead of him, then turned to walk backward. "I am happy tonight."

He said nothing. But he smiled suddenly, and her heart tripped.

She whirled, dancing away from him and laughing.

He snagged her arm. "Hasn't anyone told you that young ladies should be submissive of temper and meek of spirit?"

She wrinkled her nose at him. "That isn't me."

"No." The smile left his face. "That isn't you."

She bent over to pick a moonflower from out of the scrub. Laughing, she tucked it behind his ear. She regarded her handiwork with an impish grin. "You look silly."

"And you're acting silly." He removed the flower and pushed it through her hair, his fingers trailing across her temple and down her neck. His eyes, above the flaring bones of his cheeks, glowed red, like banked fires. "It's a blue moon tonight," he said. "Do you know what that is?"

She thought she might have known once. But her blood was running so thick, her heart beating so loudly, she couldn't think. "It's orange," she said. "The moon is orange tonight, not blue."

His face had taken on a strange, heated look. "Have you never heard the story? How once upon a time there was a bal-maiden so beautiful she made all who saw her glad to be alive, especially the shepherd boy who was her lover. But one night she was captured by a witch who coveted the handsome shepherd boy for herself. A witch so ugly even toads turned their faces away in horror—and don't laugh. This is a very serious story, and if you persist in giggling your way through it, you will spoil the whole effect."

Jessalyn sucked on her bottom lip. "I'll be good. I promise."

He stared at her mouth, and a silence stretched taut between them. Sea and wind sighed, like lovers' panting breath.

"Where was I? Ah, yes . . . The evil witch turned the bal-maiden into a hare, casting the spell so that the only time the girl could assume human form again was when the moon rode the sky in its full glory for the second time in one month. She thought she was making it impossible for the girl ever to be human again, but she had forgotten about the nights of the blue moon—those rare months when there are two full moons. And so from time to time the bewitched hare became a girl again and she and her shepherd boy would meet and make love. . . ." His hands closed over her arms, pulling her to him. He brought his face close to hers, and she waited, her heart in her throat, for his kiss. His voice had a husky break in it. "Once in a blue moon."

His lips, hard and hot, crushed hers, and her blood caught fire like a field of dry gorse. Her mouth opened beneath his, taking his tongue, giving him her own. Their lips and tongues stroked and mated, mouths melding in a desperate effort to become one.

"Jessalyn," he breathed into her open mouth. His fist tangled in her hair, pulling her head back. His lips slid down her jaw to the throbbing pulse in her throat, and Jessalyn thought she would die. "Oh, God, Jessa," he said, his voice raw. "Jessa, I want . . . I have to . . ."

He shuddered and stiffened, thrusting her away from him so hard she nearly fell. "I'm taking you home," he said, almost snarling the words.

She clung to his shirt. "Why? I don't understand."

"You are too young, dammit! And I promised—" He cut himself off, drawing in a violent breath. "You are too young."

I am not too young, she wanted to cry. *I'm not, I'm not* . . . And if he was what he claimed to be, what others said of him, her youth wouldn't matter.

"You are such a fraud, Lieutenant Trelawny," she said, the words roughened by her breathing. "You pretend to be a rakehell. But underneath that thatch-gallows manner of yours, there beats the heart of a true gentleman." She flattened her palms against his chest. She could feel the beat of his heart, frantic, like a trapped bird. "A man of honor—"

"Don't attempt to whitewash me, Miss Letty." His hands came up between them, closing around hers. He held her hands pressed hard to his chest a moment, then flung them off. "There are other names for men like me, names little girls like you can't even begin to guess the meaning of. Have you any idea how old I am?"

She shook her head. She had often wondered. But she hadn't dared ask for fear of reminding him of how young she was.

"I am twenty-five." He emitted a ragged laugh at the look on her face. He didn't know that it wasn't shock she felt, but relief. Nine years were not such a great difference at all. Her grandfather had been fifteen years older than Gram.

"Twenty-five is not so awfully old," she said, smiling.

He laughed again, shaking his head. "It feels it. It feels bloody old. As old as sin. I look at you, and I see . . ." He stroked her cheek with the backs of his fingers, a touch so light and brief she barely felt it. "I was ten the year my father died and I went to live with my brothers. My father was not the best of parents, but my brothers . . ."

His chest hitched, stopping the flow of words. He searched her face with eyes dark and desperate, as if he both dreaded and longed for her to see him exactly for what he was.

"They ruined me," he rushed on, his voice harsh. "You don't know, you can't imagine, what they did. . . . They exposed me to every vice to be bought or taken in the stews of London. By the time I was your age I had broken every law, violated every decency of God and man except 'Thou shalt not kill,' and the army quickly rectified that little oversight." His mouth grew queer and tight. "I'm a Trelawny, little one. We're a sorry, degenerate group of bastards."

She felt so sad, for him, for herself. For things once done that could never be undone, and because she could not change what he believed in his soul without changing what he was. And yet . . .

"And the man who built the steam locomotive," she said in a voice choked with unshed tears. "Who is he?"

The bitter tilt lingered on his mouth, and shadows had consumed all the light in his eyes. "He's a fool. A bloody fool."

But he's you. He's the man you are meant to be, Jessalyn could have said but didn't. For those were words he couldn't bear to hear.

He watched the girl skip along the beach, her rusty laughter clashing against the rhythmic rush of the sea. He called her name.

She whirled, her laughter cracking like the squawk of a hungry bird. "Clarence!"

Picking up her skirt, she ran toward him, and a warm glow suffused his chest, for she seemed glad to see him. Words tumbled out of her as she stopped, breathing hard, in front of him. "What are you doing here? I've barely seen you all summer."

Clarence slapped his tan kid gloves against his leg. He stared out over a sea that was a pale opal green. The light breeze smelled of seaweed and fish. It flattened her skirt, outlining the slim contours of her legs.

The warmth he'd felt on first seeing her dissipated, and an irritation took its place. It would never occur to her that he had been busy working, making his fortune. She had no conception of the value of money. *She's like all the others of her class,* he thought with an inner sneer. *The impoverished gentry with their long pedigrees and short purses, living on their three percents and a few acres of land.*

He turned on her, feeling a sudden flash of anger; he wanted her to be different. But then he looked at her smiling mouth and knew he could not really be angry with her for long. "How have you been, Jessalyn?"

Her smiled widened, and her gray eyes lightened to the color of the sea beneath a hot, glaring sun. "Oh, brave, brave. The pilchards came last night. You should have seen it."

There was a smear of sand on his ginger yellow boots. He flicked it off with his gloves. He spoke to the ground. "Trelawny won't marry you, you know. He's only out for a lark."

She said nothing. Encouraged, he pressed on. He was consumed with the need to make her see, to force her to understand that behind his handsome face and his aristocratic name, McCady Trelawny was only a shell of a man, a man with no principles, no scruples. A man incapable of giving and receiving love.

But of course, she would never see it; she had been gulled by that ravishing smile, that seductive charm. So he must use reason instead.

"A lieutenant in His Majesty's army clears maybe twenty-eight shillings after expenses. That's *all* his income, Jessalyn. His wastrel brother gives him no allowance. He gambles, of course. All the Trelawnys do, and they all have the same abysmal luck at it. They gamble with their heritage, and they gamble with their lives. When his brother, the earl, finally kills himself through overindulgence in all of his notorious vices, the only thing Mack will inherit will be his debts. And his disgrace."

"And the title."

"Is that what you're angling for—to be a countess?"

"Of course not!"

She had said it with such vehemence he believed her. He bent over and picked up a shell, tossing it at a heron that stood brooding at the tide line, its head buried in its feathers, its wings humped. The shell missed its mark, and the bird didn't even stir.

"*If* he inherits the title," Clarence said. He watched the heron because he couldn't bear to look at her. "Caerhays is unlikely to marry; no decent woman would have him. But Mack must still manage to outlive him, and they say the West Indies is a deadly place. And these pipe dream inventions of his—these iron horses and horseless carriages—"

"They are not pipe dreams! They are the future, only you are all too blind to see it. And so you persecute him for his vision."

His head jerked around, and his gaze searched her face. He saw what he expected—shining hero worship for a man who deserved nothing but her contempt.

"His *visions* consume what little money he does manage to accumulate, and they could well end up killing him someday. If he does outlive his brother and become the earl, he won't marry you. He will marry for money then because he will be the last of that God-cursed family, and though he might be irresponsible in every other way, he will do his duty by his name. It's another Trelawny tradition, the only thing that has kept their line from dying out years ago. And there is no end of rich cits' daughters who will sell soul and body to be called *my lady*."

As he ought to know. His mother's sister had been one of them. And his own mother had sold her soul and body to be called *my lord's mistress*.

He felt her eyes on him, those enormous gray eyes that saw so much. And yet so little. "Why do you hate him?" she asked.

Clarence watched a ripple of the sea advance over the dry sand. He had felt so empty lately, filled with this terrible sense of loss. As if he had been the one to give up his innocence.

"I don't want to see you hurt," he said.

"Then don't talk to me about him. I don't want to talk about him with you."

He looked at her, at the willful set to her chin. He couldn't understand what there was about her that drew him. She wasn't pretty. She had red hair, and she was too wide in the mouth, too tall, too wild and exuberant, too . . . much. Yet he remembered the feel of her lips, soft and warm and tasting faintly of Midsummer's Eve ale, and he wanted to feel them again.

But he was afraid that if he tried to kiss her now, she would turn her mouth away from his. And if she did that, he would not be able to bear it.

11

The cat Peaches had been trying all afternoon to take a nap on the sun-warmed bricks in front of the kitchen door, but her kittens were giving her little peace. They crawled all over her, nipping at her ears, butting their noses into her belly, searching for a nipple. From time to time she would lift a lazy paw and bat one of the pesky creatures away from her.

The smell of soured cream drifted out the door, and the ground began to vibrate with the steady thump-thump of a butter churn pump. Peaches got up, arched her back in a big stretch, and sauntered inside to investigate, her kittens trailing after like rags on a kite. Except for the littlest one, who couldn't make it over the doorsill.

The runty kitten had thrived under Jessalyn's mothering. She called him Napoleon because though small, he was a fierce little tacker, and he liked to bully his other brothers and sisters. The black-backed gull didn't know, of course, that the kitten had been named after a man who had once been the master of Europe. Or that the little ball of orange fluff had become that summer the recipient of a young woman's fierce and overflowing love. He saw dinner, and he took it.

At the time Jessalyn was leaning against the paddock

fence, watching the Sarn't Major break Letty's Hope to the lead. He did it slowly, introducing the filly to the halter by letting her smell it and rubbing the pliant leather over her neck and around her ears. He was just about to slip the halter over the filly's nose when she skittered back in alarm as a piercing scream shattered the afternoon.

"The gull!" Becka Poole ran across the yard, pointing up into the sky. "He's snatched Napoleon. Oooh, me life an' body."

Jessalyn whirled, her head falling back. The enormous black-backed gull swooped low across the courtyard, wings spread wide, little Napoleon dangling from its powerful beak.

"I'll get the musket," the Sarn't Major said, coming up beside her.

"No!" Jessalyn cried, the word made harsh with her horror. "You'd only end up killing them both." The gull banked in a broad, sweeping turn, making for the cliffs. Picking up her skirts, she ran after it.

Becka and the Sarn't Major watched their young mistress race across the headland on her hopeless chase after the gull. Her hat had fallen off, bouncing against her back, and her cinnamon hair snapped like a flag in the wind. Becka wiped a tear from her eye. "She loved that silly, runty kit."

"Aye," the Sarn't Major said.

"That gull will eat anything," Becka said. "He'll be consummating us next. The ravishing scavenger."

The Sarn't Major's answer was a grunt. But as he walked back to the paddock, his thick lips twitched, almost cracking into a smile. Then he thought of how Miss Jessalyn would mourn the loss of that runty kitten, and he went to get the musket. He was bloody well going to kill that bloody gull.

Jessalyn's steps slowed as she reached the cliffs. She breathed in great, gasping gulps, one hand pressed against the thrusting beat of her heart. The gull had disappeared. The cove was empty except for a fishing boat with copper-colored sails. Clouds, their bellies black like coal dust, lay low and thick on the sea. White-tipped waves stippled the sand, and suds swirled between the rocks.

The wind whipped at the cliffs, making high-pitched, wailing sounds like mourners at a funeral. She almost didn't hear it, the squeaky meow that came from Napoleon in a temper.

She scanned the pinnacles and pillars of rocks, which were tufted here and there with thrift and stunted gorse bushes. A splash of orange sitting on a jutting narrow ledge stood out among the plain grays and browns. The big bird must have lighted on the stony outcrop, released its prey, and flown off. Perhaps she'd made enough noise to frighten it away, but if so, it was bound to return.

She glanced out to sea, looking for the gull. The boat was tacking closer to the shore. She squinted against the glare of the water, trying to see more clearly. A young man stood at the tiller. Tall and lean, he wore a white shirt, the sleeves rolled up to reveal strong, tanned arms, and the wind tossed his dark hair. A black-haired girl sat beside him, and she must have said something at that moment because he half turned and looked down at her, and he laughed. The sound of his laughter, deep and husky, carried to Jessalyn on the wind. She gasped, nearly doubling over as suspicion blossomed into a terrible, stabbing pain in her belly.

Napoleon yowled.

Jessalyn swallowed, found her breath. "I'm coming, m'love." Straightening, she pushed her wind-lashed hair out of her eyes. *I will not cry,* she told herself. *I will not.* She cast one last agonized look at the boat, then started down the cliff path, blinking hard against the tears that kept threatening to come anyway.

The path sliced like a narrow, diagonal scar across the face of the cliff. It didn't pass close to the ledge where Napoleon sat, still yowling his displeasure. Since she couldn't reach him from the path, she would have to climb down the bluff, using the seams and pocks in the rocks like rungs on a ladder.

She removed her gloves for a better grip, then descended backward, feetfirst, feeling for and finding first one niche, then another. This would have been a difficult, though not an impossible, feat for a girl who had spent her childhood climbing all over the crags and steeps of the Cornish coast. But the fog had been heavy that morning, and the shale and granite rocks were wet and slippery.

She had gone about ten feet, out of reach now of the path, when the gull came back.

The great bird screeched and dived at her head. She caught sight of the white flash of his wings out the corner of her eye. Screaming, she flung out her arm to knock the bird away . . . and lost her balance.

She slithered down the rough rocks, banging her shins and knees. Her scrabbling fingers grasped at a naked furze bush, and she clung to it, swinging like a weather cock in the wind. She looked down at the sea, tumbling and foaming across the stony beach, and felt a rush of dizziness so strong she nearly retched. She shut her eyes, and the darkness seemed to intensify the sounds: her own harsh breathing, the smacking slap of the waves, Napoleon meowing, demanding to know what was taking her so long . . . and something else. Something distant, but coming closer.

The flap of wings.

As if he were possessed with a malevolent intelligence, the gull dived at her bare hands, pecking and slicing with his sharp, curved beak, then soaring up and away from her. Jessalyn screamed again in pain and terror, but she did not let go.

She waited, blood streaming down her outstretched arm from the gash in her hand, her breath sobbing in her throat, and then she heard it again, beneath the roar of the sea. . . .

Flap . . . flap . . . flap . . .

"Oh, God . . ." She pressed her face against the slick rock and steeled herself for the bird's attack.

But it was the flap of lowering sails that she'd heard. Then the scrape of a boat's keel across the shingle and McCady Trelawny calling her name.

"Lieutenant!" she cried, her voice cracking in her relief. "Please don't let that plaguey bird come back."

"He's flown off. Miss Letty, how did you . . . Never mind. Just don't let go."

He seemed to be a long time in coming, and her arms grew tired. "Are you going to rescue me or not?"

"Not." He appeared on the cliff path overhead, looking tall and stark, silhouetted against the sooty sky. He had brought a bowline from the boat, and he dropped it down to her. "I am going to stand here and watch you fall to your death. Not only would it be far more amusing but it's what you deserve for being so bacon-brained as to try to climb down sheer rocks when there's a perfectly good path—ugh!" He grunted as she grasped the rope with both hands and swung outward, trusting that he would bear her weight. Instead of climbing straight up, she went down first, to get Napoleon.

She had no trouble making her way back up the bluff with him pulling on the rope. Grasping her under the arms, he hauled her to her feet. But when she put her weight on her right leg, she drew in a sharp breath, sucking on her lower lip. "I must have sprained my ankle somehow, I—"

She looked up to find his gaze fixed on her mouth. A muscle in his jaw clenched. With no warning, he swung her into his arms and carried her up the path. It felt so wonderful being held, being touched by him. Jessalyn wrapped one arm around his neck and let her cheek fall against his chest. His shirt was wet with sea spray and smelled like him.

He deposited her on top of the stone hedge that ran along the headland. "You are quite safe now, Miss Letty," he said. His fingers grasped the arm she still had fastened around him. "There is no longer any need to cling to my neck like a blowfly."

Her cheeks burning, she pulled away. She always got caught doing such foolish, reckless things whenever he was around. He must wonder if she did them deliberately, to get him to notice her. The possibility that he would think so made her squirm. She filled her lungs and expelled the ache in her chest with a breath.

Jessalyn set little Napoleon down next to her on the hedge, and he immediately wandered off after a beetle, completely oblivious of how close he'd come to being gull food. Lieutenant Trelawny stood between her spread legs, his hands on his hips. Unable to meet his eyes, she stared at his chest instead. The wind plastered his shirt against his body. His flesh showed dark and muscular beneath the thin, wet cloth. Her heart was pounding so hard she was surprised he couldn't hear it over the boom and hiss of the surf.

"Is it too much to ask what the bloody hell you were trying to do—fly to France?" he said. "Did you wake up this morning thinking you were a gull?"

Her head jerked up. His mouth was set in a thin, taut line. "I was rescuing Napoleon," she said, then laughed as his eyes widened and his brows lifted. "My kitten, you silly goose. Not the emperor in exile on St. Helena."

The creases beside his mouth deepened. "Of course," he said. "How stupid of me to think otherwise." He stepped back, bending over, and his shirt pulled across the broad width of his back. "Let me take a look at that ankle."

His hand encircled her ankle, and the touch of his fingers even through the stiff leather of her half boots sent a shiver up her leg. "I'm probably going to have to cut your boot off," he said.

Her breath came out in a great gush. "Oh, do try not to. Gram will flay me with her tongue for going through two pairs of boots in one summer. Is Sheba Stout your lover?"

His fingers tightened, and she sucked in a sharp breath. "Ouch!"

"Whom I take to my bed is none of your concern," he said.

"I was only making conversation."

"That wasn't conversation. That was vulgar curiosity." He jerked at the laces of her boot.

"Ow! Bloody hell, that hurts!"

"Shut it." He worked her bootheel back and forth, trying to pull it off, but his touch had gentled. "And clean up your attle gutter language while you're about it," he said. "It's obvious you've been keeping bad company."

She looked down at his bent head. She wondered how it would feel to press her lips there, where his hair curled over the nape of his neck. She touched it instead. It was surprisingly soft, like a child's, and damp from the sea air. "You've taught me other things besides how to curse like a soldier," she said.

His head went still beneath her hand.

"For instance, I have learned how to tell when a man wants to kiss me. You want to kiss me now, Lieutenant."

He let go of her ankle and straightened, backing a step away from her, as if she were a fire that had suddenly grown too hot. "For God's sake," he said, his voice so taut it cracked, "you are behaving worse than a Covent Garden doxy."

Her heart was thrusting so heavily in her breast she could barely breathe. She knew she played a dangerous game. Pushed too hard, he might not stop with a kiss. He would take her, fiercely and hungrily, the way a man took a woman he wanted. Her throat went dry, and she trembled at the possibility, but whether from fear or excitement even she didn't know.

She eased off the hedge and took a hopping step to put herself right up against him. "Tell me you don't want to kiss me."

His eyes flickered away from her, then settled back on

her face. Cold, empty eyes, dark, like mine pits. "I don't want to kiss you, *little girl.*"

But she knew him now. Knew that he never said what he meant, and his eyes never showed what he was really feeling.

She curled her hands into the front of his shirt, feeling the solid flesh burn underneath the cloth and the way he shuddered. She wanted his arms around her; she wanted to yield to all his frightening strength and power. By yielding to him, she could make him hers. By touching his man's body, she could touch his man's soul.

She slid her hand up his chest, around the strong, tense curve of his neck, her fingers tangling in his damp hair. His hands closed around her upper arms, his fingers gripping hard enough to bruise. Tremors shimmied through him, his whole body vibrating like a wire pulled too tautly.

"I'm stopping this," he said on a harsh gasp as if he were in pain. She swayed, leaning into him, and he tried to shove her away. "Stop it!"

She pulled his head down until their lips were a breath away from touching. Her mouth parted open. "McCady," she said, and that was all.

He covered her lips with his, smothering his own ragged moan. His mouth was hot and wet and tasted of him. He made a low, wanting sound deep in his throat. He was hungry for her, fierce for her. The kiss he gave back to her was all raw and savage longing. It was like swallowing fire.

The force of his weight pushed her against the hedge, the stones digging into her back, but she didn't feel them. He gripped her hair so that he could hold her mouth in place while he thrust his tongue in and out. She clung to his arms, her fingers digging into the tense, rigid muscles, and the blood pounded in her ears, drowning out the slam and roar of the surf.

He tore his mouth from hers, and her head fell back. His lips trailed down the taut tendon of her neck, sucking and licking, and fire crackled over every inch of her skin like tiny balls of summer lightning. His hands were all over her breasts, his fingers pressing her taut nipples through the thin cloth of her dress. It almost hurt, but not quite, and all her muscles coiled up tight, tight, tight, and she thought she would come flying apart, burst all to pieces, and die.

He raised his head and looked at her out of dark, tortured eyes. "Jessa, for the love of God, I'm only a man. God help me, I don't think I can stop—"

Stones clattered on the cliff path, and he snapped away from her like the backlash of a whip.

Bathsheba Stout appeared over the top of the bluff. She pushed the tangled black mass of her hair out of her eyes and stared at them a moment, unsure, her mouth in a soft pout.

She shrugged, her breasts lifting and pushing against the faded material of her worn frock. "We'd best be getting the boat back, sur. If me da notices it missing, he'll be takin' the strop to me."

Lieutenant Trelawny leaned against the hedge, his chest heaving as if there suddenly weren't enough air in all the world. His face was flushed, and a pulse jumped in his temple. His sex, thick and rigid, strained against the confines of his tight breeches. As if he felt her eyes on him, on that part of him, his head swung around, and Jessalyn took the impact of his gaze like a soft blow to her belly.

His eyes were like raw wounds in his face, hot with fury and lust. And something else . . .

Something akin to hate.

Jessalyn limped through the back gate, the kitten clutched tightly to her breast. Something was not quite right. The Sarn't Major stood in the middle of the courtyard, a musket in his hand, the big gull lying dead and bloody at his feet. The sight was odd, but odder still was what came toward them across the barren, broken moorland. A lone man riding a black hack, a stranger who lolled and bounced in the saddle, as if he weren't used to having a horse between his legs.

Jessalyn hugged the kitten to her chest, watching the figure on horseback come closer. A vague dread built within her, cutting off her breath. They never got visitors at End Cottage, and she had never seen this man before.

The Sarn't Major made an odd choking sound, drawing her attention away from the coming horseman. Tears streamed into the seams and cracks of the studmaster's face, and he kept shaking his head back and forth, in a slow, ponderous movement. "She be dead," he said. "The filly be dead."

"Dead?" Jessalyn repeated, thinking that he'd made a mistake, that he must be talking about the gull.

The words spilled out of him, more words than she'd ever heard out of his mouth all put together. He had shot the gull, and the sound of the blast had startled Letty's Hope. There must have been a weakness in the filly's heart because it had given out, just stopped. One moment she had been galloping around the paddock, kicking and lashing out with her hooves and tossing her head, and then she had plunged onto her knees and fallen over dead.

Jessalyn stared at him, her eyes wide and confused. A part of her understood what he was saying, but she couldn't make the words seem real. She heard the clatter of hooves on stone, and she twisted around. The stranger had reached the gate now and was turning in. She kept thinking that all she must do was wait for him and then everything would be all right. As if the stranger could save her from what the Sarn't Major was saying.

The man dismounted and came up to her, removing his hat to reveal a head of thick hair the color of ripening corn. He had a long face and gray hollows beneath his eyes, and his forehead was pleated with deep lines. "Miss Letty?" he said, his voice rising upward in uncertainty.

Jessalyn nodded. A part of her was aware that the Sarn't Major had left and was now walking toward the stable, and

Letty's Hope was acting strangely, lying in the paddock next to the rubbing post, not moving. The kitten squirmed, meowing and scratching her hand. But she didn't put him down. She didn't dare put him down because the black-backed gull might come back. Except the gull was dead. She stared at the mangled heap of blood and feathers, reassuring herself of this fact.

The strange man with the haggard face and thick thatch of white-blond hair looked her over, taking in her dirty, ripped dress and the bloody gouge on her hand. "Miss Letty?" he asked again, as if still not quite sure that he had the right person. "My name is Geoffrey Stanhope. I am your mother's, er . . . friend."

Jessalyn shook her head once in a sudden jerking movement. "But I don't . . ." Something—a sort of bewildered hope, mixed with fear—squeezed at her chest. "My mother?"

"Yes." A door opened behind Jessalyn, and the stranger's gaze fluttered away from her. His eyes reminded her of a deer's, soft and brown and liquid. "After he—after your father died, your mother, uh . . . chose to abide with me," he said.

"Aye, the pair of ye have been *abidin'* together in sin for years." Lady Letty came toward them, her cane rapping on the stones that paved the courtyard. The old woman's speech had taken on a rough country burr, straight from the slag heaps of Wheal Ruthe. "Is the slut worth it? Do ee get much pleasure from a woman who'd make a cuckold of her lawful husband on his very deathbed an' then desert her only babe?"

The man licked his lips, which were full and soft, almost womanly. His deer-eyed gaze fastened on to Jessalyn's face. "We couldn't help falling in love, your mother and I. I would have made her my wife after he—after your father died. But I was married myself to—to someone else." A soft sigh blew out his lips. "Am still married to someone else." He turned to Lady Letty and held up his hand as if pleading with her to understand. "Emma and I . . . Our love could never be sanctioned by God and society, but we couldn't bear to be apart. We thought the child would be better off here with you. Away from the scandal of our, uh . . . liaison."

Lady Letty snorted. "An' so she was. Better off. What are ye doing here now? What does yer slut want?" Her outthrust chin suddenly trembled, and her arm wrapped hard around Jessalyn's waist as if she could physically bind her granddaughter to her. "She'll not be getting the gel back. I'll see her dead first."

"She *is* dead. Emma's dead." His voice cracked on the last word. His gaze went to Jessalyn. "I thought you should know." His head swiveled back to Lady Letty. "The girl is her daughter after all. She has a right to know."

Jessalyn couldn't move or speak. The Sarn't Major had entered the paddock and was walking toward Letty's Hope, dragging a blanket behind him. For a moment she wondered what was wrong with the filly, why she was lying so still like that in the middle of the paddock. And then she remembered: The filly was dead.

The stranger was talking again, and she struggled to pay attention. "There's a house in London," he said. "By right, it belongs to you, for your father purchased it shortly before he . . . It's heavily mortgaged, of course, but there it is. We had expenses. It's expensive, living in Town. There was also some money, but I'm afraid most of it's long spent. And horses, Thoroughbreds. We had to have a dispersal sale a while back, just before she got . . . sick, and so most of the good stock is gone. Still, she's left you a racing stable of a sort."

"Why?" Jessalyn said.

The man blinked, and his lips sucked inward as he drew in a deep breath. "Well, you are her daughter. Her only child."

"She never came to see me. Not once. She didn't even write to me. Why?"

His gaze shifted away from hers. Color mottled his cheeks like two identical raspberry stains, and his big hands crushed the brim of his beaver hat. "The scandal. We thought . . . she thought . . ." His breath eased out of him in a sigh. "No matter what, you are still her daughter."

But it hadn't been the scandal, Jessalyn thought. Not one visit, not one letter in ten years. She had been in the way. In the way of her mother and her mother's life with this man.

"Not anymore," Jessalyn said to the stranger. Her mother's lover. The kitten was purring now. Jessalyn rubbed his furry body against her cheek. He was warm, and she could feel the fluttering beat of his heart. "I haven't been her daughter for a long time now."

She turned away from the stranger and walked toward the paddock and the Sarn't Major. And the blanket-covered mound that had been a filly called Letty's Hope.

The wind was quick and salty. It fluttered the ribbons on her hat and flattened her skirt, revealing her leggy slimness.

The tide had gone out recently. The man in scarlet regimentals limped toward her across the wet sand, leaving footprints like scars behind him. He stopped beside her, not speaking. She didn't acknowledge his presence but stared out at a sea that was striated with ripples of colors, from green to blue to the cool, clear gray of her eyes.

"Miss Letty? Becka told me about your mother, and about the filly. I—"

"Don't tell me you're sorry. Whatever you do, don't tell me you're sorry." Wisps of hair blew across the sunburned skin of her cheeks, and the smell of her came to him, of sun-drenched beach and hot, earthy longing. He felt overwhelmed with an aching need to gather her into his arms and hold her.

But holding her was not all he ached to do to her, and that was the trouble.

The sun moved from behind a cloud, tinting her skin so that the blush of freckles across her cheekbones glinted like gold dust. His gaze traced the sharp flare of a brow, the straight slope of her nose, the deep indentation above her wide and puffy lips. He had never thought her pretty, but he saw now that in a few years she would be strikingly beautiful. It didn't matter anyway, for the things about her that so intrigued him were already there: the sunbeam smile, that unrefined, raucous laugh, her gamine warmth. She drank of life. She gulped it down as if it were a big glass of bubbling champagne and then held out her hands for more, laughing . . . all the while laughing.

She was not laughing now.

The sea brushed the beach in a gentle caress. She turned to look at him, searching his face. "Why are you here, Lieutenant Trelawny?"

She spoke as if her throat hurt, and her heart was in her eyes, those deep eyes that were the wells of her soul. Life hadn't taught her yet how to keep her feelings hidden. Life hadn't been cruel, until now.

"I've come to tell you good-bye," he said, deliberately making his voice cold. "I'm off to Plymouth, where I'll board a ship to rejoin my regiment."

She stared at him a moment longer, then looked away. "There are some officers, surely, who take their wives to the West Indies."

"Only a fool or a man with little regard for his wife. It is too unhealthy a clime for women."

"But there are some, surely, who have wives who wait at home for them."

"Those that can afford wives."

"I do not need much."

Something swelled within his chest so that he could barely breathe, let alone speak. What she was asking, what she wanted, was impossible. It couldn't have been more impossible than if he were a shepherd and she a bal-maiden turned into a hare. At least then they could have had their nights of the blue moon.

He reached across the short distance that separated them and brushed her face with his fingertips, then wished he hadn't. For just that briefest of touches fired a raging hunger in him that left him trembling.

But that was all it was. Hunger. He could appease that hunger now; he could bear her down onto the sand and take her and then walk away without looking back, because he knew all about hunger. And he knew himself. And she . . . she thought she loved him, but what she thought wasn't real and never lasted, *couldn't* last. Because love didn't exist in the first place. It was an appetite, nothing more, an appetite satisfied in bed and gone by morning. He'd known this truth since he was twelve years old.

"You need more than I can give you," he said, shocked at the way the words tore at his throat. "You deserve more."

"But you don't understand." She turned to face him, pain and yearning stark in her eyes. "I don't want to *save* myself for some dull, steady man. A man who will marry me but love his mistress, who will go to church on Sundays and ride to hounds on Fridays, and be drunk on port every other night of the week. The sort of man who will give his servants a whole extra shilling come Christmas and expect to be *thanked* for it."

"Who is this paragon? Perhaps I ought to marry him myself."

"Oh, God . . ." A ragged gasp of laughter tore out her throat, turning into a sob. But the enormous gray eyes that looked at him shone with a fierce light. They were filled with an emotion he didn't understand, something that struck terror deep within his soul. "I want to spend my life with you," she said. "*You.* With your hard and sulky mouth, and your rough and gentle hands, and that wonderful, irreverent way you have of looking at the world. I want the man who built an iron horse and then dared to take me for a ride on it. . . ."

She was looking at him as if he were the most marvelous man who'd ever lived. She had no idea what he was really like, the things he'd done. . . . And she had no earthly idea of what it was to follow the drum, moving from post to post, living in hovels and shacks, in tents, trying to stretch his meager pay from month to month as the babies started to come. If he took her with him, she'd only end up leaving him someday. The day the hunger died. He knew that as surely as he knew that night followed even the sunniest of days, and warm, sweet summers turned into bitter winters.

He drew in a deep, steadying breath. "You don't know—"

"I do! I know what you are going to say, and it doesn't matter." Tears started from her eyes. She dashed them away with the back of her hand. "You are the man I want to marry. I don't care what you are, or what you think you are, or how young I am, or how old you feel. I don't care if we're poor—"

"Well, I do! When I marry, it will be to a *woman,* not a scrawny, carrottop barely out of the schoolroom. She'll be a woman with breeding and money, not some provincial miss without even two beans to boil together to make soup."

She stood still, and there was no sound but the whisper of the water across sand and stone. Yet there was a scream on her face, as if he'd ripped out her heart.

"But I love you," she said at last, so low her voice might have been a part of the suck and curl of the sea. But he didn't need to hear the words to feel them.

"Too bloody bad, Miss Letty. Because I don't love you."

He spun around and left her, while he still had the courage. He was running away from her, away from all that she thought she could be for him. And all that he knew he could never be for her.

"McCady!" she cried after him. "You can't leave me, I love you!"

He lengthened his stride. It was better to hurt her once, cleanly, than to hurt her over the years a thousand times, in a thousand ways. That warm and shining light he'd seen in her eyes wouldn't last. It would die the day the hunger died. She would hate him then and hate herself for having been such a fool. And he didn't want to be around when that happened because he would not be able to bear it.

He stopped halfway up the cliff path and turned to look back. She stood with her shoulders hunched, her face buried in her hands, and he knew she was crying. He must have heard that wonderful rusty laugh of hers a thousand times this summer. He wished his last memory of her didn't have to be one of tears . . . tears over him. She was just so bloody young, too young to know better than to let herself care for a man like him. Young enough still that she would get over him.

He had meant to keep walking, but at the top of the bluff he paused. She stood straight and tall now, her slender figure a stark and lonely sentinel against the milky Cornish sky. The wind whipped the trailing ribbons of the hat that he had given her, the hat with its posy of yellow primroses. He supposed there would come a day when he could take a walk along a beach of white sand and blue water and not think of this moment.

But he knew that no matter how long he lived, he would never be able to bear the sight of yellow primroses.

PART TWO

12

Shawls of fine rain fell on Newmarket Heath.

It was a steady rain. The kind of sneaky, stubborn rain that penetrated the thickest of wool greatcoats until one's very bones felt soggy enough to be wrung out into a bucket. It had turned the clipped green turf of the racetrack into a muddy quagmire.

Lady Letty sat beneath the leaking leather hood of a ramshackle cabriolet and scowled at the dripping sky. She fastened a spyglass to one eye, focusing on the starting post. "'Twill be at least a half hour before they're off. Time enough for us to lay another pony on our nag."

"Oh, Gram . . ." Jessalyn drew in a deep breath, wrinkling her nose. The rented carriage reeked of mildew and stale tobacco smoke. "We cannot afford to risk another twenty-five pounds."

"What? Speak up, gel."

Jessalyn cupped her hand around her mouth and leaned into her grandmother to shout. "If you are growing deaf, Gram, I shall have to get myself a speaking trumpet!"

"Humph."

"And if we become much more in the suds, I shall have to borrow from Mr. Tiltwell."

"I forbid it," Lady Letty stated, proving, as Jessalyn well

knew, that she'd been hearing every word. "A Letty never borrows from her lover." She rapped Jessalyn sharply on her knee with the spyglass. "One would think I hadn't raised you proper."

Jessalyn rubbed her stinging knee. "Clarence is not my—"

"I know what the boy is to you, blast it, and I don't like it. One does not marry the Clarence Tiltwells of this world, m'dear. It is understandable that you might want him—there's a certain appeal there if one likes 'em pale and fair, which I, personally, do not—but at least have the sense God gave you to wait until you are safely wed into your own class. *Then* you may take him to your bed—"

"I do not want Clarence in that way!" Jessalyn nearly shouted again. "I want him for my husband," she quickly added as a shrewd look shot into Lady Letty's eyes. It was no use. She'd had this argument with Gram before, and neither of them, being stubborn Lettys, was about to budge.

Ironically, it was for Gram's sake that she had accepted Clarence Tiltwell's proposal in the first place. By marrying him, she would ensure a life of luxury for her grandmother for all of her remaining days. No, she must be honest with herself. It was not only for Gram. Someday Gram would be lost to her, and Jessalyn did not want to spend her life alone. She wanted a home, a husband, children. Clarence could give her all those things, she told herself for the hundredth time, everything she could ever want or need. And she was fond of him, truly she was. Their friendship had roots that went back to their childhood. They would deal well together as husband and wife.

And he loved her. He told her often how much he loved her.

Yet Jessalyn was frowning as she peered through the drizzle at the prancing line of Thoroughbreds and jockeys in rainbow-colored taffetas. The twenty-five pounds her grandmother wanted to wager was the last of the household money that Jessalyn had set aside to see them through the winter until her marriage next spring. If they lost, they could well be reduced to selling watercress bunches in the grimy London streets.

But they wouldn't lose. Not this time.

Jessalyn descended from the carriage into mud that had the consistency of hasty pudding. She turned her face up to the gently weeping clouds, loving the feel of the soft rain bathing her cheeks like spray from an eau de cologne bottle. "Are you hungry, Gram? Shall I bring you back something to eat?"

Lady Letty sat lost in thought, massaging the blackthorn handle of her cane. In the dim light the skin of her face shone pale and translucent as an eggshell. In that moment she looked more than her eighty-three years.

"Gram?"

Lady Letty blinked and focused gray eyes that were as hard as tin ore on her granddaughter's face. But her voice held none of its usual tartness. "Nay, gel." She reached down and brushed Jessalyn's cheek, a touch that was tender and so uncharacteristic that Jessalyn had to swallow around a strange thickness in her throat.

Lady Letty's hand fell to her lap. It looked boneless against her heavy black skirt, a long and narrow hand with bent fingers, old and frail. Jessalyn was filled with a familiar fear. She felt alone and afraid, six years old again and about to be tossed aside like a suit of old clothes.

"Now quit your shilly-shallying, and get along with you, gel," Lady Letty said, grimacing a scowl, an expression that was oddly loving for all its fierceness.

Jessalyn squeezed her grandmother's hand. She felt its reassuring and familiar strength that was there, still, beneath the fragility of age. "This is our lucky day, Gram, I just know it. We'll risk it all, neck or nothing," she said, laughing, and at the squeaky, joyous sound of it people turned to look, and they, too, smiled.

Whirling around, she set off with a spring to her step to

bet their last twenty-five pounds on the next race, neck or nothing.

" 'Ware the sharpers and pickpockets!" Lady Letty called after her.

Jessalyn walked down a path littered with soggy race cards, past the hazard tables that were sheltered from the rain by a low-slung canopy. Water dripped from the red-striped canvas, bleeding into puddles. A boisterous group of young bucks, barely old enough to shave, pressed around the gaming tables. Any fool who frequented the Turf knew the dice were cogged, the games run by crooked sharpers. But there always seemed to be a fresh flock of pigeons to gull. As she plunged into the crowd of men on foot and horseback, Jessalyn gripped her reticule so tightly the linked steel rings bit through her kid gloves. At racing meets, pickpockets and cutpurses were as thick as crows in a cornfield.

Smells of jellied eels and ripe cheese and snatches of laughter wafted out the open doors of the many gin tents. A huckster strolled by, hawking penny tots of gin and meat pasties that steamed in the cool air. Jessalyn's stomach growled. She didn't stop, though, for she was intent to place her bet before the runners had all gathered at the starting post.

The first time Jessalyn attended a racing meet, Gram had accused her of behaving like a gapeseed, staring open-mouthed at every sight. Newmarket was a network of interlocking courses covering four miles over spacious, level meadows of thick, short grass. But it wasn't only a place for horse racing. In many ways it was like a fair, with horror plays and peep shows, dancing dogs and cockfights.

This afternoon's contest was called the Crombie Sweeps, after the Scottish lord who had organized it. It was a sweepstakes race for two-year-olds. Each owner who subscribed to the race had had to put up fifty sovereigns, and the winner would take the pot. But the Lettys, true members of the Turf, weren't content just to risk their stake money. For one thing, the expense of keeping even their small string of four horses, the cost of fodder, straw, and hay, and the stabling outlay, couldn't be covered alone by the stakes they won. They had to bet to live.

As Jessalyn strode toward the betting post, her stomach spasmed with a fear that left her feeling queasy, for their luck had been running so sour of late. A gelding they had planned to race in the Rowley Mile meet last month had been laid low with the colic the night before. Then Nancy Girl, their most profitable runner to date, had mysteriously broken a bone in her knee while turned out to grass and had to be put down. In another race their entry had been leading by three lengths when a handbill had blown across the track, startling him so that he reared, tossing his jockey headfirst into the turf. Two other times this season their horses had had disappointing outings, running sluggishly and finishing well back in the pack.

Indeed, the Letty luck had truly been abysmal, Jessalyn thought. But it was bound to turn today. Especially in this race, with this horse. From the day the blood bay colt had first put in his appearance in the world, she had *known* that he would be the one to win them the Derby someday. It wasn't that he had been born with the configuration of a racer. In truth, he still wasn't much to look at, for he had enormous feet and the short cannon bones that denoted more strength than speed. But every time Jessalyn looked into those bright, intelligent eyes she saw burning within the ruthless, driving will to win that made a champion.

She had named him Blue Moon.

The betting post, a thin white pole, could barely be seen through the crowd of gentlemen milling around it, most on horseback. They called out their wagers to the blacklegs who made the book, laying and taking bets at varying prices. The legs, sheltering today beneath a large sagging lean-to, shouted back, loudly naming their odds.

Black Charlie was the only female leg in England. An enormous woman, she overflowed around her stool like a bullfrog sitting on a stone. It was said she was worth ten thousand pounds a year, though she dressed and talked and looked like the Spitalfields washerwoman she had once been. Jessalyn was careful to stop downwind of her, for she smelled worse than a basket of rotten eggs. She had once told Jessalyn that she'd already had a lifetime of soap and water and never intended to get near the stuff again.

"Come to lay more blunt on yer pretty boy, have ye, Miss Letty?" Black Charlie said, smiling around the bit of a clay pipe she had stuck between tobacco brown teeth. "'Ow much this time?"

"A pony. To win."

Black Charlie noted the twenty-five-pound wager on the running tick she kept. Money would not change hands until later. "You and yer granny'll be living high as fighting cocks if yer lay pays off, eh? Pity it is that I can't be givin' ye better odds, but that Blue Moon of yers is a tiptop goer and no mistake. Ye watch if he don't make all them other 'orses look like donkeys."

Out of habit Jessalyn checked the list of runners and their odds, which was chalked on a large piece of slate posted above Black Charlie's head. Blue Moon was down as the favorite, for in the two contests he'd run in his young life he had defeated all comers. Her eyes scanned the rest. "Who's the late entry?"

"Eh? Oh, ye mean Rum Chaser. His owner has just now come up to scratch with the stake." Black Charlie jerked her three chins at the men who straddled stools alongside her. "Yon legs're laying five to two on 'im at starting." She heaved a derisive snort that set her chins to trembling. "Rum Chaser's of a showy turn, ye mind. But my tout says 'e ain't fit. 'E ain't had a sweat for a fortnight." She paused to puff on her pipe and winked a great, fleshy eye. "And he weren't fed on no milk-soaked bread and fresh eggs last night like yer Blue Moon was."

Jessalyn waved away the malodorous smoke that billowed from Black Charlie's pipe. She was careful to keep her face blank, but inwardly she was torn between laughter and dismay. The Sarn't Major would be furious to know that Blue Moon's dietary secret was out. But then Black Charlie's touts were the best on the Heath at spying on the racehorses in training and picking up tips.

"Rum Chaser's training has been neglected, ye see, ever since the earl popped off," Black Charlie was saying. "'Tis said he put a barking iron in his mouth and blew 'is noddle off, the earl did."

"Rum Chaser's owner shot himself?" Jessalyn asked, only half listening. She was trying to see if she could spot Blue Moon at the starting post.

"Aye. 'Twas done in some gaming hell," Black Charlie went on. "Played deep and then got caught playin' dirty and took the 'onorable way out. 'Tis said the earl's heir were once a penniless soldier afore fortune smiled upon 'im. I'll tells ye this, he's as much the deep plunger as his brother ever was. 'E laid a thousand quid on his runner to place, did the new Lord Caerhays."

"Lord *who?*" Jessalyn's voice cracked as her heart thrust up into her throat. "Rum Chaser belongs to the earl of Caerhays?" Dear life . . . She sucked in a deep breath and felt her heart begin to beat again in loud, hard thumps like a Cornish tin stamp. "Is he here? Is Lieut—is Lord Caerhays here?"

"Standing right behind ye, he is." Black Charlie's cackle split the air. "'E looks a rum un. The sort of man ye'd trust to guard yer back, but not yer daughter's virtue, eh?"

Jessalyn whipped around so fast she nearly stumbled. Her gaze was filled with the wide back of a tall man with a caped greatcoat slung in a negligent fashion over his shoulders. Just then he turned half toward her, and Jessalyn felt a wrenching pain in her chest, a pain so sharp and thrusting so deep she nearly cried aloud.

The years had hardened his high-boned face, but he was still disdainfully handsome. A woman catching a glimpse of him from across a ballroom would look again. And then again.

But for Jessalyn just to see him once was more than she could bear. Yet she could not have looked away, not even if the whole world had ignited into a blazing conflagration behind her. His skin had been bronzed by the sun, and his hair hung in shaggy strands from beneath his glossy high-crowned beaver. He lifted his head slightly, looking toward the starting post, and something glinted like a bright coin beneath the curved brim of his hat. A thin gold loop that pierced the lobe of his left ear. He hadn't changed, oh, he hadn't changed . . . Still wicked and dashing and irreverent. A scapegrace Trelawny to his very bones, and to the devil with you if you didn't like it. She imagined how Society's matrons must swell up like frogs at mating time at the very idea of a peer of the realm sporting a pirate's earring.

And then the inevitable happened. He turned his head, and their gazes met. He stared at her a long time, his face dark and intent. He made a movement as if to leave, then changed his mind and came toward her.

He still walked like a lazy cat, with that sauntering sway of lean and manly hips, ruined at the last moment by the hitch in his stride. He hadn't changed, hadn't changed. . . .

When I marry, it will be to a woman, not a scrawny, carrottop barely out of the schoolroom. She'll be a woman with breeding and money, not some provincial miss without even two beans to boil together to make soup.

But I love you.

Too bloody bad, Miss Letty. Because I don't love you.

Humiliation washed over her, as fresh as if it had happened only yesterday. She had laid her heart at his feet, and he had walked away. How amusing she must have seemed to him, how he must have laughed—silly Miss Letty with her moony ways, falling over cliffs and down mine shafts, and begging him to marry her. Silly child . . . How she had loved him then.

And how she hated him now.

Her first instinct was to turn and run, but she made herself stand tall and straight until he was almost upon her. He had left her so little pride that summer, had left it tattered and in shreds, but she wrapped it around herself now like an old mended cloak. She lifted a composed face, and the heavy serge skirt of her walnut brown redingote, and sailed past him, cutting him dead.

A footman in purple and gold satin livery dashed past her, nearly knocking her down. Suddenly she was enveloped by a whole gaggle of running footmen. Some gentlemen, bored with waiting for the sweepstakes to start, were matching their servants in a human race.

One of the footmen, his roly-poly body sausaged into tight crimson and silver satin, his periwig askew over one eye, lagged far behind the others, and his master was riding along beside him, ordering him to pick up his legs and move his bloody arse, dammit. The footman, puffing like a locomotive, leaped high and landed in a puddle. Muddy water splashed through the air. Jessalyn stood, stunned and dripping, until a hand closed around her elbow, guiding her out of the way.

"Well, well, if it isn't Miss Letty in trouble as usual. Somehow I always thought that if I should ever see you again, it would be in a place where you don't belong."

She had to swallow before she could speak. Her tongue felt rough with rust, and it seemed she had forgotten to breathe. She looked up into his face, so handsome above his tall, starched collar and cleverly tied cravat. Into his eyes, so dark and compelling. At his mouth, a mouth that she knew could be hard and then sulky by turns.

A mouth that had once kissed her.

"But I do belong here," she said, pleased that her voice betrayed none of the turmoil within her breast. "My horse Blue Moon is entered in the Crombie Sweeps, and I am here to see him run away with the prize, Mr. . . . Pray forgive me, but though your face is familiar, your name has slipped my memory—no, I have it. Trelawny. Lieutenant Trelawny."

Anger flashed in his eyes. Raw and ragged anger that was swiftly covered up. "It is Lord Caerhays now, and you remembered damn well who I am, Jessalyn. You didn't used to be so good at nasty, cutting sort of games."

"I was taught how to play by an expert." She gathered up her skirt again. "Do accept my condolences on your brother's death, and now if you will excuse me . . ."

She took a step, but he took a larger one, planting himself in front of her. His lips curled up at one end in an arrogant smile. "No, I will not excuse you. Miss Letty. At least not until we exchange a few more polite banalities. You shall ask me how I am faring, and I shall say: 'Tolerably well, thank you.' Then I shall ask how you are faring."

She made her eyes go wide and guileless. "I beg your pardon. I hadn't thought to be rude. I merely assumed that the state of my health is a matter of utmost indifference to you . . . since I harbor not the slightest interest in yours."

He leaned into her, so close she could see the beginning shadow of a beard on his lean cheeks and the shadows stirring in the dark pools of his eyes. "Now there you are wrong," he said, drawling the words in a deliberately seductive fashion, "for I have thought of you often in the last five years."

"I thought of you, too, my lord. In the beginning. But then I came to see that you were right: We did not at all suit. And so my thoughts moved on to other things."

To her shock his head fell back in laughter. "Well put," he exclaimed. "Cut to the bone, I've been. Skewered like a Christmas goose, pricked like a pincushion, sliced like an onion, stabbed like a—like a . . . dear me, I seem to have run out of metaphors. Tell me, Miss Letty—it *is* still Miss Letty? Or should I be addressing you as someone more matronly? Mrs. Respectable, perhaps? Mrs. Dull?"

The words built in her mouth to tell him about her betrothal to his cousin, for more than anything that would show him that she had survived what he had done to her heart and to her pride. But as she tilted her head back to speak, she caught his gaze upon her. The twin exploding suns blazed bright in his eyes, as disturbing as ever, and even after all this time she felt her heart pick up a beat.

She stared up at him, hating him for doing this to her— for knocking down in five minutes all the walls she'd spent five years building. "You've grown up, little girl," he said, his voice husky but with an underlying edge that promised a danger she was, oh, too familiar with.

Grown up . . . she must remember that she was a woman now, no longer the silly barefoot girl who had once made such a fool of herself over him. She had acquired a bosom that filled out her redingote. Beneath her fanciful Gypsy hat, her hair was pulled neatly back into a braided chignon. But it was still red, and her mouth was still too big for her face.

When I marry, it will be to a woman, not a scrawny, carrottop barely out of the schoolroom. . . .

Jessalyn's stomach clenched into a tight knot. Away . . . she had to get away from him before . . .

But before she knew what he was about, he had taken her arm and was leading her over to the painted white markers that lined the home straight. His touch was light, impersonal, but she felt it deep within her like a bruise on the bone.

His hand released her to wrap around one of the posts. He gripped the wood so tightly the veins and sinews of his wrist stood out and the leather of his tan gloves pulled taut across his knuckles. She shot a quick glance at his face. He was staring at the tall white pillar that marked the starting point where the runners were gathering. A muscle jumped in his cheek.

The jockeys, bright as popinjays in their taffetas, were jostling for position. Through the misty drizzle, the horses were barely distinguishable from one another, their coats all dark and sleek like otters with the wet.

Out the corner of her eye she saw him move. He even started to walk away from her, and she let out a soft breath of relief. Then he whirled and took two hard, jerky strides. His hands fell on her shoulders, pulling her around. "Why did you name him Blue Moon?"

Whatever she had expected, it was not that. For a moment the shrill cries of the hawkers and legs faded away. She saw herself dancing before him, laughing, picking a moonflower to tuck behind his ear. She heard the sigh of the surf and felt the sea wind . . . that night of the blue moon, when he had taken her in his arms and kissed her the way a man kissed a woman he wanted. Hard and rough and hungry.

In spite of all her hard-won control, she felt the walls crumble some more. She looked into his eyes, to see if he remembered, too, and saw nothing there but shadows. "I named him Blue Moon because he's rare and special," she said, the words matter-of-fact, telling the truth, but only part of it. "This one will do it, my lord. He is going to win the Derby for us, for Gram and me. Now if you will please be so kind as to take your hands off me. I dislike being touched by people I scarcely know."

He opened his hands, fingers spread wide, and lifted them off her shoulders in an exaggerated motion. "I do beg your pardon, Miss Letty. I shall try to refrain from *touching* you in the future." He brought his face so close to hers his breath disturbed strands of her hair, and Jessalyn's heart thrust hard like a fist against her breast. "At least," he said, "until we come to know each other again."

She felt the shock of his words deep in her belly. *Again* . . . Unconsciously, her hands clenched. No, not again. Never again.

He hadn't moved, nor did he take his eyes off her face. The sleeve of his greatcoat brushed her arm. The wind whipped the bottom of her redingote open, slapping it against his leg. She heard him take a breath; she imagined she could feel his heartbeat.

"I hope your Blue Moon wins you many races," he said, and there was still an edge of rough anger to his voice. "But not today's. I already have a coper interested in buying my Rum Chaser, and he'll be worth far more as a stud if he can go out a winner. Not to mention the fact that I have a bloody fortune riding on his hide."

"You should not have plunged so deeply, my lord. For he'll have a hard time beating Blue Moon. Especially in this weather."

"A mudder, is he?" The creases alongside his mouth deepened into a sudden and unexpected smile, and Jessalyn's treacherous heart pitched and dipped.

"Blue Moon runs like the wind on anything."

He stared at her, his eyes on her mouth. The air vibrated between them like the strings of a viola tuned too tightly. She stared back at him, at the taut set of his face. She felt his heat, smelled him.

She stepped back and turned aside, suddenly afraid. Tension thickened the air until she couldn't breathe. Her chest felt heavy with a quiet despair, yet her heart was racing. It was as if she were falling down a mine shaft and her scrabbling fingers could find no purchase. Falling down, down, until she was back again in that bittersweet summer, not herself anymore but the girl she had been. Poor silly Miss Letty, loving him, needing him. Losing him. The first time had almost killed her, but she had survived. *Again . . . again . . .* She would never let herself be hurt like that again.

She licked her lips, tasting the rain, which was cool and tinged with smoke. I must be going," she said on an expulsion of pent-up breath, already turning away. "Gram will be wondering—"

"Wait!" The urgency in his tone stopped her. But when she looked back, his eyes were empty and as unfathomable as the sea. "The race is about to start," he said.

She looked to see if what he said was true. The runners were still lining up, a procedure that had been known to take up to an hour. She searched for Blue Moon and his jockey, Topper, and spotted them easily. The boy in the Letty colors of black and scarlet; the horse's bay coat looking almost bloodred in the murky light. The field was large, and the jockeys had to fight for a place in the lead, kicking and hitting one another in the face with the butt ends of their whips. The horses pranced and lashed out with their hooves. The jockeys bounced on their backs, their bright taffeta-covered skullcaps bobbing like fishing corks.

He was standing close to her again. She sucked in a deep breath. The wet, mulchy smell of the turf seemed to wash over her like a wave, then receded. "Which one is your brother's horse—"

"My horse."

"Yes . . . I'm sorry."

"You needn't feel sorry for Rum Chaser. I assure you that while I have many vices, I am invariably kind to animals. It is my one soft spot."

He had done this the first time they'd met, talked in circles around her so that she'd emerged from a conversation with him feeling dizzier than a top. "I meant that I am sorry to learn of your brother's death," she said.

"Why should you be sorry? No one else is. He put a pistol in his mouth and blew his brains all over the pink-flocked wallpaper, leaving me not only his title and champion racehorse but all his bloody debts as well. And further upholding the proud Trelawny tradition of dying young, violently, and in disgrace."

She looked up into his face, noting the bitter slant to his hard mouth. "And will you uphold the tradition now that you are the earl of Caerhays?"

He pinned her with his gaze. "Probably."

For a moment she thought she saw real pain smothered behind the shadows of those dark eyes. She turned abruptly away from him. "You never said which one is your horse. My lord."

"Rum Chaser's knight is wearing green and yellow. Miss Letty."

Around the Turf the jockeys were called knights of the pigskin. Jessalyn had always loved the fanciful expression, which came from the pigskin saddles the jockeys rode on. She spotted the green and yellow taffeta of Rum Chaser's knight mounted on a dark chestnut with four white socks. The jockey seemed to be having trouble holding the horse in check. The big chestnut was curvetting and rearing and tossing his head. His massive hindquarters revealed his power and speed, and his arched neck his pride. Black Charlie had been right: Rum Chaser was of a showy turn. Jessalyn could only hope the leg's touts were also right about his not being fit.

The wind blew, bringing with it not the smell of the turf this time but the scent of the man beside her—of maleness and danger and of something that fanned a flame low in her belly. He had the whole wide heath to move about in, yet he was standing so close to her that they could have shared the same coffin. She smiled at the absurd thought.

"I still hate it when you do that," he said.

Her head snapped around. "Do what?"

"Smile as if you know something I don't know."

But I love you.

Too bloody bad, Miss Letty. Because I don't love you.

"Since you ask, I was thinking I really ought to thank you for turning down my rash and thoughtless proposal of marriage all those years ago," she said with a bright, careless smile, although inside she was aching, aching. "It is amazing—is it not?—the mistakes one makes when one is young and foolish."

His face did not change expression; he didn't even blink. His eyes were empty, dark, and still as an underground pool. "But we must have a care," he said, "not to make the same mistake twice."

Whose mistake was he talking about? she wondered. Hers or his? She felt an unwanted tightening in her chest.

In that moment if there had been any softening in his eyes, any indication at all that he had cared for her that summer, even a little, she might have forgiven him everything.

But his gaze remained flat and impenetrable, and she had taken to heart the bitter lesson learned the day he had left her. That loving someone is not enough if he refuses to love you back.

The starting bell clanged. They both whipped around as a flag flashed beside the distant post, white like a gull's wing against the green turf, and suddenly the horses were off.

The screams of the spectators slammed against Jessalyn's ears like the roar of a hundred hungry lions. But she didn't even breathe. Her eyes were riveted on black and scarlet colors and Blue Moon's distinctive ungainly stride.

They were well in the back of the pack. For all his courage, Blue Moon had a disconcerting habit of trailing lazily along in the rear, waiting until the last possible second to put on his tremendous burst of speed. His crafty mind understood that to have his head in front was enough; he saw no point in exerting himself to win by a furlough when a whisker would do. But this made for some excruciatingly nerve-racking moments for those who had their hopes and their money riding on his blood bay hide.

Jessalyn swayed on her feet, as if the cheers of the crowd were buffeting her. The course was an undulating mile and a half long, twisted and cruel as the devil's heart. The horses' hooves flashed silver, tearing like scythes into the sloggy turf. The jockeys' bright taffetas wavered in and out of the driving mist, blurring into streaks of living fire.

A black gelding named Candy Dancer had quickly taken the lead and was holding it. Jessalyn reminded herself that the touts had Candy Dancer pegged as a fast starter that often had no pluck for the hard finish.

They were now at the far end of the course, where it curved sharply back around like a bent elbow. Shrouded by the rain, the horses were black shadows, indistinguishable.

Suddenly they burst out of the white mist like arrows shooting through a gauzy curtain. The man beside her stiffened as Rum Chaser emerged from the pack along the inside to challenge Candy Dancer.

Hooves pounded the turf like a thousand drums, vibrating the ground beneath Jessalyn's feet. She looked for Topper's black and red skullcap and spotted it, bobbing a full five lengths behind the leaders. *Too late,* she thought. *He's left it until too late.* Then, just when it seemed the race was lost, Blue Moon put on his flying speed, coming around the outside, gaining, gaining, gaining. . . . Five hundred yards stretched before them to the winning post, and the three Thoroughbreds, black and bay and chestnut, were now running stride for stride, straining every muscle and sinew toward victory.

As was the custom, many of the spectators on horseback galloped onto the course to join the runners. Without the bright colors of the jockeys' skullcaps it would now have been impossible to distinguish which horses were actually a part of the race. Jessalyn began bouncing up and down on the balls of her feet. She knew she was wriggling like a pilchard, but she didn't care.

"Come on, Blue Moon. Come on, come on . . ." she chanted, as if the words were an incantation, her voice rising to a crescendo along with her excitement.

She glanced at the man beside her. He watched with a controlled intensity, only the tight set of his mouth revealing how much he had invested in this race. She was lost a moment in looking at him, and so she missed seeing the beginning of what happened. Only the horrible finish.

The crowd's cheers of excitement shattered into screams as Rum Chaser went down in a tangle of white socks and hooves. Blue Moon swerved, his legs slipping sideways out from under him in the mud. He slid along on his belly, unable to collect his crazily skating feet, then overbalanced onto his nose . . .

And lay absolutely still.

13

Jessalyn stood frozen in horror as men and horses surged around her, spilling onto the track. She took one stumbling step, and then another. It felt as if she were in a nightmare, running through the boggy turf and getting nowhere. Blue Moon still lay on the ground, unmoving. *God, oh, God, he's dead,* Jessalyn thought. Topper was crawling through the mud toward the horse, his mouth open in a shout that Jessalyn couldn't hear over the shrieks and the pounding of hooves, over the pounding of her own heart.

Suddenly Blue Moon jerked into movement, struggling back onto his feet. Jessalyn sobbed with relief. He'd only had the wind knocked out of him by the fall. But Rum Chaser still rolled on the ground, thrashing and neighing in pain. His jockey, bright green and yellow taffeta now smeared with mud, swayed groggily to his feet. The earl of Caerhays stood stiff and still beside him, his head bent beneath the pelting rain.

The clang of the referee's bell rent the wet air, announcing Candy Dancer the winner. Followed seconds later by a flapping noise, like sheets in the wind, of the pigeons carrying the results to London.

Someone handed McCady a pistol.

"No!" Jessalyn cried, stumbling toward him.

He swung around to her, and she recoiled from the killing rage that blazed in his eyes.

His hand lashed out, his fingers biting deep into her arm. "Come here, damn you," he snarled, hauling her roughly up against him. "You started it, so you may as well see the bloody end of it."

The great Thoroughbred's cannon was broken so badly the jagged edge of the bone had torn through the thin flesh. He was screaming from the pain. "Oh, God," Jessalyn cried, turning her head aside.

McCady put the barrel of the pistol against her cheek and forced her head back around. He brought his face close to hers. His breath washed over her, hot as a caress, but his voice was like shards of ice. "You watch, dammit."

For one suspended moment he kept the pistol pressed hard against her cheek. Her whole face felt stiff and cold. Rum Chaser's screams faded until she heard only a rushing in her ears, like the surf at End Cottage. Oddly the smells she breathed in were homey ones, of horse sweat and crushed grass.

He turned and pointed the gun at Rum Chaser's head and squeezed the trigger.

The sound of the shot smacked against her. Jessalyn flinched, but she didn't cry out. The chestnut's big body jerked and was still. The air stank of sulfur. She lifted her gaze to McCady's face. She could see his fury in every hardened line of his body; she could feel it radiating from him in waves, like heat from a Midsummer's Eve bonfire. But she couldn't understand why it was directed at her.

His voice slashed through the air like a dueling blade. "How much did you win?"

"Win! We lost a hundred and twenty-five pounds, plus the race stake. We lost."

"I don't believe you lost a bloody farthing." His grip tightened, squeezing so tightly she had to set her jaw to keep from whimpering. "Either your jockey was got at or you paid him yourself to crimp the race, because you had your blunt riding on Candy Dancer instead. You probably planned to lose the easy way by running a dog race, but when Rum Chaser entered at the last minute, you had to take more drastic measures. And *this* is the result." He flung the pistol to the ground, next to his dead horse.

Jessalyn stared up at him, her eyes wide and blank with shock. He was a peer, and thus his status would carry weight with the Jockey Club, the awesome body that regulated the English racing scene. If the club were to put any credence into his accusation, she and Gram could be warned off Newmarket Heath, even permanently barred from the Turf altogether.

"No!" she protested. "I didn't . . . I would never—"

He flung his head back and then with a vicious jerk brought her crashing against his chest. His eyes flared, and his gaze fell on her mouth. His head dipped down, and she had the strangest thought that he was about to kiss her. But then he thrust her away as if touching her disgusted him. He spun around and strode through the crowd.

She had to run to catch up with him. Grasping his arm, she pulled him around to face her. "How dare you accuse me of such a hateful thing! I am not to blame if you were such a fool as to wager a thousand pounds on a horse that wasn't fit."

He pried her fingers loose from his sleeve, then dropped her hand. "I know what I saw, and that collision was deliberate."

"Indeed?" She lifted her chin. "Go ahead and make your accusation then. But after I have proven you wrong, I shall expect a public apology for the slur you have cast upon the Letty name with your smearing lies." Her lower lip curled into a sneer. "Or is *honor* a concept too far beyond a Trelawny's understanding? My *lord.*"

His face whitened, and a muscle bunched along his jaw. He stared back at her with eyes as stony black as the granite cliffs of Cornwall. Then he spun around on his heel and walked away. She watching him go, feeling battered and bruised inside, but this time she had matched him blow for blow. *You are silly Miss Letty no longer*, she thought, feeling proud of her woman's self.

But unfortunately, when it came to McCady Trelawny, her treacherous heart had a tendency to care nothing of pride.

The Sarn't Major had taken charge of Blue Moon, putting a hood over his head to calm him, layering rugs over his sweating back. Jessalyn ran up as the trainer was about to lead the Thoroughbred off to the thatched lean-tos where the horses were temporarily stabled on race day. The bay's left hind leg was curled up beneath his belly, the big splayed hoof only skimming the ground.

She searched the Sarn't Major's grim face, appealing to him mutely with her eyes to tell her that the injury wasn't serious.

He shook his head. "Got a badly twisted hock," he stated in his usual terse manner.

Jessalyn ran her hand over the swollen joint. She was shocked at the heat that radiated from the horse's flesh; it was like holding out her palm to a coal fire.

"He'll not be racin' anymore this year," the Sarn't Major said. "'Tes a proper question whether or no he'll ever be fit t' run again."

Jessalyn pressed her face into Blue Moon's neck, rubbing her cheek against the rough wool of the rug. As if sensing her despair, the horse turned his head and looked at her, his great intelligent eyes staring calmly at her out of the black hood. Jessalyn blinked hard against a rush of tears.

She asked the Sarn't Major if he had seen the accident.

"Aye," he said.

"Do you think . . . did it look to you as if it were deliberate?"

"Aye," he said again. "It had the look of bein' a crimp race."

"But Topper wouldn't—"

"Nay. Not Topper. I said it had the look of bein' a crimp race. I didn't say 'twere one."

Jessalyn bought a meat pie and rice pudding wrapped in paper, paying a boy a shilling to carry the food and a message to Lady Letty. She went with the Sarn't Major to see Blue Moon safely settled in his box with a bag of oats and a nourishing dram of canary wine. Then she went looking for Topper.

She spotted him talking with the winning jockey beside the gibbetlike weighing scales. He had already changed out of his colorful riding taffeta, but his small, wiry body was still clothed as flamboyantly as a costermonger in an orange shirt, blue-checked waistcoat, yellow breeches, and purple neckerchief. A red felt hat, sporting a pheasant feather, covered his snow blond hair.

Jessalyn thought Topper loved such flashy togs because so much of his early life had been spent in a world of gray and black. The youth was one of Lady Letty's strays. One day four years ago, shortly after they had moved into the London house that Jessalyn inherited from her mother, the parlor chimney had caught on fire and they'd had to hire a man to put it out. The chimney sweep had brought a climbing boy along with him to send up the narrow flue. The child was naked and emaciated, caked with soot and grime. His hideously callused knees and elbows were scraped raw and bleeding; his enormous blue eyes filled with fear and a dull acceptance. Lady Letty had taken one look and bought the boy off the sweep for two guineas. They had thought his hair was black until they'd given him a bath.

They had also thought him about six or seven—he was so small—but he told them he was sure that he was at least thirteen. He had vague memories of another life, a cottage in the country and a white pony. He didn't know his name, but the sweep had called him Topper. It was the Sarn't Major who had first put Topper on a horse and had discovered the boy's natural balance and sensitive hands.

Jessalyn caught Topper's eye now and waved. He bade

good-bye to the other jockey with a jaunty salute, walking around the weighing scales. Jessalyn came from the other side to meet him, almost planting her half boot in a pile of steaming horse dung.

"Ere now, watch yer step, Miss Jessalyn," he said in thick accents that revealed his rookery childhood. As he reached out to assist her, a grimace of pain twisted his elfin face.

"Oh, Topper. Were you hurt in the fall?"

"I got me a gammy arm, but I reckon I'll live." His mobile mouth split into a wide grin, revealing the gap in his front teeth that had been lost to the butt end of a whip during his first race. Missing teeth were a badge of honor among the knights of the pigskin. "Don't tell Becka about it, ye mind. She'll dose me up with one of them boluses she's always tryin' to force down me throat." He pulled a face. "Gawblimey, some of that stuff tastes worse'n rat bane. Ye got a frown on ye down t' yer knees, Miss Jessalyn. Blue Moon's got a gimp hock, 'tis true, but he's a game un. He'll run again, ye'll see."

She forced a smile. "Topper, Rum Chaser's owner is accusing you of deliberately causing that accident in order to throw the race."

Topper turned his head aside and spit through the hole in his teeth like a coachman. "Too risky, by half. If I was to crimp a race, see, I'd nobble me horse with a physic aforehand. Duck shot made up with putty or opium balls ud do the trick. To ride foul is bleedin' crazy, not t' mention dangerous to me 'ealth."

He squinted at her through his pale lashes and wrinkled his sharp nose. "I ride honest, and ye can say as much to his bleedin' lordship. It was his knight what caused the bust-up, not me. It was his man what was boozed so deep he was lolling in the saddle like a walleyed dog right before the off. Mebbe it was his high and mighty lordship who had a bit laid off on the nag what won."

Jessalyn closed her eyes, picturing the scene. Rum

Chaser's jockey had certainly looked dazed. He could have been drunk, but he also could have simply been concussed from the fall. And McCady—Lord Caerhays . . . there was no doubting that his fury was genuine, a fury born of despair. He had behaved like a man badly dipped, who had wagered more than he could afford to lose.

A sheet of wind-driven rain slapped her face, and she rocked on her feet, shivering. For the first time she realized how wet and cold she was.

Topper's voice came to her as if from the bottom of a mine pit, and she opened her eyes. ". . . I promised me mates I'd meet 'em at the Laughing Footman for a tot or two of the wet stuff."

She remembered suddenly that Topper's share of the winning purse would have been ten pounds, and she fumbled with her reticule. "I have a few shillings with me."

He stilled her hand. "Never ye mind, Miss Jessalyn. I've plenty of tin."

With a final grin he sauntered away, whistling through his broken teeth. Frowning, Jessalyn watched him go. Topper could never have deliberately sent Blue Moon crashing into Rum Chaser. He loved the horse too much to risk hurting him.

No, Topper couldn't have crimped the race. Angry and disgusted with herself for allowing McCady—Lord Caerhays to plant the ugly suspicion in her mind, she hurried to where Gram waited for her in their shabby rented cabriolet.

A lone man leaned against the betting post, deserted now in murky twilight. At the sight of him, her step slowed. Shadows darkened the hollows beneath his flaring cheekbones, and his eyes glittered at her, black and empty. He had looked like that the first time she had seen him. A fallen angel.

She turned her back on him and walked away, her head high.

* * *

Clarence Tiltwell could never enter Brooks's without feeling immense satisfaction. It was as if his membership in the exclusive men's club had become a symbol of all that he had accomplished. He would stand inside the marbled entrance hall and breathe deeply of the odor of beeswax, scented candles, and old money. And he would think of his father. Or rather, of the man who was nominally his father.

It pleased him, oh, how it pleased him, to know that Henry Tiltwell—with his rough country accent and tutworker's hands—would never be allowed through the club's hallowed front door.

That evening Clarence's thoughts did not dwell long on Henry but moved inevitably to the other man who might have been his father. The first thing he had done upon becoming a member was to search for the earl's name in the betting book. It appeared many times, along with those of his three sons. The Trelawnys were profligate gamblers to a man. Why, just this afternoon, or so he had heard, the twelfth earl of Caerhays had hazarded an incredible one thousand pounds on a horse that had not even managed to cross the finishing post.

Before long, Clarence thought—with grim satisfaction and a piercing quiver of guilty joy—the only trace of a Trelawny to be found in Brooks's would be their names, fading on the pages of the betting book.

A servant appeared and relieved Clarence of his walking stick, hat, and gloves. He crossed the hall, his bootheels clicking on black and white tiles. He paused to check his appearance in a gilt-framed mirror, adjusting his intricately tied cravat and smoothing back his blond hair. He mounted the stairs, past Roman busts resting stone-faced in their niches. Tonight he felt like those Roman Caesars—a conqueror.

He entered a small parlor on the second floor. The only other occupants were two men checking the Weatherby Racing Calendar off against the studbook. They nodded a greeting, then went back to their serious calculation of the horses and their odds. Clarence asked the wine steward to broach a bottle of the best port.

The room was all masculine refinement: crimson damask wallpaper and red brocade curtains. Clarence flicked back the tails of his coat and sat down in one of a matching set of tufted green leather chairs before the fire. He adjusted the buff and blue cockade in his lapel, which proclaimed him to be an avid member of the Whig party.

Two years ago he had been elected a member of Parliament, representing the Cornish borough of St. Michael. He had an income of more than thirty thousand pounds a year, and in another two years he expected that figure to double. Recently he had purchased a house on Berkeley Square between a baron and a marquess, where soon he hoped to be setting up his nursery with Jessalyn as his wife. And now, something he hadn't even allowed himself to think of before, something he wanted so badly that he knew already he would be devastated if it didn't come to pass. . . . His patron had hinted over dinner last night that a knighthood might one day be forthcoming.

A rush of exquisite pleasure thrummed through him. *A knighthood.* Sir Clarence Tiltwell. Sir Clarence.

He turned his head at the soft fall of footsteps on the green and red patterned carpet. The club's majordomo approached, followed by the tall dark presence of the twelfth earl of Caerhays.

"This way, my lord," the majordomo said.

My lord. Clarence noted the deferential way the servant treated his titled cousin, which was slightly less deferential than the way the servant had treated him. Oh, it was nothing overt—a flicker of an eyelid, a certain set of the mouth —but Clarence was aware of it. He swallowed down a sour taste in his mouth.

The cousins' eyes met, and McCady's dazzling smile broke across his tanned face, like the sun coming out from behind a cloud. As always, Clarence found himself irresistibly drawn to that smile. He looked up at his cousin, and his chest felt tight with a strange and convoluted mixture of love and hate, envy and longing.

"Mack. Sit down, please. Some port?" he said as McCady settled with lazy grace into the facing wing chair. The rich leather made a sighing sound as it absorbed his weight. Clarence deliberately hadn't addressed his cousin by his title. The truth was he couldn't choke it past his throat. A knight, he thought with bitterness, was nothing to an earl.

McCady leaned forward, reaching for the port, and gaslight from the cut-glass luster shimmered off the gold loop that pierced his ear. Clarence frowned. An English gentleman should never make such an uncivilized spectacle of himself. *If I were the earl . . .* he thought, as he had thought so often in his life. But no matter what he did, no matter how lofty his accomplishments, nothing would ever correct the appalling injustice surrounding the circumstances of his birth.

But then Clarence's frown faded as he reminded himself of the power he had over the man sitting across from him. His cousin, his brother . . .

"I am afraid I have some unwelcome news," Clarence said.

McCady tilted back his head and finished off the wine in one swallow. He said nothing, but the whitening of the knuckles on the hand that clutched the glass revealed his inner tension. By now, Clarence thought, hoped, McCady Trelawny, the *earl* of Caerhays, must be growing very desperate indeed.

The cousins had seen a lot of each other during the last two years. Since McCady had formed the British Railway Company, the first of its kind, for the conveyance of passengers and freight between Falmouth and London. Since Parliament had set up a committee to oversee the scheme. Since Clarence Tiltwell had maneuvered for himself an appointment on that committee.

Thus far Parliament had granted the BRC permission to lay only a single, experimental line between Plymouth and

Exeter, a distance of some forty miles. Yet the cost of laying those forty miles of track had been staggering, for it had required huge engineering feats: a viaduct, numerous cuttings and embankments. The tunnel alone had taken almost six months to dig—all done by navvies with pick and shovel. It was an enormous gamble for McCady and his company. For only if the committee deemed the experiment viable would Parliament grant the BRC the right to build the remainder of the line.

The committee, Clarence thought, *my committee*, had the power of life and death over McCady Trelawny's railway. Over McCady's dream.

"A division has developed within the committee," Clarence now said, his gaze focused on his cousin's taut face, "a division between those favoring steam power locomotives to operate the new railway and those who want the more traditional method of rope haulage by a fixed engine."

McCady's arrogant mouth tightened slightly. "Rope haulage? You cannot be serious."

"Very serious, I'm afraid. We have voted that the way to resolve the disagreement is to hold trials to determine which method is most effective."

McCady muttered a foul word beneath his breath, and Clarence bit back a smile.

"You can still build your locomotive and run it in the trials," Clarence said. "But others will be allowed to compete as well. The trials will be held in August, over twenty miles of the completed portion of the line. There will be rules and stipulations—I won't go into those now. The winner will be granted the license from Parliament allowing him to supply the British Railway Company with the engines necessary to operate the public tramway."

"That contract was to come to me," McCady said, his voice deceptively soft, and Clarence felt a clenching of fear in the pit of his stomach. He would rather have faced a regiment of highwaymen on Hounslow Heath than Mc-Cady Trelawny in an angry and dangerous mood.

Clarence wet his lips. "There are those on the committee—"

"Bugger your bloody committee."

"—who don't trust your judgment," Clarence went on. The fear was fading; he mustn't forget that the power was all his now. This wasn't a knoll in Belgium, and McCady couldn't slash through his enemies with a sword. "They find it difficult to put their faith in an ex-lieutenant from a rather unfashionable line regiment, just recently come into a bankrupted title. A title you inherited from a brother so reviled for his degeneracy that even the devil would cut him dead if he met him on the street. A brother who shot himself, leaving twenty thousand pounds' worth of gaming vowels that have yet to be paid."

"I am not my brother. And the vowels will be paid."

With what? Clarence wondered, though he didn't say so aloud. "Of course, you are not the complete rakeshame your brother was." He allowed himself a small smile. "But then neither can you claim to be a saint. In truth, there are only one or two on the committee whose feelings against you are so personal. The others merely believe steam locomotion is dangerous and unworkable. You must admit it has not proven very effective thus far."

"That is because it has never been given a chance—" McCady cut himself off. He stared at Clarence with a furious intensity that lifted the fine hairs on the younger man's neck. "Are you one of those *others*, Clarey? Dammit, I deserve that contract. The rail line wouldn't exist if it weren't for me. I *built* the bloody thing!"

The other two men looked up from their studbook as McCady's harsh voice disturbed the genteel silence. "Shhh," one hissed. McCady cast a look in their direction that said, *Bugger off.* He had never cared what others thought of him. There were times, many times when Clarence envied his cousin the freedom that such indifference must bring him.

"There is no need to shout at me," Clarence said, pitching his voice low and hoping his cousin would follow suit. "You can be assured that I argued your point of view. But we must tread warily, Mack. The truth is, Parliament are still very nervous about this whole railway affair. And there are powerful interests opposing it most vigorously—landowners, barge- and stagecoach operators, toll collectors . . . well, I hardly need name them to you."

"Christ, Clarey." McCady leaned forward, his elbows on his knees. He looked like a man with his back to a cracking dike, trying to hold back a flooding tide with his fingertips. "I cannot wait until August for that contract. I need to raise ten thousand quid by the first of July to meet the interest on my notes or the BRC goes under, and I go with it."

Clarence's chest puffed with righteous anger. "And did you think the way out of your difficulty was to take the thousand pounds you did have and hazard it all on a deuced *horse?*"

The reckless smile of the born rebel flashed across McCady's face. "Desperate circumstances require desperate measures. If the bloody nag had won . . ." He lowered his head, thrusting his fingers through his hair. "Ah, hell, Clarey."

Clarence looked from his cousin's bent head into the dark, winking red eye of his port, hiding the satisfaction he felt. He brought the glass to his lips, savoring the fruity bite of the wine on his tongue. Clarence walked past Fleet Prison nearly every day; he had stared often at the poor wretches thrusting their tin cups through the iron bars, begging for pennies. *Pray remember us poor debtors . . .*

A sudden, sick elation filled him as he reached for the decanter, pouring them both more wine. An ancient name and title would not spare McCady Trelawny from conviction in a bankruptcy court. And for a man of his fierce arrogance and pride, such a place as Fleet Prison would break him. The way you broke a seasoned hickory stick . . . by putting your foot on it and pushing hard and slowly, until it cracked with a noise like a scream.

"I saw Jessalyn Letty today."

The statement, coming from nowhere, so startled Clarence that he jerked, nearly knocking over the decanter as he went to set it back on the table. In all these years, not since that ghastly summer, had McCady ever once mentioned Jessalyn. Clarence tried to keep his face blank, but he doubted he succeeded very well. "Really? And where was that?"

"Newmarket."

Clarence frowned. He might have known McCady would come across her there. It illustrated just the sort of scaff and raff she exposed herself to by frequenting the racing scene. He bridled at the thought of all the money wasted on those so-called Thoroughbreds that Jessalyn had inherited from her mother. Coddled in their expensive lodgings, eating their heads off, all for a chance in a few races a year, which they invariably lost. He laid the blame for the entire nonsense at Lady Letty's door. Once Jessalyn was his wife, he would put a stop to it. He would dispose of every one of those worthless nags and forbid her to set foot within a mile of a racecourse.

"I suppose she lost as well," Clarence said, his frown deepening. Jessalyn's propensity for gambling was another thing he would curb once he became her husband.

McCady shrugged. "Miss Letty and I did not part on the best of terms five years ago, and thus our reunion was not a congenial one. Pity that, for she grew up to be exceptionally beautiful."

McCady toyed with the stem of his wineglass, looking almost bored, yet there was a brooding set to his mouth, and strange shadows moved within the dark depths of his eyes. Clarence felt a shudder of alarm. McCady might have scrupled to seduce Jessalyn when she was only sixteen, but at twenty-one she would be fair game. That terrible summer would start all over again. Once more he would be forced to stand aside and watch while the girl he loved succumbed to that powerful and degenerate Trelawny charm.

But not this time . . . He was no longer the calf-hearted boy he had been that long-ago summer. Now he was rich and powerful in his own right, and Jessalyn Letty was *his*.

He felt his lips stretching into a tight smile as a place deep within him grew hard and cold. "What a happy coincidence that you should mention Miss Letty, Mack. Indeed, you might wish to offer me congratulations, for I have just this week asked Jessalyn to do me the honor of becoming my wife and—"

The fragile port glass shattered in McCady's hand. Dark ruby wine dripped off his fingers, looking like blood.

Clarence half stood, holding out his handkerchief. "Good God, man, you don't know your own strength."

McCady took the delicately embroidered linen, wiping his hand. "She has accepted you?" he asked, his voice so devoid of emotion they might has well have been discussing the weather.

Leaning back, Clarence put three fingers into his fob pocket. He rubbed the two gold sovereigns he always carried for luck. "Of course, she has accepted, but then it was always understood between us that we would marry someday. We've set a date for the first week in June, but truthfully, old boy"—he leaned forward and put on a just-between-us-men smile—"I don't think I can wait that long."

McCady pinned him with his fierce gaze. Suddenly there was something dark and dangerous in the room, and Clarence wished he hadn't gone quite so far. After all, Mack had wanted Jessalyn very badly at one time.

"You will be good to her, Clarey," McCady said.

"I—I love her," Clarence answered, startled.

A ripple of feeling stirred in those dark eyes. "Don't tell me you love her. Love is a fool's emotion, another pretty word for lust and a moral excuse to fuck. All I care about is how you treat her. If you ever hurt her, Clarey, I will kill you."

"If anyone hurts her, it is likely to be you!" Clarence blurted, his face flushed.

"I will kill you," McCady said again.

Clarence stared into eyes that were utterly savage. The back of his neck and ears grew hot, and he jerked his gaze away. He cleared his throat. "I realize the committee's decision has been a bit of a setback for you," he said, desperate suddenly to shift McCady's mind off Jessalyn. "But it is really only a matter of stretching the company's assets until your locomotive can win the trial."

A fleeting emotion quivered in his cousin's face. Clarence suddenly had the unpleasant feeling that McCady was laughing at him.

Clarence cleared his throat again. "Unfortunately, with me serving on the committee, any financial transaction between us would present the appearance of collusion on our parts. Some could even look upon it as in the nature of a bribe." He studied the toe of his boot. "I have plenty of surplus capital lying around just itching to be invested in a worthy cause. A pity there isn't some way I could put it to good use and help you over this little setback." He lifted his head. "After all, Mack, even for cousins we are extraordinarily close. In some ways you are like a brother to me."

Clarence searched the face of the man across from him. *Say it*, he thought, *look at me and acknowledge that I could be your brother.*

McCady did look at him with those shadowed dark eyes, but he said nothing.

Clarence got to his feet, pulling out his repeater's watch and making a big show of being an important man with important things to do. He thought he should feel triumph, and he could not understand why all he felt was desolation.

At the door he paused and looked back at the man who stared, brooding, into the fire. He felt a pang at the sight of that harsh and elegant profile, the haughty cheekbone and sullen curve of that hard mouth. The beloved and hated face of his cousin . . . his brother.

Oh, McCady had found a few starry-eyed dupes willing to invest in his foolish dream, but the bulk of the debt was his. Only one bank had dared to risk lending the money to back his fledgling company.

Sometime toward the end of June, McCady Trelawny, the twelfth earl of Caerhays, would come to the Mechanics Bank of London, hat in hand, begging for an abeyance of the interest due on his promissory notes until the locomotive trials had been run. But he wouldn't get it. Clarence knew he wouldn't get it. Few people were aware of it, in truth, only two others knew of it besides himself, but . . .

Clarence Tiltwell *owned* the Mechanics Bank of London.

14

A rocket shot across the sky, exploding overhead like a shattered star. Glittering blue fire rained down, silhouetting the trees, transforming branches into witches' claws and shadows in capering demons. Although the night was mild, Jessalyn shivered, huddling deep within the folds of her cloak.

"Are ye cold, miss?"

She shook her head, then heaved an enormous sigh. "Oh, Topper. I don't think I can go through with this. Dear life . . . if Gram were to hear of it, she would never forgive me."

"And who's to tell her, eh?" The young jockey was leaning against the trunk of an elm, his arms folded across his chest. Red globe lamps hung from the branches above, casting a ruddy glow over his face. "No one can see who ye are in them togs. Ye could be the bleedin' queen of Sheba. We need the blunt," he reminded her.

Jessalyn flinched as a Roman candle ignited with a boom and a hail of fire clusters. The Vauxhall pleasure gardens were suddenly as bright as a meadow at high noon, and she touched the spangled, lacquered mask she wore as if to reassure herself that it was still in place. Nervous fear sat on her stomach like sour wine.

The colored globe lamps in the elm trees winked red and blue and yellow eyes. The whistle and bang of the fireworks drowned out the lilting strains of a waltz. Arcaded colonnades surrounded a leafy bower where beggars mixed with bankers and dukes rubbed elbows with cobblers, and prostitutes and pickpockets fleeced them all. Within small discreet booths, gentlemen and ladies partook of flirtatious conversation and expensive suppers of muslin-thin slices of ham, tiny chickens, cheesecakes, and syllabubs.

And soon now, as soon as the fireworks show was over, many in the crowd would drift into the nearby wooden rotunda for the night's entertainment, and Jessalyn would . . .

Her stomach clenched again. She would do what she had to do. The money she was about to make would go a long way toward feeding them all in the coming months, not to mention the four racehorses that were even now consuming a fortune in oats in their rented stable at Newmarket.

A serpentine exploded above, spitting flames. A hand touched her shoulder, and Jessalyn whirled, her heart leaping into her throat. Topper, his gap-toothed grin splitting his face, held out a glass of the famous Vauxhall punch. "I bought ye a drink, Miss Jessalyn. Wet yer gullet with enough of this, and ye could waltz with the devil and not turn a hair."

Jessalyn's hand shook as she reached for the glass, but she managed a smile of thanks for the boy. She started to drink and nearly choked as pungent fumes swirled up her nose. The punch burned like liquid fire going down, but when it hit bottom, she felt all warm and tingly inside.

It gave her the courage to go around to the back of the rotunda and join the other sequined, spangled, and plumed performers awaiting their cue at the stage entrance. A pudding-paunched man waddled up to her. His hair was oiled and brushed behind his ears in stiff wings, and his collar points were starched so high Jessalyn feared he would cut off his head if he had to turn it suddenly. He was Mr.

O'Hare, who that afternoon had hired her to be the opening act in his Equestrian Spectacle.

"Miss Brown?" he said. His lips, thin and tight as a buttonhole, twisted into a knowing smirk. She had not been very original with her alias. "You're late."

Jessalyn said nothing; her mouth was too dry for speech. "Take off the cloak."

Her hands tightened in the thick material at her neck. Then she loosened the barrel snaps and let the cloak slip off her shoulders. Mr. O'Hare had provided her with the costume, and Jessalyn suspected it had once belonged to a boy. It consisted of tight-fitting sequined white hose and a scarlet doublet shot with gold thread, like the court clothes of a cavalier from a long-ago era. Her mask was in the shape of a bird's head, with what looked like real parrot feathers beneath the lacquer. It had a great curved beak that was coming loose and wiggled when she touched it.

Mr. O'Hare's bold gaze roamed down the length of her exposed legs, then up again. Jessalyn's cheeks flushed hot behind the mask. His mouth parted in a smile, revealing a gold tooth that flashed in the lantern light. "You'll do. Oh, aye, lassie. You'll do."

He motioned to a stable lad, who brought over the horse she would perform on tonight. It was a circus horse, a rosinback—a mare with a broad level back and a coat as white as frothed milk. She had a wide leather strap called a surcingle cinched around her belly and ostrich plumes fastened to her head.

Jessalyn murmured sweet nothings in the mare's ears, checked the tightness of the surcingle a dozen times, and did a lot of fussing and fidgeting, while a wire walker, a juggler, and a sword swallower warmed up the audience. Too soon she heard the revel master's voice echoing out of the rotunda's doors . . . *death-defying equestrian feats.* Jessalyn checked the surcingle again and thought she might get sick.

Suddenly Mr. O'Hare was flapping his arm at her. She

sent the mare forward with a soft click of her tongue. Grasping the surcingle, she vaulted onto the horse's back and pulled herself into the kneeling position. She extended her right leg behind her, pointed her toe, and lifted her head high just as the mare burst through a paper hoop and into the rotunda's ring. A loud crack of sound smacked into her, and she nearly fell off from the shock of it. She thought someone had set off a rocket within the building. Then she realized it was the noise of hundreds of hands clapping.

The people in the boxes and gallery and the smoking, fluttering torches blended into a dizzying swirl of light and colors as she cantered around the small ring. Thumping canes and snapping snuffboxes, talk and laughter all blended into a frantic buzz, like a busy hive. Fear and excitement tightened her muscles. Her palms went wet with sweat. She sucked in a deep breath and let it out slowly, centering herself to the movement of the horse. Soon the noise receded until it became nothing more than a whisper, like the distant wash of the sea across sand. Her senses became focused on specific things: the dusty smell of the sawdust that covered the floor of the pit; the smooth, oily feel of the leather surcingle; the dry, chalky taste in her mouth that came from nerves.

She performed her tricks flawlessly—the Flag, the Mill, the Scissors, and the "death-defying" Cossack Hang. It was while performing this feat, hanging sideways and upside down over the left side of the horse, with her left leg pointed skyward and her arms dangling over her head toward the ground, that she saw him.

It was only a fleeting glimpse, when her gaze had wandered from the rotating cherubs on the domed ceiling to the spinning tier of the upper boxes. But she could have picked out his face from among multitudes, even upside down. She took a better look when she righted herself and cantered around the ring again to the accompaniment of thunderous applause and cries of "Huzza!" He was in a front box with a party of two other men and three women. She wondered which of the women was his.

His expression looked reckless and dangerous, and his dark gaze speared her as if he knew, *knew* that it was she beneath the bird mask. Her whole body went hot, and she was possessed with a violent longing to gallop out of the ring and keep going until she rode off the end of the earth.

Once more she cantered around the ring, and as if pulled by invisible reins, her head lifted and her eyes were drawn up to his. He'd always seen her as a silly, bumbling, beetle-witted child, and his opinion was unlikely ever to change. But her heart was safe from him now; she would make sure that this was so. If she didn't allow herself to care what he thought of her, he could no longer hurt her.

She had one last death-defying feat left to perform and she knew which one it would be—the Standing Somersault, the trick she had shown off for him the day that he had first kissed her. The day that she had fallen into Claret Pond, and fallen so deeply in love that she had become lost and never found her way back.

But this time there were no rabbit holes to spoil the ending. She did it perfectly. She landed upright on the mare's back, standing tall, her arms lifted above her head as the mare leaped back through the ring and out of the rotunda, and wave after wave of applause washed over them.

Jessalyn jumped from the horse onto legs that suddenly felt as loose and quivery as jellied eels. She hugged the mare, planting a kiss on her pink nose. "Scrape off the sweat, and rub her down good," she said to the boy who came running up. The night breeze chilled her own sweating body. She wrapped up in her cloak as she searched for Topper in the crowd milling outside the arena door.

A hand clamped down on her wrist, jerking her around so violently she was flung onto his chest and had to grasp the lapels of his coat to keep from falling. Her head fell back, and her gaze clashed with hard, shadowed eyes.

"You're coming with me," he said.

She struggled to pull free of him. "How dare you presume to order me about. You are not my brother or my guardian. You are nothing to me." She liked the sound of that so much she said it again. "You are nothing."

"You are coming with me now," he said again.

"I am not. I have another performance—"

The rest of her protest caught in her throat as, slowly, he lowered his head, bringing his face so close to hers she could feel the heat of his breath and see the yellow sunbursts in his eyes. "The hell you do," he said, and Jessalyn thought the devil's voice would probably sound like that.

He strode down the broad treelined walk, pulling her after him. Stones bruised the soles of her thinly slippered feet. She clawed at the hand that was clamped like a vise around her wrist. "Let me go or I'll scream," she protested, but as soon as the words were out her mouth, she felt like a fool. They had sounded so silly, like something the heroine of a blue book would wail just before the villain ravished her.

"Go ahead, indulge yourself," her particular villain retorted in a mocking drawl that had her clenching her teeth. "Young ladies scream in Vauxhall Gardens all the time. It is practically a mating call."

He was right. The gardens were latticed with dark walks bounded by high hedges and hidden ornamental ruins that were havens for seduction. The night air was filled with the tinkle and gurgle of fountains, the rustle of wind-stirred leaves, and the squealing and shrieking of ladies losing their virtue.

The smell of lilac lay heavy on the breeze. Lamps winked like fairy lights in the trees, and the moon rolled across the sky, round and shiny as a new penny. It was a beautiful night, a night made for love. McCady's fingers crushed her wrist as he dragged her down the walk. She jerked hard against him, trying to pull free, and succeeded only in nearly wrenching her arm off.

He hauled her out of the front gate, then down to the

riverfront, walking fast and jerking her along hard behind him, so that if he hadn't had such a death grip on her wrist, she would have fallen headfirst down the rickety wooden steps to the quay. "Oars!" he bellowed, and a moment later a small wherry bumped up to the dock, splashing stinking, oily water onto the warped boards.

His hands closed around her waist to lift her into the boat, and she lashed out with her foot, catching him high on the thigh, missing her aim.

"Bloody hell, Jessalyn." He grunted as she landed a good one on his shin, but it didn't stop him from tossing her like a sack of turnips into the wherry. She landed hard on the poorly cushioned thwart, rattling her teeth.

The ferry landing was marked by a red-and-blue-striped pole and a flaming link torch. The torch flared in a sudden gust of wind, filling the air with the reek of tow and pitch and highlighting the harsh bones of his face. For a moment fear overwhelmed Jessalyn's anger. He was capable of anything, was McCady Trelawny. He acknowledged no rules, answered to no one. Then her anger, like the torch, flared again.

She struggled to stand up in the rocking boat, but McCady held her down with a bruising grip on her shoulder while he paid the ferryman his sixpence. "Are you blind?" she shouted. "Can't you see that this man is abducting me?"

"Aye." The ferryman hawked and spit into the water. "They all say that at first. And they all comes to likin' it in the end." He pushed the wherry away from the dock, and it was gripped by the river current.

"Where are you taking me?" Jessalyn demanded. Her voice caught on a slight tremor, and she tried to swallow it back down into her chest, where the fear resided.

For answer she got the slap of oars in the water. Lights from the gilded barges of the livery companies and the spanning arc of Westminster Bridge twinkled and sparkled, so that it seemed as if all the sky's stars had fallen into the river. There were people on the bridge, in those barges. Yet she knew she could scream herself hoarse and no one would come to help her.

They landed near a stand of hackney chariots, and he hailed one. His hand gripped her elbow, pushing her up the steps into the carriage. She fell onto the cracked leather seat, thrusting her cold feet into the straw on the floor, shivering, rubbing the bruises he had put on her wrist. He spoke to the driver, then climbed in beside her. She sat unmoving, stiff as a pit prop. The carriage started forward, clattering over the cobbles.

"Take that ridiculous thing off your face."

Her hands flew up to the bird mask. She fumbled with it, knocking the loose beak askew. She untied the strings and let it fall into her lap. A night breeze, smelling of London soot and river sludge, blew under the hackney's hood, cooling her burning cheeks. The flaring gas jets in the street spilled intermittent light into the carriage, casting his features into sharp bones and dangerous shadows.

The hackney slowed to turn a corner, and a boy ran up alongside, tossing a handbill into the earl's lap. He crumpled the paper in his fist and tossed it out again, swinging his head toward her, his earring winking like a golden eye.

His hand lashed out to fling open her cloak. He stared at her forever, and she felt the strangest awareness of her own body within the exotic clothes. Her breasts, taut and aching, pressing against the stiff satin of the doublet. Her legs, covered only by the thin silk hose and quivering as if they were naked.

He spoke through tight lips. "You have always had a propensity for trouble, but even at sixteen I doubt you were capable of hatching such a half-baked, bird-witted scheme that could so ruin you in the eyes of the world."

She jerked the cloak from his grasp, hugging it close to her chest. She hadn't wanted to ruin herself; she only wanted to earn some money to see her family through the next couple of months, until her marriage next June.

"Say something, damnation."

Her head snapped around. "Why should I? You're making enough clack for both of us. My lord."

A muscle jumped along his jaw, and his fists clenched. "Tomorrow I shall have a word with the man who operates that—that circus. I assure you that he will no longer be requiring your services."

"Thank you very much. My lord. And while you're about it, perhaps you will tell me how we're all supposed to eat without the twenty shillings a night Mr. O'Hare was going to pay me."

"I should have thought you had plenty of blunt. After your big winnings at Newmarket the other day."

"I told you that we did not crimp that race." She looked into his eyes, alternately shadowed and then starred in the flickering light. "It could have been you. Indeed, it is just the sort of cheating, dishonorable behavior you Trelawnys are known for."

If she had meant to wound him, she hadn't succeeded. His face was more of a mask than the one in her lap. She had never been able to tell what he was thinking when it mattered.

"If you are really so desperate, why didn't you apply to your betrothed?" he said. "Cousin Clarey has enough tin to feed half of London and not feel the pinch."

So Clarence had mentioned their betrothal to his cousin; he had known it all along. And though she was loath to admit it, especially to herself, it hurt to realize that the earl of Caerhays didn't seem to care.

She lifted her chin. "We Lettys do not borrow from our friends. Or lovers," she added. She cast a sideways glance to see what he would make of that.

He seemed to make nothing of it at all, merely shrugging. "I might be badly dipped myself but I can still spare a pound or two. Enough to keep you and your grandmother from starving."

"I wouldn't take the world's last crust of bread if it came

from you." It was another silly remark, and she knew as soon as the words left her mouth that he would pounce on them.

He didn't disappoint her. "Instead of joining the circus," he drawled, "you should have gone on the stage. You have such a flair for the melodramatic delivery."

"It was not a circus. It was an Equestrian Spectacle."

"It was indeed a spectacle."

"And you are a vile . . . an odious . . . a despicable . . ." Words failed her. "An utter cad," she finished lamely, thinking that once again she was sounding like the beleaguered heroine of the worst sort of blue book.

He leaned into her, and something menacing flickered in his eyes. She felt the power of him that was a heat in the night, and she was drawn to that heat the way one would hold out cold hands to a flame. She could understand what had so attracted her at sixteen—the dark side of him that was wicked and lawless, exciting in its very danger. It attracted her still. She wanted to taste that danger, to see if she could tame it. She wanted him. It was primal in its power, this wanting. Seductive in its inevitability.

Her head told her there was no future with him. Yet in the charged silence she licked her lips, tasting fear and excitement . . . wanting him.

His gaze fastened on to her mouth, and she knew from the taut look on his face and the lazy-lidded heat in his eyes that he wanted her as well. Her head told her a man could desire where he did not love. Yet deliberately she wet her lips again.

He lowered his head, and his hand stole up to frame her face. His thumb stroked the line of her jaw. Mesmerized, she watched the creases alongside his mouth deepen as his lips moved. His breathy words caressed her cheek. "If you want me to kiss you, Miss Letty, why don't you just ask? It is no great distance after all from the circus ring to the brothel—"

She swung a fist at his head. His hand shot up, grabbing

her wrist. His lips parted in a hard smile. "I wouldn't do that were I you. I just might be the sort of vile, odious, despicable, and *utter cad* who would hit you back."

She tugged against his grip. "Let go of me, you bloody bastard."

He clicked his tongue, shaking his head in mock dismay. "Such naughty language, though hardly original. Have you been keeping bad company again?"

Their rough breathing filled the carriage as they glared at each other in aroused hostility. Muttering an oath, he swung his head away from her. He called to the driver on the box to pull up, and the carriage jolted to a stop. As if awakening from a trance, Jessalyn looked around to see where they were. They appeared to be in the middle of the market piazza of Covent Garden.

The driver let down the steps, and McCady descended first. He held up his hand to her. "Get out," he said in a voice of silk and steel.

Jessalyn deliberately ignored his hand. She climbed down, stepping onto paving stones that were slick with walnut husks and rotting cabbage leaves. Her left foot shot out from under her, and she grabbed him to regain her balance, her arm sliding around his waist beneath his coat. She felt the sinewy muscle that encased his ribs, felt it tauten as he sucked in a sharp breath, and she thrust herself hard away from him.

She saw his chest jerk, heard the rasp in his breathing. Her heart seemed to be wedged up in her throat, choking her. Whatever had been between them five years ago was still there, stronger than ever.

A roasted chestnut man rolled his cart toward them, shaking his pan, and the air was filled with the smell of burned nuts. The theaters were just letting out, and the streets were crowded with playgoers. Fruit sellers shoved among them, offering their wares with a cry: "Chase some oranges! Chase my nonpareils!"

An untidy collection of lean-tos and tumbledown sheds

covered the piazza. It smelled of overripe melons and rotting onions, for Covent Garden was the site of London's
vegetable market. In a few hours the square would be
crowded with carts and wagons heaped with fresh country
produce, costermongers in their gaudy waistcoats and
greengrocers in their blue aprons. But at night the place
was given over to revelry and sin. The once noble mansions
that surrounded the square had long ago been converted
into penny gaffs and chophouses, bagnios and brothels. Sex
in all its permutations could be bought within sight of the
fat columns of St. Paul's Cathedral.

The lamplights looked like big, shiny flat sequins in the
hazy darkness, casting a golden pall over the scene. A Fashionable Impure wearing a magnificent plumed headdress
strolled slowly across the church portico. Her soft white
arms and rounded breasts were displayed to the cool night
air, and the material of her gown was so diaphanous it was
more suggestion than substance.

A young blood dressed to the nines joined the woman on
the portico. He said something to her and squeezed her
exposed breast as if testing for its ripeness. Then the two of
them descended the steps and rounded the corner, disappearing into the night.

McCady's boots crunched on the shells and husks as he
came up behind her. "Flying around Vauxhall's rotunda in
spangles and hose makes you little better than her," he
said, his breath rustling her hair, but his voice was edged
with a raw anger. "Is that what you want, Jessalyn?"

She stiffened. "I fail to see the correlation, my lord. Indeed, I find your insinuation insulting."

"Dammit, Jessalyn. If your behavior tonight ever gets
out, you will be utterly and completely ruined, and you
know it."

"Only you know that it was I behind the mask. A gentleman would vow to keep a lady's secret."

"A *lady* would never indulge in such scandalous behavior in the first place. A lady would never have taken the

risk. If your Mr. Clarence Tiltwell, MP, ever got wind of it, he would be forced to repudiate you publicly—"

"Clarence would never do such a thing. He loves me."

"Clarence loves himself. And in his position he cannot afford even a breath of scandal. He would cry to the skies how you had deceived him, and by the time he was through, there would be men piled up outside your door nose-high like pilchards in August offering you proposals. And they wouldn't be marriage proposals."

She caught a note of something in his voice, something she didn't dare to trust. But it was almost as if he *cared* what happened to her, cared about her reputation and her future happiness. She wanted to push him, to see how far his caring would go. But this path led to heartache, and she had been down it before. She thought of one of Gram's favorite sayings: that only an addlepated fool bit into the same rotten apple twice.

Still, she had to know. . . .

She turned to face him, arching her brows and arranging her lips into a soft moue. "In truth, I had not considered entertaining those sorts of proposals," she said. "But now that you put me in mind of it, my lord, I can see where becoming some wealthy man's—how do you young bloods put it?—some man's *ladybird* is indeed an alternative."

He did not react as she had hoped. Instead he lifted one brow in turn and looked her over slowly as if judging just how viable an alternative. "Look around you then, Miss Letty. You'll find quite an aviary of ladybirds here at Covent Garden, from plump white doves to the scrawniest crows. You should understand the value of what you're selling and price yourself accordingly. For instance, if you were a virgin under thirteen, you could fetch upward of two hundred pounds. But a virgin at twenty-one—you are still a virgin?"

"I might be. It is no concern of yours."

"It will be the concern of the man who buys you. He should know what he's getting. A dried-up old maid . . ."

He paused, but she did not rise to the bait. "On the scale of
virgins a dried-up old maid is worth a lot less than a nubile
ingenue fresh out of the schoolroom."

"Why should I care what scale the man uses, since I shall
be the one to do the choosing, not he? He will have to be
well breeched, of course." She flicked a finger at the gold
band in his ear. "Not one up to his pretty earring in debt.
And he must be handsome as well, with no fat around his
belly and no bald spots on his head." She gave these por-
tions of his anatomy a scathing look as if he were already
going to seed.

"A woman past her prime with red hair and freckles cannot be too particular."

"I am hardly in my dotage and—"

"Positively antiquated, I would say."

"—and I no longer have freckles."

He caught her jaw with two fingers and twisted her head
around, so that the flambeau from a nearby cigar-divan
shone full on her face. He rubbed his thumb across her
cheekbone. "Liar. I see a good two dozen right here."

His gaze moved over her face as intimately as a caress,
and the constant noise in the crowded piazza seemed suddenly to still. The wind snatched the hem of her cloak and
wrapped it around his leg. His head dipped, and her lips
parted, waiting, no longer breathing, waiting until even her
heart seemed to pause in anticipation of what was to come.

He let her go, and she squeezed her eyes shut against a
sudden plunge of disappointment. "I—I shall insist he give
me jewels," she forced out through her tight throat. "And a
house with the deed in my name."

"Very wise. Because your attractions, dubious as they
are, will probably only last another three years. Perhaps
four."

"Gram says I have enduring bones."

"Enduring bones or not, he'll soon grow tired of you.
You'll be older then, and used. You will not be able to be so
choosy the second time. In another year or two, another

man or two, you'll become like that little dolly-mop over there."

She followed the direction of his gaze. A woman in low-cut, gaudy satin and a fringed shawl clung drunkenly to the arm of an old man in a greasy greatcoat. Her face was caked with yellow powder, her cheeks rouged orange like marmalade stains.

"Her jack will take her into a dive behind the colonnade there. He will consummate the arranged transaction—which, if she is fortunate, will be a normal consummation and not the nasty sort of play that can only be described in Latin phrases. Then he will pay her five shillings, four of which will go to her abbess, or her pimp. She has already started on the downward slide, you see. Into the gutter with her."

He nodded toward a brick wall covered with faded, peeling posters. At first all Jessalyn saw were shadows. Then the shadows stirred and became a woman in a ragged duffel cloak and rusty black poke bonnet.

"She has to ply her trade in parks and alleys because she is so diseased that no house or pimp will have her. She gets two pennies, and if I told you what she is willing to do for them, you wouldn't believe me."

The prostitute, sensing their interest, pushed off the wall and sauntered out into the piazza. She stepped into the circle of light cast by the flambeau, and Jessalyn sucked in a shocked breath. For the woman was not a woman at all, but a girl no older than fifteen. Her mouth was covered with weeping sores, and someone had recently beaten her, for liver-colored bruises ringed both eyes. "Buy yer pleasure, yer honor?" she whined, plucking at McCady's clothes with scabby fingers. "Anything ye wants, yer honor. Any ways ye wants it."

He put a coin into the girl's hand and waved her away, and Jessalyn could tell from his face that he felt no shock or horror. In truth, he felt nothing at all. He had been exposed to the stews of London too young, had partaken of their dark pleasures too often, ever to be shocked or horrified by anything again. He turned, and his gaze—fierce and arrogant, and perhaps a little wary—pierced her. She had thought it all a game, but he had been deadly serious. He had set out to teach her a lesson again, and this time he had succeeded. Succeeded better than he knew.

"Well, Miss Letty? Have you seen enough?" he said in a mocking, cutting voice, and in that moment she hated him.

She hated him for showing her that some sins had consequences too terrible to bear and that even innocence had a price. She hated him for showing her that love could be ugly.

She whirled to run, but he seized her from behind, wrapping one powerful arm around her and flinging her around. She fought him, going for his face with her nails, and he encircled her wrists in a bruising grip, twisting her arms behind her back. She opened her mouth, and he covered it with his own.

Beneath his kiss she tasted bitter, smoldering anger, yet her mouth opened wide to his. His lips softened, gentled. He let go of her wrists to tangle his fingers in her hair, bending her head back so that he could probe her mouth with his tongue. She seized his mouth like someone starving, tasting him, drinking of him. She kissed him back with all the passion of a girl's lost love and all the hunger of a woman yearning, needing, to rediscover love again. And the pain of it was too much, too much.

She tore free of him, backing away, her head shaking wildly back and forth. "Not again . . . not again."

She took off running, turning into an alley, not knowing where she was going, not caring. A dandy in purple-and-green-striped pantaloons spilled out the door of a smoke-filled coffeehouse, and she slammed into him.

He clasped her arms to steady her. "Well, well," he said. His breath, reeking of brandy and tobacco, wafted over her face. "What have we here?"

"Let her go," McCady said in a voice she had never

heard before. The dandy's gaze shot past her, and his fingers opened, releasing her. He held his gloved hands palms out in front him as he backed up. Then he spun around and walked rapidly away out the back end of the alley.

Jessalyn stood unmoving now, panting, fighting back tears. She kept her back to McCady as he came up to her. But when he planted himself in front of her, she slowly lifted her eyes to his. The face of the devil in a rage would look like that, she thought. Not hot but searing cold and utterly merciless. His hand clamped around her arm, his fingers digging into her flesh and heating the blood in her veins until she burned inside. He was being deliberately cruel, and all she could feel was a sweet, piercing pleasure at his touch.

She stared down at the fingers that gripped her so cruelly, those scarred and burned inventor's fingers, and the thought hit her with a violent jolt that she had never stopped loving this man. Even while hating him, still she had loved him. This man with his shadowed eyes and dark soul, and his stirring visions of iron horses and horseless carriages. This man who owned her heart in a way that no other man ever would.

Who owned her heart and didn't want it.

"Take your hand off me," she said.

His mouth tightened into a hard smile. "I am done assaulting your bloody virtue for tonight. But neither am I going to let you indulge in a childish tantrum and run alone through the streets."

He led her back out into the piazza. The fingers that had clasped her arm so cruelly now rubbed gentle circles on her bruised skin.

"I won't run. Just, please . . . don't touch me," she said, her voice choking.

He cast her a sharp look, but he let her go, whistling for the hackney. She heard him give the driver her direction, and she didn't even think to wonder how he came to know where she lived. They rode the short distance in a silence that crackled with tension. In the silvery flashes of light that penetrated beneath the carriage's hood, his expression seemed sharpened, more dangerous than ever.

The hackney was still rolling to a stop when she jumped out, not waiting for the steps to be lowered. She hit the pavement hard, stumbling a bit, then regained her balance, racing down the Adelphi Terrace that fronted the river. "Jessalyn, wait," he called after her. She fumbled with the front door of her town house, praying that Becka had remembered to leave it unbolted. His footsteps pounded on the stone behind her. The latch lifted, but one of the hinges was stiff; it had needed oiling for months now. Swearing like a drunken tinner, she pushed with panting desperation against the door, and at last, at last, it swung open. "Jessalyn!" His shadow, cast by the flaring streetlamp, fell over her, consuming her. "Jessalyn, goddammit . . ." She slipped inside.

He closed his hand around the jamb to keep her from shutting the door.

She shut it anyway, slamming it as hard as she could.

He snatched his hand back, cursing. She shot the bolt and sagged, gasping for breath, pressing her flushed cheek against the smoothly painted wood.

She thought she heard his receding footsteps, and she straightened to peek through the judas-hole. He stood across the terrace, leaning against the grilled railing that overlooked the river, his hair falling over his forehead. He was sucking on his knuckles and looking like a hurt and lonesome little boy. She wanted to go back out to him and hold his head to her breast and comfort him. She turned around and, pressing her back against the door, slid slowly to the floor. She hugged her legs, rubbing her face across the hard bones of her knees. A wetness seeped through her spangled hose. She touched her cheeks, shocked to discover they were wet and sticky with tears.

Napoleon came out from his bed beneath the stairs. He entwined himself around her legs, his loud purr grating like a watchman's rattle. But when she went to pet him, he bit her hand and streaked off, orange and white tail flying high. Even her cat didn't love her. The ridiculous thought brought out a soggy laugh and got her on her feet.

Becka had left a candle burning on the newel-post. On her way to her bedroom Jessalyn paused to open her grandmother's door. The old woman lay flat on her back on the bed, her hands outside the covers, straight at her sides, lying so still that Jessalyn went into the room and held her fingers to her grandmother's lips. She was not aware of the depth of her fear until she felt the knee-quivering wash of relief that came with the warm caress of her grandmother's breath. Lady Letty had to take so much laudanum now for her rheumatism that she slept like the dead through the night. Like the dead. Fear clutched again at Jessalyn's chest, the same fear she had felt that afternoon at Newmarket. It was a dread of loneliness, she knew. She couldn't bear the thought of life without Gram, of spending the years alone.

Once in her own room, she did not undress for bed. On the top shelf of her walnut wardrobe, shoved way in the back, was a bandbox. She had to stand on a chair to fetch it down. Inside was a little cottage bonnet made of chip straw and decorated with a posy of yellow silk primroses. The straw was cracked and unraveling at the brim, the silk flowers drooping and faded.

She put the hat on and studied herself in the round looking glass that was inset into the wardrobe's door.

It was a pretty little hat, but it was meant for a much younger girl, a girl just emerging from the schoolroom, awkward and giggly and apt to take herself much too seriously. A tightness squeezed Jessalyn's chest as she thought of the girl who had worn this hat that long-ago summer. For the first time she understood just how incredibly young she must have seemed to him.

Turning away from the mirror, she pulled off the hat with

a savage gesture. It was an old, useless thing, meant for the rubbish heap; she shouldn't have kept it.

Yet with care now, and gentleness, she put the hat back in the box, and as she did so, she noticed, beneath the tissue that lined the bottom, the corner of a green leather book. She took the book and went with it to the window seat. As she ran her palm over the embossed leather, the smell of mildew wafted up at her. She saw where splotches of black fur marred the gold gilt. The sight of the decay filled her with such a deep sadness her chest ached.

A primrose lay pressed against the flyleaf inside. It was nearly transparent, so dry she feared that if she so much as breathed on it, it would crumble into dust. Taking extra pains not to disturb the flower, she turned to the first page. The ink had faded, but she could still read the words.

I met a man today . . .

15

The front door opened with a squeal of its unoiled hinges, and Jessalyn jumped at the noise. She scooped up the stack of tradesmen's bills, shoving them beneath a pillow. She sat on the pillow, then snatched up Napoleon and the Weatherby Racing Calendar and planted them both in her lap. Settling back in an Egyptian couch with crocodile claw feet, she assumed what she hoped was a look of angelic innocence.

She heard Becka's voice in the front hall. That would be Gram coming home. Gram, who persisted in giving away money they didn't have. Just this afternoon she had gone to deliver a new pair of crutches to the rag-and-bone dealer's crippled son. And she had taken to buying so many baked potatoes from the thin, ragged girl who sold them on the corner that even Becka professed herself to be heartily sick of them. But Jessalyn couldn't ask Gram to economize on charity, and she didn't want to worry her. So she kept the mounting bills a secret and prayed for a turn in the abysmal Letty luck.

Jessalyn heaved a gusty sigh. The movement disturbed Napoleon, who let his displeasure be known by digging his claws into her thighs. He had grown into a crotchety cat, though still runty. He did not like London and had yet to forgive her for bringing him here.

Four years ago the Sarn't Major had come to Gram and said it was now or never if they were going to make one last run in the big races. So he had walked their string of horses to Newmarket, and she and Gram and Becka had taken the stagecoach. They had moved into her mother's house here in London, one in a square block of contiguous town houses called the Adelphi.

Outside, the house was made of brick, delicately ornamented with pilasters in the honeysuckle design. Inside, the beautiful classical rooms had been turned into something only Cleopatra would feel at home in. Lotus bowl chandeliers and walls papered with hieroglyphics and sphinxes, sideboards with water lily carvings, and chair backs shaped like coiling serpents. In the dining room stood a table made of a single piece of white marble in the shape of a sarcophagus.

Lady Letty couldn't enter a room without shuddering, and Becka claimed all the sphinxes and crocodiles gave her hillas. But Jessalyn secretly loved the house. She would wander the rooms, wondering about the woman who had lived here, the woman who had betrayed her husband and deserted her child to follow a Grand Passion. She would study her face in the looking glass, searching for that woman in herself. But her big mouth and fiery hair, her long lankiness were all Rosalie the bal-maiden's. She was a child of barren moors and sea-battered cliffs. Of that mysterious, exotic woman who had liked lions and lyres, she saw nothing.

That woman, the mother of her memory, had been fair and dainty with a whispering voice and an elusive, musical laugh. That woman had held her to her breast and kissed her forehead when she had fallen on the stairs and bumped it on the newel-post. It was the one clear memory she had of her mother. That woman must surely have loved her. But not enough to keep her.

The door to the drawing room opened, and Jessalyn lifted her head, expecting Gram.

"Oooh, me life and body!" exclaimed Becka Poole, exhaling a deep, shaky breath. She stood in the doorway, a goose wing duster in one hand and a piece of paper in the other. The scar was as red as a whiplash on her pale cheek.

Jessalyn jumped up, spilling Napoleon onto the floor. He hissed and swiped a paw at her skirts. "Becka? Have you taken ill?" A sudden fear stole her breath. "Is it Gram?"

Becka's raisin-colored eyes focused slowly on her mistress. "Twere a man."

"A man?

"A gennelman's gennelman. He brought this letter for ee." She held out the piece of paper clutched in her fist.

Jessalyn reached for it, but the girl wouldn't let it go. "Becka?"

"Eh?" Becka started, releasing her grip on the letter. "That gennelman's gennelman, miss—he were the hand-somest man I ever did see, with golden hair and strange eyes, all pale shimmery brown like brandy. Sadlike, they were. They put me in mind of the crucifixated Jesus in that painting what's in St. Paul's Cathedral. He looked at me with them eyes, an' I felt these contraptions low in me belly. Spasmslike." She started to rub her stomach, then noticed the duster in her hand. She stared at it as if she'd never seen it before. "Never have I felt such a wambling of me innards afore. Mebbe he be the devil in the disguise of an angel what tried t' put a hex on me. 'Tes a good thing I be wearin' me hagstone."

She shuddered dramatically, touching the leather cord at her neck. "Cor, miss, I looked up into them eyes of his an' nearly perspired right there at his feet!"

Jessalyn deftly turned a laugh into a cough. "Perhaps you ought to lie down for an hour or so to calm your nerves."

"Ais, miss. A lie down would do me proper. Me nerves be scattered something fierce."

Becka left, moving like a sleepwalker. Jessalyn smoothed

out the crinkles in her letter. She felt a shiver of excitement, for no one had ever sent her a letter before. It was expensive hot-pressed paper, creamy and gilt-edged. She broke the wafer and unfolded the paper, and a bank note floated to the floor. There were five of them—five ten-pound bank notes. His direction was embossed at the top, but the only thing written on the paper was a signature: "Caerhays" in bold black handwriting.

A cold anger filled Jessalyn as she left the drawing room and climbed the stairs to her bedroom. With calm deliberation, she changed into an old kerseymere walking dress with a matching spencer. There was an ink stain on the cuff, and the cloth was of a color that resembled the sludge that collected in the London gutters when it rained. She could not remember when or where she had acquired the hideous thing, but it would certainly serve her purpose today. Today she wanted him to see that she cared not the slightest whether she impressed him or not, as she set about telling him where he could go with his bank notes and what he could do with them when he got there.

Her hair was braided in a coronet on top of her head, and she left it alone, merely covering it with the ugliest hat she could find, a plain black poke bonnet. Within a bare ten minutes she was in a sedan chair, being carried to a certain earl's lodgings on St. James's Street.

They had just turned off Piccadilly when the chair was dropped with a sudden jolt that rattled her teeth. She could hear shouts and the pounding of feet; then something hit the chair with a thud, rocking it so hard it nearly tipped over. Fearing a riot, she cautiously raised the window shade and leaned out.

A coal wagon had run into a huge dray loaded with chickens in crates, spilling black briquettes and squawking fowls into the street. It seemed that all London, including her chairmen, had converged on the scene to make off with the chickens and the fuel to cook them with.

Jessalyn got down to walk the rest of the way, leaving the

money for her fare tucked in the frayed satin seat. Chicken feathers swirled and floated in the air. The fog had worsened considerably since that morning. It was like being smothered by heavy, foul-smelling fleece. Her eyes burned, and she tasted coal soot when she swallowed.

At last Jessalyn spotted the building she was looking for. But a group of young bloods was between her and it, lounging against the stone bollards that separated the sidewalk from the street. In unison they lifted their quizzing glasses and ogled her, clucking like the chickens as she came toward them.

Jessalyn stared through them as if they did not exist. One thrust his walking stick into her path, and she went around it. Another stuck out his boot, catching her skirt with his spur. She jerked, and the material came free with a rip. She was shaking, and her palms were sweating in her limerick gloves by the time she gave the iron bellpull a tug.

The stranger who opened the door was the most beautiful man she had ever seen, with gentle golden brown eyes and a finely sculpted head topped by short blond curls. He was wearing only a shirt and buckskins, and the muscles in his arms and legs were like anchor chains. He could have been cast in bronze and mounted in a museum and not looked out of place. Jessalyn realized suddenly that she was staring at him with her mouth gaping open.

"Guid afternoon, Miss Letty," he said, his voice melodious with a Scottish lilt.

Jessalyn hesitated, surprised the man seemed to know her. "Is this where Lord Caerhays— Is he expecting me?"

"His nibs's precise words were—begging yer pairdon, miss—that once I had delivered his missive, I should expect ye here within the hour, clacking like a dog with a can tied to its tail. If ye come in, I'll go and wake him."

"So Caerhays is still abed in the middle of the afternoon, is he?" Jessalyn said, stepping into the narrow vestibule. "Did his lordship get foxed last night?"

He turned his eyes on to her, eyes that were the exact

color of brandy when warmed by a candle flame. Yet they held a tinge of sadness, like those of a gentle and forgiving priest who still couldn't help being disappointed by the foibles of his flock. "Aweel," he said softly, "far be it for me to comment on his nibs's nocturnal habits, miss. But he spent the wee hours in a Jermyn Street hell. Drinking, gaming. He tells me such things are what earls do."

"They are the sort of things the mad earls of Caerhays do," Jessalyn said.

He let loose with a sigh as mournful as a funeral bell. "Tis in the bluid, I fear. When the bluid wears thin, it becomes susceptible to mental afflictions. This way, if ye please, miss."

With an air of stately gloom he led her up the narrow stairs to the modest bachelor lodgings. Jessalyn followed, wondering if the man was playing some game at her expanse, for he was unlike any manservant she had ever encountered, with his beautiful face and his salty Scottish brogue peppered with London cant.

He ushered her into an apple green parlor that was cheerful even in the dim light of a foggy day. The room was elegantly appointed, with carved pine paneling and light satinwood furnishings. But it also had a lived-in look: A pair of boots lay kicked off beside a reading chair; riding gloves and a crop had been left on the mantel. A patent lamp cast a warm glow over a desk, where that morning's *Times* lay ironed and cut, beside a dog-eared issue of *Mechanics Magazine*.

The door opened behind her, and Jessalyn whirled, her heart thudding.

But it was only the manservant, back again and bearing a tray. The smell of coffee and toasted crumpets filled the room.

"If ye've come to return the blunt, miss," he said, "ye might want to suggest to his nibs that he toss a wee bit of it in my direction. We've been so let to pockets around here I've holes in my stockings ye could put a fist through." He had set the tray down on the desk, and now he pointed to a glass of cloudy liquid that sat next to the japanned iron coffeepot. "And see that his nibs drinks his tar-water. For if he awakes with the very devil of a heid, I should not be surprised."

Jessalyn thought she saw laughter lurking in the man's remarkable eyes, although his mouth remained turned down like an inverted bowl. "How long have you been with Lord Caerhays, Mr . . . ?"

"I go by the moniker of Duncan," he said, and suddenly she could have sworn that he winked at her. "Although I'm not saying I was born with it, ye mind. I was his nibs's batman in the war. Now I'm his valet when he wants to act all dukey and put on airs. Aweel, life was simpler before he became a swell, that I can tell ye. Give him a hot supper and a dry cot and he'd purr like a kit. Now he's got a railway to build and debts so's he can't sleep come night— no matter that 'tis on a feather mattress—and a bruither what goes pegging off and leaves him with a title he don't want and even more debts. 'Tis enough to choke a man." He paused at the door to heave a great mournful sigh. "The army was simpler, miss. Then all I had to worry aboot was him getting some beef-witted notion in his noddle to be a hero and get himself killed."

Jessalyn said nothing. She didn't want to hear about Mc-Cady's troubles. She didn't want to start feeling sorry for him when feeling anything for him at all was so dangerous to her vulnerable heart.

The door closed behind the manservant with a gentle click. Left alone to wait, Jessalyn made a slow circuit of the room.

Thrust into one corner stood an old table heaped with draft drawings. Half of the scarred oaken surface was taken up with the model of an iron horse that ran around a minia-ture circular track. The locomotive was similar to the one she had ridden on that long-ago summer, except this boiler was more streamlined and the—the *cylinders,* he had called them, now slanted upward at sharp angles, so that they resembled a grasshopper's legs. The model engine had tiny carriages and wagons hitched to the back of it. A tightness squeezed Jessalyn's chest as she imagined cartloads of people and goods being whisked from one end of England to the other on McCady Trelawny's incredible invention.

McCady Trelawny's incredible folly.

For that was what they were calling it—Trelawny's Folly. Although she could never forgive the callous, jaded lieutenant who had rejected her, there had been times during the years while reading the ridiculing stories in the newspapers when she had wanted to weep for the young man with a fire in his eyes who had taken her for a ride on his marvelous locomotive.

Experts had been quoted, saying that crops would be ruined by the belching smoke and fields set afire by spewing cinders. Cattle would be scared into infertility by the dreadful noise. The passengers and freight Trelawny hoped to carry on his infamous railway all would be blown to smithereens. One man had even attempted to prove, with charts and diagrams, how all that steam being released into the air would affect the tides, causing a great wave that would rise up and swallow the whole island of Britain.

Lieutenant Trelawny, the papers said, had threatened to drown the man in a horse trough. And Jessalyn, reading it, had ached for him. She kept seeing his face the way it had been on that day of the Tiltwells' Midsummer's Day house party, when the passionate fire in his eyes had been doused by ridiculing laughter.

Only once had she read anything the least positive about the potential of rail transportation. The article had mentioned all the innovations in Trelawny's new steam locomotive. Most had been too technical for her to understand. Except for one: He had invented a new type of rail that rested on sleepers made of rolled iron that would not crumble under the heavy weight of the engine the way the Tiltwells' tramway had broken into pieces that summer. No longer were passengers in danger of being tossed out onto their dairy-airs and into prickly gorse bushes.

She was smiling as she thought of this when something spangled caught her eye. It was partially covered by a crumpled piece of draft paper. It was the bird mask that she had been wearing last night, with its lacquered feathers and crooked beak. She picked it up—

"Good afternoon, Miss Letty."

She stood in profile to him, the light from the wall sconce illuminating her face so that it looked soft and smooth like clotted cream. An ugly black hat covered her hair, yet tiny wisps had fought free to lie against her cheek like licks of flame. Five years of trying to forget, and all it had taken was one look at her and he had never wanted any woman more.

At his greeting, her fingers squeezed the mask so tightly it cracked, making a sound like the discharge of a pistol. Now she turned slowly to face him. Dark smudges lay like old bruises under her eyes, and her lower lip looked even fuller than usual. Deliberately he kept to the shadows of the doorway. He thrust the tips of his fingers into the waistband of his riding breeches and leaned against the jamb. A tense silence filled the room; it thrummed like a battle drum in his blood.

"How did you know it was I?" she finally said. "Last night, I mean . . ."

His gaze went to the mask in her hands, then back to her face. "I would know you anywhere."

The words were the most intimate he had ever spoken to her. He wished he hadn't said them because in the end they were only words. The bruised look didn't leave her face, and the mask trembled in her hands as she laid it back down on the table.

He came toward her, then past her. He was not dressed; that is, he wore only a shirt and riding breeches. Nor had he shaved. He wasn't in the mood to play the part of the gallant today.

He picked up the glass of tar-water off the tray, grimaced at it, then poured it into a pot that held a pathetic fern with curling brown fronds. It was where the tar-water disappeared every morning. Duncan thought the plant had some sort of mite. He'd been dosing it with julep elixir all summer.

Since he could not trust himself to look at her, McCady stared out the window. Fog had condensed on the glass, trickling down in miniature rivers. A laundress walked by in the street below, a bundle of dirty linen lashed to her head. The clap of her clogs on the cobbles echoed in the thick air beyond the window, almost drowning out the tick of the gilt clock on the mantel.

At last he turned around. She stood in the center of the Turkey carpet, rail-slat thin and wearing something that looked as if it had been plucked straight off the back of a Spitalfields washerwoman, and still, he wanted to take her face in his hands and kiss her mouth, and he almost hated her for it. He didn't need her in his life, couldn't *afford* to need her, and that was the end of it.

He studied her out of angry, narrowed eyes. "That dress is utterly appalling," he said.

"Do you think so?" She looked down at herself, and a secret little smile hovered at the corners of her mouth. "I'm actually rather fond of it."

He started to laugh and wound up wincing as pain shot through his head. "Bloody hell . . . Do sit down, Miss Letty."

Not waiting for her to obey him, he sprawled into the chair behind the desk, leaning his elbows on the stained blotter. He pressed his thumbs into his closed lids. The pounding in his temple was louder than a bal-maiden spalling ore. "God." He sighed, rubbing his hand over his beard-roughened face and up through his hair. "I have—"

"The very devil of a heid?"

He lifted his aching head to stare up at her out of eyes that felt as dry and brittle as seed husks.

She laughed then, a sound that was breathless and rusty. His chest tightened, making it difficult to breathe. "Such are the wages of sin, my lord," she said, and laughed again. "Pity you couldn't bank them, for you would be a rich man."

"Sit down," he snapped. "And quit looking so bloody smug."

She settled gracefully into a chair and folded her gloved hands in her lap. Her gaze met his, soft and gray and cool as a dawn sky. Her composure surprised him. He wanted to rip into it, to tear it in two like a pocket handkerchief.

"What are you doing here?" he demanded. "Aside, of course, from courting trouble again like a lusty scullery maid."

Her eyes widened, and the gray sky darkened. "Why, whatever do you mean? My lord."

"I mean, Miss Letty, that ladies do not come unescorted to a gentleman's lodgings. Should anyone of any consequence at all have seen you enter my door, your reputation will no longer be worth a tin cup to spit in. You will be utterly destroyed in Society's eyes."

She actually had the audacity to smile at him. "For an avowed rake you seem overly concerned lately about Society's eyes. But I did not came here to bandy words with you. I came for—"

"Seduction."

That stiffened her spine like a ramrod. "Seduction?"

"Your purpose in coming here. Why else would a woman come alone to a man's lodgings unless it is for the purpose of allowing herself to be seduced?"

She jerked open the ties of a battered red morocco reticule and pulled out the folded bank notes he had sent her that morning. From the expression on her face he expected her to fling them at his head. Instead she stood up, laid them on the desk before him, then sat back down again. "I will not be your ladybird."

Smiling suddenly, he leaned back. He stretched out his

legs, linking his fingers behind his head, elbows spread
wide. The movement pulled his shirt open at the neck. He
could feel her gaze there, like a warm sigh.

He pitched his voice low. "But I could make you sing
with pleasure, Jessalyn."

Her bosom swelled as she sucked in a deep breath. She
swallowed, hard. "I am not a green girl anymore. I'm not as
impressionable. I'm not as impressed with you. My lord."

"I am devastated to hear that." He stood up and circled
the desk, coming toward her. Came until his thighs pressed
against her knees, pressed until he could feel the heat of
her. "Because I"—he leaned over and rested his hand
against her face, tilting her head—"still have a weakness"
—he played his thumb against the corner of her mouth
until her lips softened and parted. Slowly he lowered his
head, bringing his lips within a sigh of hers—"for leggy
redheads." He kept his mouth close to hers, breathing on
her lips until her lids began to flutter.

He plucked a feather off the brim of the ugly black bonnet. He picked another off the front of her bodice, where
her breasts pushed out the braided front of her drab spencer.

He brushed the feathers along the bone of her jaw.
"Have you been cleaning out a chicken coop?"

She held herself still, as if she thought she would break if
she so much as breathed.

He brought the feathers up to caress her lips. He heard
her trap a moan deep in her throat. The scent of her, of
Pears primrose soap and warm woman, swam to his head
like brandy. His breath faltered and then came back, fast
and uneven. *Seduction.* He had set out to seduce her, and
he was the one being seduced.

"I want you," he said. He dropped the feathers and
traced the wide line of her mouth with his fingers this time.
Her mouth . . . whoever drank of her mouth was thirsty
forever. "I want you in my bed, Jessalyn. And you want to
be there."

All the color seemed to have collected in bright bands across her cheekbones, leaving her lips bloodless. She shook her head slowly, back and forth. "No."

"Yes."

Her breasts shuddered with her uneven breath. She looked up at him out of eyes that were as dark and turbulent as an autumn rainstorm. She started to push herself out of the chair at the same time that he grasped her arms to haul her out of it. Her reticule slipped from her lap to the floor, spilling its contents, but neither of them noticed. He touched his lips to hers.

And the world caught fire. Desire and need surged through him with such force that he swayed, his fingers gripping deep furrows in the rough material of her spencer. His tongue slipped between her parted lips to fill her mouth, and nothing had ever tasted more wonderful than Jessalyn, sweet Jessa . . .

A moan vibrated deep in his throat. His palm slid down to the small of her back, and he pressed her into him, grinding his hardness against the softness of her belly. Her roaming hands burned him, claimed him.

She slanted her mouth away from his, her breath blowing hot on his cheek. "McCady, please . . . we must stop." Her fists gripped his shirt, but instead of pushing him away, she pulled him tighter against her. "I love you too much. I—"

Every muscle in his body went rigid, and he thrust her away from him. "Don't say that."

She certainly hadn't meant to say it. Her fist was pressed against her mouth. Her eyes looked haunted by something so deep it was beyond words.

But then her hand fell from her mouth, and she lifted her chin into the air, a woman prepared to do battle. And if he could have, he would have smiled. "I can't help what I feel," she said. "I love you."

He gave a sudden sharp jerk of his head, backing away from her. "Don't feel it. Don't even think it." He backed another step until he bumped up against the edge of the desk. He shook his head again, trying to clear it of the roaring blood still pumping hard through his veins. "What you think you feel—it doesn't exist beyond a commodity for sale in Covent Garden. No different from a head of lettuce or a basket of oranges. And just as perishable, just as cheap." He drew in a deep breath and expelled it slowly, trying to ease the tightness in his chest. "Jessalyn . . . I can't give you what you want."

She regarded him carefully out of solemn gray eyes, her head slightly cocked. "What is it that you think I want, McCady?"

"What all women want. Promises no man can ever keep —forever and happily-ever-after." *Love,* he thought. But he didn't believe in the word, so he was careful never to use it. He had never told a woman he loved her. It was part of not making promises he had no intention of keeping. "You want marriage." His hand slashed through the air, cutting off any protest she might have made. "I can't give it to you, Jessalyn, even if I wanted to. My brother has saddled me with a gaming debt that honor demands I must pay at a time when I've barely a groat to bless myself with. My grand scheme to build a railway is a national joke, and I am on the precipice of being flung into debtor's prison. To put it bluntly, sweetling, I need a rich wife."

For a moment a trace of a strange smile softened the grave curve of her mouth. "And I still haven't two beans to boil together to make soup."

She stood tall before him, her eyes, calm and wise, searching his face. This was not the same Jessalyn who had stood on a beach of white sand and blue water and begged him not to leave her. And still, he ached for her with a hunger that was a heavy, hollow feeling in his gut.

"Very well," she said. "You cannot love me, and you cannot offer me marriage. Then what *can* you give me?"

The blunt honesty of the question startled him, but the answer rose easily to his lips. It was an answer he had given many times before, to many other women. "Pleasure," he said. "For as long as it lasts."

Again that strange little smile. "You want me to be your ladybird. Until you tire of me."

His mouth took on a cynical twist. "You are much more likely to tire of me first."

She turned her back on him, going to the window. She held aside the mulberry brocade curtain. Her hand looked slender and vulnerable against the heavy dark material. He could see the white of her face reflected in the watery glass, but not her expression. His body felt heavy, his blood thick with desire.

"I want you, Jessalyn," he said, and saw a shudder ripple across her back. "I want to kiss your mouth. I want to hold your naked breasts in my hands. I want to lay you down on my bed and bury myself inside your wet heat and make you mine."

She was trembling at his words, but she wouldn't look at him. He pictured himself crossing the room and taking her in his arms. He knew that if he did that, she would be unable to resist what was between them, what had always been between them. But as always with her, something held him back: strange protective feelings he didn't want and didn't know what to do with.

He began to measure the lengthening silence with each tick of the clock. At last she turned to face him. He could see nothing in her eyes now but himself, reflected into eternity. "I deserve more, McCady. And so do you."

She knelt on the floor to retrieve her reticule. She stayed in that position a moment, her back curved and taut, like a bow strung too tightly. He wasn't going to beg. He had never begged a woman before, and he wasn't going to start now.

She pushed herself to her feet and headed for the door. "Jessalyn."

She turned, and the sconce caught the brittle shimmer of unshed tears in her eyes.

He picked the bank notes up off the desk. "You will take these with you."

Mutely she shook her head.

"Take them, Miss Letty. Or I shall have a word with my starchy, sobersides cousin. He should find it most edifying to learn that his betrothed is in such straitened circumstances that she was forced to gallop around the Vauxhall rotunda in spangled tights."

She sucked in a sharp breath. "You would not dare to stoop so low as to tell Clarence."

"When one is as sunk in the depths of depravity as I, one gets used to stooping." He gripped her wrist and pressed the stiff paper into her hand. He could feel the beat of her blood, hard and fast, beneath the softness of her skin. "Take them."

Her fingers opened, and the notes floated to the floor. "Tell Clarence the whole, then, if it pleases you to hurt me. But I will not take your money. Not even if I had chosen to become your ladybird would I have taken your money, my lord."

He let go of her wrist, but the pounding of her pulse echoed in his blood. He nodded to her, his head stiff. "Duncan will see you home in a hackney."

The manservant appeared on cue, a grim look on his handsome face. "I've got one all ready and waiting, miss. Those loungers who gave ye that wee bit of trouble earlier are still littering the street. Young coxcombs and fribblers, with nothing better to do than . . ." He trailed off as he caught the expression on his lordship's face. "Now, don't ye go getting all murderous on me, sir, else ye'll be winding up in gaol sooner than they can bankrupt ye there, and with a hanging charge wrapped around yer neck. I'll see the lass comes to nae harm."

McCady's hands uncurled as the desire to smash his fists into nameless faces slowly faded. Duncan would see her safe. He didn't want to let her go, but every line of Jessalyn's body shrieked that she wanted to be away from him.

He watched her follow Duncan down the stairs and out the door. Back within the apple green parlor he went to the window. The hackney driver ran up to lower the steps, and she paused. Her face, turned in profile, shone like a half-moon in the fog. A tendril of hair, bright as a sunrise, slashed across her cheek.

He gripped the curtain as if he needed it to hold himself up. He wanted her so badly he could scarcely breathe from the pain of it.

The driver closed the door and climbed into his box. The hackney rolled into the street with a jingle of harness and a clatter of wheels. Yellow fog swirled and eddied, swallowing the black carriage, and she was gone.

Hands clenched, he threw back his head, the tendons of his neck standing out like ropes. "Jessalyn!" he shouted.

And slammed his fist into the window. He didn't hear the shattering tinkle of falling glass, or see his blood splashing in bright starburst patterns on the parquet floor. She was gone, and all that was left was a vast emptiness and the echo of his heart, knocking like a wheel out of gear.

He wanted her, wanted her, wanted her. . . .

16

The two hundred doeskin bags made a pile the size of a hayrick in the middle of the thick Brussels carpet in Aloysius Hamilton's elegant coffee room.

"Quite a sight, ain't it?" the corn merchant said. He hefted one of the bags in his big hand, then let it fall with a satisfying jangle. "Twenty thousand pounds in gold. Don't suppose you'll be wanting to count 'em, eh?" He bellowed a laugh, which trailed off when the man beside him did not even furnish an answering smile.

"Are you certain you wouldn't prefer to take a promissory note after all?" Aloysius felt obliged to ask, though he fervently hoped not. Just the logistics of converting the twenty thousand pounds into gold sovereigns and conveying them to his Mayfair mansion had taxed even his considerable organizational skills. And he'd spent all of last night sweating like a spit goose with fear that thieves would make off with the fortune, in spite of the veritable army of Bow Street runners he'd hired as guards. He hated to think that it could now all have been for naught.

Yet the earl didn't seem either pleased or displeased with the proof of Aloysius Hamilton's efforts. He merely stared at the hill of money bags, an attitude of weary disdain on his highbred face. "Let's get on with it, shall we?" he said.

Aloysius led his guest to the end of the room, where a pair of imperial chairs addressed each other across the expanse of an elegant walnut desk. He wondered at the earl's limp, but given the man's morose mood, he thought it best to keep his wonderings to himself. They took their seats, and Aloysius positioned a document adorned with ribbons and seals before the earl.

"Just affix your name to the last page, my lord, directly after mine."

After the briefest hesitation the earl reached for the weighty papers. "If it wouldn't inconvenience you, I should like to read it over one last time."

"Eh? Oh, aye, aye. Of course. Take your time. All the time you need."

A thick silence settled over the room. Aloysius toyed with the jeweled rings and gold seals on his fob, then busied himself with twisting the tightly curled ends of his waxed mustaches. His wife kept nattering at him to shave them off, said they weren't fashionable. But he would almost rather walk into the Bank of England with a bare arse than bare his upper lip. He was never going to be one of the Bow Street set anyway. He was a nabob; whatever small social status he achieved, he had to buy.

Aloysius stole another look at the earl. A gold earring winked in the dark hair that hung ragged and long over the stiff velvet collar of his fashionable tail coat. The man looked like a damned Gypsy, yet somehow he managed to carry it off. Such a thing was bred into one's blood and bones, Aloysius supposed: how to dress, how to behave, how to think. Take this matter of honor. The man might be a scapegrace, but he possessed a strict code of honor that Aloysius, the corn merchant, only dimly understood. The twenty thousand pounds, for instance—*all* of it would go to pay off the gaming vowels of the earl's brother, who had been caught cheating at cards and so had put a pistol to his head.

Honor. Tailor and butcher bills could go unpaid for

years, but gaming vowels were debts of honor and had to be settled before all others. His father could die in a drunken stupor, his brothers could turn themselves into opium eaters and whoremongers, but honor dictated that as the heir to the title the young earl must now make good on every shilling of those vowels. As an English gentleman he could do no less.

"I trust you find it all in order," Aloysius said when the earl looked up from his perusal of the document.

The earl said nothing, merely reached for the standish, and Aloysius noticed for the first time the bloodstained bandage wrapped around the knuckles of the man's right hand. "Been engaging in a bout of fisticuffs, eh?"

The fingers of the injured hand curled slightly. "Only with myself."

"You ought to have a care with it. I had a brother who died of a cut that became septic. . . ." Aloysius's voice trailed off. The earl in his arrogance would doubtless have little sympathy for the fate of a poor collier's son.

Aloysius's jowls sunk back into the starched points of his shirt collar as he watched the fine-boned fingers ink the pen. He bit back a smile of satisfaction at the scratching sound of the nub moving across the paper. Until this moment he had been half convinced that when it came right down to it, his mount would balk at the fence.

The earl's hand shook slightly as he replaced the pen in its stand. Slowly he raised his head, and for a moment Aloysius thought those dark eyes glittered with a raw and savage pain. But then he shuttered them with his lids.

Aloysius nodded at the pile of money bags. "That lot all goes to pay off your brother's vowels, does it not?"

"Money easily earned is easily spent," the earl said with a wry twist of his lips.

"And have you considered, then, my other offer—to buy the BRC from you?"

The earl lifted a haughty brow. "You have just acquired my body and soul. Isn't that enough?"

Aloysius had not become one of the richest men in England by being timid. When he got a man down, the man stayed down—even a damned peer of the realm.

He fixed the earl with a hard stare. His eyes were the color of spittle, and he knew how to make them go empty and cold. "Rumor has it you need to come up with at least ten thousand pounds in ten months or your company goes bust and you go to gaol. The way I see it you have little choice, dear boy. You're going to sell it to me either now or later." He flicked a finger at the sheaf of papers that lay between them. "Because if you insist upon using the twenty thousand I have just paid you to buy back your precious honor, then you're going to have to make short work of it, dear boy, to *earn* the remainder of the settlement before July."

The earl leaned forward, and something wild and desperate and dangerous flashed in his eyes. "When you buy yourself a stud, *dear boy,* it is for one thing only. I wager you a thousand pounds the girl is breeding within a month after the wedding."

"Done, by Jove!"

Leaning back, Aloysius hooked a thumb into his fob pocket and barked a laugh. He'd bought himself a peer, by God—body and soul. And he'd have the lad's company, too, in the end. Aloysius Hamilton might be a corn merchant, but a man did not become one of the richest men in England by putting all his eggs in one basket. And he had more than a few of those eggs nested in coaching inns the length and breadth of England, coaching inns that would lose a lot of trade should bleedin' railways start crisscrossing the countryside like a chess board. No, as Aloysius saw it, there were only two ways to deal with competition like that: either absorb it or destroy it.

All in all, Aloysius thought, he was pleased with this evening's work, though it had cost him a tidy fifty thousand pounds. Twenty in exchange for a signature on the nuptial settlement, and an additional thirty to be paid over on the day the first boy child made an appearance in this world. In some ways, he hardly cared whether it happened as soon as ten months, thereby costing him his wager and a shot at the railway company. For on that blessed day, he—Aloysius Hamilton, nabob corn merchant and son of a collier—would become grandfather to a title.

A flash of white muslin flickered in the window, catching his eye. Aloysius stood, tugging his silk pistachio-and-cream-striped waistcoat down over the bulge of his stomach. "Come, my lord," he said, gesturing at the French doors that opened onto a pleasing vista of clipped evergreens and leaden statues, and a young woman with gilded hair and a shy and gentle smile. "I believe you have something of particular import to ask my daughter, eh?"

It was more of a heaven than a hell.

Or so thought the young bloods who frequented the Jermyn Street house—it was what heaven would be were God a gaming man.

It wasn't much from the outside, with an iron-grilled door that required a password to get through. But inside spread a palatial hall ablaze with chandeliers and scented candles. In the dining room the board groaned beneath such delicacies as roasted swan with chevreuil sauce and larded sweetmeats. Upstairs were mirrored ceilings and satin sheets and women of easy virtue to enjoy them with.

But the gaming room was the pulsating heart of the house. There the dark paneled walls stood bare of ornament and paintings, so as not to distract the players from their game. There tense silence reigned, broken only by the ring of a crystal glass, the click of a snuffbox, the rattle of dice. There the play was very deep and only a little dirty.

And there Lady Margaret Atwood, mistress of it all, floated around the room in a black sarcenet evening dress, a sable tippet, and a choker of twelve diamonds that were each as big as a man's thumbnail and very real.

She would stop to whisper in an ear here, to caress a

cheek there, but she always kept a careful eye on the play. She watched to see that the croupiers were fleecing her customers and not herself and that the flashers were busy earning their keep, luring fresh pigeons into her net.

It was hard for her to remember sometimes that she had been born to gentler pursuits. The daughter of an ambitious vicar, she had been married at sixteen to a viscount three times her age. He had been a four-bottle man, had Lord Atwood. Every night after dinner he sat alone at the worm-eaten table in his moldy castle and put away four bottles of claret. One night he broached a fifth and didn't live to see the morning. That was when she had learned that a widow's personal property could be sold to cover her husband's debts.

That was when she became a whore.

Oh, she minced no words about what she was. A woman who sold her body for money was a whore, whether she did it for five shillings or a gaming house on Jermyn Street. She didn't have to sell her body anymore, but when she looked in the mirror, she still saw a whore. It was the eyes. When you did certain things, when certain things were done to you, it left shadows in the eyes that never went away.

Lady Atwood paused to watch the play at a whist table. One of the players was her man, a puff, who bet deeply with the house's money and thus encouraged others to follow suit. The puff was working on a plump young pigeon— Lord Sterns, who was heir to a dukedom with a handsome allowance, a gaming habit, and little skill at the cards. Tonight the lordling looked more the fool than usual, for he was wearing his coat inside out to bring him luck. He was going to need it. He was playing against Nigel Payne, who was very good indeed and merciless with his victims. It was Nigel who had taken poor Stephen Trelawny for twenty thousand pounds and then hounded the man to suicide by accusing him of cheating and demanding that the vowels be settled at once.

Nigel flashed a sly grin as he glanced up at Lady Atwood

from beneath the broad-brimmed straw hat he wore to cut
down the glare from the chandeliers. At the moment there
was only a modest stack of ivory fishes next to the candle
dish in his corner, but she knew the pile would grow considerably before dawn lightened the sky. The trouble with
Nigel was that he had a tendency to pluck *her* pigeons.

Nigel adjusted his leather cuff protectors. He was about
to deal the cards when the door opened and the already
quiet room fell still as a church on Monday morning.

The earl of Caerhays entered the room, and it was as if
something wild and fierce had been let loose to prowl her
house. Lady Atwood felt her heartbeat quicken, a thing that
hadn't happened to her in quite some time.

The earl was followed by a strapping blond fellow, carrying a musket in one big hand and a pistol tucked through
his belt for good measure, and Lady Atwood feared there
was about to be blood spilled on her expensive Axminster
carpet. The golden god was followed in turn by men wheeling barrows loaded with dozens of small brown leather
bags.

Caerhays stopped before Nigel and blessed him with a
languid smile. "Evening, Payne." He picked up one of the
leather bags, pulled open the string, and emptied it on the
table. Gold sovereigns spilled across the green baize, winking and spinning in the bright light. "Twenty thousand
canaries. Would you care to count them?"

Nigel's narrow eyes flickered to the money, and he
cleared his throat. "Course not, Caerhays. Trust you. Word
of a gentleman and all that."

"Quite. Might I suggest you use some of it to buy yourself a pistol."

Nigel's face turned the color of old suet, and a muscle
began to tic beneath his right eye. "Do—do you mean to
call me out?"

"Whyever would I want to do that?" Caerhays drawled,
with a mocking lift of one dark brow. "On the contrary, it is
the matter of your continued good health that concerns me.

It is dangerous to carry such a large sum through the streets of London. Such a target for thieves and footpads, don't you know."

"But what am I . . . my God. Banks are closed." Nigel's gaze widened as he took in the size of the barrows and the number of bags each contained. He suddenly realized that the big fellow with the barking irons and his cronies all had vanished, leaving him holding the bag. Two hundred bags, to be precise. Two hundred bags of gold, to be even more precise. "Can hardly expect me to—to—I protest this, sir . . ." But he was speaking to the earl's disappearing back.

The silent room suddenly erupted into chatter and nervous laughter. Lady Atwood gave the gamester a gentle pat on the shoulder. "Darling Nigel, I am certain you'll be wanting to remove yourself from my premises at once. My servants will see you and your golden canaries to the door," she said, with emphasis on the last word, thereby implying that the door was the farthest they would see him to. Once out on the street, Nigel would be on his own.

The gambler would be on his own, and all his gold be snatched, disappearing into London's wretched rookeries. It was a sardonic stroke of revenge worthy of a Trelawny. The debt of honor would be settled, and London's poor would eat heartily and sleep warmly tonight at Nigel Payne's expense.

Lord Caerhays had almost escaped by the time she caught up with him. She slipped her arm through his and steered him down the hall. "McCady, you naughty boy, you cannot possibly be leaving. Not when I haven't seen you for ages."

At a sharp nod of her head, a handsome young footman resplendent in livery and powdered wig opened the door to the green salon. "Fetch us some champagne," she said, not bothering to look in the servant's direction.

The room was too hot, and she moved the pole screen in front of the fire. A faint memory of hashish lingered in the air from last night's debauch. Its scent of sweet decay clung to the opulently upholstered furniture and the heavy green velvet curtains. The windows ought to have been opened that afternoon, and the wilting flowers that graced the cut-crystal vases and bowls replaced. Such lack of attention, she vowed, would cost the majordomo his job on the morrow.

After the servant had poured the champagne and quit the room, she lounged back on a midnight black sofa. She knew the opaque velvet complemented the vivid brightness of her henna-washed hair and the whiteness of the skin she bathed nightly with distilled pineapple water. She sipped at the sparkling iced wine, enjoying the tingle of it on the roof of her mouth and the sight of McCady Trelawny looking blatantly virile in a dark blue tail coat and thigh-hugging cream pantaloons.

There was a wildness about him tonight that stirred her. She wondered what he had done to get his hands on so much money, for she'd heard he hadn't a feather to fly with. She hoped it wasn't anything that would land him in New-gate, though in truth she wouldn't put it past him to have robbed the National Treasury.

She had known all three of the Trelawny boys for years— much too handsome for their or anyone else's good; sullen, proud, and filled with such joyless restlessness. Hell-bent on self-destruction, they drugged themselves with pleasure and flirted with danger, courting their destiny of disgrace and violent death with wild abandon. But a part of her had always hoped that McCady would somehow find a way to escape his fate.

She had never forgotten the first time she had seen him, the night his older brothers had brought him to this house. So young he had been, a mere boy. Too young to understand what was being been done to him. Until that next morning—after a night of debauchery that had put even herself to the blush—when she had seen the shadows in his dark Trelawny eyes and known that deep within him something that was gentle and good had been brutalized beyond repair.

"McCady?"

He turned, still lost in thought, and for a moment all his defenses were down, and she was shocked by what she saw in his eyes.

She had seen those eyes hard and sharp as an ax blade as he wagered more than he could afford on the turn of a card. She had seen them looming above her in the night, hot and glowing with passion. She had seen them turn dull and remote with self-disgust the morning after. But she had never seen them as they were now, filled with such raw pain. Whatever or whoever had hurt him—it had gone soul-deep.

He noticed her studying him, and he lowered his lids, hiding his thoughts. His mouth curved into a cynical smile. Only she, who knew him well, saw that it lacked his usual bravado.

He tilted his champagne glass at her in a mocking toast. "You ought to congratulate me, Maggie. I'm about to become a married man."

She felt a sharp and unexpected pain in her chest. "So it has happened to you at last," she said, and her smile felt tight. "What is she like—this girl who has managed to capture a wicked Trelawny's heart?"

He lifted a shoulder in a dismissive shrug. "I haven't the vaguest notion what she's like. I only met the chit for the first time two hours ago."

"The money. I see . . ." The odd tightness in her chest eased somewhat. She rubbed her finger around the rim of the champagne glass, making it sing a mournful hymn. "Haven't you ever felt it, McCady? That breathless excitement when someone enters the room. That hot surging in the blood. That tingly, dizzying, wild and frightening feeling called—"

"I take the girl to bed, and it's gone by morning."

"Love," she finished softly.

This time his smile was cruel. "You're slipping, Maggie. A good whore should never allow herself to become sentimental over what she sells."

She arched a perfectly plucked brow. "Are you describing me or yourself?"

An emotion flared behind the shadows in his eyes, gone before she could read it. He set his champagne down untouched. "It's too late anyway," he said, so softly she wasn't sure she'd heard him right or for that matter what he meant by it. "It's too late," he said again, and shrugged as if he didn't care. But even separated by the width of the room, she could feel a tension vibrating along every inch of his whipcord-taut frame.

She went to him. She used her little finger to trace the beautiful, sulky curve of his mouth. It had been a long time. Years. "Share my bed tonight, McCady."

"I am not in a generous mood."

"Then take."

His fingers closed over her wrist, and he brought her hand to his lips. He smiled, but shook his head. He bade her a polite good-bye, and when the door had shut behind him, she pressed the hand that he had kissed against her cheek.

It was a sentimental thing to do, and she sneered at herself for it, but she went to the window for one last glimpse of him. She knew somehow that he would never return to this house again.

He stood in the spill of a streetlamp, the light shining full on his face. He did nothing, simply stood there, and she had never seen anyone look more alone.

Jessalyn Letty peered out the carriage window at the long line of stanhopes, landaus, and phaetons winding ahead of them. "We shall be another hour at this rate," she said, as their red-lacquered vehicle rolled forward a few more inches, then swayed and jolted to a stop. "We could have walked there by now ten times over."

"Tain't the done thing, gel," Lady Letty pronounced, "hoofing it to a ball." She flicked open a silver plate snuffbox and took a pinch, then offered some to Clarence Tiltwell, who declined. The sharp smell of ambergris and bitter almonds filled the carriage, making Jessalyn's eyes water.

Lady Letty blew a loud sneeze into her handkerchief. "What a sad crush." She sneezed again. "One would think all of London is determined to attend this Hamilton person's rout. What is the world coming to? The man is a mere corn merchant."

"Aloysius Hamilton is also a banker," Clarence said. "A lot of people owe him money."

Lady Letty heaved a great whistling snort, like a boiling kettle. "Aha! So you're in hock to him, are you?" Using her quizzing glass, she appraised the blue satin and black leather interior of Clarence Tiltwell's town coach. It was top-of-the-line and ruinously expensive. "Just how badly dipped are you?"

Clarence's gentle laugh echoed in the roomy carriage. "I am a banker as well, Lady Letty. People owe *me* money."

"Tain't the done thing, Tiltwell, to bring up a subject so crass as debts and money whilst in polite society," Lady Letty said, completely oblivious of the fact that she had been the one to raise the subject. "If you are ever to rise above your tutworker origins, you should know that, boy."

"Oh, Gram . . ." Jessalyn cast a glance at Clarence, but if his feelings had been wounded, his face didn't show it. No color mottled his fair complexion, and his eyes, reflecting the light from the roof lanterns, merely looked amused.

The coach, which had been rattling across the cobbles, suddenly quieted as they pulled onto the bed of straw that had been laid in the street to cut the noise in front of the Hamilton Mayfair mansion. Lights blazed from the unshuttered windows, and lanterns flickered on decorated poles. A linkboy ran down carpeted steps to open their carriage door.

No sooner had they descended into the street than a ragged urchin squirmed his way past the footmen and postilions to shove a rusty tea tray up into their faces. "Buy me gingerbread, yer honors!" he cried. "Fresh and 'ot!"

Lady Letty opened her reticule, but the postboy drove the child off with a crack of his whip. "Don't," Clarence said, stilling the old woman's hand. "For if you buy from him, there'll be a hundred others to take his place. You cannot feed them all."

It did indeed seem as if a hundred gaping faces crowded around the carriages. These thin, pale faces of the poor who had come to witness the lavish sight of Quality arriving at a ball. The stink of their unwashed bodies and pawned clothes hung over the street, mixing with the smell of horse dung. Their murmuring voices and occasional cries reminded Jessalyn of the sea slapping the Cornish cliffs and the screams of the gulls.

She slipped her arm through her grandmother's, drawing her into a comforting embrace. In the smoky light of the flambeaux, Lady Letty's face looked pinched with pain. It was the children, Jessalyn knew. Even after four years of such sights, her grandmother could not bear the plight of London's children. For Rosalie, the bal-maiden, had never forgotten what it was like to go to bed on a pile of rags with a belly swollen and cramping from hunger.

The linkboy ushered them up the stairs and through the front door. The earthy smells of horse and sweat were replaced by the honeyed fragrance of the best wax candles and the floral and spice of many perfumes. They were passed on to a groom of the chambers in powdered wig and glorious livery, who announced their arrival in stentorian syllables.

The Hamiltons stood at the top of a long, curving white marble staircase to receive their guests. Mr. Hamilton was a fat little squab of a man with a great pair of mustaches that if uncurled would reach thrice around his head. Mrs.

Hamilton was draped with gobbets of jewelry and rouged to the eyes.

The ballroom shimmered in the illuminated brilliance cast by the latest gas chandeliers. Dozens of faceted watch balls hung from the ceiling and window niches, reflecting the dazzling room a thousand times over. Plumed headdresses were *le dernier cri* for evening wear this year, and the room was full of feathers, undulating and swaying like wheat blowing in the wind.

"Gram has discovered the faro tables," Jessalyn said as she and Clarence faced each other in the first quadrille. "I cannot imagine where she found the stakes. I hope she isn't playing with vowels."

He drew her in a graceful circle in time with the music that floated down from the minstrel gallery. "Actually I lent her a few pounds," he said. "I thought she would enjoy the evening better." His lips parted in a wide smile, revealing the boyish gap in his front teeth. He looked especially handsome tonight in a bottle green velvet coat that matched his eyes and set off his buttercup yellow hair.

"That will teach you to admit that you're a banker," Jessalyn said, laughing and feeling a deep rush of fondness for him. And a wrenching guilt for promising to marry him when all along her heart still belonged to McCady, and always would. "I shall, of course, pay you back. Otherwise, when Gram loses it all, which she is bound to do, she will try to sell you one of her snuffboxes—"

"I shall buy it and sell it back to you later. How is that?" His smile was so warm and caring. An odd tightness squeezed her throat, making it difficult to speak.

"Clarence, I . . . You are a true friend."

The dance had ended, but Clarence kept hold of her hand. His eyes bored into hers. His face was taut with an intensity that made her uncomfortable. An intensity and a hunger. "I hope that I am more than that," he said.

She withdrew her hand. "I . . . It has grown rather warm in here. Perhaps a glass of champagne punch?"

He stared at her as the silence stretched between them. She held her breath, afraid that he would voice aloud the thoughts she could read in his eyes. But then his gaze shifted away from hers, and the moment passed.

"Yes, of course," he said, and, bowing, left her.

She watched the whirling dancers, and her chest tightened with a bittersweet ache. She thought of her first grown-up party of that long-ago summer, dancing with Mc-Cady, the way he had teased her when she tripped over his feet and then made herself dizzy staring at the ceiling, the way he had—

It was as if he'd come walking out of her memory. Suddenly he was there in the doorway and looking over the ballroom as if he were the dark prince and everyone else his subject. Everything inside her seemed to give way, and for a moment she forgot to breathe.

He turned slightly, to greet his host, and Jessalyn stared at his proud profile. With his too-long hair and pirate's earring, he didn't look quite civilized. His sharp-boned face and hard body were too masculine for his elegant clothes. *He doesn't belong here*, she thought. Not in London with its boring crushes and oppressive rules. He belonged in another time when men wore armor and conquered kingdoms and lived by no rule but that of the sword.

I want you, Jessalyn.

Wanted her but could not love her.

Her emotions waged the same war as they had that day he had so coldly asked her to share his bed. Her Letty pride had demanded she slap his face, the hurt child in her had wanted to scratch and claw at him and hurt him back, but her woman's heart had wanted to fling herself into his arms and love him anyway. Love him hard enough and long enough until he had no choice but to love her back.

She was never going to get over him. It didn't matter whether they were in the same ballroom or on opposite sides of the world, she could feel the dangerous desire to give in, to give in to the temptation to believe that she alone out of all the women in the world could change him. That she alone could possess his heart.

Another quadrille had formed on the floor, blocking her view of him, and her heartbeat slowed. Only to stop completely when she saw that he was circling the room, in that lean-hipped, slightly hitching saunter that was uniquely his, and coming right at her.

She looked around with wide, frantic eyes and spotted a window alcove furnished with a marquetry side table that bore an enormous white glass vase and a smoking pastille pot. She made for it like a rabbit for a bolt-hole. She slipped into the alcove, craning her head around to see if he followed, and struck the table with her hip, sending the vase crashing to the floor.

"Bloody hell," she exclaimed beneath her breath.

"It *was* a rather hideous thing, wasn't it?"

Jessalyn whipped around, startled to find that her bolt-hole was already occupied by a young woman with pattern-card perfect features and silvery gold spindrift hair styled into a short cap of curls. Diamonds sparkled in her plumed headdress, and her silver lamé dress shimmered in the bright candlelight. She twinkled like a skyful of stars.

Jessalyn remembered shaking this young woman's hand at the top of the stairs, and the flush that stained her cheeks burned hotter. "I am so sorry, Miss Hamilton. Please, you must allow me to replace the vase."

"Oh, pray do not consider it." Wisteria blue eyes danced with amusement. "We have put the wretched thing in every room in the house in the hope that some accident would befall it. My aunt Lucinda gave it to us, you see. She means well, the poor old dear, but she has a squint—can't see a thing, no matter how ugly it is, unless it's directly beneath her nose."

As a sign of the Hamilton wealth, the window curtains were cut extra long to puddle on the floor. To Jessalyn's astonishment the girl lifted the heavy brocade and swept the glass shards underneath with her feet. "There now."

She dusted her gloved hands together and sent Jessalyn a conspiratorial smile. "If anyone asks us what has happened to the wretched thing, we shall deny all knowledge of its existence."

"You must still allow me to replace it with something," Jessalyn said. "I insist."

"Why not make it something truly ugly, then, and we can give it to poor Aunt Lucinda?" She had a lilting laugh that curled up on the ends like flower petals. "I'm afraid you've caught me in an act of a most shameful cowardice, hiding in here. But if I have to perform one more curtsy tonight, I know my knees will give out." She peered out into the crowded ballroom, releasing a delicate sigh. She had an enviable bosom that swelled over the blond lace tucker that edged her stiff stomacher. "You are a friend of Mr. Tiltwell's. Miss Letty, is it?"

"Yes, but I am surprised you remember. You must have greeted five hundred people tonight, and surely you couldn't name all of them as an acquaintance."

"You don't know Mamma. I have been shown off like prime breeding stock at every crush, rout, and ball for the last three Seasons. A lure for a Title." She said the word with bitterness and as if it were possessed of a capital letter. "Of course, it is not my blood that is the bait but the enormous sum of money that is to be my dowry."

"I shouldn't mind an enormous dowry," Jessalyn said, and was pleased when Miss Hamilton laughed. She felt an odd sort of kinship with the other girl. It was one of those rare instances, she thought, when you know you have just met someone who is going to become a good friend.

Again Miss Hamilton leaned out of the alcove to scan the room. Jessalyn wondered if she was looking for someone in particular. She was nervously twisting a small hand-painted fan in her fingers. It was the sort of elegant trifle a girl's beau would give her when he paid a call.

Miss Hamilton noticed the direction of Jessalyn's gaze, and she lifted the fan, spreading its leaves. A waltzing couple was painted on the stiff silk. A smile played around her small mouth. "I shall tell you a secret," she said, "although it is not to be a secret much longer. A—a man has asked me to be his wife. He is very handsome, and he does have a title."

"You must be very happy."

Miss Hamilton's purple-blue eyes darkened. "I would be if The Title weren't so obviously marrying me for the settlement. Until three days ago we had never laid eyes on each other. And he is not the sort of man to pretend feelings that he does not have."

But already she loves him, Jessalyn thought. *Poor girl.*

A bedizened and bejeweled woman in beaded puce was working her way down the length of the room, searching in all the window niches. "Oh, drat, there is Mamma." Miss Hamilton heaved a heartfelt sigh. "She is wise to all my little tricks." She looked at Jessalyn, and a brightness lit up her blue eyes—wisteria bathed with sunshine. "I should like it very much if you would call on me sometime, Miss Letty," she said, and though the smile remained bright, there was a loneliness in her voice.

Jessalyn smiled in return and held out her hand. "Please, my name is Jessalyn."

She gave Jessalyn's hand a gentle squeeze. "I am Emily."

They walked together out of the alcove, and Emily went forward to intercept her mother. She was so small and dainty, and she moved with a fluid grace that Jessalyn longed to emulate. Mrs. Hamilton had her fingers firmly fastened around the arm of a man, a long-nosed man with thinning blond hair and a haughty demeanor. The Title, Jessalyn supposed, and she felt a rush of pity for Miss Emily Hamilton. For he looked like the sort of man who would keep his wife in a gilded cage, while he amused himself with an aviary of ladybirds.

Suddenly a rough hand seized her wrist, pulling her around. She looked up into a dark angel's face, and her heart knocked against her chest. "What are you doing?"

"Waltzing with you," he said in a voice as gentle as a dawn wind. His arm slid around her waist, a possessive hand pressed into her back, and he swept her out into the middle of the dance.

For a moment her startled gaze locked with that of Clarence, who stood just inside the doorway with two glasses of champagne punch in his hands. But then they were swallowed up by the rest of the dancers.

She met McCady's gaze, and she felt the concussion of it like a blow. His mouth was set in that hard, tight line that always made him look a little cruel. "Are you still going to marry him?" he demanded.

"Yes," she lied, and looked away from him, down at her feet, which were moving as stiffly as stilts across the floor.

"If you ask me," he said, "you're making a mistake."

"I haven't asked you, and now if you will be so kind as to release me . . ."

"Come now, Miss Letty. Where are your party manners? When a gentleman begs for the honor of a dance, it is impolite to deny him."

"You hardly begged. You didn't even ask."

"A small oversight." He lowered his head until his breath stirred in her hair like a sea mist. "And you, Miss Letty, still can't waltz without looking at your feet."

To her shock she started laughing. It was nerves, and she tried to make herself stop, but she couldn't. Her laughter, wild and lusty, floated up to the ballroom's gilded ceiling. She didn't see, for her head had fallen back, but his eyes squeezed shut, and his mouth winced as if he were in pain.

The arm that was lightly resting around her waist tightened. "Jessalyn . . . remember that summer and the night of the blue moon?"

Her startled gaze fell to his face. There was an uncertainty, a vulnerability in his eyes that she had never seen before. As if for just a moment the shadows had opened to reveal a part of his soul. She swallowed around a thickness in her throat. "I could never forget that night."

Although the music hadn't stopped, he eased her out of his arms. "Neither will I," he said, a strange roughness in his voice. "As long as I live. No matter what I must do . . . what happens, I will never forget that night. Or you."

She stared at him, trying to divine what he was telling her. It was almost as if he was saying good-bye.

17

Clarence stood before her with a glass of champagne punch in each hand and a baffled look on his face. "But we can't possibly leave now," he said. "It's barely midnight. What will people think?"

"I do not *care* what—" Jessalyn drew in a deep breath. "Tell them Gram has taken suddenly ill."

"If it's Caerhays, if he's insulted you, I'll demand satisfaction."

"Will you challenge him to pistols at dawn?" Jessalyn retorted, though she instantly regretted it. She pushed a great sigh out of her chest. "Oh, Clarence . . . we only danced."

Only danced. She didn't know why she had been left with this terrible sense of loss. She only knew she could no longer bear to be here among all the gilt and laughter and music. "Please, just take us home."

Clarence thrust the glasses of punch at a passing footman and slipped his hand beneath Jessalyn's elbow. "Very well. But I thought you understood how important it was for me to be here tonight. Aloysius Hamilton might not possess a title, but he has influence in government circles that most of your precious dukes and *earls* could only dream of. As my future wife you should be giving a thought, my love, to the advancement of my career in Parliament."

Jessalyn had to swallow back the need to tell him that she could never marry him now. But this wasn't the time or place to jilt the man who was, despite it all, still her dearest, her very best friend in all the world.

They had almost forced their way through the crush blocking the door when a great blasting toot slammed through the air, and silence descended in the room, sharp and sudden, like a clap of thunder.

All eyes turned toward one end of the grand ballroom, where Aloysius Hamilton stood mounted on a small dais, with a sheepish grin on his face and a brass coaching horn in his hand. "Now that I have your attention," he said, and his startled guests broke into relieved titters of laughter.

Aloysius launched into a rambling speech, most of which Jessalyn couldn't hear, but she supposed this must be the announcement of the big secret—Emily's betrothal to her title. And indeed, Emily soon joined her father on the dais. Aloysius took his daughter's hand and raised it to his lips. He kept her hand in his as he beckoned with the other to someone in a crowd of people to the left of him.

In spite of the heavy sadness pressing on her chest, Jessalyn could not help smiling as she watched her new friend, Emily Hamilton, hold out her free hand and draw a man up onto the dais with her. She was smiling still as she watched that man lift Emily's hand and kiss her fingers, before laying them on his bent arm. Smiling, smiling, smiling as a wash of pain froze her breath and blinded her.

Beside her, Jessalyn heard Clarence suck in a gasp of shock. Voices battered her ears: *Betrothal . . . marrying an earl, Caerhays . . . They are all rakehells, but this one is mad. He's laying down rails from here to Cornwall, and he thinks to run iron horses . . . riding for a smash. And Hamilton, the bloody rich nabob, will have himself an earl's get for a grandson. . . .*

Although every eye was on him, he stood still and looked

slowly around the room. His gaze stopped only when it found her. Their eyes clashed and held. She saw nothing in his face. Nothing at all.

If she had any pride at all, she would go up to him now and she would smile and wish him happy, wish them both happy, and act as if she were happy, happy, happy, without a care in the world. Oh, God ·. . .

She looked around for Clarence, but he had disappeared. She tried to push through the crowd of guests all trying to go in the opposite direction, toward the dais, to offer their congratulations. Suddenly she felt suffocated, as if all these people were a great weight crushing her, pressing her into the floor.

Someone touched her, taking her arm. It was Clarence. Oddly his face was blanched with shock, and a small tic was throbbing beneath his right eye. "He only got enough upon the betrothal to pay off his brother's gaming vowels," Clarence said, and though it made no sense to her, Jessalyn thought she heard a note of strained relief in his voice. "The rest of the settlement won't be his until after the heir is born."

Her own face felt so stiff, as if she'd been dumped in a vat of starch. She had to get away before she started cracking in a million pieces.

"Clarence, please . . . take us home now."

He stood within the shadows of the portico's pillars and watched her leave. The street was still clogged with carriages and swearing coachmen, for most of the guests would not depart for hours yet.

He watched until Tiltwell's scarlet town coach rolled down the street on well-oiled wheels, turned the corner, and was gone.

"Lord Caerhays?"

He turned. Emily Hamilton stood within the pool of light cast by the flickering torches. A look that was half worshipful, half fearful marred her pretty face.

"What do you want?" he demanded. Then immediately regretted the harshness of his words when he saw her flinch. They had been betrothed for three days, yet she couldn't bring herself to call him by his first name. Doubtless she would be calling him Lord Caerhays on their wedding night.

"My father wishes to speak with you, my lord." Her mouth trembled into a sweet smile that he tried, and failed, to answer.

He wanted to hate her, but he couldn't. It wasn't her fault that she wasn't somebody else.

"I cannot imagine why you and Tiltwell wanted to attend that crush in the first place, gel," Lady Letty said as Becka opened the door to them. "But once there, the least you could have done was stay above an hour or two. Instead you insisted upon leaving just when my luck was about to turn. There is nothing for it—I am going to bed."

"I'm sorry. Good night, Gram," Jessalyn said to her grandmother's departing back. She stood unmoving, half in, half out the open door. A breeze blew in off the river, and she turned her face to it. She yearned suddenly for Cornwall and the sea. She wanted to go *home*.

There was such a weight of unshed tears in her chest that needed to come out. She was going to start crying soon, and when she did, she was not going to be able to stop. Her tears would flood the world until she drowned in them.

"Evenin', Mr. Tiltwell, sur," Becka said. "Ye be lookin' handsome this night. Done up to the nines ee be. 'Tes enough to set a girl's heart to fluctuatin' in her breast, just to look at ee." She giggled, then winked, then followed Lady Letty inside.

Clarence touched Jessalyn's arm. "Walk with me out on the terrace?"

"Unchaperoned?" she said, forcing a smile. "That wouldn't be proper. Think of your reputation."

Clarence didn't smile with her. As usual he had not un-

derstood her teasing. Poor Clarence, everything in his
world was all so ponderously serious.

"Jessalyn, I have known you your entire life," he said.
"When have I ever behaved toward you in any manner
other than what is considered proper?"

She swallowed a sigh. "Never," she said. Almost never.
He had kissed her twice. Once on the day she had accepted
his proposal of marriage, and once before the Midsummer's
Eve bonfire the summer she was sixteen. The summer she
had been taught all about love, but not by him.

She allowed him to lead her toward the iron railing that
faced the river. Beneath the terrace were great arched stor-
age vaults, empty now except for the river scavengers who
lived like moles within them. On calm nights she could
hear the crackling of their fires and occasional snatches
of drunken laughter. Tonight the river was flat and tinseled with silver ribbons from lanterns on the boats and
bridges.

Clarence cleared his throat. "Jessalyn, I wonder if you
have given any more thought to the idea of moving up the
date of our wedding?"

"Oh, Clarence . . ." She spun around to face him. Then
wished she hadn't, for she knew that even in the cloaking
darkness he could see the dismay on her face.

"I had reason to believe that you were as anxious as I to
begin our life together," he said stiffly.

"Oh, Clarence, I'm so sorry . . ." She laid a hand on his
rigid arm. "You are my dearest friend, and I love you. But I
have come to see that it is not in the way you want. In the
way it should be between husband and wife. I—"

"Are you trying to tell me that you are experiencing second thoughts?"

She dragged in an aching breath. "I'm sorry."

"I see." He turned away from her. His gloved hands
wrapped around the railing. He spoke into the night, his
voice calm, assured. "Your debts here in London and at

Newmarket are mounting, although I know you've been trying to hide the direness of your circumstances from me and from your grandmother. But you cannot go on like this much longer, Jessalyn, and then what are your choices? To become a governess to a passel of screaming brats. Or the paid companion of a crotchety old dowager with smelly pug dogs and numerous disgusting ailments."

She thought of her silly self, riding around and around the rotunda at Vauxhall Gardens, turning somersaults in her bird mask with its wiggly beak. "I should run away and join the circus before it comes to that," she said, and a strange gurgle escaped out her tight throat.

He jerked around to glare at her. "Are you laughing at me?"

"No, I'm not. I'm sorry." *That's all I seem able to say,* she thought. *I'm sorry, sorry, sorry . . .* There was this thick, unrelenting ache in her chest. She tried to expel it by pushing out a sigh. But it remained, making it hard for her to breathe.

"My circumstances are not as dire as you make them out to be," she said. "We shall get by until spring, when we will go to End Cottage so that Gram can get a dose of the sea air. Then, if Blue Moon is recovered, we shall come back up to Epsom and race him in the Derby. The winning purse is a thousand pounds."

He barked a harsh laugh. "If you win it! Ah, God, Jessalyn . . ." His head fell back. He squeezed the bridge of his nose with his fingers, then let his hand fall helplessly to his side. "I love you. I've loved you for years. All that I've done—the seat in Parliament, the house in Berkeley Square, the fortune I am building, a possible knighthood— it was all done to make myself worthy of you." He clasped her upper arms, startling her with the strength of his grip and the fierceness in his voice. "Jessalyn, I love you."

I love you.

She squeezed her eyes shut. He was her friend and she

was hurting him and she couldn't bear this. "P-perhaps I just need a little more time," she said, and knew she was being a coward. But she just couldn't bear any more pain right now.

His grip tightened, hurting her. "How much? How much time does it take to decide if you want to become a man's wife?"

She opened her eyes. His face showed everything: bewilderment and despair, and the last desperate glimmerings of hope. She had known this man since she was six years old. They were friends. They were . . .

"Just a little more time, Clarence. Please. Give me until spring, like we planned."

McCady . . . Lord Caerhays would be married to his heiress by then. She would have accepted it by then. She would be used to it—oh, God, how was she ever going to get used to it?

Clarence released her, straightening his cravat and the lapels of his coat, as if he had to put himself back into order again after that uncharacteristic outburst. "I know that you will give all that I have said fair consideration, Jessalyn," he said. "You're only experiencing those nuptial eve fears that all young brides go through. They'll soon pass. You'll see if I'm not right." She heard the relief in his voice and felt ashamed.

He cupped her cheek, tilting her head back. "Just think of the life I can offer you and your grandmother. But most important, think about how much I love you."

She looked up into Clarence Tiltwell's earnest face. She could feel the cracks in her heart widening. The pain was coming now, and it was unbearable.

Great pots of golden chrysanthemums decorated the choir and high altar of St. Margaret's, Westminster. The sun shone through the stained glass window of Christ Crucified, casting red and blue and yellow patterns on the stone floor. It was, the guests all agreed, a beautiful day for a wedding.

The bride stood before the chancel rail, looking radiantly beautiful in a dress of white and silver lace and a veil weighted with hundreds of seed pearls that flowed over her arms to sweep the floor. The groom looked dashingly handsome in a blue town coat with long tails and straw-colored trousers. His hair hanging long beneath his silk top hat and the gold ring flashing in his ear gave him a piratical air that stirred the heart in more than one feminine breast.

There was to be a breakfast after the ceremony, and most of London that counted had received the engraved gilt-edged invitations. But only the Hamiltons' most intimate friends were at the church for the ceremony. They stood now within boxed pews, and the men envied the groom the dowry he was getting. The women envied the bride her groom. Fifty intimate friends invited to witness the indissoluble bond of matrimony.

And one who was not invited.

She stood to the side, half hidden behind a pillar and a pair of tall iron candlesticks. Up until this moment she had not really believed the wedding would take place. It was as if someone had told her she was about to die.

Although she had come, now she could not bear to watch it. She looked up at the twisted face of the stained glass Christ. Her eyes squeezed shut. *Oh, God, I do want to die. Please, God, let me die.*

The pastor's voice echoed in the stony, hollow emptiness. "By the laws of God and the British Commonwealth, I pronounce you man and wife."

McCady Trelawny, twelfth earl of Caerhays, did not look at his countess. He turned, his eyes searching, as if he sensed her presence. Across the gray shadowed church their gazes met. Her heart lurched as she saw his face change, saw it become raw and naked with despair . . .

As if his soul had been stolen.

She walked away from him, down the long nave, the

soles of her kid slippers making no sound on the stone floor. She began to run.

She was halfway down the steps when the bells began to toll.

18

The first primroses of spring were blooming the week she came home to Cornwall.

Jessalyn walked to church that Sunday morning down a lane lined with high hedges exploding with the yellow blossoms. Seeing no one about, she picked up her skirts and climbed on top of the stone wall. She spread her arms wide and tilted her face to the sun, filling her lungs with a deep breath. The air had an applelike smell, crisp and green. Laughing aloud, she spun around and took off running along the top of the hedge the way she used to do as a child, and the wind whipped her hair and numbed her cheeks and carried her laughter out to sea.

The first primroses of the year. It meant that winter would be over soon. It meant a new beginning. She would pick one later, she thought, to show Gram. There hadn't been any primroses in London.

The wind was blowing a gale by the time she arrived at the church, the sea running thick and heavy, presaging another storm. But for the moment the sun shone and the primroses bloomed, and Jessalyn rejoiced in being alive.

The church that served the tinners and fishermen in this corner of Cornwall was called St. Genny's after St. Genesius, an early Celtic saint who had been beheaded for his faith. It was said he haunted the moors with his head tucked like a bread loaf beneath his arm. Years ago Jessalyn and Clarence had once spent a summer night lurking among the gravestones with a fishing net, hoping to catch him. But instead all they'd caught had been a lecture from Reverend Troutbeck, and poor Clarence had gotten another thrashing.

Made of gray stone splotched with moss, the tiny church had a crenellated square tower that looked as if it would be more at home on a fortress. Inside, the squat nave smelled of mildew and of the bats that lived in the belfry. On rainy days one had to take care where one sat, for in spite of numerous grinning contests over the years, the roof still leaked.

Jessalyn brought a great gust of wind into the church with her that rattled the pages in the psalters and nearly snatched the wig from Dr. Humphrey's head. She slipped into a worm-eaten pew just as the Reverend Mrs. Troutbeck's wavering soprano launched into the final notes of "O come, let us sing to the Lord."

The Reverend Troutbeck, wearing a surplice stained with the muggety pie he'd eaten for breakfast, mounted the pulpit. He sucked in a deep breath, his corset creaking like an old pair of bellows, opened his mouth, and held it open as the door squealed and another great gust of wind filled the church.

Everyone turned in unison to stare, and Jessalyn's heart lurched up into her throat. The earl of Caerhays stood within the doorway. The morning sun shone full on his reckless face with its flaring cheekbones and shadowed eyes. In his snuff-colored riding coat and buckskins, he looked as if he'd decided only at the last minute to attend the service. His young wife stood beside him, bundled head to toe in a blue Angola hussar cloak and blushing prettily.

His gaze collided with Jessalyn's. She sat stiff-backed, her chin lifted high, refusing to look away, while the old familiar ache squeezed at her heart. Love was not a matter of will; she couldn't make what she felt for him lessen or go away. She could hate him, and she did, for hurting her, for leaving her, again and again. But she would go on loving him with each breath she took until she died. And even then it would not end. For if there was such a thing as a soul, then hers would go on loving him throughout eternity.

He stared back at her, and his face might have been carved of the same rock as the Cornish cliffs.

Just then Emily noticed her. The girl's face lightened with a surprised smile, and that was Jessalyn's undoing. She jerked around, dropping her psalter. As she bent over, fumbling for the book beneath the pew, she saw his glossy top boots and Emily's kid slippers walk together down the aisle. Tears filled her eyes. She stayed hunched over for a moment, blinking and swallowing hard, until she could raise her head and look dry-eyed at the Reverend Trout-beck in his pulpit.

Not an inspiring preacher in the best of times, the village parson was so disconcerted to have such an exalted person-age as an earl in his church that he grew nearly incoherent. As he rambled through the lesson, Jessalyn sat in breathless tension, watching the sand trickle through the hourglass grain by grain. She didn't look at Lord Caerhays again, but he might as well have been sitting beside her, his shoulder and thigh pressing against hers, his breath stirring her hair, so aware was she of his presence.

The wind gusted against the church, rattling the loose shingles, as the reverend launched into a final prayer. "It seems, O Lord," he intoned, "that you are about to visit us with another storm. We pray thee that no wrecks should happen. . . ." His voice dwindled to a squeak as he began to perceive the chasms opening beneath his feet. It wasn't too many generations ago that the notorious Trelawnys, al-ways strapped for money, had been known to lure ships deliberately to their deaths on stormy nights by lighting false signals on the cliffs above Crookneck Cove.

Everyone—those who hadn't already been gawking at him throughout the service—turned to look at the earl. He had kept his eyes cast downward on the gloved hands folded across the ebony handle of his walking stick. Now he lifted his head and pinned the unfortunate curate with his fierce dark gaze, and his cynical drawl filled the tiny church. "We pray, of course, that no wrecks should happen," he said, "but if by chance a wreck should be ordained to happen, then we pray that God will guide it to happen at Crookneck Cove. Is that not so, Reverend?"

A silence followed this pronouncement, a silence so still Jessalyn could hear the bats rustling overhead. Then someone emitted a smothered giggle, and a second later the entire congregation of tinners and fishermen was laughing. The Reverend Troutbeck flushed and hemmed and launched into another prayer wherein he dropped a broad hint about the need for a new roof.

Jessalyn bolted from the pew before the last notes of the closing hymn had faded into echoes. The sun, pale in a paler sky, dazzled her eyes, and she kept having to blink away tears as she hurried from the church down the stony path. The wind shrieked like a demented witch. It was thick with the coming storm, tasting of sea salt and sand and chilling rain. She had just reached the lych-gate when she heard her name.

"Jessalyn? Miss Letty?"

Jessalyn turned. Emily Hamilton—Emily *Trelawny*—emerged from the shelter of the portico. The wind whipped off the fur-lined hood of her cloak, and her fair hair glittered like a crown. She came alone. The earl had stayed behind to speak to the reverend.

Jessalyn stood beneath the lych-gate, waiting. She would not be a coward. But it had become so hard for her to breathe through the heaviness in her chest, and the sun and wind kept making her eyes water.

"Lady Caerhays," she said as Emily stopped before her. Emily's smile faltered a bit. "Oh, no, you mustn't do that

—you mustn't call me Lady Caerhays. I had thought . . . well, that we were friends."

Somehow Jessalyn was able to dredge up an answering smile. "Hullo then, Emily."

"We thought you still in London, my lord and I." Emily looked behind her, as if seeking her husband's confirmation. Jessalyn couldn't stop herself from looking as well. He had his back to them; she couldn't even see his face. It didn't matter. He would forever have the ability to make her blood run hot and thick simply at the mere thought of him. More than ever she would have to take care not to let it show. Dear life, she mustn't ever again let it show.

"The country air must agree with you," Emily was saying. "For you are looking splendid. My lord said as much."

"Did he?" This was so unlike the man she knew that Jessalyn could not believe it.

Emily's soft laugh was snatched away by the wind. "Well, *I* said as much. But he agreed with me. How long have you been in Cornwall? Ourselves we've been at the hall nearly three months now, since after Christmas." She sighed and looked around her, her rosebud mouth curling into a smile. "It is so beautiful here, and yet so wild. . . . When Caerhays said he wished to take up residence at his principal seat, well, I confess I didn't want to come. But now I don't think I shall ever want to leave."

Jessalyn drew in a deep breath, trying to loosen her throat. She had known, for Clarence had told her, that McCady had come to Cornwall with his new wife. He had been borrowing heavily again, to make the hall livable and to build at the foundry in Penzance a new locomotive for competing in the upcoming trials. He was even reopening an old played-out mine, Clarence had added, shaking his head in dismay. "He's trying to save his railway company by starting up a *mining* venture of all things. Only a Trelawny would dare such a risk."

Jessalyn looked now at the woman who had married the man she loved. A serenity softened Emily's face, a quiescence that was at once both steely and gentle and that had drawn Jessalyn to the other woman since first they met. She shouldn't hate Emily or blame her for her own pain. But it was so hard, so hard.

"I am glad you have found happiness here," Jessalyn said.

"Happiness? Yes, I suppose I have. . . ." But Emily's gaze sought out her husband, and an odd sort of anguish darkened her eyes.

A gust slammed against them. Emily swayed, nearly falling, and Jessalyn grabbed her arm. The wind caught the edge of the girl's blue cloak, whipping it open, and revealing a belly swollen with child.

"We are expecting a baby in four months' time," Emily said, color rising in her cheeks.

We . . . Pain wrenched at Jessalyn's chest, so sharp she thought it must have cracked in two. For a moment she was back in the Hamilton ballroom, hearing Clarence's censorious voice above the shattering of her heart. *He only got enough upon the betrothal to pay off his brother's gaming vowels. The rest of the settlement won't be his until after the heir is born.*

"How fortunate for his lordship," she said aloud to Emily. But as soon as the words left her mouth, she felt small and mean. "Rather, how wonderful that after all these years there is to be a new baby at Caerhays Hall."

Emily blushed again. "The doctors keep insisting my health is delicate, but in truth, I have never felt better. Still, I mustn't ride or walk too far. Perhaps you would come to call on us soon."

Lord Caerhays had ended his conversation with the reverend and was coming toward them, limping heavily. Jessalyn wondered if like Gram's rheumatism, his wound was especially painful in damp weather. His *wife* would know; perhaps she should ask his *wife.* Oh, God, she couldn't bear this.

"Please, I—I must be off," she said quickly. "My grandmother has been unwell. The trip down from London is so arduous for one of her age."

Emily's face clouded. She patted Jessalyn's arm, offering a sweet and genuine sympathy. "Oh, I am so sorry. Pray, give her my respects."

"Thank you. I shall. . . ." He was nearly upon them. Their gazes clashed again, and his hard face wavered and dissolved as tears filled her eyes.

She whirled, running down the lane. Stifled sobs burned her throat, clogging her breath. She stopped beside the hedge, leaning against it, gasping and swallowing and trying not to cry. She pressed her clenched fists so hard into the rough stones she broke the skin, yet she didn't feel the pain. She told herself not to look back, but she couldn't help it.

The earl of Caerhays and his lady wife stood side by side beneath the lych-gate, not touching. But the malevolent wind, as if to remind her, blew open the blue cloak again. Pain stabbed at Jessalyn, so fierce she nearly cried aloud. She had stood in St. Margaret's and watched them marry, and still a part of her had not believed he was well and truly lost to her.

Until now.

Home, she thought. *I want to go home.* So badly did she want to be back at End Cottage, where all was familiar and safe and the way it had always been, that she could almost taste it. The way she could taste the sea on the wind. She began to run, the wind making her eyes tear again, turning the primroses, the first ones of the spring, into a yellow blur. She didn't stop to pick one.

And the next morning they were gone, destroyed during the night by the storm.

They said in Cornwall that the sea had moods. That night the sea was wild and angry.

The storm drew him down to Crookneck Cove. A fierce

wind whipped at the sand and waves, throwing up a gritty haze. A pregnant sky loomed, dark and heavy with rain.

The wind snatched at his hair. He had come bareheaded and without a coat, wanting to feel the full fury of the storm, for it matched the wildness surging in his blood. He wanted to roar the way the sea was roaring, to beat and lash at the rocks like the wind. He tasted the rage of the sea in the salty spume that swirled around him.

A movement down the beach caught his eye. His breath stopped; his whole body tensed. Yet he wasn't surprised to find her here. In his memories of this place she was always bare-legged and running free across the sand, her hair billowing behind her like a cinnamon cloud.

Tonight she stood alone at the edge of the wild surf, as if challenging the sea to do its worst. An enormous wave smashed against the beach, deluging her with spray. She stood unmoving still, soaked, her wet dress plastered to her body. She might as well have been naked.

He couldn't keep the desire at bay, not always, not forever. No man had that much will. He allowed himself to feel, just for a moment, what it would be like to go to her and take her into his arms, to bear her down on the sand and make her his in a way that was as wild and enduring as the raging sea.

He allowed himself to feel, and it was a mistake. His hunger for her, his need, drove him limping toward her across the sand. A solitary gull echoed a warning cry. She whipped around. His intent must have shown on his face, for he saw the fear dawn in her eyes. Fear and a horror that drove like a fist into his gut.

She ran, passing by him so closely her hair whipped across his face.

"Jessalyn!" he cried. But although he could have, he didn't try to stop her. She tore up the cliff path as if all the demons of hell chased after her.

He stayed at the beach a long time, watching wave after

wave tighten, curl, and break. The gull cried again, but it was drowned out by the scream of the wind.

Lady Letty snorted and thumped the ground with her cane. "Who'd have thought we'd ever see the day? Cheeky devil. The Trelawnys have always been cheeky devils."

"I should think you'd be pleased to see the mine reopened, Gram." Jessalyn looked across the bluff at the enginehouse of Wheal Patience. It was decorated with red and white flags that snapped in the breeze, sounding like a hundred clapping hands. The enginehouse looked good as new, with whole bricks replacing the broken ones and the window frames painted a bright daffodil yellow. Smoke from the chimney stack spiraled into a sky so blue it hurt the eyes. "Think what it will mean to the men of Mousehole," she said, "to have work all the year round."

Lady Letty snorted again, although she looked pleased. "All well and good, but he's been spending money as if 'twere cuckoo spit. And they say the marriage settlement won't come due till the heir is born. He's been borrowing on future expectations, mind you. Riding for a fall, he is—typical Trelawny. What if it's a girl, eh? What if it's born dead? You can tell she ain't a breeder. Too delicate by half."

Emily indeed appeared too delicate and fragile to bear a child. She looked like a child herself, standing beside her tall, broad-shouldered husband on the bob plat, the unrailed wooden platform high above the crowd. New mining ventures were launched just like ships, and everyone breathing within miles was on hand to witness the event.

The earl and his lady had climbed to the bob plat on the top floor of the house to christen the great beam. The chimney stack and enginehouse were built on a promontory between the sheer bluff and the sea, reached only by a narrow cliff path. Jessalyn was surprised Lord Caerhays had allowed his pregnant wife to make the dangerous climb. Perhaps Emily had insisted, wanting to share in his moment. In her place Jessalyn would have done the same.

In her place . . . Memories assailed Jessalyn, pulling at
her heart. Memories of the day they had come here together to explore the mine. They had quarreled, and he'd
left her behind, but she had gone after him and fallen, like
a clumsy fool, down a shaft. They had found Salome's baby;
in the excitement she'd never thought to ask afterward if
he'd found tin. She had known even then that one day he
would start up a new venture. But in her dreams, in her
silly schoolgirl dreams, she had been the one standing beside him on the bob plat.

The church choir silenced the crowd by singing "God
Save the King." The Reverend Troutbeck stepped to the
front of the platform and called upon the Lord to bless the
endeavor with lodes of high-grade ore. Beneath him the
engine moaned as it began to raise steam. Lord Caerhays
then took the reverend's place, framed by the daffodil yellow window behind him. He shouted a speech into the sun-
dappled air that soon had the tinners and tutworkers laughing and slapping one another's backs.

Since everyone else was staring openly, Jessalyn was
able to fill her heart with the sight of him. He looked magnificent in a well-cut coat of blue superfine, pale yellow
pantaloons, and a white waistcoat with pearl buttons. The
breeze plucked at his hair where it curled beneath his top
hat, the sun glinting off the gold ring in his ear.

Cheers erupted into the air as the earl finished his short
speech. He turned, drawing his wife to his side. Emily's gilt
hair shone like a saint's halo in the sun. For a moment the
crowd went utterly still, awed by her beauty. She looked up
at her husband, smiling tentatively, her face filled with love
and a bewildered yearning.

Jessalyn looked away.

Emily kept her gaze fastened on to her husband as she
raised a bottle of smuggled French brandy and broke it
over the great beam. Shattered glass and drops of brandy
shimmered in the sun, as if it were raining diamonds. The
villagers cheered, the core bell clanged, and Lady Letty

thumped the ground with her cane. Only Jessalyn stood stiff and silent.

McCady lifted his head, and his gaze searched her out, crossing the distance between them, shutting out the world. She had always been able to feel his gaze on her, like a touch, as if he were caressing her with his mind. Unconsciously her body swayed, and a soft sigh escaped her slightly parted lips as if he were running his hands over her body. His face turned stark with an emotion so deep it remained nameless, a yawning need that wrenched at her heart. But in the next moment his mouth hardened, and he turned away, and Jessalyn wondered if she had imagined it all.

The earl himself opened the exhaust regulator on the new engine that he had built, and steam escaped with a sigh, rising white and misty into the air. The pump rods fell, and up swung the great balance bob, then down fell the bob and up came the rods, again and again, thrust, thump, thrust, thump, thrust thump, and the boiler moaned and sighed.

But in the mine below all was black and still. In the mine below where untold riches might lie waiting. Riches and risk.

Becka Poole waited until the others had already helped themselves before she approached the trestle tables piled with food and drink. People she knew, people who were used to her face, she didn't mind so much. But there were many strangers here this day, men from as far away as Truro who were hoping to be taken on at the new mine. Miss Jessalyn said they didn't mean to be cruel when they stared. And in truth, it was pity she mostly saw in their eyes. But she hated the pity. Nasty taunts—well, she could give back as good as she got. But pity, that she could hardly bear.

Even though she went last, there was plenty of food left over: good Cornish fare, not like what they'd had to make

do with in London. Whelks and jellied eels, ginger beer
and bee wine, curlew and muggety pie. Lord Caerhays was
a generous man when it came to putting out the victuals.
But Becka wasn't sure she liked the earl. He frightened her
with his harsh face and those fierce dark eyes. Devil's eyes
they were, and she touched the hagstone around her neck
to ward off the evil thought. Dear life an' body, the way he
was looking at Miss Jessalyn today, 'twas a wonder the air
didn't catch afire. Becka wished a man would look at *her*
that way, so hot and hungrylike. It would never happen,
though. Not with her scar an' all.

She had just bitten into a nice big slice of the muggety
pie when a shadow fell across the ground in front of her.
She first saw his boots, polished to such a shine her face
was reflected back at her. She pulled her hair over her
cheek, hiding the scar, and slowly lifted her eyes, following
the long, slender length of him up to a pair of brandy-
colored eyes, fringed with long lashes tipped golden by the
sun. Dear life an' body, it was *him*—Mr. Duncan.

She swallowed the bit of muggety pie in her mouth. It
tasted like a wool ball and stuck in her throat going down,
and she choked.

He patted her back; she choked harder. "Have a care
now, Miss Poole," he said in his soft Scottish brogue. "'Tis
drinking something ye ought to be doing." He pressed a
leather jack brimming with ginger beer into her hands.

He'd called her Miss Poole. Nobody had ever called her
Miss Poole. She'd always been just Becka. But he'd called
her Miss Poole as if she were *somebody*.

She gulped the beer down so fast she nearly started
choking again. "Cor, I be thirsty as a cat with nine kits,"
she said when she could breathe. She wiped the foamy
mustache off her upper lip with the back of her hand. She
watched him out the corner of her eye, careful to keep her
ruined cheek turned away from him. It hurt to look at him,
he was so beautiful. "A proper slap-up to-do this is," she
said, for lack of anything better.

"'Tis a fine day for a celebration, it is," he agreed. He had a nice voice, gentle, like his eyes.

"Oh, aye, aye, 'tis a proper day for a celibate."

A startled look came over his face. "I beg yer pairdon?" he said.

She blushed furiously. "Mr. Duncan. Sir," she added, cursing herself for her lack of manners in not addressing him respectfully. She gripped her blue linsey-wool skirt, trying to still her shaking hands.

A silence came between them. He was looking at her, but there wasn't pity in his eyes. That time in London, when she'd opened the door to him, she hadn't seen pity then either. Yet he must notice the scar. He was too just well bred to let on. He was a gentleman's gentleman after all.

And, oh, so handsome. She stared up at him in awe through the curtain of her hair. 'Twas a wonder no woman had snapped him up long afore now. But then perhaps he was married after all, or perhaps he had himself a guinea hen stashed away in London Town. It suddenly occurred to her that she knew nothing about him, except that he worked for Lord Caerhays. And she didn't see any pity in his eyes.

He glanced toward the bonfire, where almost everyone was now gathered, drinking noggins of gin and treacle and waiting to get at the roasting potatoes. He shifted his weight from one foot to the other.

"Ye ought t' try a bite of the star-gazy pie," she said quickly, to keep him from leaving.

He looked down at the table where she pointed, and his eyes widened. She hadn't thought how star-gazy pie could be a sight if you weren't used to it. What with the pilchards' heads sticking out of the crust like that, their little beady white eyes staring blankly up at you.

Indeed, his gloriously handsome face had turned the shade of the green snakes that lived in the gorse. "Uh . . .

nae, thank ye," he said. "Truth to tell, I havena much of an appetite at the moment."

"The sea air makes ee bilious, do it? It often affects a body in that way," she said, pleased to find herself on firm conversational ground at last. Beyond discussing her own delicate health, Becka loved nothing better than to sympathize with the ills and tribulations of other unfortunates. "For indignity of the innards, I do recommend polycrest and rhubarb."

"Indignity of the innards?" His voice sounded strained. The poor man must truly be feeling unwell.

She nodded vigorously. "Rhubarb and polycrest an' ye'll be brave in no time. I've been prostitute with a bad rheum meself. Been up nights with it for a week, I tell ee. First, I gets the sweats, when the flesh runs off me like a fat goose. Then I gets the chills, and the next thing I knows me chest starts to rattlin' like a pot lid. I wake up absolutely expired."

"Expired?" An odd expression had come over his face, a sort of pained look. She hoped he hadn't suddenly suffered a rupture.

"Ais. Tired and so weaklike I couldn't wrestle me own shadow. Expired."

He cleared his throat. "Aye, of course. It sounds a dangerous state of affairs, yer rheum. Ye'd better be having a care, or it could turn into the morbid sore throat, ye know."

"Don't I just! I've tried dosin' meself with tar-water and cobweb pills and rubbin' me chest with adder fat. But them cures bain't workin'."

His blond brows drew together over his straight nose in thought. "My maether has a surefire cure for the rheum. An ointment, it is, though I don't know all of what goes into it. But she claims 'tis even been known to cure the hooting cough. I have some with me now, back in my room at the hall." She watched, mesmerized, as his sensuously shaped lips curved into a sweet smile. "I could bring it over to End

Cottage later, and ye'll feel grand again in nae time. Though I shouldna be coming much before midnight."

A gull screamed and dived at the star-gazy pie, making off with one of the pilchards, but Becka didn't even notice. Her stomach had gone all fluttery, as if she'd just swallowed a thousand butterflies. "Tedn't proper for we to be meetin' after dark," she said, giving him an arch look.

Three more gulls wheeled overhead, eyeing the food. "I do assure ye, Miss Poole," he said, shouting a bit to be heard above the screams of the birds, "my intentions are strictly honorable. 'Tis yer health that is concerning me, lass, nae yer virtue."

"Eh? Oh . . ." Becka felt all her hopes break into pieces like a dry biscuit. What a ninny-hammer she was to be thinking he'd want aught to do with her. Not Becka Poole, with her scarred face. He was a gentleman's gentleman, and as beautiful as a church painting. Too good even to be passing the time of day with the likes of her, a drunken tinner's ugly daughter.

The steady throb-throb of the engine vibrated the ground beneath McCady Trelawny's feet, as if the earth had a heartbeat. He stood within the mining house and shut his eyes, listening to a sound that was as familiar to him as the rush of his own pulse.

He felt himself dissolve, become one with the hard, driving power of the engine. The pounding thrust of the pistons, the hiss and suck of the valves, the throbbing sigh of the spent steam. He felt the heat of the firebox like a breath against his face. He breathed in deeply the hot, wet smell of steam. . . .

And Pears primrose soap.

He opened his eyes and saw her reflected in the engine's great brass cylinder. He drank in the sight of her, at once both delicate and wild. She stood at the window, the one that faced the sea. A nimbus of light surrounded her so that she seemed an illusion that would vanish if he so much as breathed. He couldn't see her face, only the slender curve of her back and one gloved hand that rested on the sill. For a moment he thought he saw a hat with yellow primroses sitting there beside her. But it was only a trick of the light or perhaps of memory.

He went to her, ducking under the great beam as it swung down. The bootheel of his crippled leg scraped on the stone floor. She started and spun around. Her face paled, and he saw fear leap into her eyes.

"Don't!" he cried, flinging out a hand. He barely brushed her arm, but something surged and crackled between them, as powerful as the charge of a lightning bolt. She rubbed the place where he had touched her, although her beautiful, intent eyes never left his face. "Don't run away," he said.

Her eyes widened, and her chest hitched as she sucked in a sharp breath. "I'm not running away. I'm not. . . ."

Now that he had her attention he didn't know what to do with it. There was nothing he could say to her. It was ludicrous to think they could ever be friends. A man did not become friends with a woman whose laugh, whose smile, whose very smell left him hard and aching with want.

In the silence that had fallen between them, he became aware once again of the slow, sucking noise of the pump. It was a slithery sound, like skin rubbing against hot, moist skin. Her gaze flashed to his face, then away again, too swiftly for him to read her thoughts. She moistened her lips, drawing his own gaze down to her mouth.

"Did you build this engine? My lord."

"Yes. Miss Letty."

She looked the pump engine over, nodding grimly as if this confirmed her worst expectations of him. But then she surprised him by saying, "It is a fine engine."

"Thank you. . . . I didn't think you'd be coming back to Cornwall," he said. *God,* he thought, *this conversation is inane.* Why couldn't they talk about what really mattered?

Why had he never been able to talk to anyone about what mattered?

Her wide mouth quivered, nearly smiling. There had always been such a joy within her, he thought, a fire that could never be doused no matter what life forced her to endure.

"We're only here for a short time, my lord. We'll be going up to Epsom Downs come May, for the Derby."

"Blue Moon is healthy then? He'll be able to compete?"

"The Sarn't Major thinks so." She raised her head and fastened her wide, smoky gaze onto his face. "You are still convinced we crimped that race, aren't you? My lord."

"I believe the collision was deliberate, yes. I shouldn't trust that jockey of yours were I you. Miss Letty."

Anger darkened her eyes to the color of the sea at night. "Topper would never do such a thing."

"Your loyalty is admirable, Miss Letty. I wonder . . ." A strand of her hair had come loose to wrap around her neck. He lifted it between two fingers. It felt like silk and looked like liquid fire. He tucked the curl back up beneath the rolled brim of her hat, allowing his fingertips to linger at her temple. He could see her trembling. "I wonder, if you truly cared for a man . . . I almost think you would forgive him anything."

He saw understanding flash behind the flat grayness of her eyes. He waited, breath suspended, for her response. Although he didn't know what she could possibly say that would ease the ache in his chest.

"No," she said. "Not anything . . ."

"Lookit, Miss Letty! Lookit!"

A little girl in pink pinafore and black pigtails burst through the door. She wore a gap-toothed smile so wide the corners of her mouth nearly touched her ears. In one grubby fist she clutched what to McCady's eyes looked like a bunch of weeds.

She skidded to a stop and held the scraggly posy up to Jessalyn. The weeds had been pulled up by the roots, and they trickled dirt onto the newly swept floor. "I picked these for ee, Miss Letty."

Jessalyn accepted the bouquet of weeds with a smile that pierced straight through to McCady's heart. "They're beautiful," she said softly. "Thank you, Little Jessie." She brought the posy up to her face, her nose wrinkling as she fought to hold back a sneeze. McCady caught a pungent whiff of wild garlic. He turned his head to hide a smile.

A pair of jackdaws flew across the open window, black wings flashing, drowning out the thump of the engine with their raucous cawing. "Look!" Little Jessie cried.

McCady's head jerked around, following the direction of the little girl's pointing finger. The sky was empty now, but something had disturbed the jackdaws. He strode to the window, leaning out. He caught a fleeting glimpse of a man running down to the sea, slipping in and out among the rocks, a thick-chested, shaggy-haired man in a miner's coat and ragged drill trousers.

"It was Grandda!" Little Jessie cried, her voice shrieking louder than the crows.

"Jacky Stout," Jessalyn said. She shivered, and McCady was surprised to see fear shadow her eyes.

"Who?"

"Jacky Stout." Jessalyn gathered the little girl against her legs, resting her palm on her head. "Little Jessie is the baby we found here in the mine that day." Startled, McCady looked down at the child. The pale, fey face that stared back up at him stirred a distant memory. She had a sharply pointed chin and tilted catlike eyes. Her black braids hung nearly to her waist, and a hole in her pantalets revealed a scabbed knee. Surely this child was too old. But then it had been over five years. "Jacky Stout is her grandfather," Jessalyn said.

"I remember him. I thought he'd been hanged for poaching."

"I don't like Grandda," Little Jessie said. "He hit me

once an' called me a—a bastid. Mam says he's good for nothing but gallow's fodder."

McCady hunkered down on his heels so that he was eye to eye with her. Little Jessie. Without thought his hand came up to cup her cheek, as if needing to touch her to prove that she was real. For so long that summer had seemed more dream to him than memory.

"I doubt it was your grandfather," McCady said softly. "It was probably some curious tinner come from far afield and looking for work."

"It was Grandda," Little Jessie insisted.

He looked up at Jessalyn, and although her face had gentled, he caught the lingering shadows of fear in her eyes. He wanted to ask her about Jacky Stout and why she was so afraid of him when she had not been afraid that summer. But his wife came tripping through the door just then, her pretty face alight with happiness. Jessalyn stepped back with a guilty flush, as if she'd been caught doing something wicked just by speaking with him.

"Oh, you must come see!" Emily cried. "Jessalyn . . . my lord." Color blossomed on her cheeks as her gaze fell on her husband. "You must come. They are having a *hurling* contest. Some of the miners are trying to see who can heave an old pit prop the farthest." She captured a smile with her hand. "I have never known the like."

Shrieking with excitement, Little Jessie ran to Emily, and Jessalyn followed more slowly. McCady straightened but remained where he was. The engine tender came in to stoke the fire, and the place suddenly seemed crowded.

The engine tender threw open the damper, releasing a great blast of heat. He shoveled in more coal and the fire blazed higher. The two women and the child stood within the great arched doorway, backlighted by blue sky and green sea. Laughing, Emily said something to Jessalyn. McCady waited, his heart suspended for Jessalyn's answering laugh. But it didn't come.

* * *

After that he told himself he would stay away from her. But he felt as if there was something alive inside him that had to be fed and instead he was slowly starving. So he kept seeking her out, with his eyes, with his nerve endings. And when he saw her break away from everyone and walk alone to the cliffs, he followed her.

The swiftly running tide swallowed the narrow beach, making a soft, rushing sound, like a pulse. She sat upon a rock hoary and shaggy with weeds and lichen. He sat beside her. She stiffened, but this time she made no move to run away. There were only the two of them and the gulls.

His hands trembled to touch her. He clenched them into a fist between his spread knees.

He spotted a single primrose growing in a bit of dirt within the cleft of a rock. He plucked the flower, twirling the stem between his fingers. The moon was coming up early in the afternoon sky, pale and half spent. It was not a blue moon.

"It is so wild and beautiful here," she said, breaking the silence between them. "Yet I was thinking of how this will all look in a few months, covered with mining attle and gritty black slag heaps."

He did not look where she did—at the yellow water gushing from the adit at the foot of the cliff, already staining the sand, swirling like spilled paint into the sea. He looked at her. Wisps of hair, the color of a campfire at night, curled about her face. Her skin was so pale it was almost translucent. Her mouth . . . her mouth . . .

He looked down and saw that he had crushed the primrose in his fist. He opened his hand, letting the bruised flower fall into the muddy sea. "I thought you would be pleased that I have opened the mine," he said.

"Oh, I am, I am. I was only being selfish."

A moment passed in silence as they watched a small plover scurry over the dripping rocks, a sand eel wriggling in its beak. She started to push herself up, and he helped her with a hand beneath her elbow. A gentleman's touch, an acceptable touch, a proper touch. But once they were on their feet, when he could have let go, when he *should* have let her go, he did not. He could feel her heat through the thin muslin sleeve of her dress, feel her trembling.

"Jessalyn . . ."

She pulled her arm from his grasp. "I wish—" She stopped the words by sinking her teeth into her lower lip, hard enough to leave imprints like tiny cuts.

He stared into her face. Her wide gray eyes impaled him, piercing his heart. "What do you wish?" *I would bring you the stars in the palms of my hands if I thought that it would only make you laugh again.*

"I wish that you would leave me alone, my lord. I wish that you would go away forever and leave me alone."

"Cor, Becka girl. Ee've got about as much sense as a peahen with no head."

Becka Poole pulled her fringed shawl close beneath her neck and folded her arms across her chest, hugging herself. He wasn't coming. He had said he would, but he wasn't going to come. Like as not he was back in his room at Caerhays Hall right this very minute, sitting afore the fire, toasting his toes, and laughing to think of her outside all alone at midnight, a prey for corpse lights and with a gale abrewing.

She touched her hagstone for luck just as lightning flared in a liverish sky. The wind had come up, high and thick with salt. It whistled like a pierced pig's bladder and set the boughs of the hawthorn and wild nut trees streaming out like flying witch's hair.

She huddled against the stone wall of the little dairy where she had arranged to meet him. Inside, some cheeses were starting to ripen, and their smell came to her on the wind. As did the sweet scent of lavender water. She had splashed a whole bottle of it all over herself before she'd changed into her best Sunday meeting frock. She hoped she hadn't overdone it.

Something curled around her legs, and she caught a scream with her hand before it could come flying out of her mouth. It was that wretched cat, Napoleon. She had just managed to calm her thudding heart when for some reason known only to himself the beast started yowling as if he'd just caught his tail in a mousetrap.

"Hist yer noise," she whispered loudly, flapping her hands at him. Dear life, she had to shut him up, or Miss Jessalyn would be out in two shakes to see what had him so overset. "Shoo, now. Off to bed with ee."

The runty orange cat streaked across the courtyard and leaped onto the front parlor windowsill. The window must have been left open a crack, for he pushed it with his paw and disappeared inside.

"Miss Poole?"

Becka whirled around, nearly leaping out of her skin. She pressed her hand against her breastbone because her heart was beating fit to burst out of her chest. Lightning flashed. He looked like a painting she had seen once of the Archangel Gabriel, his golden hair swirling in the wind, his tall, broad-shouldered body silhouetted against a black sky.

"I was thinking 'tis nae likely I'd be finding ye out this night after all," he said. He was wearing only a shirt that fluttered with his hard breathing. She wondered if he'd run all the way. She hoped not. Running wasn't good for the lungs, especially when they got to heaving like bellows against the walls of the chest. "Nae with this wind," he added.

"Oooh, this wind! 'Tes blowin' so hard a body needs two hands to hold down the hair on his head."

His smile glimmered like a silver trout in the dark. He had the straightest teeth, and they were very white. It occurred to her suddenly that she didn't often see him smile.

"Were ee born on a Wednesday?" she asked. "'Tesn't

good to be born on a Wednesday. I were born on a Tuesday. Wednesday's child be full of woe. Tuesday's child—"

He took her arm leading her deeper within the shelter of the dairy's low-thatched eaves. Her heart started to hammer again. It was beating so hard Becka feared she was having a heart stroke.

"Do I seem woeful to ye, Miss Poole?"

"Well . . . ais, ee do, betimes." She looked up into his face, struck nearly breathless suddenly with fear and excitement and a growing wonder. She was out here alone in the dark with a man who was handsome enough to be a prince. And who was lowering his head and parting his lips as if he were about to kiss her.

His mouth captured hers, held it fast a moment, then began to move with gentle, insistent pressure. When he ended the kiss an eternity later, Becka sucked in a great draft of air as if she'd been drowning.

"Cor!" she exclaimed. "Why did ee do that?"

He brushed her lips with his again. "It seemed the moment called for the doing of something frivolous."

Suddenly he lifted his head, sniffing the air. She thought he was going to sneeze. She hoped he hadn't caught her rheumy chill by kissing her. Her lips still tingled from where they had touched his. His lips had been the strangest combination of soft and hard. And they had been hot, too, and sort of melting, the way the top of a candle is just after you blow it out. In truth, she had rather liked the feel of them. She wondered how she could get him to do something frivolous again.

"Do ye smell smoke?" he said.

"Eh?" She drew in a deep breath, wrinkling her nose. She smelled the cheese and the sea and lavender water . . . and, aye, she smelled smoke. "Mebbe Miss Jessalyn couldn't sleep and she got up to stir the fire."

He stepped out from beneath the shelter of the dairy, and she went with him. She noticed something odd at the parlor window where Napoleon had slipped through earlier. An orange light, looking fractured and wavy through the mullioned glass.

She was just about to point this out to him when the roof erupted into flames.

19

His hot breath seared the back of her neck.

She ran down a path choked with brambly vines that burst into fiery pinwheels and sent sparks shooting into the air. She ran and ran, and still he was there, breathing against her neck, burning her skin. Tongues of hellfire licked at her legs, scorching, melting. A red-hot wind roared and crackled, consuming her screams. Yet she could hear him still, calling out to her, offering sweet promises she knew were lies, and she would not stop running, she would not turn around to look into his face. Because once she saw his face, she would be forever damned.

He laughed his devil's laugh. *You may as well look, Jessalyn, oh, yes. Because you cannot escape me. You can never escape me. You surrendered your soul to me when you were sixteen, and I* own *you now. So you may as well look . . .*

He seized her around the waist, enveloping her in a lover's embrace, and where he touched her she turned into fire. He spun her around, and his hot breath bathed her face, and though she kept her eyes squeezed tightly shut, she knew he smiled his devil's smile. *Mine. At last, at last you are mine . . . kiss me, Jessalyn. Become one with me and you will live forever.* Her will dissolved, betrayed by old powers, dark longings. She opened her eyes and looked into bright sunbursts floating in black pools, burning sunbursts, devouring sunbursts. His eyes, his eyes, McCady's eyes . . .

She screamed . . .

And woke up in hell.

The wall at the foot of her bed was a sheet of fire. Thirsty flames licked at the old silk paper melting it into instant ash. Black smoke billowed like wind-tossed clouds. Orange and yellow lights danced, reflected in the looking glass and windowpanes.

She sat up, blinking in confusion, not sure if she was dreaming still. Then she felt the heat and sucked in a breath choked with smoke, and she knew the fire was real. Throwing off the bedcovers, she leaped from the bed.

"Gram!"

At the door she paused. Smoke curled beneath the threshold in ghostly fingers. Flickers of eerie red light shone on the polished floor. Her hand reached out, hovering, afraid of what lay on the other side of the door.

The brass latch was so hot it seared the skin off her palms. She screamed from the pain and from terror, flinging open the door. The flames, fed by fresh air, flared with a whoosh.

The sudden fierce blast of heat drove her back, sucking the breath from her lungs. The fire hissed along the black oak floorboards, raising blisters that popped and curled like thick boiling soup.

She plunged through the flames and ran down the smoldering Turkey carpet to Lady Letty's room. Heat undulated in waves from the front stairwell. A pall of ocherous smoke hugged the ceiling. In the kitchen below, something was whistling and popping like the fireworks at Vauxhall Gardens.

Jessalyn reached for the latch, whimpering in expectation of the pain, but although the metal was hot, it wasn't burning. She pushed open the door and slammed it quickly behind her.

The fire had not reached this room yet, but the smoke was so bad it was like trying to peer through a wool blanket. Years' worth of varnish in the wood paneling released noxious fumes that blinded her eyes and tore at her throat, stealing her breath. Choking, Jessalyn groped her way to the bed.

It was empty.

"Gram!"

She fell to her hands and knees, searching the floor with her outstretched hands. Gram wasn't in the room, she wasn't here, oh, God, what if she left and Gram was still in here somewhere, unconscious, suffocating, burning . . .

The ceiling above her head exploded into flames.

"Gram!"

Sobbing, Jessalyn pushed herself half upright. She banged into the nightstand by her grandmother's bed, bruising her hipbone. She didn't even feel it. Pain was everywhere, with every breath.

Something clawed at her ankle, and she screamed before she realized it was Lady Letty. She fell back down to her knees again and wrapped her arms around the old woman's thin shoulders. She felt Lady Letty's chest jerk with her harsh breathing.

Streams of smoke were now pouring beneath the door. She tightened her grip on her grandmother. The old woman reached up, grasping her hand. "Leave me . . . too old . . ."

A jar of barley water sat on the nightstand above her. Jessalyn ripped pieces off the bottom of her night rail and soaked the cloth strips, tying one over her nose and mouth and doing the same for Gram. For a moment the sweet malty smell of barley filled her nostrils, but it was soon replaced by the smoke.

She hauled her grandmother upright as easily as she would lift a portmanteau. Fear and youth and determination made her strong.

Bearing almost all of Lady Letty's frail weight, Jessalyn

carried her to the door. The only way out of her grandmother's bedchamber was into the hall and down the stairs.
The room's large double mullioned windows overlooked
the courtyard, a straight two-story drop onto granite stone.
She could perhaps survive such a fall with only a broken
bone or two, but not Gram.

Jessalyn staggered through the flickering tongues of fire,
bent over, half dragging Lady Letty toward the stairs. Her
throat was raw. Every time she swallowed it felt as if she
were eating the flames. The heat seared the inside of her
lungs and roasted her skin. Her ears hurt from the roaring
noise the fire made, louder than any wind, louder than the
angriest of seas.

Snakes of flame curled up the stair banisters and slithered along the steps and risers. Jessalyn stopped and
looked down, and it was like staring deep into the heart of a
blast furnace. The fire was a living thing. Red and orange
and yellow flames fed and consumed and went on to feed
again, growing ever brighter and hotter and hungrier. The
world below had taken on a red glow, as if it had been
submerged in a pool of blood.

Lady Letty dug her nails into Jessalyn's arms, shaking
her. "Can't get out that way, gel," she choked.

Jessalyn blinked and shuddered. She looked down and
saw only death. Panic squeezed out what little air she had
left in her lungs. Gram was right, they would never make it
down the stairs and out the front door alive. There remained only her room. It was a short drop from the window
onto the roof that sheltered the front parlor, and a longer
drop to the ground, but to dirt, not stone.

They turned back. A fiery beam fell from the ceiling,
barely missing Jessalyn's head. She didn't even see it. She
burned her hand on the door latch again; this time she
made not a sound. The old-fashioned box bed, where she
had gone to sleep last night and all those nights of her
childhood, was now a flaming pyre. She propped Lady
Letty against the wall beside the window, the only wall not

burning. Using a chair as a battering ram, she broke through the wooden casement and thick diamond panes. The raucous fire drowned out the sound of shattering glass.

Jessalyn hefted Lady Letty over the ledge, out onto the roof, then turned back with some half-formed thought of trying to make it up to the attic to save Becka. Suddenly the door exploded, and flames roared into the room as if out of the mouth of a fire-breathing dragon. Searing heat buffeted her, throwing her back against the shattered window frame. Sobbing and choking, Jessalyn crawled on her hands and knees out onto the rough cedar shingles, and though she cut herself on the broken glass, she didn't feel it.

They stood together, straddling the blunted peak of the gently sloping hipped roof, sucking in drafts of sweet, cold air. The sea wind whipped at Jessalyn's hair and the ragged skirt of her night rail; it felt like ice against her blistered skin. But the fire blazed on in the parlor below, and the thin cedar strips beneath her bare feet were hot and growing hotter. She knew that it was only a matter of seconds before the shingles, too, would burst into flames.

A flutter of movement in the paddock below caught her eye, and she heard her name, snatched away by the wind.

"Becka!" she cried, shocked that it came out only a croak. "Get the ladder! In the stables!"

Becka was shouting and pointing. Jessalyn saw Prudence, the only horse still living at End Cottage, gallop out the open door of the stables, followed by a man with the ladder beneath his arm. She heard a sizzling crackle, felt a wave of heat break against her legs. The parlor roof had caught fire.

And then the man was on the burning roof with her, taking Gram from her arms. It was Duncan, the earl's manservant.

She followed him down the ladder. Her bare feet touched the earth, cool and moist, and her legs began to tremble. Her head reeled, and she swayed on her feet. "Miss Jessalyn!" Becka cried, seizing her around the waist.

"Oooh, Miss Jessalyn, don't ee faint here. Come over where 'tes safe."

Duncan carried Lady Letty to the grove of wild nut and hawthorn trees, out of harm's way of the flying cinders and choking smoke. Jessalyn, supported by Becka, followed.

He propped Lady Letty against the trunk of a tree. In the red glow cast by the fire, the old woman's face looked smeared with blood, and her gold-tasseled nightcap gave her a macabre look. Kneeling beside her, Jessalyn touched her cheek. "Are you all right, Gram?"

Lady Letty looked once at the blazing house, then turned her head aside. "Die . . ." She choked, her chest shuddering and jerking as she gasped for air. "Should have left me to die."

Fresh tears spilled from Jessalyn's burning eyes. She sat back on her heels, rocking, as the tears streamed down her cheeks. "Oh, Gram . . ."

Lady Letty's chest convulsed with another bout of racking coughs.

"The auld lady's swallowed a lot of smoke," Duncan said to Jessalyn, but she didn't seem to hear; she just kept rocking and weeping in a terrible silence. He straightened, and his big hands settled on Becka Poole's shoulders, pulling her around to face him. "Can ye run fast, lass?"

Becka swallowed hard and nodded.

"Run then and fetch the doctor."

Her eyes wide on his face, Becka nodded again. Duncan bent his head and planted a kiss that was hard and rough on her lips before he spun her around, giving her a little shove. "Off wi' ye then, my wee one."

Becka took off, running along the cliffs, just as a horse came galloping down the lane from the direction of Caerhays Hall. For a moment it seemed he would not stop, that the earl of Caerhays would send his horse plunging into the flames. Terrified by the fire, the animal reared so far back on his haunches his hind legs shot out from beneath him. The earl rolled off the horse's bare back and got to his feet, shouting. He threw back his head and bellowed like a man gone mad, "Jessalyn!"

Duncan reached him in time to stop him from dashing into the flaming house. He grasped Caerhays by the shoulders much as he had held Becka only moments ago. The earl wore only breeches and boots, and the manservant's fingers dug deep into hard flesh that was hot and slick with sweat.

"She's out, man. She's safe."

Dark eyes stared back at Duncan, crazed eyes that reflected the flames. The earl's head fell back, his lids squeezing shut, and his chest jerked once, hard, as if he were repressing a sob. Or a scream.

Something *was* screaming. Duncan flung his head back and looked up. A small orange cat paced the peak of the highest roof, yowling in fear and fury.

"Napoleon!"

Jessalyn Letty came flying out of the trees. By the time they understood what she was about, she was already halfway up the ladder. Duncan got to her first, hauling her back down. She flailed, sobbing hysterically. He wrapped his arms around her, trying to still her. The cat screeched.

Caerhays started up the ladder.

"Sir, no!" Duncan thrust Jessalyn away from him and grabbed the earl's boot. Caerhays kicked him in the chest and sent him staggering backward. "For mercy's sake, sir," Duncan shouted as the earl went over the top of the head step, "'tis only a cat."

Lord Caerhays swung around, and his mouth twisted into a crooked smile, a smile that was young and full of reckless bravado, and to Duncan's shock he felt himself smiling back. "What the hell, she loves the bloody thing," Caerhays said, and he ran up the slope of the flaming roof, the leather soles of his boots scrabbling for purchase on the burned and cracked shingles.

Bending at the knees, McCady swung his arms back and jumped up. He grabbed the edge of the cornice with his fingertips and hung there a moment, then jackknifed his legs and pulled himself onto the steep slope of the higher roof.

Flames and smoke swirled around him; it seemed impossible that he would not catch on fire. Something snapped inside Jessalyn then, and she came to herself. Horror widened her eyes as she understood the danger the man she loved had put himself into for her sake. "McCady, no!" she screamed. "Come back!"

It was unlikely he even heard her. He crawled up the burning roof, arms and legs splayed like a crab's. He hefted himself onto the peak, lying across the pointed edge. He stretched out a hand toward Napoleon, but the frightened cat scurried out of his reach. Balancing precariously, he stood up and walked along the peak, and his tall, broad-shouldered body was silhouetted against a sky that glowed orange like a sunrise. Napoleon crouched, gathering himself, preparing to leap onto the tall ornamented chimney stack. McCady lunged, seizing the cat by the scruff of its neck just as the ridgepole and rafters collapsed beneath him in a billow of fire.

"McCady!" Jessalyn screamed as he was swallowed by flames that shot into the sky like rockets. An arm wrapped around her waist, and she clawed at it. "McCady!" she screamed again, and it felt as if she were tearing her lungs out along with his name. She wanted to throw herself in the fire, to die with him. A pain gripped her, so intense she couldn't bear it. She turned her head, as if not seeing would make the pain go away, burying her face in the rough linen of Duncan's shirt.

It seemed an eternity of hell passed; then she felt Duncan shudder and heard the rumble of his voice echo within his chest. "Praise God."

She looked up. McCady Trelawny emerged out of the flames like a fallen angel passing through the gateway of hell, walking through what was left of her bedroom window, and struggling to hold on to a clawing, biting, yowling ball of singed orange fur.

She waited for him, laughing and crying, as he climbed down the ladder. He went to put the cat into her arms, like a trophy he had won in a joust, but Napoleon was having none of that. Scratching and hissing, he launched himself into the air and bolted for the trees.

Jessalyn ran her scorched palms over McCady's bare chest and arms, noting the bloody gouges left by Napoleon's claws and the raw blisters from the fire. "You silly pea goose, look at what you've done to yourself."

He gathered her to him, and they turned together to watch the fire consume what was left of End Cottage. The pretty yellow and red brick walls collapsed inward, sending a final flaming tower roaring into the sky. The faded purple settee where Gram always sat to take her afternoon tea, the beehive chair where Peaches once nursed her kittens before the kitchen hearth, a girl's straw bonnet decorated with a posy yellow primroses—all were gone now, reduced to ashes and memories.

She leaned against the hard wall of his chest and drew her strength from his. Later she would think this was wrong, to be in his arms, touching him. But in that moment there was no room for lust or passion, only for comfort.

This he gave her, while she stood within the circle made by his body and watched her childhood die.

Jessalyn's voice was nothing but a hoarse whisper. "Set? But who would want to set fire to End—"

A violent fit of coughing racked her chest, and she smothered her mouth with a wet handkerchief. Gentle fingers pushed the hair out of her face. "Here, drink this," McCady said.

Cupped in a strong, lean hand that was blistered as hers were from the fire, a glass of brandy appeared before her. She took the glass from him without meeting his eyes.

Their fingers touched. She drew back from his nearness, which was suddenly too overwhelming.

She took a huge swallow of the brandy and nearly choked again. The alcohol seared her raw throat but seemed to loosen some of the tightness in her chest. She took another swallow. "The Lettys have lived here for generations in peace with everyone," she croaked. "No one has a reason to burn down our house."

"Duncan believes he saw a man skulking about the kitchen wing at the time he noticed the fire. A big, shaggy-haired man dressed like a tinner."

Jessalyn repressed a shudder, hugging the wool blanket that she wore around her shoulders like a cloak. Beneath the blanket she had on only a tattered night rail, ripped and scorched. She had to remind herself that she was safe now, safe within the newly renovated library at Caerhays Hall. The room was chilly, but the grate remained empty; the earl had not called for a fire to be lit.

She could still smell smoke; it was in her hair, in her skin. Every inch of her body throbbed with pain, but her hands hurt the worst. She went to one of the tall French windows that looked north, toward End Cottage. Where End Cottage used to be. Columns of black smoke mushroomed against the bottom of clouds that were heavy and gray in the dawn sky. The wind sent water slashing against the panes, and the view before Jessalyn's eyes wavered. Too late it had started to rain.

She turned away from the window. She poured herself more brandy from the cut-glass decanter. As she returned the decanter to its place on a satinwood console table, the faceted crystal caught and reflected the candelabra flames, and she flinched. Her legs began to tremble, and she subsided into a nearby chair. Her hand shook as she brought the glass up to her lips, slopping brandy onto the blanket and just missing the chair's citron-striped chintz.

Dear life, I mustn't stain Emily's pretty new furniture,

Jessalyn thought wildly, barely suppressing a hysterical giggle.

The room had grown so silent she could hear the tick of the ormolu mantel clock and the rain beating against the windows. McCady Trelawny, wearing only his breeches and boots, had come riding like a demon out of the night to save her. He stood beside her now, half naked, and she could feel his seductive heat. He was like fire, she thought. Dangerous, destructive, beautiful. Tension thrummed through her like a high-pitched scream.

"Jessalyn." He touched her shoulder, and she flinched again.

Her singed hair fell back into her eyes, and she brushed it out of the way. She could not make her hands stop shaking. Her distracted gaze wandered around the room. "What was Duncan doing at End Cottage anyway?"

"He was visiting with your serving girl and—"

Her head snapped up. "Visiting Becka? At midnight? I will not allow this, my lord. Becka is a good girl, a decent girl, not some trollop to be taken advantage of by your valet, who is much too handsome to be allowed to run loose around the countryside—"

"Dammit, Jessalyn. Will you gather your scattered wits together and attend to what I'm saying?"

He turned abruptly away from her and threw himself into the leather chair that sat behind a heavy pedestal library table. He stretched his legs out, lacing his fingers behind his head, elbows spread wide, exposing the dark shadow of the hair beneath his arms, mysterious, erotic. Candlelight glinted off the sheen of sweat on his chest. *Someone ought to tell him that earls do not have such chests,* Jessalyn thought, *muscled and brawny like a Billingsgate porter's.* Her gaze jerked up to his dark angel's face, with its flaring cheekbones and arrogant mouth. His face that haunted her days and her nights.

Dizziness overwhelmed her, and she blinked. The brandy had gone straight to her head. She jerked her gaze away from his, as if appearing to be suddenly fascinated with the blue-patterned tobacco jar that sat at the far end of the tabletop. The room seemed too small.

"I hear what you are saying, my lord. The man who set the fire was Jacky Stout. It has to be he. He was caught poaching about two years back. He was going to be transported, but that prison hulk up in Plymouth is like a sieve. Ever since that day we found Little Jessie in the mine, he's blamed me for all his misfortunes. He is convinced I peached on him to the squire's gamekeepers."

Jessalyn thought of Jacky Stout running loose about the countryside, setting murderous fires. "She'll get hers!" he had bellowed as the gaolers led him away. "She'll get hers, that Letty bitch!" She hadn't paid much attention to the threat at the time. She still found it hard to believe the man had come back to Cornwall to wreak such destruction.

McCady got up and circled the table, coming toward her, and her whole body tensed. She could barely breathe from the pressure in her chest.

"You could be right about Stout," he said. "I'll look into it. In the meantime, you ought to be in bed. You've had a shock and—"

She thrust herself so hard out of the chair that it teetered, bringing herself up right next to him. So close their chests almost touched. "I cannot possibly stay here!" she cried, choking on the last word.

He breathed an impatient sigh, and she felt his chest move. "You heard what the doctor said. Your grandmother has congestion of the lungs from the smoke she inhaled. She is to remain in bed for at least a fortnight."

Jessalyn had heard, but she hadn't wanted to think about the consequences of the doctor's diagnosis. She tried to imagine herself here in this house, where she was liable to come upon him at any time. This house, an earl's great hall. She looked around the tastefully furnished room. Beneath the decay had been beautiful oak floors, covered now with a red and buff carpet. The broken windowpanes had been

replaced and framed with curtains of rich cream silk padua-
soy. The fireplace had been furnished with a modern steel
grate. Emily was making a pleasant home for him, Jessalyn
thought, and he had never really had a home. Emily was
making him a good wife.

Jessalyn felt weighted with a deep, dark sadness. What
she felt for him was never going to go away, but it was
wrong now, immoral and wicked. She was wishing for,
waiting for something she could never have, ought not to
have, and she was making herself miserable with the wanting.

He saw the fear in her eyes, but he misunderstood the
reason for it. "Nothing more is going to happen to you,
Jessalyn. I won't allow it." His arm started to come up, as if
he were going to reach for her, to draw her close, but then
he let it fall without touching her. "It will be easier for me
to protect you if you are here at the hall."

She drew in a deep breath, trying to relieve some of the
tightness in her chest. "I haven't any clothes," she said
suddenly. The immensity of what she had lost struck her
then, and a great sob welled up in her throat.

His hand settled on the small of her back to propel her
forward. His touch was worse than fire. She couldn't bear
it. "Come," he said. "Emily is having a bedchamber prepared for you and a bath drawn. And she'll find you some
clothes. Later, after you are rested, we will make plans for
what you are to do."

"I seem to have little choice, do I?" Jessalyn said, her
voice brittle. At the door she stopped, moving out of his
light embrace. "Order your manservant to stay away from
Becka."

"Duncan isn't the sort to take advantage of an innocent
girl's susceptibilities."

"If he allows her to fall in love with him when he does
not really want her love, that is all it takes to break an
innocent girl's heart."

She had the satisfaction of seeing his face tighten with a

flash of pain before she turned away. But it did little to
mend the pieces of her own broken heart.

She got as far as the stairs before she fainted. Although
she didn't know it, he caught her before she hit the floor.
And though she didn't feel it, he kissed her forehead, but
not her lips.

One storm after another came in from the sea, and time
dribbled more slowly than sand through the hourglass on
the Reverend Troutbeck's pulpit.

Jessalyn paced before a dying fire, too restless to sleep.
In the two days that she had been at Caerhays Hall, she
had managed to avoid coming face-to-face again with its
master. Pleading smoke-induced headaches, she had taken
all her meals on trays and spent the afternoons sitting with
Gram. But it did little good. His presence was everywhere:
in the smell of his shaving soap, which lingered in the hall
outside his bedroom door, in the soiled cravat left carelessly draped over the newel-post at the top of the stairs, in
the deep timbre of his voice heard across the stableyard.

The wind lashed at the house. Candle flames fluttered in
their glass globes, and the maroon curtains on the big four-
poster rustled as if stirred by an unseen hand. Drafts of
damp air swirled around the room in spite of the embroidered silk Chinese screens set before the door and windows.

Jessalyn shivered, pulling the quilted satin collar of her
borrowed night robe tighter around her neck. She went to
the velvet-draped window, drawn to look out at the storm-
ravaged night. She could see little of the wild, overgrown
gardens below; sea spume carried inland by the wind had
left the panes crusted with salt like pickled herrings. Water
splashed against the glass. At End Cottage, when it stormed
like this, they'd had to lay rags along the windowsills to
catch the leaks.

She supposed the same was probably true for much of
the rest of Caerhays Hall. Only a portion of one wing had

been renovated thus far. And even then Jessalyn imagined the cost must have been enough to make a rich man wince, for the great old house had been allowed to deteriorate for too long.

The changes were all Emily's doing. Her presence, too, was everywhere, and although Jessalyn tried hard to avoid the lord of the hall, she found herself seeking out the company of its lady.

That afternoon she had come across Emily in the drawing room, arranging daffodils and bluebells into a milk glass vase. She looked fruil and delicate in her almond green merino morning dress, even though it was cut full beneath the bosom to allow for her pregnancy. Her short silver blond curls shimmered like a wind-stirred lake in the shaft of rare sunlight that came through the chintz-draped windows.

Jessalyn told herself she was being foolish, but she felt as dowdy as a brown hen in a puce fustian that had been borrowed from Squire Babbage's wife, who next to herself was the tallest woman in the county. The dress hung on her like a wet sail, and there was still a gap of three inches between the padded hem of the skirt and Jessalyn's slippers.

But Emily's smile was warm and friendly as Jessalyn paused in the doorway to the drawing room, unsure of her welcome.

"Jessalyn! I trust your headache is better." Emily returned to her arrangement, cupping a sun yellow bloom in her palm. "These spring storms play havoc with a flower garden. I should like to replant the conservatory someday. But that is for the future."

Jessalyn entered a room that was decorated in a soft color scheme of ocher and citron and a mismatch of styles that all somehow seemed to go together. "You have done wonders with the house already," she said.

Emily flushed as she set the vase of flowers on a pier

table between a pair of silver candlesticks. "Much of this furniture came from my mother's attics."

It occurred to Jessalyn that she knew all about catching pilchards and training racehorses, yet she was sadly lacking in domestic talents. Emily might be a corn merchant's daughter, but she was better suited to be an earl's wife than Jessalyn would ever have been.

"We can afford very little at the moment," Emily said in a cheerful lilt, sounding as if she truly did not care that the whole world knew her husband to be on the precipice of ruin. Yet Jessalyn noticed that she nervously fingered the fringe of the tippet she wore around her shoulders. "Caerhays says Wheal Patience should start paying its way soon. He is hoping for a windfall of profits to settle the interest on those monstrous railway loans."

"There is the baby," Jessalyn couldn't keep herself from saying. "And the settlement that will come to you from your father once the child is born."

Emily pressed her palm to the swell of her stomach. "Oh, yes, there is that. The babe might come in time, and it might be a boy. But though I couldn't bear to see Caerhays flung into Fleet Prison, I cannot help wishing he didn't have to be saved in that way. He is so proud. I think that he would so much rather save himself." The blue eyes she lifted to Jessalyn's face were shadowed with worry and a kind of sick yearning. "He is not the sort of man to have married for money. Oh, I know he claims it is a Trelawny tradition, but he says it with such a bitterness in his voice—"

Emily froze at the rap of bootheels on the stone-flagged floor of the great hall. Color flooded her cheeks, and she seemed to hold her breath. Then they heard the deep rumble of Duncan's voice and an answering giggle from Becka.

"Oh!" Emily exclaimed with a soft little sigh. "I thought it might be . . . He's gone to Penzance to coddle his precious locomotive. Something arrived by the stage from a foundry in Birmingham yesterday. Copper tubes, I believe he said, although what on earth their purpose is I haven't the least notion."

Emily's face came alive as she spoke of the earl, and her gaze kept drifting to the door as if still she hoped he would pass through it, even though he was not expected.

Jessalyn pictured the two of them discussing his inventions over their coffee cups at breakfast. Or they could have walked along the beach at Crookneck Cove, chasing the gulls and the waves and laughing while he promised that she would be one of the first to ride on his new locomotive. Perhaps it was at night, when he held her in his arms, that he whispered of his dreams, asking her to share in them, while she touched his man's body, touched his man's soul.

And Jessalyn had had to look away from Emily's bright and lovely face because she could not bear such thoughts.

Yet now, in the dark and empty hours of the storm-ravaged night, they came to her again, unbidden, unwelcome, unbearable. Emily lying in McCady's arms, touching, touching . . .

She pushed herself away from the window. Suddenly she wanted to feel the violent fury of the rain beating against her face, to be swallowed by the black night, to be buffeted and plundered by the wind. She wanted to fling out her arms and embrace the storm, to be ravished by it.

She threw off her night clothes and struggled into Mrs. Babbage's rough fustian dress, not bothering with shift or stays. She had no cloak, but she knew there would be a set of oilskins and seaboots in the kitchen, for no Cornish house would be without them. Taking up a candlestick, she stepped into the hall.

Only a single glass taper lamp lit the dark walnut-paneled passage. She passed Emily's door and then his. They did not share a bedroom, but then no fashionable couple of the *ton* did. Somehow she found herself pausing in the middle of the hall, ears tensed for a sound, his voice, his footstep, beyond the old-fashioned iron-banded barrier to his chamber.

The door swung open, so startling her that she nearly dropped the candle. Hot wax splattered, missing the dish and burning her hand. She stared up at him, eyes wide, as she sucked the stinging web of skin between her finger and thumb.

The room was dark behind him, except for the flickering orange glow from the fire. Shadows lay like blades across his face. He was bare from the waist up. A light mat of dark hair limned the bulges and hollows of his chest. He stood with one arm braced, his hand pressing so hard against the jamb that the veins stood out against his skin. She could imagine the power of him, how he would feel beneath her hands.

"What are you doing still up?" he demanded in a voice as dark and shadowed as the rest of him. "I thought you had a headache."

Her breath came out in a soft whistle. "I—I thought to go for a walk along the cove."

"It's high tide. The sea is battering the cliffs, and there's no beach to walk on. It's too dangerous."

He took a step closer to her, into the hall. Water dripped from his long, windblown hair, and his wet buckskins lay plastered to his flesh, slick and shiny like the coat of a seal.

She wet her lips, swallowed. "Yet you braved the storm."

He said nothing.

"Well, perhaps I'll read then. If I might borrow a book?"

He shrugged, and the naked muscles of his chest flexed. "Of course."

She turned and walked with stately dignity down the hall, although her insides were frothing and frizzing like a glass of effervescent lemon. Behind her the old wood creaked like dry bones.

She stopped and spun around so abruptly he nearly walked into her. His hand grasped her arm. He let it go immediately, but it was not soon enough. Jessalyn had to fight for the breath to speak.

"I can find my own way down."

He gave no answer, and when she turned and descended the stairs, he came after her.

He opened the door to the library for her. But he straddled the threshold, so that she had to walk by him, so close her sleeve brushed his bare chest. He smelled of the rain and wet leather and the cool night air. Her nipples, naked of a modest shift, tightened and scraped against the coarse fustian. Never before had she been so aware of her own body. She felt all tight and hot, as if her flesh were swelling and pressing against her skin.

He lit an ormolu patent lamp that sat on the massive pedestal desk. Papers were spread in disarray beneath it. Cost sheets, she noticed, for Wheal Patience. Covered in red ink.

He splashed brandy into a toddy glass, drank it down, and poured another. Carrying the freshened glass, he went to the hearth and tossed more coal onto the fire. Flames leaped up the chimney, brightening the room and bronzing his skin with a soft golden glow. Never had she been more aware of him as a man. The strong, slender sinews of his sun-browned hands. The way his naked chest expanded and subsided with his every breath. The way the damp leather breeches clung to his slender hips and long, lean thighs.

He spun around suddenly, and the firelight danced off the facets of the glass in his hand. He lifted it and one brow in a silent offer.

Her mouth was so dry she had to swallow before she could speak. "No. Thank you."

He took a step toward her, and she scooted around him as if he were a snake lying across her path. She put the desk between them and pretended to be fascinated with the contents of the podium bookcases, which were mostly empty.

His voice came from behind her. "We haven't much of a collection, I'm afraid. The Trelawnys have never been ones for scholarship, and books are easy to dispose of when one is sadly dipped and in need of the ready in a hurry."

She lifted her head and saw his reflection in the grilled glass doors. His face was dark and brooding. Their gazes met and held as if locked, and Jessalyn stopped breathing. Outside, the wind moaned and the rain beat violently against the tightly closed shutters.

She fumbled open the case and pulled out a slim red leather volume, not even bothering to check the title.

He set the toddy glass down with such force it chimed like a dinner bell. When she turned around, he was in front of her, blocking her escape. She backed up until her bottom struck the sharp corner of the desk. Her name, carried to her on the sudden wash of his hot breath, was drowned out by the howl of the wind.

Rivulets of water had trickled from his hair onto his shoulders and chest. It glistened on the bare flesh, matting the hair into swirls around his nipples, funneling down over ridges of muscle, following a dark arrow to the waistband of his tight, low-slung buckskins, where they gaped open, the top two buttons left negligently undone.

She jerked her startled gaze back up to his face.

He took a step toward her, and her breath left her chest in a low, keening moan. His mouth had taken on a ruthless slant, and the yellow sunbursts flared bright and hot in his eyes. He smelled of brandy now and a feral heat. A leashed violence seemed to shimmer in the air around him like heat waves off a smithy's forge. As if he were a wild animal that had been caged too long and had gone suddenly mad from his captivity.

He will take me, she thought, *take me here on the floor of the library with his wife upstairs.* He would take her, fiercely and hungrily, the way a man took a woman he wanted.

And she would let him.

Suddenly he spun away from her. His back shuddered, and the words sounded torn from him. "Get out of here, Jessalyn. Now."

Jessalyn fled the room and didn't stop until she was safe

within her own bedchamber with the door shut and bolted behind her. She leaned against the wall, her chest jerking with the effort to get enough breath.

Nothing had happened. He hadn't touched her, barely spoken to her, only looked at her. Yet she felt ravished.

20

Jessalyn walked across the soot-dusted stones of the courtyard, her wooden pattens clattering, echoing like pebbles
dropped down an empty well.

All that was left of End Cottage was the tall ornamental
chimney stack. With its scalloped cap and red and yellow
checkered brickwork, the chimney looked sad and lonely
thrusting up among the broken, blackened beams and
charred rubble. Like a gaudy strumpet long past her prime.

Jessalyn tasted the grit of ash on her teeth. The smell of
burned wood pinched her nose. The sadness and loneliness
were there, too, within herself. She had known love in this
house, and security. She told herself that it was not the
house that had made her feel these things. The essentials in
her life remained: the people she cared for and who cared
for her and Cornwall, with its moors and cliffs and, always,
the enveloping sea.

The patch of primroses still bloomed against the paddock
fence. She picked one, stroking the starburst of yellow petals across her cheek, closing her eyes to let its faint, sweet
scent banish the scorched smell of destruction.

An angry yowl broke through her thoughts. Napoleon
streaked across the courtyard until he was almost upon her,
then skidded to a stop and sauntered slowly, as if he hadn't

been all *that* pleased to see her. Laughing, she bent to pick him up. "Where have you been, you wretched cat?" she said, rubbing noses with him. He'd been missing since the fire, and she'd feared he had run off for good.

Napoleon burst into a raucous purr. But after a moment the fickle beast squirmed to be let down. Tail swishing, he began to stalk a robin that was searching among the stones for moss to build a nest.

Jessalyn set out across the headland toward the cliffs. The rain had started the gorse to blooming, so bright a yellow it hurt the eyes. The moors were a palette of earthy colors from the pea green of new grass to the light biscuit brown of salt-scrubbed rocks. But the sea was all sulky gray, muttering and grumbling across the sand. In the cove below a flotilla of fishing boats was dressing sails to catch a sudden shift in the wind. A pair of sea gulls flapped across the sand, fighting over a fish head.

A patch of familiar blue linsey-wool fluttered on the sea side of the cliff hedge. Jessalyn called out Becka's name.

The girl started to run, then stopped, turning her face into the stones. Her shoulders shuddered, and Jessalyn heard choked and strangled sobs. She approached slowly, not wanting to frighten the girl into hying off.

She touched her bent head. "Becka, m'love. What has happened?"

Becka's answer came out muffled by tears and a red cotton kerchief.

Jessalyn used her fingers to stroke the sweat-damp strands of hair off Becka's face. "Is it Duncan?"

Becka blew loudly into the kerchief, then took her nose out. It was pink as a gooseberry, and her plump cheeks were white and blotched with tears like a soggy bun. But the scar looked red and welted, newly cut. "Me heart, she be b-brokennn!" she cried, the last syllable ending in a wail.

Jessalyn gathered Becka into her arms, stroking her

heaving back. "If he has compromised you, m'love, I shall compel him to marry you."

Becka shied away from her. "Ooh, God spare me. I bain't never marryin' Mr. Duncan. Never!" Her eyes grew round as jingle wheels. "Ee can't force me, can ee?"

"No, of course not. Not if you don't want to."

Becka's plump chin took on a stubborn tilt. "Good. 'Cause I doesn't. Why, what would he be wantin' with the likes of me? I'd be of no more use to him than a mule with a wooden leg." She flung back her hair, twisting her face toward the merciless eye of the sun. "Look at me! What man wants a woman what looks like this?"

"Someday there will be a man, a decent, kind man, who will love you for what you are," Jessalyn said softly.

Becka dashed tears out of her eyes. "Oh, aye, mebbe if he be ugly as a two-headed toad hisself, but not un like Mr. Duncan." She drew in a deep, shuddering sigh. "And he hasn't complicated me neither, 'cause I haven't been lettin' him do no coosing around. Well, mebbe I did allow him to kiss me oncet. Mebbe twice. But no more. And though me heart be broken into a million crims, ee won't see me going all historical—ascreechin' and atearin' out me hair over a man. Look at me hands, calm they be."

The hands she held out were red and work-chapped and nail-bitten, and tears welled in Jessalyn's eyes. She closed her fingers around Becka's rough ones, but Becka jerked away from her and took off running down the cliff path. Jessalyn thought about following, but she could offer the girl little comfort. It was that wretched Duncan she had to see and get set straight on a thing or two.

She returned to the hall, only to be told by one of the earl's two stable hands that the manservant had gone down to Wheal Patience. Something had got to rattling in the pump engine, the boy said, and Duncan was one of the few coves around these parts, besides the earl, who knew how those infernal things were put together. Determined to

have it out with the man immediately, Jessalyn set off for
the mine.

She passed a mule train, heavy with panniers of tin
bound for the coinage hall in Penzance. Perhaps some of
the red ink on the earl's cost sheets would soon be turning
to black, she thought. As she got within sight of the mine,
she heard a party of bal-maidens singing in the washing hut
and the thump and clatter of the tin stamp.

The engine had just been coaled; thick smoke belched
from the chimney, drifting across the scarred moors. Behind it rolled the sea, a bottle green, the color of Clarence
Tiltwell's eyes. Odd that she would think of him now. Or
perhaps not so odd, after all this talk of marriage. If she
married anyone now, it would be Clarence. Yet still she
straddled the fence, unable to tell him yes or no.

She found Duncan within the enginehouse, hunkered
down before the boiler. A piece of the brass plating had
been removed, and he had his hand thrust inside a mess of
tubes so tangled they looked like a plate of Italian noodles.
He was wrenching at something with a spanner, and she
wondered how he kept from scorching his fingers. Steam
hissed and plopped in scalding drops onto the floor, and
she could hear a steady throb thump and the suck and
splash of water, which meant the pump was working.

The enginehouse had lost much of the gaiety of opening
day. It was the hub of a working mine now, filled with
strips of canvas, miners' picks and shovels, storm lanterns,
and kegs of blasting powder. Already the whitewashed
walls were turning ocherous from the coal smoke, and the
miners' dirty boots had left tracks of congealed grease and
dried mud on the stone floor. Duncan, however, looked
magnificent—stripped down to shirtsleeves and a yellow
swansdown waistcoat that matched his hair, the muscles of
his arms and back bunching with each twist of his wrist.

The mine was between shifts, and so the house was
empty of people. Besides Duncan, there was only a single
tinner, who was even now climbing onto a round iron

bucket the Cornish called a kibble, lurching into the shaft, bumping out of sight, and leaving Jessalyn alone with Mc-Cady's manservant.

He turned and looked up at the sound of her footsteps. "Miss Letty? If ye're looking for his nibs, he's gone down—"

She stopped before him, her hands fisted on her hips. "You have broken Becka's heart, and I demand to know what you are going to do about it."

He tossed the spanner onto the stone floor with an angry clatter. He stood up, wiping his palms on a stained rag. "Her heart is no more broken than mine be. She willna have me."

Jessalyn's eyes widened in surprise. "You've asked her to marry you?"

"Aye, I've tossed her the handkerchief a'right," he said, the words coming out in a bitter rush. "And she tossed it right back at me. She told me she was a drunken tinner's ugly daughter, and I shamed her with my offer because I didna mean it, and if I meant it, I'd likely regret it. She said I'd soon get so pucky-sick of her scarred face, I'd be out for a lark with any moll or whore-bird who caught my eye, thereby shaming her even worse."

"Oh, Becka . . ."

He jerked his head. "Oh, aye. She thinks 'tis nae but lust as put the words into my mouth. She thinks some sort of witch she calls a knacker has put a lust spell on me. She even gave me something to counteract the magic." He tugged open his shirt and drew out a shriveled brown-green lump that was strung through the middle with a bit of twine. He held it up, shrugging. "Aweel, I had to put it on. I'd ae hurt her feelings otherwise. Do ye know what 'tis?"

"It's a mummified frog."

He dropped the charm as if it had suddenly been jolted into life with one of those electric currents and had tried to leap out of his hand. Jessalyn laughed, and after a moment his laughter joined with hers, though he sobered first. "Oh, Becka . . ." Jessalyn sighed. She stared at the man's averted face, at the finely sculpted nose and cheekbones, the sensual lips. "You must know you are a very handsome man, Duncan. I should imagine you are . . . well, that women might . . ."

His beautiful mouth twisted into something that was not quite a smile. "Aye, ye've the right of it. I shave this phiz of mine every day. I know I've got what ye might call pleasing features. And I won't deny there's been a time or two when I've used them to get beneath a woman's skirts. But a straight nose and a well-shaped mouth . . . they're all chance. A good heart doesna lie behind a handsome face, no more than evil goes about dressed as ugliness." He looked at her out of tawny eyes that were pure and deep as springwaters. "There is in Miss Poole a sweetness, a good-ness of heart the like of which I've never met before. I would count myself the luckiest man in the world if she would consent to share my life. And I would spend that life making sartain she never regretted her choice."

"Oh, Becka . . . Perhaps if I talked to her, I might convince—"

He shook his head, and his mouth softened into a gentle smile. "Nay. Don't ye worry, Miss Letty. I'll talk her round to my way of thinking, given time." The smile deepened, crinkling the tiny fan lines around his eyes. "And my word as a gentleman's gentleman: I willna take her to my bed till it can be as my wife."

But Jessalyn was beginning to wonder if perhaps more ardent lovemaking on Duncan's part might be just what was needed to convince Becka of the sincerity of his feel-ings. She had opened her mouth to offer a delicately worded suggestion when the stone floor shivered beneath her feet as if the earth had caught an ague.

Her startled gaze flew to Duncan's face. He had his head cocked toward the main shaft. A heartbeat later a great blast shook the enginehouse, and the ground heaved violently, knocking Jessalyn to her knees. Clouds of brown dust billowed out of the pit. A faint odor of sulfur singed the air.

Shouts rebounded up the walls of the shaft; boots rang on stone. Through a haze of dust and smoke, Jessalyn saw a head top the ladder, eyes blinking molelike in a blackened face. In the stunned silence that had followed the explosion, Jessalyn could hear water dripping. The candle in the miner's hat flickered in the gloom.

"There's been a fall on the seventh level!" he shouted as Duncan sprang forward to help him. "A bad un. There's four, mebbe five trapped." He hacked a cough. "Air's gone thick with dust. And 'tes flooding."

Another man climbed out the pit in a temper, jerking the hard hat off his head and flinging it at the wall. "The shorings all come down on the back half of the winze. Some bleedin' fool set off powder down there."

More miners spilled out of the black hole in the ground, looking like bog creatures with their muddy faces and wet, filthy clothes. One especially, with his squat-legged, thick-bellied body and greasy, shaggy hair. He held a hand up to his hat, shading his mud-splashed face with his arm. Hunching his back, he ducked under the great swinging beam rod, disappearing behind the pump engine. But for a flash of a second their gazes had met—and Jessalyn could almost have sworn she'd been looking into the snake gray eyes of Jacky Stout.

Just then someone cried out from below that a man was coming up on the kibble with a broken arm. Jessalyn had hurried over to the shaft head to see if she could help when an echo came to her as if carried along on the gauzy ribbons of smoke and dust: *If ye're looking for his nibs, he's gone down—*

She seized Duncan's arm so hard she nearly pitched the both of them into the pit. "Where is Lord Caerhays?"

The face he turned to her was ash gray. "One of the tutworkers discovered a new tin-bearing lode. His nibs and the mine captain went down to see it for themselves." The color seemed to blanch from his eyes as he spoke. "The seventh level. He's on the seventh level."

Jessalyn shook her head hard, as if by doing so she could shake off his words. "No. Oh, God . . ."

Something pressed against her chest, cutting off her breath. He was down there, in the ground, buried beneath tons of rock and dirt, the black water rising, filling his mouth, smothering his screams. . . . Get him out, she had to get him out.

A pile of mining gear and tackle lay heaped in one corner. She ran over to it; her hands clawed through metal and wood. She picked up a shovel, then saw something better: a rock drill. She started back to the shaft head.

Duncan tried to pry the heavy iron drill from her shaking grip. She tugged back. She couldn't bear the thought of McCady's dying down there while she did nothing. "Let go of me, damn you."

"Ye canna go down there, Miss Letty," Duncan said, laying a big hand on her shoulder, stilling her. "Ye'd only be in the way. And there's Lady Caerhays, she'll be needing ye."

Her chest heaved; she couldn't seem to get enough air. At last she sucked in a great breath, and with it came a raw and impotent fury. Damn him. Damn McCady Trelawny for trying to leave her again. Always, always he left her. "I shall never forgive him for this," she raged aloud. "What was he thinking of? He's the earl now, he's not supposed to be going down into mines."

Duncan expelled a deep sigh. He plucked a lantern off a peg on the wall and slammed a hard hat onto his head. "They said the load looked rich. And he's that desperate for the blunt, Miss Letty."

Jessalyn let the drill clatter to the floor. She pressed back tears with the heels of her hands; she knew there wasn't anything she could do. Except wait.

* * *

"Is he dead?"

Emily tottered down the cliff path, the wind whipping at her blue hussar cloak, flattening it against the bulge of her stomach. Her face was the thin, translucent white of an eggshell. "Please tell me he's not dead."

Jessalyn took her arm, steadying her. She felt so frail, as easy to blow away as a dry leaf. "He's been trapped by a fall, but they're digging him out." Saying it aloud, she could believe that it was true, that he would come out of it alive and whole.

She tightened her grip on Emily's arm as Dr. Humphrey lumbered past them on the narrow path, the long tails of his frock coat slapping his legs. He carried his black bag in one hand, while the other kept his wig anchored to his head. Emily swayed, buffeted by his wake.

"You mustn't try to make this climb," Jessalyn said, gently pushing her back up the path. "It's too dangerous, and you've the babe to think of. Come, I'll wait up on the bluff with you."

They sat, side by side, with their backs braced against the rocks where the land fell sheer to the sea. The tall brick tower that was Wheal Patience thrust up from the promontory below them, like a rocket poised to fire. The sun set behind it, limning the bricks with a silver light.

The sea wind cooled Jessalyn's face. She rubbed a chin that was tacky with dirt and the sweat of fear against her drawn-up knees. She could still taste the brown dust in her mouth, like chalk. Beneath her bottom, the ground vibrated with the steady pulselike throb of the engine, pumping water from the depths of the earth where he lay buried, but not dead. . . . Please, God, not dead . . .

The core bell hadn't clanged that evening, but the men on the night shift were already there. Word of the fall had spread, and they had come, carrying their picks and shovels and drills. Their women had arrived, as always, in the late afternoon to get hot water for their washing and had stayed to keep the vigil.

Only a faint bit of daylight showed now on the horizon, dying behind clouds that were torn and ragged like a beggar's cloak. Frothy waves flashed white and sharp like knife blades.

The darkness made the waiting worse. Down there, where he was, the dark would be utter and absolute, smelling of death. Her fear for him was a scream in the back of her throat that kept threatening to burst out. She wrapped her arms around her bent legs, hugging herself.

Beside her Emily stirred. Her voice came, gentle on the wind. "You love him, too, don't you?"

A tightness squeezed Jessalyn's chest, and tears stung her eyes. She was too soul-weary to lie. "It seems that I have loved him my entire life."

The tide washed against the rocks, again and then again. Emily ripped up a handful of marram grass, sending a tiny avalanche of pebbles splashing into the sea. "I am his wife, but you are his . . . I was going to say heart, but that's not it. His obsession, I suppose."

Jessalyn held herself still, afraid to move, afraid to speak.

Emily twisted around, and her face in the deepening twilight looked brittle as old parchment. "But he is my husband. Caerhays is mine."

Jessalyn's breath stopped in her throat. "I know . . . I know."

Emily's shoulders hunched, and she smothered her mouth with her knuckles. "Oh, *God*, I love him so. He is my night and my day." She pulled down her fists, tilting her face to the night sky. "And he—he is kind to me, but that is all."

Emily's fingers pleated and unpleated the soft wool of her cloak. "That night of the fire, I started to come into the library, and for some reason I got distracted—it was Duncan, I think, coming to tell me that the rain had doused the flames, and there was no longer any danger of its spreading. And I heard Caerhays shouting through the closed door. 'Dammit, Jessalyn,' he said, bellowed really, and I could tell that he was quite angry with you. He is never anything but unfailingly polite with me, no matter what I do or say. The few times I tried to provoke him into feeling *something* for me, even if it was rage, he simply left the room." She vent her frustration on the grass, tearing it up by the roots. "Kindness! I think that it is possible to kill with kindness—"

"Miss Letty!"

The tinners' women had gathered within the shelter of a copse of wind-twisted hawthorn. Little Jessie had broken away from the group and was toddling across the sward, lugging a basket almost as big as she was. "Miss Letty, lookit!" A big grin split her face as she raised the wicker lid, revealing an earthenware plate piled with lardy cakes, a battered teapot, and two tin cups.

"Me mam said ee would be needin' vittles to keep up yer strength." From the pocket of her pinafore, she produced a mashed lump wrapped in newspaper that turned out to be a smoked pilchard sandwiched between chunks of black bread. "This un's mine, but ee can have it, too."

Jessalyn's fear had churned her stomach into a permanent state of nausea, but she took the sandwich and even managed a smile. "That is very kind of you, spud."

"I can pour. Lemme pour." Little Jessie squatted beside them, knees spread wide, her lips pouched in concentration as she filled the cups. Steam wreathed her fey, pointed face. The tea was hot and black, smelling strongly of jasmine.

Jessalyn took the tea, warming her fingers on the hot tin. "Have you seen your grandfather again since the opening, Little Jessie?"

The child shook her head so hard her braids whipped her chest. "No'm. Mam said I musta been mistooken. He scampered off, did Grandda, on 'count of the runners bein' after him. Went to America. Should I be leavin' the basket, Miss Letty?"

"Yes, please. Thank your mam for me."

Emily watched the little girl run off with a flash of white pantalets. "Little Jessie. Was she named after you?"

Jessalyn breathed a shaky laugh. "Yes, the poor little thing." She broke off a piece of the lardy cake and flung it into the sea for the shorebirds. "What a namesake to have to live down—the scrapes I got into when I was her age . . ."

"She is the baby you and Caerhays found in the mine," Emily stated. Jessalyn kept her gaze on the lardy cake, breaking off another piece. "He spoke to me once of that time," Emily said. "He said they were the happiest days of his life."

Jessalyn swung around in surprise. "But it was only one summer."

"A summer that changed his life. I believe he thought that if he ever married anyone, it would be you."

Jessalyn stared out at a sea that was still and black, as if it, too, existed only to wait. "I asked him to marry me that summer. I as much as begged him. He wanted nothing to do with me, and he told me so in most unflattering terms."

"I think men must be different from women in how they love," Emily said, "in how they show their love. For us being in love is a haven. For some men it can be a most tormenting kind of hell."

In the dark all Jessalyn could see was the purity of Emily's profile and her cropped hair faintly tinseled by starlight. Her chest felt sore with a grief unspent. She wondered if this was a punishment from God, for clinging to her love even after he had married. It was sinful to covet what was Emily's. And she could not begrudge the man she loved another's love and care simply because it did not come from her. He was already out of her life. She made a silent vow to God that if He would let McCady live, she would banish him from her heart as well.

She started to reach out, to take Emily's hand, but in the end she pulled back. "You are his wife, and I am nothing to him now," she said, her throat full. "He might not know it yet, but Caerhays is blessed to have found you."

Emily's head lifted, and for a moment Jessalyn thought she would smile, but then she tensed, her face seeming to shatter like ice under a mallet. She grabbed Jessalyn's arm, her nails digging deep. "They're bringing somebody up."

Jessalyn jerked around, jolting to her feet. Lanterns bobbed and dipped before the enginehouse. Men were climbing the cliff path, carrying a body on a piece of canvas stretched between two poles.

Emily tried to run and stumbled, falling with a rattling jar onto her hands and knees. Jessalyn stopped to pick her up, and they waited, arms wrapped around each other, for the rescue party to crest the bluff.

Because he was taller than the others, Duncan's golden head topped the rise first. He walked beside the litter, holding aloft a pitch torch, and in the sudden flare of light Jessalyn could see that the body had hair that was the washed yellow color of an old saddle. And the hand that dangled lifeless was spotted with age. The men laid the litter on the ground, covering it with a blanket. One of the tinners' women started to wail.

Jessalyn felt Emily's spine stiffen as she drew in a deep breath. She stepped forward, her head high, and in that moment Jessalyn thought she had never looked more the earl's wife. "Have you found my husband?"

Duncan shook his head, his gaze on his boots. "We'll keep digging, m'lady." He paused, as if undecided whether to say more. "There's still hope, m'lady." But he hadn't been able to keep the lie out of his voice.

"Yes, of course," Emily said. "Thank you, Duncan. And thank the others for me as well, please. For all that they are doing."

Duncan and the men returned to the mine. McCady's women stood on the bluff together and watched them go. After a while Emily slipped her arm around Jessalyn's waist, leaning her head on Jessalyn's shoulder . . . waiting.

They brought him up an hour later.

They carried him up in a litter like the others. But unlike the others, he lived.

At the sight of him Jessalyn swallowed back a sob in a throat skinned raw from fear and worry. He might be alive, but he looked near death, with his eyes shut and sunk deep into the sockets, the flesh pared from the bones of his face and white as whalebone. His chest heaved, drawing thinly at the air, and blood oozed from a gash in his head.

Emily made a little chirping noise of pain and grabbed Jessalyn's hand. McCady opened his eyes.

His gaze flickered over the faces surrounding him, fastening on to one. "Jessalyn . . ." He sucked in an agonized breath. She thought he looked bruised. Deep inside him, where he would never heal. But then, incredibly, he smiled. "I got a . . . trifle lost . . ."

Tears spilled from Jessalyn's eyes. "You silly goose. No one can be a trifle lost."

Emily squeezed her hand tightly in silent comfort. But after a moment Jessalyn pulled free and dropped back, leaving Emily to walk alone beside the litter that carried her husband.

They had gone only ten more feet when Emily jerked and spun around, collapsing onto her knees. She stretched out her arm, her fingers curling into a rigid claw, and Jessalyn felt a scream building in her chest. *He's dead*, she thought. *Oh, God, he's dead.*

But it was Emily who screamed.

21

Rain dripped off the roof of the lych-gate, rattling on the shiny, lacquered wood of the coffins, soaking into the ebony velvet bunting of the hearse. The horses' black plumes drooped, soggy with the damp. It was fitting weather for a funeral.

The whole countryside had gathered at St. Genny's cemetery. Some were drawn as always by the enactment of a tragedy, but most were there out of respect for the earl. Hadn't he brought work to these parts? said Salome Stout to her mistress, the Reverend Mrs. Troutbeck. And he one of the scapegrace Trelawnys, them as never cared a tuppence for Cornwall before. Well, the mining venture had ended badly to be sure, but give the man his due, he had tried.

The pallbearers carried the caskets one at a time to where the freshly turned earth lay black in the spring grass among the leaning salt-pitted gravestones. It did not take as many hands to lift the second one, small as it was. 'Twas no bigger than a lobster basket, Little Jessie Stout said, earning a shush from her mam. If the babe had lived, so Dr. Humphrey said, it would have been a boy.

They spoke in reverent whispers of how Lady Caerhays had miscarried her babe on the bluff above Wheal Patience that terrible night of the fall and of how she had died, bleeding and feverish, two days later. The earl had not even been in his right head himself when the poor thing had slipped away.

Miss Jessalyn had been with her at the end, though, and there was another tragedy. Burned out of house and home she and old Lady Letty had been, and this hardly a week gone by. Left with scarcely a rag to stand up in. Still, she had trimmed her hat with black mourning ribbons this day, out of proper respect for the dead, so Mrs. Troutbeck pointed out to Mrs. Childrens, the baker's wife. She had grown up a proper lady, had Miss Jessalyn, for all her earlier harum-scarum ways.

The Reverend Troutbeck fumbled through the service, twice losing his place. Not many noticed, though, for they were too intent on studying the earl. The women thought he looked romantic, like a hero out of a blue book, what with the way the white bandage around his head set off his dark good looks. And such a torment burning in his eyes, they whispered. How he must have loved his pretty young wife. The men—those who knew that he was burying all hope at thirty thousand pounds—thought how well he might be grieved to the point of madness.

Jessalyn stood beside him, looking up at him out of gritty, pain-darkened eyes. She saw a face that was all sharp bones and hollow shadows. He was still and drawn deep into himself, his eyes utterly empty and seeing nothing but the coffins . . . and another failure.

He is flagellating himself with it, Jessalyn thought, *like a monk beating his own back with a knotted rope, until he bleeds and does penance for his sins.* She wanted to lean her body against his, to press his head to her breast. To take the whip from his hand and kiss his scarred and bruised fingers one by one. And she was afraid that if she so much as touched his arm in sympathy, he would turn away.

The Reverend Troutbeck spoke of dust returning unto dust, and ashes unto ashes. The rain came down harder now, beating a tattoo on the caskets. Jessalyn's gaze was drawn to the lych-gate, where the hearse waited, where she and Emily had stopped to speak that windy Sunday, the day the primroses had first bloomed. Emily had been so happy that day, laughing, blossoming herself in her pregnancy, and with her newly discovered love for Cornwall. *I don't think I shall ever want to leave. . . .*

A great sadness swelled within Jessalyn's breast. She swallowed hard, trying to keep it down, but a gulping little cry escaped her. McCady flinched, as if she'd touched him after all.

She lifted her head, seeing him through a wash of tears. His gaze lashed back at her, sun-bright with fury. He spun on his heel and strode away from her and the caskets of his wife and son, his right leg dragging heavily and leaving a groove in the thick green grass.

The pale linen of his shirt shone stark against the tin gray sky. The sea rolled in heavy black waves, tumbling over his boots, breaking into foam.

She sloughed toward him through the wet sand. The rain slashed at the beach, making a rough, purring sound as it stippled and pocked the water. He faced the sea. He had discarded his coat somewhere; his shirt clung to his back, so wet she could see the darkness of his skin underneath. She licked her lips, tasting salt and fear, and spoke his name.

She didn't think he heard, for he stood unmoving still. She shivered, wet and cold in the pouring rain, for she was wrapped only in a delicate cashmere shawl that Emily had given her after the fire. She thought she would leave and instead took another step toward him.

His voice lashed at her, hard and biting, above the sea's raucous, gasping breaths. "You can no longer place any dependence on my playing the part of the honorable gentleman, Miss Letty. From now on, if you know what is good for you, you will stay the bloody hell away from me."

She took another step and laid her cheek against his back.

He whirled, almost stumbling as he took all his weight on his bad leg. He flung out his arm, pointing down the beach. "Go, damn you!"

Tiny tremors shook her legs, and tears burned her eyes. She felt suffocated with yearning. She would not leave him.

His dark hair hung plastered to his head, dripping over the white bandage. Rain ran over the sharp bones of his face. Haunted and slightly wild, his eyes glowed at her. His hand curled into a tight fist, and he drew it back against his chest. "Oh, Christ, Jessa. Please . . ."

"I love you."

He seized her in a grip that hurt, hauling her up against his hard chest with such force it knocked the breath from her. He lowered his head, smothering her mouth, and the sea slammed and broke around them. The rain poured.

His kiss was rough, frantic . . . hot. She clung to his shoulders, her fingers digging into his rigid flesh, while he devoured her lips. He yanked off her poke bonnet, then jerked off her shawl and hurled them onto the rocks. He thrust his fingers through her hair, pulling her chignon loose from its netting and pins. He held her head fast with one hand, while he kneaded her breasts with the other. His fingers tugged and pulled at her nipples through the thin, rain-slick material of her muslin bodice and cotton shift.

He was being too rough and fierce, hurting her, but she didn't care. She had wanted this for so long. She was afraid to move, afraid to make a sound, for fear that he would stop.

He tore his mouth from hers and dragged her down with him onto the wet, foam-laced sand.

He loomed above her. The gold ring in his ear caught a flash of some ethereal light, so that it shimmered like a star caught fast in the dark night of his hair. His eyes were dark and sun-faceted in a world of gray rain. There was no tenderness in them, no mercy in the hard and hungry mouth that seized her lips. Only a deep and terrible need.

She surrendered to his kiss. Not even the crashing roar of rain and sea could drown out the tumult of her heart. Her hands roamed over him, seeking, yet she already knew the shape of him, the taste of him. She had always known these things, even before she knew of him.

A wave broke hard against the beach, dousing them with salty spray. He said something fast and harsh that she didn't understand, as he pushed up her skirt and shift. He gripped her thighs, spreading them. He knelt between her legs, rising above her. His face was so hard, so intent, he looked cruel. He cursed as he wrenched at the flap of his pantaloons, and then his breath left him in a soft, keening sigh. His sex sprang free from the concealing shadows of hair and cloth. Her glazed, unfocused eyes caught but a glimpse before he lowered himself over her again. His fingers probed for the slit in her drawers, and when he found it, he hooked his fingers in the opening and ripped.

She gasped with shock and then arched, gasping again, as he slid his finger deep inside her. He went utterly still, and she seemed to hang suspended with him, in a universe of wondrous feeling, connected only to his hard, burning finger. A wet heat spread in a growing pool from that part of her, as if she were melting down there.

He shuddered, and a harsh, tearing sound erupted from his throat. "God, I have to . . . Jessa, sweetling, I can't. I'm sorry, but I can't . . ."

She didn't know what he meant; she was afraid he was going to stop, to pull away from her. The thought was unbearable. She wrapped her arms around his back, her nails gripping at the wet thin linen, holding him tight to her. "Please," she whispered.

He pushed another finger inside her, opening her. She felt a searing pain, and she stiffened against him. Something smooth and hard and hot pushed between her legs, probing her woman's flesh, stretching her impossibly wide.

She knew a moment's fear, and then he drove into her. And she pressed her mouth into his shoulder to smother a cry.

He thrust again, burying himself deeper. She felt the fullness of him; he was thick and hard and throbbing inside her. It hurt, yet there was something else there—a hot, spiraling pressure that went beyond the pain into pleasure. It felt right for him to be so deep within her, to be a part of her.

He moved, pulling almost out of her, then pushing in again, a rough thrust and drag that struck a fire deep within her, like a spark off flint. She clung to him, straining upward, as the pressure within her grew, burning hotter. He pumped his hips, and the breath came from him in harsh, tearing gasps. "Please . . ." she said again, wanting something more, not knowing what it was.

His head flung back, his eyes clenching shut, his face contorted. He gave one last mighty thrust that seemed to pierce her heart as he shuddered violently, surging long and deep within her.

He collapsed heavily on top of her. She could feel the thudding of his heart and tiny tremors quivering across his chest. She reveled in the crush of him against her, the feel of his weight. Love for him squeezed at her heart, bringing tears to her eyes.

Slowly his breathing quieted. He drew out of her and rolled onto his back in the sand, leaving her feeling empty.

The rain poured over her face, into her parted, panting mouth. The sea spilled over her legs, pounding and sucking, in and out, pulsing to the heavy beat of her heart. She sat up. Her skirts were rucked up around her waist, and she pulled them down, suddenly embarrassed.

She dared a glance at him. He sat with one leg bent, his elbow resting on his knee, his face buried in his hand, and his fingers clenching and clenching in his rain-black hair. The words *I love you* swelled up from within her, pushing against her lips, but she held them back.

He raised his head, and his hand fell, hanging limp. He

looked at the tumultuous sea, and she could see his throat move as he swallowed. He turned, searching her face. The only light in the whole world seemed to come from his eyes. "I want you again."

A sigh stretched across her chest, easing out of her. She leaned into him. "Oh, take me again, McCady. Take me again."

His arms came around her, crushing her to him, and his mouth closed over hers in a long, deep kiss that stole her breath.

After an eternity he tore his mouth from hers and buried his face in the curve of her neck. He planted soft, sighing kisses along her throat, his lips trailing over her chilled, wet skin, and she trembled. He lifted his head. His mouth tightened as he rubbed his thumb over her red and swollen lips. "I was a bloody rutting beast. I hurt you."

He had, but she didn't care. She loved the thought of him being inside her, the intimacy of it. And they said it hurt only the first time.

She smiled, tilting her face up to his, asking without thought or words for another kiss. He traced the shape of her mouth with his tongue, parting her lips. He tasted of the rain and the sea, and of wanting—hot and spicy. Their mouths mated, then parted, only to come back together, again and again, as if each breath must begin and end with the other's lips.

His fingers tangled in her hair, dragging her head back, exposing her neck to his hot, wet mouth. He rubbed his partially open lips against her throbbing pulse. "Ah, God, Jessa, Jessa . . . you taste like sin. Once started, a man cannot stop." He raised his head, pulling back a little. His eyes burned bright and hot.

With the soft pads of her fingers, she traced the severe line of his mouth. His lips moved beneath her touch, the creases deepening into a sudden, beautiful smile. "Christ, I think it's raining," he said. "And I've got sand in places one doesn't dare mention in polite society. Let's find a bed."

* * *

It was dim and damp inside the gatehouse.

He lit a lantern, hooking its handle over a wall peg. The room held little furniture: a scarred and ring-marked table, two ladder-back chairs, and an old wooden bed made up with a brown army blanket and rough huckaback sheets that looked worn but clean. A stack of dry faggots lay next to the swept hearth. The place was freshly scrubbed and smelled faintly of fried bacon and tobacco.

She felt shy and nervous, being alone here with him, knowing what was coming, knowing that he was thinking of it, as she was. "Does someone live here?" she asked.

He was crouched on one knee, laying the fire. His doe-skin pantaloons pulled tautly across his hard thighs; his wet shirt clung to the powerful muscles of his back. "No one now," he said. "Duncan slept here at first, until we could fix a place for him up in the hall."

The wood caught with a lick of flame and curl of smoke. He straightened and came toward her, where she stood in the middle of the room. It was ridiculous, but she had to tighten her muscles to keep from running away. There was a roaring in her ears, as if they were still being battered by the rain and the sea. He stopped when only a hand space separated them. So close she could smell his shaving soap and the wet starch in his shirt. And a hot male smell that went with what he had done to her on the beach.

"Take off your clothes," he said. Commanded.

"M-my clothes?" She had not thought about this, that he would want her to undress. She had never bared her body to a man before. Not even Becka had seen her out of her shift. Yet there was a wet stickiness between her legs to remind her of the intimacy she'd already shared with this man.

His fingers spanned her chin, tilting her head to meet his eyes. They caught the light of the fire, glowing like hurricane lamps in the stormy passion of his dark face. "I want to see you naked, Jessalyn."

Her hands trembled as she reached behind her back, working at the hidden laces that fastened her bodice. She was afraid he wouldn't like her body. She was so thin and bony.

She had trouble working loose the tight long sleeves, the wet muslin seemed to cling to her arms. But then the dress slid into a dripping pool around her ankles. She wasn't wearing stays, only a shift and drawers. Drawers that were ripped from front to back so that she could feel cool air bathing those most intimate parts of her body.

His breathing had changed, coming in quick, shallow gasps. "Everything," he said, the word a coarse whisper.

She swallowed hard around the dryness in her throat. She untied the drawstring to her drawers, and they joined her dress on the floor. She pulled the shift over her head, letting it fall from her outstretched fingers. Her wet hair hung in clumps over her shoulders, water running in rivulets over her breasts and belly. The water was cold, yet her skin sizzled. She couldn't look at him.

"I've wanted you since you were sixteen," he said, the words hoarse. "When you were all legs and no tits and with a sunburnt nose and freckles on your cheekbones."

He was staring at her breasts, and she felt a rush of tingling heat spread through her, like swallowing brandy. She looked down. Her nipples stood out hard and round and dark like two pebbles. "They still aren't much to look at."

He breathed a laugh. "Oh, no, there you are most wrong, Miss Letty." His hand trembled slightly as he combed the hair away from her face, following the length of one thick curl where it curved beneath a smooth, upthrust breast, sticking to her wet skin, skin that seemed suddenly to have caught on fire. "As an acknowledged rake I happen to be a connoisseur of women's breasts." He cupped one in his palm, lifting it, and she stifled a moan behind her teeth. "And yours are splendid. All round and golden, as if sprinkled with cinnamon." Together they watched his long, hard fingers, dark against the whiteness of her skin, trace the contours of her pliant, aching flesh, gently teasing the nipple until it seemed to throb and quiver. "I've dreamed about what it would be like to try and lick every cinnamon fleck off with my tongue, one by one."

Her body felt weighted, her skin too hot and tight. Her legs trembled, wanting to sink to the floor. She had to touch him as well. She laid her palms flat against his chest, rubbing them over his wet shirt, marveling at the way his muscles tightened and expanded with his heavy breaths. The way he felt, rugged as the cliffs, yet yielding, too, beneath her hands like the soft black earth. "You are so strong," she said. "So hard."

His head fell forward, and he groaned her name against her hair. He swung her up into his arms and carried her to the bed.

The old rope springs moaned beneath them. The army blanket was rough under her back; every inch of her skin felt flayed, too sensitive to bear so much as a breath. He lay beside her, partially covering her, and his shirt brushed against her breasts, tormenting her nipples. His hand stroked the length of her, and his gaze followed, fire scorching along the path of fire.

"I knew the hair between your legs would be this color," he said. "Like a burning torch." His fingers lightly, lightly touched her there, and she gasped and arched up off the bed, as if he'd lit a fuse, setting off a rocket inside her.

He seized her mouth in a long, fierce kiss, then pulled away from her and sat up. He tugged at his boots, cursing them when they resisted. He yanked his shirt over his head, popping buttons that clattered and rolled on the floor. He stood up. He hadn't bothered with refastening his pantaloons; they gaped open at the waist, revealing a dense triangle of dark curling hair. He stood sideways to her, and she could see plainly how the tight wet doeskin cradled the heavy bulge of his sex. He peeled the wet cloth down over his hips, baring to her fascinated gaze the curved, muscular moon of one buttock . . . and his swollen member, bursting free. It was thick and ridged with veins, purple-red, almost glistening. Her breath escaped through her parted lips in a tiny, whistling sound.

"Is that a gasp of fear or awe?" He stood, grinning, before her. Blatantly virile and arrogantly aware of it.

Laughter bubbled up and poured out of her, raucous and squeaky as a rusty gate—and dying when she noticed the purple-red weal that curved around his thigh. She reached up and ran her finger along the length of the hard, puckered ridge. "You could have been killed," she said. The thought terrified her. That life was so precarious. That she could lose him. Even the little of him that she had could be lost to her forever.

He removed her hand and brought it to his lips as he eased down onto the bed beside her. He stared at her, and the skin across his cheekbones seemed to tauten, his lips to tighten, as if he were in pain. "Laugh again," he said.

"Why?" He grinned at her, and she giggled. "No one—" She giggled again. "No one can laugh on command. It isn't—" A hooting snort burst out of her, sounding like a dull saw going through wood.

He laughed along with her, smothering his face between her breasts. "God, I love the way you laugh," he said. "I get hard sometimes just hearing you laugh."

She looked down the length of their two bodies, lying side by side: his hard and sun-browned, hers cream pale and softer. At his manhood, lying thick and heavy against her hip. "You're hard right now."

He rose up and rubbed his sex over her belly. "Feel it. This is what you do to me, Jessalyn. Are you pleased with yourself?"

She was rather pleased with herself. And curious about him. She touched his hard length lightly with her fingertips, surprised at the silky slickness of his skin and the burning heat. She felt him shudder, heard his sharp intake of breath.

He took her hand and wrapped it around him. "Hold me. Grip me tight."

He filled her hand. She squeezed him gently, instinctively making a fist and stroking his thick length to the root. He made a harsh sobbing sound, like an animal in pain.

She let go of him. "Did I hurt you? I didn't mean to hurt you."

He laughed, nuzzling her neck. "Ah, Christ, no, you didn't hurt me. That felt so good, so good. . . ."

For one long suspended breath out of time, he stared at her, as if etching her face into his memory. Then he lowered his head and licked the curve of her breast where it swelled beneath her arm. His tongue traced the shape of it, stroking underneath, following the gentle upward slope to the quivering peak and he sucked it deep into his mouth.

Dear life . . .

She had never felt anything like this before. Oh, God, he had her nipple in her mouth, suckling on it like a babe. She didn't know men did this; it was wicked, it was wonderful. Fireworks shot off in dizzying whirls inside her, falling and dying into a throbbing heat low in her womb.

He lathed slick, hot kisses all over her breasts and down her belly, sucking at places she didn't even know she had. His long hair brushed her skin, tickling, igniting little gorse fires. His breath bathed her in fiery gusts. His back trembled and grew taut and slick with sweat beneath her roaming hands.

She almost screamed when he palmed her mound. His fingers tangled in the red nest of hair, tracing the grooves of her body where her legs joined. He pushed a finger deep inside her, then pulled it out, in and out, in and out, in long, rhythmic thrusts that seemed to match the wild pumping of her heart. With the pad of his thumb he stroked the lips of her sex, pushing upward, touching some exquisitely sensitive place deep inside her that stopped her heart. Her hands clawed at the blanket; her head thrashed. She undulated her hips, pumping them against his stroking, probing fingers as the most terrible pressure built inside her. She opened her mouth to tell him to stop and whimpered instead. Dear life . . . she was going to die if he didn't stop. She arched her back, bucking hard against his hand, begging for, begging for, begging . . .

Her chest heaved with the effort to breathe. His mouth was on hers, kissing her. He spoke into her. "Not yet, Jessa. Not yet . . ."

And then she felt his burning hardness probing at the wet, quivering place where his fingers had been.

His hands slid beneath her bottom, raising her hips. She felt a tiny tremor of fear now, for it had hurt so the last time. He entered her slowly, pushing into her inch by inch, until he was buried to the hilt.

"Don't move," he said though his clenched teeth. "Wait . . . a moment . . ." His head bowed, his hair lapping at her breasts, as he drew in short, panting breaths. "God, you are so tight. Wet and hot, like a mouth."

A deep, tearing moan escaped him as he settled deeper. Instinctively she wrapped her legs around his hips, pulling him deeper still. He began to move within her. He flattened his palm against her stomach, his fingers inching down, finding her in the tight tangle of red curls, rubbing her in rhythm with his pounding thrusts. The pleasure was so exquisite it raised a scream in the back of her throat. The old rope springs squeaked and groaned, and the wooden bedstead knocked against the wall, pounding, pounding, and she couldn't bear it, couldn't bear it, couldn't—

She exploded inside, shuddering, shattering, dying. . . .

She awoke to the smell of him. But when she stretched out her hand, the space beside her was empty and cold.

She pressed her face into the pillow, afraid to open her eyes and discover she was alone. But then she heard a soft sound, like a sigh, and slowly she turned her head.

The fire, too long ignored, had gone out. There was no light in the room except for a muted dawn filtering through the single window. He stood, a black silhouette before it, his back to her. McCady Trelawny, this dark-souled man, whom she loved with all the depth and power of her woman's heart.

She watched him, afraid to breathe. For one afternoon and a night he had been hers, his rough and tender touch, his hungry kisses, his man's sex buried deep inside her. She had always known that by giving him her body, she would be giving him the power to hurt her beyond measure. Yet she had never been able to change what was in her heart: She loved him so much. Beyond pride and shame and regret.

He must have felt her eyes on him, for he stiffened and turned. His dark angel's face looked fiercely beautiful in the diffused light and as remote as the stars.

He took a step toward her, then stopped. He was dressed, and she felt suddenly shy in her own nakedness, vulnerable. She pulled the sheet over her breasts. "I'm leaving for London this morning," he said.

Pain slammed into her like a fisted blow. She shut her eyes to hide the rush of tears and swallowed down rising sobs. She would not cry. Nor would she ask him why, but he answered her as if she had.

"Because I must make one last, useless, wasted effort at trying to save my railway company. Because I have business in London anyway that must be seen to before the August trials. And because"—his breath caught, and naked pain flashed across his face—"because I want you so bloody badly I can scarcely breathe when you're near me, so how could I possibly go on living in the same house without touching you?"

She straightened her legs and pushed herself up onto her elbows. There was a burning soreness between her thighs. And an odd pulsing deep within her belly, as if the shudders and tremors that he had wrenched from her again and again throughout the night lingered in her still, echoing.

"I shouldn't want to live at all if you weren't here to touch me."

"Jessalyn . . . you don't understand." There was a faintly bitter tilt to his mouth. Her chest tightened with panic, cutting off her breath. She was failing him, losing him, and she didn't know what to do to stop it, what it was that he wanted from her. "I'm done for, dished up, cut all to pieces," he went on, the words mocking, but the pain lingering in his eyes. "I don't know why it is that I have been able to bed other women and walk away from them without a moment's thought. But with you I've always . . . Ah, hell, Jessalyn, I keep trying not to hurt you, and all I seem to do is bring you pain. Within six weeks I'm likely to be carted off to debtor's prison. I cannot take you down into ruin with me."

Her voice was hoarse from the pain in her throat. "And if I don't care what becomes of me as long as we're together?"

He came to her. He stood above her, looking down at her, and his eyes seemed to penetrate through all the effort she was making not to weep, not to beg, penetrating into her soul. "*I* care," he said in a ragged voice.

He leaned over to brush a kiss past her mouth, so light and fast she barely felt it. Until afterward, and even then it was but the lingering trace of a memory on her lips.

"I love you," she said. But by then she was speaking to an empty room.

22

Pale arms groped through the iron bars. Dirt black hands clawed at the air. Jessalyn bit back a scream, stepping out of reach. The face that peered down at her was hidden by a tangle of white beard. Black eyes burned, looking slightly mad.

But the voice that spoke was sane, educated. "You wouldn't perchance have a penny to spare a poor debtor, child? Nay, even a farthing to ease the lot of a benighted soul, condemned by a cruel vagary of fate to this hell upon earth."

Jessalyn fumbled in the bottom of her reticule until her fingers felt a half crown. She tossed the coin through the bars, rather than put it into the man's hands. With a cackle of glee, he disappeared after it.

She hurried across Fleet Market, but she could not help looking back over her shoulder. She felt mean for having treated the poor wretch as something less than human, but he'd had the look and stink about him of gaol fever.

Hell upon earth.

Fleet Prison. Massive walls, pitted and black with soot, looming out of the yellow fog. Somber walls, unrelieved by the small iron-barred windows of its crowded, vermin-ridden cells. Such would be McCady Trelawny's fate if she failed in her plan to save him.

At first it had been only a half-formed idea. But with every rattling mile of the mail coach ride to London; with every dawn hour spent in torchlit yards, bolting down mugs of ale and treacle; with every village passed, horses' hooves clattering on stone and the echo of the postboy's horn in the air, the idea had coalesced into a resolution. She would find a way to save him.

Still she could not shake off her grandmother's warning, given that morning, the morning McCady had left her.

She had found Lady Letty sitting up in bed, wearing a voluminous cap decorated with love knots and ribbons, and caught in the act of hiding a snuffbox beneath the sheets.

Leave it to Gram to have already borrowed or stolen a box from someone, since the few she'd had with her here in Cornwall had all been lost in the fire. Luckily, the bulk of her precious collection was still safe in the London town house.

"Gram, you are incorrigible," Jessalyn scolded. "You know what the doctor said about indulging in that bad habit, a woman of your age."

Lady Letty's snort ended with a sneeze. "*Living* is a bad habit for a woman of my age."

Jessalyn sat on the lemon-striped chintz bedspread, picking up the old woman's hand. "You must concentrate on getting well. You'll want to be strong enough to make the journey to Epsom next month for the Derby."

She looked up to find her grandmother's tin gray eyes intent on her face. "So he made a woman of you last night, did he?"

Jessalyn's cheeks burned, and her gaze dropped to her lap. Does it show that badly? she wondered. Had he left a mark on her like a lingering illness? A fever in the eyes, a weakness of the heart. Bright sunlight streamed through the windows, but at the moment she longed for some obscuring Cornish fog.

"Ha! At least you can still blush. He'll wed you now, gel, or I'll see him in hell."

Jessalyn said nothing. She could hardly tell her grandmother that far from marrying her, he was even now refusing to have her as his mistress.

Lady Letty pushed herself farther up the mound of pillows, dusting brown powder off her bodice. "You'll do well with Caerhays. They say rakes make the best husbands, know how to pleasure a woman. Lord knows your grandfather did." She reached beneath the sheets, pulling out the snuffbox. She rubbed the lid with her finger, a faraway look misting her eyes. "He loved me, the addlepated fool. Though he never thought to say the words—not once, till he lay dying. Nearly killed him then myself for waiting so long. Men never know whether they're thinking with their heads or their cocks."

"Gram!"

Lady Letty snorted a laugh. "In my day we knew all the words and used 'em, too. So how was he, eh? Did he bed you well? He's always looked at you as if he wanted to devour you. I 'spect last night he did."

Jessalyn's blush deepened. She struggled to gather her scattered wits, bringing up the original purpose of her visit. "Gram, I must go to London."

A crafty look stole into the old woman's eyes. "Chasing after him, are you? I'll countenance your going only if you take Becka with you. Appearances, gel. And though it might be shutting the paddock gate after the horse has bolted, you are to give me your word you'll stay out of his bed till he meets you at the altar."

"I am not chasing after him. He isn't even to know I've gone. And I will not leave you here alone—"

"Caerhays's housekeeper can look after me. We get along. She grew up next to the slag heaps just like myself." Her gnarled, mottled hand reached out to cover Jessalyn's slender pale one. "He's dished up proper, isn't he? That's why he won't marry you. He's given up, and so you think there's nothing for it but to save him yourself."

Jessalyn sighed. There was no hiding anything from Gram. "I'm going to try," she said.

Lady Letty grunted. "Have a care in the saving of him, mind, that you don't damage his man's pride in the process. He'll not forgive you that."

"Then I shall just have to take care he never finds out."

. . . take care he never finds out.

Jessalyn turned her back on Fleet Prison. She pulled her cottage cloak more tightly around her throat, dug her hands deep into her fox fur muff, and bent into the wind. The fog was frozen and heavy, smelling fouler than a tannery. It was weather more suited to January than April.

She walked past brick houses garbed in soot and packed together like books on a shelf. Past shops selling bootlaces and tea trays. Past smells of boiled cabbage and roast potatoes.

The direction she was searching for turned out to be a seedy warehouse by the river that smelled of hemp and tea. It butted up against a gin shop, whose open door spilled raucous laughter and tobacco smoke into the chill air. Something stirred beneath the stoop, and Jessalyn pulled back her skirts, expecting a rat. Then she saw a woman crouched there, holding a screaming baby in an egg crate lined with straw. She watched in shock and horror as the woman filled a sugar-tit from a gin jug and stuck it in the baby's mouth.

Her stomach spasmed with nerves. An iron grille covered the warehouse's single window, and the black paint on the door was peeling. If it weren't for a small plaque etched with the words *Tiltwell Enterprises,* she would have doubted she had the right place. She hesitated a moment, debating whether to knock, then pushed down the door latch and entered a small dim room.

A row of clerks perched on stools facing the wall, quills

waving madly in the air as they scribbled. It was as cold in the room as it was outside. The men all had potato sacks wrapped like shawls over their patched coats, and the fingers poking out of their ratty mittens looked blue.

One of the men creaked to his feet and came to greet her. He wiped his sleeve across his dripping nose. It was red and round, like a copper knob. "I would like to speak to Mr. Tiltwell, if you please," Jessalyn said, her breath wreathing around her face in tiny white puffs.

The clerk peered at her through a pair of horn spectacles, greasy with thumb prints. "He's out just now. Collecting the rents."

"Then I shall await his return."

The clerk snuffled a sneeze into his neckcloth and motioned for her to follow him.

The room he showed her to was somewhat warmer, for a small coal fire burned in the grate. It was sparsely furnished with a few battered cabinets, a wooden coat-tree, and a plain dark oak desk. The walls were hung with shabby paper, broken only by a single dirt-streaked window. It looked out on a dark courtyard that was empty except for a soggy ash heap and a rusty water pump.

A few moments later Jessalyn heard voices. Clarence's, the clerk's, and another, deeper voice with rough country accents.

The door opened, and Clarence entered, bringing the chill and smell of fog into the room. He looked splendid, tall and handsome in a merino greatcoat and top hat. Yet the sight of him did not make her legs tremble or her stomach tingle, and the ache in her heart came from sadness, not yearning.

He flashed a gap-toothed smile, and his bottle green eyes lit up at sight of her. "Jessalyn, what a pleasant surprise!" He removed his fur-lined gloves, slapping his hands together. "Brr. It's a mortal cold day out."

"And your clerks are starved with it. Really, Clarence, I

cannot believe you're such a nipcheese that you won't provide those poor men with a fire."

"A little chill in the air keeps them on their toes. It takes hard work, Jessalyn, to get where I've come," he said even as he tipped some more coal onto his own fire. He straightened and looked around the room, as if seeing it for the first time. "Where is your footman? Surely you didn't come here on your own."

"I haven't a footman, Clarence. You know that."

"Your abigail then. You should have at least brought that girl with you, the one with the hideous scar."

"Becka isn't well. She says she has a gouty pain in her head. Really, Clarence," she snapped, her nerves making her irritable with him, "I did not come here for you to read me a lecture."

Clarence shrugged out of his greatcoat, which he hung on the wooden tree. Although it had only been a couple of months since she'd last seen him, he looked changed. He was wearing his hair different, brushed up to give its growing sparsity more fullness. And there was an odd tightness about his mouth.

"I am sorry to scold you," he said as he came up to her. "You know it is only my deep regard for you that—" He had started to raise her fingers to his lips, and now a look of surprise crossed his face. He turned her hand over to examine her palm. "Whatever have you done to yourself? These look like burns."

She curled her fingers over the scabbed pads. The blisters were healing, but they still pained her too much to wear gloves. "End Cottage caught fire. Gram and I were fortunate to get out alive."

"You were *in* the house at the time. But—" He cut himself off. Distress had darkened his eyes to the color of stone moss, and Jessalyn felt touched by his concern.

She removed her hand from his clasp and went to the window. There was a man in the yard, bent over the trough, sloughing water over his head. For a brief moment, as he straightened, he turned, and Jessalyn saw a pitted, jowly face beneath shaggy, dripping hair. Then the man spun around and walked off, disappearing through a door in the mews.

Jessalyn stiffened, sure that—but no . . . Dear life, since the fire it seemed that everywhere she looked she saw the face of Jacky Stout.

She turned from the window. Clarence was watching her, a frown drawing a crease between his brows. "I must say, Jessalyn, you look fair done up. Has something happened?"

"Clarence, I . . ." She gripped her hands behind her back and forced herself to meet his eyes. "I have come to tell you that it is impossible for me to be your wife."

He held himself very still. Then his breath left him in a gentle sigh. "I see. And what has made it impossible?"

"Oh, Clarence. I tried once to tell you . . . I am fond of you, you are a dear, dear friend, but I simply don't love you in that way. And I understand now that I never shall."

"You will forgive me if I do not share your certainty. I had hoped that with time—"

"Clarence, I shan't marry you. Ever."

He squeezed the bridge of his nose between two fingers, his eyes wincing shut. Then he flung back his head and swung away from her, his fists clenched at his sides. The room grew so quiet she could hear drunken singing coming from the gin shop next door. Jessalyn's teeth sank into her lower lip as she stared at his stiff back. As hard as that had been, this next part was going to be even worse.

She sucked in a deep breath, as if she could draw courage from the air. "I know that it is very bad form of me to turn down your offer and then beg a boon in return, but . . ." She swallowed around a terrible dryness in her mouth. Dear life, but this was cutting at her pride like a whiplash. "But I find myself in somewhat straitened circumstances. Clarence, I—I wonder if I might apply to you for a loan."

His fists unclenched, and he coughed. He walked away from her, toward the desk. He hitched his hip onto one corner and looked down at his clasped hands. His face was as white as the bleached linen of his shirt. "How—" His voice broke, and he had to stop to clear his throat. "How much do you need?"

Jessalyn's fingers were trying to twist knots in her skirt. "Ten—ten thousand pounds. I'm afraid I've little to give you as collateral. The Adelphi house is mortgaged from cellar to chimney pot. But there are the horses." A flash of pain stabbed at her chest, but she ignored it. "As they are, they aren't worth much, but if Blue Moon wins the Derby . . ."

He was swinging one long booted leg back and forth. He raised his head. Though his mouth quirked into a little smile, she saw to her dismay that his eyes shone wet with suppressed tears. "My dear. You know that if you marry me, you could have your every whim gratified, no matter how outrageous or expensive. And if you are in the suds . . . well, as your husband I shall be obliged to settle all your debts."

"I have explained why I cannot marry you, Clarence. The reasons for my needing the money are—are personal."

"Jessalyn, Jessalyn . . ." He shook his head, as if admonishing a slow-witted child. "Do you take me for a fool? You want it for *him*—for Caerhays. He finally has done it, hasn't he? He's made you his Trelawny whore."

A rush of heat spread up her throat. "How dare you?"

"The man is married. Have you no shame?"

"Emily is dead!" Jessalyn blurted, guilt making her shout the words.

Clarence straightened with a snap, and his pale face took on a sudden animation. "Dead, by God! And the brat? Would it have been a boy?" He threw back his head and hooted a laugh at the ceiling. "Poor cousin, to be so close and then *phit*"—he snapped his fingers—"it's gone." He paced the bare plank floor, chuckling to himself. Suddenly he swung around and his gaze refocused on her. "And you think he'll marry you—teetering as he is on the verge of ruin and disgrace? He hasn't a hope or a prayer of escaping prison, now that his little heiress is dead."

Jessalyn stared at him, seeing the fair, slender face of the boy she'd ridden bareback with across the moors, the boy she'd challenged to a diving contest in Claret Pond, the young man who had given her her first kiss before a Midsummer's Eve bonfire. Surely that Clarence would have emptied out his purse to save his cousin.

She lifted her hand to him, as if reaching across time to the boy he had been. "Oh, Clarence, I can understand why McCady's pride has forbidden him to ask it of you. But what has stopped you from offering to lend him the money he needs?"

"My dear, he owes it all to me in the first place. It is *my* bank that holds his notes." He paced the room, pumping his arms, then grasping his hands together as if in prayer. "By God, I have waited years to bring McCady Trelawny to his knees. If there was truly any justice in this world, he would soon go the way of his brothers, and I could come into the title, but as it is, at least I can have the satisfaction—" He stopped, swinging around, and a crafty look narrowed his eyes. "He must be getting quite desperate now if he has sent you to me."

"He didn't send me. And you mustn't tell him, Clarence, please. You know how he is, his pride. He would never forgive me if . . ." Her voice trailed off. She was speaking to him as if he were the old Clarence. But she didn't know this man.

A withdrawn look had settled over his face. He adjusted his neckcloth, smoothed down the lapels of his coat, as if regretting now his earlier outburst. He went back to his desk and settled into the chair. He shot his cuff, dipped a quill into the inkpot, and began to write in a red leather ledger.

Jessalyn drew in a breath to speak, then expelled it in a

silent sigh. She retrieved her cloak and muff off the coat-tree and went to the door.

"I shall give you the ten thousand pounds, Jessalyn."

Her hand fell from the latch, and she turned. She stared at his bent head, not daring to breathe. He continued to write, the pen scraping roughly across the paper. "Will you, Clarence? And what must I give you in return?"

He tossed down the pen and leaned back in his chair, fingering the coins in his fob pocket. His gaze was as cold and merciless as a winter wind. "You will give me yourself, of course."

"I see." Tears filled her eyes, but she blinked them back. She lifted her chin. "I know all about these sorts of transactions, for someone once explained them to me in great detail. I am to become your ladybird. For one night? Or do you wish for a more permanent arrangement?"

"Oh, no, my dear. I still want you for my wife. I will *have* you for my wife."

Jessalyn's breath caught in her throat like a clap of bellows. It was odd, but the thought of being this man's wife was a hundredfold more intolerable than being his harlot. "No," she said.

He raised one languid blond brow. "Not even to save your lover's life? It costs to *live*, you know, even in Fleet Prison. Warm blankets and food and gin and the rope mats they give you to sleep on—they all must be paid for. You must even pay to have the irons struck off your ankles; otherwise you are left chained to the floor. They all cost, Jessalyn, and he'll not long survive if he doesn't get them."

Jessalyn's mouth tasted like burned paper. She did not want to listen to Clarence's words. She did not want to have to make such a choice.

He picked up the quill and began to rub the feather back and forth across his palm. "And what is it the philosophers say—one cannot live on bread alone? One needs plans, ambitions, dreams. Already he has had to grovel, to sweat and bleed to lay those forty miles of track. He's even swung a pick himself if the stories are true." His voice turned soft and menacing. "You would be preserving his dream, Jessalyn."

"But I don't . . ." Slowly she shook her head. She felt weighted with a great inertia, like a butterfly trapped in a bucket of treacle. It seemed to be taking all of her energy just to think. "I don't understand. Why do the very thing that will save the man you've set out to destroy?"

"Because more than his ruin, my dear, I want you."

Memories came to her one after the other, like chains of paper dolls. McCady riding a wooden horse, his face alight with laughter while lights whirled around his head like stars; his long, scarred hands cradling a tiny baby, *Babies and winsome virgins always put a quiver in my knees and a quake in my heart;* steam wreathing around his dark head as he shoveled coal into a firebox, *I should like to come along with you, Lieutenant Trelawny.* . . .

Dark eyes, sun-bright with passion, seeing beauty in her body, touching her, *I have wanted you since you were sixteen.* . . .

Jessalyn clasped her hands behind her back and held herself tall. She lifted her chin and stared down her nose at this tutworker's grandson. "Then you may have me, Mr. Tiltwell," she said. "But ten thousand pounds is not enough. You are to settle *all* his notes, not simply forgive the interest. All of his debts, down to the last farthing."

His head flung back. "But you're talking about over forty thousand pounds!"

"That is my only offer. Take it or leave it."

He stood up and came to her, trying to intimidate her with his man's authority. A frown thinned his mouth, and a muscle tightened along his jaw as he stared at her, gauging her resolution. Jessalyn stared back at him. Beneath her corded muslin skirts, her legs were shaking. But she didn't blink.

He pursed his lips, pushing out a breath. "Very well, Jessalyn." He held up his hand, and the soft menace returned to his voice. "But I have a condition as well. Once you are my wife, you will not go near him. Nor will you mention his name, to me or within my hearing. To us it will be as if he has died."

It felt as if a bone were caught in her throat. Unable to speak, she jerked her head in a sharp nod.

"We have an agreement then. You will become my wife, and I will give you his promissory notes, fully settled, on our wedding night."

She looked up at the pale, thin face of the man she had once thought of as her dearest friend. Tears blurred her eyes. She tried to hold them back, but they overflowed, spilling down her cheeks. "Why, Clarence? I thought you loved him. I thought you loved us both."

He caught her tears with his fingers, and his face softened. "I can make you happy, Jessalyn. You'll see that I can make you happy. In time you will forget him. You will cease loving him and come to love me instead, as you were always meant to."

"I will never forget him. Or stop loving him."

Clarence's thin nostrils flared slightly, but he went on, as if she had not spoken. "We shall be married immediately. I should have no trouble obtaining a special license—"

"No. We will be married the week after the Derby."

He pressed his tongue between the gap in his teeth and slowly shook his head. "Jessalyn, what purpose would it serve—what would it serve *him* to wait?"

She backed away from him, her fingers fumbling behind her for the door latch. She had to get out of this miserable room before she was sick. "Because the Derby is *my* dream, and I will not have it sullied by living it as your wife."

He brought his face toward hers, but she turned her head aside. His fingers spanned her jaw, holding her still, while he planted his mouth on hers in a hard, punishing kiss. "You had no right to give him something that was mine," he said, his breath hot against her mouth. "It shall be a long time before I forgive you for that."

She jerked out of his grasp, wiping her lips with the back of her hand. "You do not own me, Mr. Tiltwell."

"On the contrary, my dear. I have just bought you for forty thousand pounds."

Topper walked down Fleet Street, feeling on top of the world. He whistled through the hole in his teeth at an apple-cheeked maid, who had stepped out of a tavern to empty a slop bucket. He tossed a penny into the lap of a legless man who rolled by on a three-wheeled chair, playing a pipe. A lamplighter appeared around the bend ahead of him, reaching up with his long pole, and soon small points of light began to appear, one after the other in the misty dusk. Topper fancied they looked like a string of pearls.

Tipping his hat, he stepped aside for a gentleman, who was preceded by a liveried footman with an ivory-handled cane. *Someday I'll be like that swell,* Topper thought. Someday he, too, would be rich and wear flashy togs and ride in a coach with postilions and matching pairs. And if he felt like hoofing it, well, then, he'd have a footman go before him to pave the way.

His nose twitched at the aroma of fresh hot-cross buns wafting from a pastry cookshop. He bought a mutton pie but passed up a strawberry tart for dessert. The Derby was coming up, and a knight had to watch his weight when he was riding the horses. Someday, though, he'd be able to stuff his face with strawberry tarts till he shot the cat. He'd be that rich.

Now the guv'nor—he was that rich, Topper thought as he turned off bright, noisy Fleet Street and began to wend his way through dark, narrow streets toward the river. His gaze darted to the shadows, searching for footpads; they'd as soon bludgeon your head in as spit at you in this part of town. Rich as a king was the guv'nor, though you wouldn't know it to look at where the man conducted his business. But then it wasn't smart to flash the ready when you were sitting cheek to jowl with boozing kens and tenements. 'Course, a lot of the guv'nor's money came from those same boozing kens and tenements. Two shillings a week he got from every man jack who dwelled in this particular rookery.

Topper knew well what living in those places was like: the dark, dank rooms lit only with stinking tallow dips; the walls alive with wood lice. Just as he knew what it was like to be so hungry you'd eat a rotting apple core off a sidewalk slimy with spittle. Or melt the stubs of candles into your gruel to make it thick enough to fill your belly.

A door swung open, and a sweep's boy stumbled out into the street, nearly knocking Topper down. The lad was bent double under a bag of soot, and his master was flailing at his legs with a broom handle. Topper hurried away from the sight. He knew what *that* was like, too. Being roused at dawn out of a cold bed of soot bags and straw and set to work cleaning rich folks' chimneys. To have your knees and elbows made tough as leather by rubbing them with brine, till they streamed with blood and you were screaming from the pain of it. To be forced into a flue too narrow for a rat, forced to climb until you were trapped, unable to go up or down, trapped in the dark . . .

Topper's mind shied away from these memories. Those days were over now and best forgotten. And besides, as bad as being a climbing boy had been, Topper knew there were other, worse ways of starving. Like spinning catgut in the workhouse or working for a molly-house where you had to sell your body like a girl. Or you could get caught cutting purses and be sent to gaol. Topper shuddered at the thought. The idea of being shut up in a small dark cell made his belly go all over queasy. Those times he'd been trapped, the walls squeezing in, the air black and thick, had left Topper with a mortal fear of small dark places.

There was only one thing he feared worse, and that was

getting the sooty warts. It happened sometimes to climbing boys, those who managed to grow old enough to bed girls. Not that they were able to bed girls for long after they got *that* hellish disease. Their privates were usually entirely eaten off by the time they died.

He'd noticed the sores six months ago.

Topper's mind slammed shut on the thought. They were nothing to worry about. Just something he picked up from that dolly-mop he'd bedded the night of the Crombie Sweeps, when he'd gotten stew-eyed drunk on Strip-Me-Naked gin. If they were sooty warts, they would hurt, wouldn't they? And these sores didn't hurt. They were hard and scalylike; he could poke them with a pin and not feel a thing. No, they weren't sooty warts. Just something he'd picked up from that dolly-mop.

The gin shop was busy tonight, with men standing three deep at the bar to wet their whistles with a glass of ninepenny. Topper entered the warehouse through the back way and slipped into the clerks' room. Light shone beneath the closed door of the guv'nor's office, causing the tall stools to throw weblike shadows onto the wall. A cultured voice, cold with anger, said, "You bloody fool. You weren't to have set fire to the house while she was *in* it."

"When else was I supposed t' do it 'cept at night?" came a whining answer. It was Jacky Stout, the bullyboy the guv'nor used to collect his tenement rents and do other dirty jobs. "A man can't go around puttin' a torch to a house in the bright light o' day."

Topper hesitated. He didn't want to walk through that door with Stout in there. Topper had never understood how a man like the guv'nor, so posh and educated, had connected up with a bullyboy like Jacky Stout. But then Stout claimed he and the guv'nor went back a long way together. Back to Cornwall, when the guv'nor was but a lad and had once paid him to peach on a smuggling pitch, only to turn chicken at the last minute.

Topper mopped his suddenly sweating face with his sleeve and lifted the door latch.

The guv'nor, who was sitting behind his desk, looked up, and his handsome face broke into a bright smile. "Ah, Topper, here you are. . . . You may congratulate me, my boy. Miss Letty has again promised to become my wife."

Topper tried to smile. "So the wedding's to be after all." He cast a swift glance at Stout. The pock-faced man was tossing a spalling hammer—his favorite weapon for rent collection—back and forth in his beefy hands. Stout grinned, showing teeth that put Topper in mind of a sewer rat.

Topper jerked his gaze back to the guv'nor. He forced himself not to think of Miss Jessalyn and what her fate would be married to such a man as made his fortune off boozing kens and tenement rents. "I'm to be getting me blunt then. Me five hundred quid."

"I'm afraid you haven't finished earning it yet," the guv'nor said.

"But ye was t' pay it to me on the day she gave up racing and promised t' be yer wife."

Jacky Stout laid the spalling hammer in his lap and cracked the knuckles of his big hands. Topper's spine roached up at the grating sound, but he didn't look in the bullyboy's direction. He wouldn't give the man the satisfaction.

He kept his face straight ahead, his eyes on the guv'nor. The man was leaning his chin on his folded hands, biting his thumb in thought. A fancy silver candle branch sat on the desk, and the flames guttered in a sudden draft. A thick silence smothered the room; Topper thought he could hear his heart beat.

"For one thing, she's still racing," the guv'nor finally said. "Which is why you are to nobble Blue Moon before the Epsom Derby. And make it permanent this time. If that bloody nag ever gets so much as a whisker across a finishing post again, I'll have your balls."

"But if she's agreed to marry ye, why should ye be wantin' to wish her any more 'arm? I thought 'twas the point of all this." Topper waved a hand, encompassing all the nobbled horses and crimped races of the last two years. "Making her life a misery so's that she'd turn to you."

The guv'nor's mouth lifted in a gentle smile, a smile that Topper didn't believe for a minute. "It is what's known as insurance, my boy."

Topper's head jerked back and forth. "I ain't doin' it. Not no more. There ain't enough blunt in all the world to make me do it." It made him feel good to say it and sick because he knew he didn't mean it.

The guv'nor leaned back. He reached into his pocket and took out two gold guineas. He began to turn them over and over in his pale, slender fingers. "You ever seen a spalling hammer crush rock, Topper my boy." Jacky Stout began to toss the hammer back and forth in his hands. Thump-thump . . . thump-thump . . . and the breath expelled from Topper in a whine through the hole in his front teeth. "Think what it could do to a jockey's hands," the guv'nor went on in his soft voice. "They say a jockey's talent is all in his hands—"

The hammer slammed so hard into the floor that the building shuddered.

Vomit rose in Topper's throat, and he lurched over, spewing mutton pie all over his fancy plate-buckled shoes. He remained bent over, gasping, as runnels of sweat ran down his sides. He wiped off his mouth with the sleeve of his bright yellow coat. "I'll go to the coppers," he rasped.

The guv'nor laughed. "Come now, boy. Do you think they would put any credence in your story, that they would take the word of a jockey over an MP? No, they are more liable to put you in prison. In a cell. In the dark."

Topper couldn't control his shudder, and Jacky Stout snorted, sounding like a pig feeding in a trough. The guv'nor snapped his head around. "Stubble it, Jacky. I've another job for you."

The laughter slid off Stout's jowly face like melting tallow. "Eh? But I took care of everything, sur. Her house is
burnt to cinders, an' his bloody lordship's mine is shut fer
good. It'll cost more as he's ever got t' get it going again."

"Do you know what a locomotive is, Jacky?"

"Eh?"

The guv'nor heaved a put-upon sigh. "Never mind, I'll
work out all the details and explain them to you later."

"What'd ye want me to be doin' to this loco-whatsit?"

"The same thing you did to his tin mine," the guv'nor
said, a faint, wintry smile on his mouth. "Blow it up."

23

Against a smoky red sky they were but dark shadows, like the ghost riders of legend coming to steal his soul. They galloped across the hilltop, then made a broad, sweeping turn, coming toward him across the misty downs, and it seemed that he could feel the thrum of their hooves, melding with the fierce beat of his heart. His mouth tightened when he picked out the blood bay. His hands curled, as if he were already wrapping them around her throat.

The horses thundered past a copse of old beeches, and sunlight glinted off the spyglasses in the trees, shimmering like silver raindrops. The touts were out in full force that morning, picking up tips for their legs from this last training gallop before the big race.

The blood bay peeled off from the others, joining a one-armed man who sat on a hack, watching. The rider on the bay reined up. After a moment the one-armed man turned around in his saddle and pointed.

McCady Trelawny's mouth stretched into a hard smile. She was coming.

She pulled up and dismounted, to approach him on foot. Plumes of steam flew out the bay's nostrils, wreathing her head. She was muffled up to the eyebrows against the dawn chill in a man's woolen coat and cap. Her face was luminescent in the misty light; her eyes were enormous.

She pulled off her cap and tossed back her head. Her hair fell over her shoulders, a waterfall of molten copper. He thought that he had never known anything so beautiful. He felt a sudden and terrible need to gather her into his arms and bury his face in that hair.

He yanked the folded-up *Morning Post* out his coat pocket and thrust it in her face. "Is this true?"

"Yes." Her eyes turned dark as storm-bellied clouds as they filled with some emotion he couldn't name.

He flung the paper away and seized her by the shoulders. He brought his face so close to hers he could see his breath flutter the wisps of her hair. "Goddamn you, Jessa. You are mine."

She wrenched away from him, backing up. "I belong to no one but myself! It is my *life*, to do with as I want. If I want to marry for money—"

"Money!"

Her chest hitched with a little sucked-in breath. "Yes, money. What is so terrible about that? You did it. Perhaps I'm tired of being poor."

He searched her pale, beautiful face. "You're lying."

"McCady, please . . ." She sucked her lower lip into her mouth, then pushed it back out again, and to his bitter fury he was filled with such a fierce need to kiss her that he had to clench his teeth against a moan. "Please," she said again. "Don't make this any more difficult for me than it already is."

"It bloody well *should* be difficult."

Her words didn't match the haunted look in her eyes. She was lying. He *knew* her. In some ways he knew her better than he knew himself. She would never marry Tiltwell for his fortune. She would never marry any man unless she fancied herself in love with him.

Love with him . . .

Pain and savage fury clawed at his chest. It was the worst

pain he'd ever known, so intolerable he wondered how he stood it. He wanted to kill her. He wanted to crush her to him and smother her mouth with his. He wanted to thrust himself inside her, hard and deep, until she admitted that she was his, and only his.

His hands closed around her arms, and with a vicious jerk he brought her crashing against his chest. He slammed his open mouth down hard on hers in a kiss that was rough and desperate. Her hands curled around the lapels of his coat, and she melted against him, meeting his thrusting tongue with her own and, ah, God, but he had never tasted anything so sweet. She smelled of horse and wet grass and Pears primrose soap, and for that heartbeat out of time she filled his universe.

Until she tore her mouth from his and pushed against him so hard he almost stumbled. She backed away from him, slowly shaking her head, pressing trembling fingers to her wet and swollen lips. Her eyes were like great liquid moons in her pale face.

He filled his lungs and expelled the ache in his chest into the air. "Jessalyn, for the love of God, don't . . ." The words spilled out of him, unbidden, lacerating his pride. "Are you going to marry Clarence Tiltwell?"

"Yes."

"To hell with you then," he snarled, and spun on his heel, his hitching stride cutting a swath through the thick grass.

"McCady!"

His back flinched as if lashed with a whip, but he didn't turn around. He felt the loss of her as a raw agony deep within him, a mortal illness. But he kept going, and he did not look back. Not even when he heard the sobs tear out of her chest, sounding as if they were ripping apart her heart.

The devil's heart, Topper thought. The night was as black as the devil's heart.

He sagged against the lean-to wall, his chest heaving in panic, sucking in great whistling breaths that smelled of horse sweat and fresh dung. It was so bloody dark. He yearned for a candle, but he daren't risk one, not with the Sarn't Major asleep and snoring like a hedgehog in the tiny hayloft between the rafters and the thatch.

Straw rustled as he approached Blue Moon's box, and Topper started, barely swallowing the scream that rose in his throat. He rubbed a shaking hand over his face. It was slimed with sweat, though the night was cool. Gawblimey, he was jumpy as a flea on a hot bakestone.

The big bay greeted him with a soft snort and a nudge of his velvet nose. Tears stung Topper's eyes. *I can't do it,* he thought, *I ain't doin' it*—even as he uncorked a jug and poured the contents into the bay's water bucket.

Poured a dram of canary wine laced with enough rat bane to kill every horse in England.

"Look what I've got fer ye, me bonny lad," he crooned into Blue Moon's pricked ear, and the words tasted of straw. The bay bumped his head against the wooden bucket, but Topper held it just out of reach. Blue Moon loved the wine; it was a special treat they gave him after every race or hard gallop.

I can't do it . . .

The spalling hammer had slammed into the floor with such force it had left a round dent the size of a tea plate in the wood. It was what Topper kept seeing over and over in his mind's eye, the hammer going up and coming down, again and again. On his hands.

A strangled whimper escaped out his tight throat. He clenched the water bucket so hard it slopped over into the straw. Blue Moon nickered and bumped his arm.

"I'm sorry, m'love, but I got to do it. Sorry, so sorry . . ."

He held out the bucket, and Blue Moon lowered his head.

With a harsh, strangled sob, Topper whirled and flung the bucket against the wall. It landed short, hitting a hay bale with a muffled thud and splash. But Topper didn't know it, for he'd already disappeared into the dark night.

"Topper's gone missing," the Sarn't Major said. He was looking at his boots, not at her, but Jessalyn had seen the sheen of wetness in his eyes.

She leaned her elbows on the stall door. Blue Moon stared blankly back at her, but then it was race day, and he always looked bored on race day. "All those accidents . . ." A sigh caught in her throat; she felt weighted with such an immense sadness. Clarence and now Topper —it seemed as if all the people in her world were not as she had thought them. She felt betrayed, her heart violated. "I thought it was just our dismal Letty luck. But it was Topper all along."

The Sarn't Major grunted as he pried open the bay's mouth and peered at his tongue, then sniffed at the horse's breath. "If he's nobbled him, I can't tell it. But it makes no never mind. With Topper gone missing, we ain't got no knight."

Jessalyn entered the box. She rubbed her hand over the sleek blood bay coat, down over his haunches, to the hock that had been injured last fall. It felt sound. "I shall ride in his place," she said.

The Sarn't Major spit into the straw. "Can't. Ye're a female."

"So? They can't disqualify us for breaking a rule that doesn't exist. Wearing jockey's togs, and as tall and thin as I am, no one will know. Just say I'm your new lad." Her mouth trembled into a forlorn little smile. "I don't expect we would have won anyway."

The Sarn't Major frowned at her over the bay's broad back. He pursed his thick lips, hunched his head into his shoulders, and spit into the straw again. "Me an' Blue Moon'll meet ye at the weigh-in then. But mind ye keep yer head about ye and yer mouth shut. Ye start to blatherin', and they'll spot ye fer a female quicker'n a cat can pounce."

Topper's black and scarlet taffeta shirt and moleskin breeches hung on a peg on the wall. The Sarn't Major had lovingly cleaned them himself; he'd even pressed out the wrinkles with a hot smoothing iron. The taffeta made a whispering sound as she lifted it off the peg. Jessalyn felt tears well in her eyes, and left alone now, she allowed them to fall.

At the scuffling sound of leather on gravel, she whirled, expecting the boy.

McCady Trelawny filled the lean-to's open doorway. He lounged with one shoulder propped against the wooden brace, his arms crossed loosely over his chest. With the rising sun at his back, his face was nothing but shadows. Except for his eyes, which seemed to glow like a cat's, wild and feral. Her heart swelled with such love it hurt to look at him, yet she could not look away.

He drew in a deep breath. "Jessalyn . . ."

A long shadow fell between them. "Here you are, my dear," Clarence Tiltwell said. He sauntered into the lean-to, cool and elegant in a snuff-colored riding coat and tight buff breeches. He glanced around, a frown marring his smooth high brow. "I just saw your training groom leading Blue Moon off toward the weighing house. I am disappointed in you, Jessalyn. That in spite of all my admonitions to the contrary, you are still determined to compete in this race."

"Go rain on somebody else's picnic, Tiltwell," McCady said in his most irritating drawl. "She doesn't belong to you yet." The earl hadn't abandoned his negligent pose, yet the tension in the air had suddenly grown so palpable Jessalyn could have reached out and plucked it like the strings on a harpsichord.

Humming a little ditty, Clarence peered into the empty box. "Where's your jockey? I wanted to give him a guinea for luck."

Jessalyn crushed the black and scarlet taffeta shirt to her breast as if it were a shield. "I—I can give it to him, if you like. He's waiting for me at the scales."

Clarence flashed his cousin a bright smile that revealed the gap in his teeth. "So, Caerhays. You've heard that Jessalyn and I are getting married next Friday? Are you here to wish her happy?"

McCady cocked a mocking brow. "Do you think she can be happy in hell?"

Clarence's laugh sounded brittle in the misty morning air. "Come now, coz. All's fair in love and war, isn't that what they say? What's this, Jessalyn—have you been crying?" he said, acting as if he'd only just now noticed. He brushed her cheek with the backs of his knuckles. McCady stiffened, making a sound deep in his throat like a strangled growl.

For the sake of the man she loved, Jessalyn forced herself to endure Clarence's touch. She even managed a smile. "It was only an attack of racing day nerves. My dear," she added, though the words tasted like bile in her mouth.

Clarence clicked his tongue. "Poor sweetheart. But then a woman's sensibilities ought to be of a delicate nature," he said. "Which is why, I trust, that once we are married, you will take up gentler pursuits more suited to the wife of an MP."

He patted her cheek as if she had been an obedient pet and turned to leave. He paused in the doorway and looked his cousin over, from the toes of the earl's polished top boots to the silk crown of his top hat. "Do you know what the trouble is with you, Trelawny? You don't know when to concede that you are fairly beaten."

"And the trouble with you, *Tiltwell*," the earl of Caerhays said in a bored, insulting voice, "is that you aren't a Trelawny and you never will be."

The color drained from Clarence's face, and his fists clenched. The two men glared at each other, bristling like a pair of alley dogs fighting over the same bone. Clarence pulled his lips back from his teeth in a rictus of a smile. "Will we see you at the wedding, coz? At least do come for the breakfast afterward. Who knows? Perhaps you'll be the one to find the bean in the bride's cake and take the plunge again."

Clarence Tiltwell left a silence in his wake. Jessalyn's hands shook as she gathered the rest of Topper's things. A hawker strolled by, selling eel pies; the smell of burned grease and hay came in with the breeze. She would not meet McCady's gaze, though she could feel him watching her. It was a tactile thing, like a breath against naked skin.

She had to walk past him to leave the lean-to. His hand fell on her arm, stopping her. "Don't marry him, Jessalyn," he said. "You see what he is like. He'll wind up doing your breathing for you."

She stared at his long, hard fingers, dark against the pale pink sleeve of her kerseymere spencer. Heat spread through her from his touch, melting her. Like holding a burning candle to thin silk. "I must go," she said on a sharply expelled breath.

His fingers tightened their grip. "Don't marry him, Jessa," he said again, and she couldn't miss the anguish in his voice.

"The—the Sarn't Major is waiting for me," she choked out through her tight throat, and fled. Because in another minute she would have told him everything. And then instead of saving him, she would have only have wound up hastening his destruction.

Blue Moon stood, legs splayed, on four stone slabs set into the ground, while a man measured the height of his withers with a rod. The big bay's head nodded as if he were dozing in the sun.

Jessalyn sidled up to the Sarn't Major. She felt conspicuous, sure that at any moment someone would shout and fingers would point her way, declaring her an impostor. She had pinned her hair close to her head and covered it with Topper's bright scarlet skullcap, then rubbed dirt over her cheeks to disguise their feminine pallor. Beyond binding her breasts, she hadn't needed to bother with her figure. She'd always been slim-hipped and long-shanked, and her feet had fitted perfectly into the boy's lightweight leather boots.

"How do I look, Sarn't Major?" she asked, pitching her voice low.

The trainer flicked a glance in her direction. "Ye look like a proper knight, but ye're walkin' like a regular dolly-mop. Quit swivelin' and swishin' yer hips. What ye need to do is strut."

"Strut. Right." Jessalyn affected a swaggering stance, cocking one hip. She tried to spit through her teeth and nearly splattered her boots. She eyed Blue Moon, whose head was drooping to his knees. "He looks half asleep. Are you sure he wasn't given something?"

"Our boy never perks up till he's coming down the flat and lookin' at the finishin' post. Ye know that. Ye best go weigh in now, and don't get to flappin' yer jaws while yer about it."

Jessalyn put her fingers to her lips and winked at him. He answered with a ferocious scowl, and her mouth broke into a big smile.

"Christ in his cups, don't go flashin' yer ivories!" he exclaimed. "Never been a boy born what looks as pretty as ye do when ye smile."

"Why, I do believe you have just paid me a compliment, you ol' softy. I would kiss you for it were I not in disguise."

"Hunh. Good thing then."

The Sarn't Major continued to grouse and grumble as he handed her several thin, flat pieces of lead to bring her weight up to handicap. She tucked them into the special slots sewn into her saddle for that purpose, then *strutted* over to sit on the scale plate. She kept her mouth shut, and the man barely glanced at her as he added the weights onto the opposite plate until she was balanced out. He nodded, made a tick on a slate, and motioned for her to get down.

The Sarn't Major took the kit from her hands when she rejoined him. He saddled Blue Moon in his efficient one-handed manner, then gave her a leg up. It felt as if she were straddling a mountain as she settled onto Blue Moon's broad back.

The Sarn't Major studied her seat, then decided to shorten her stirrups a notch. She looked down at his bent head, at the bald spot in his gunmetal gray hair that was clipped close to his scarred and knobby scalp. "Does Gram know what we're doing?"

"Aye. I told 'er." He glanced up, and for a moment Jessalyn could have sworn he almost smiled. "She said 'twas better to die game than to die chicken."

A nervous laugh, rusty as old bellows, burst out of her. She squelched it by sucking on her lower lip. She could feel her heart beating through the soles of her boots. "Is there anything special I should do?"

"Aye. Don't fall off."

With that admonition ringing in her ears, Jessalyn walked Blue Moon to the starting post through a crush of carriages and spectators milling around on horseback. Most of the runners were already there, and it was their knights Jessalyn worried most about, for they all knew Topper and would have expected to see him up on Blue Moon. She pulled her skullcap so far down over her ears, she could barely see out from beneath the stiff beak.

The other jockeys circled the post, making sure their girths were tight and making last-minute adjustments to their stirrup lengths. It was perfect racing weather. The sun was a hazy yellow ball in a sky the color of birch bark. The light shifted with the breeze, from brilliant sparkle to soft mist. The horses' coats gleamed like dew-wet grass.

Jessalyn had never seen so many people on hand to view a race. They sat on the roofs of their carriages, burst from the seams of the grandstands, swarmed in a thick cluster around the betting post. The royal white pavilion looked like a miniature castle with its battlements and Gothic arches. The king wasn't there today, for he was busy preparing for his upcoming coronation. Earlier that morning Jessalyn had flirted and bribed her way into obtaining a seat for Gram in the pavilion, out of the sun and the crowd.

Jessalyn's skullcap muffled the other jockeys' nervous chatter and the distant hum of the spectators. Fear and excitement tightened her muscles, and Blue Moon, picking up her mood, did a nervous little sidestep. Jessalyn drew in a deep breath to calm them both, filling her lungs with the smell of the turf, which was perfumed with wild thyme and juniper. The smooth green grass spread empty before her, looking like the baize on a billiard table. A white-railed fence bordered the course like a decorative strip of tatted lace. It didn't help to know that the posts were made thin and brittle, so that they would easily break beneath any jockey unfortunate enough to be dashed against them.

The last horse to come up to the post was the day's favorite, a dark chestnut with a starred forehead called Merlin. A richly dressed man with boot black hair and beady cockerel eyes rode alongside, imparting last-minute instructions to his jockey. "Give him a bellyful of the whip at the finish. Cut his bloody entrails out if you have to, lad. But bring him home a winner."

Jessalyn thought Merlin was splendid to look at: big, strong, and well muscled. But there was a sensitive, high-strung air about him. He didn't at all look the sort of horse that would respond well to the whip.

"Hullo, you there, boy."

A whip tapped Jessalyn on the shoulder. Startled, she spun around so fast in the saddle she nearly unseated herself. A jockey on a piebald gelding sat glaring at her out of spaniel-colored eyes. "That's Topper's pitch ye're sittin' on."

Jessalyn spit through her teeth. This time her efforts

barely missed the shiny toe of the other fellow's boots. "What's it t' ye?" she growled.

The young man's sparrowlike mouth stretched into a tight grin as he slashed the looped end of his whip at her face.

If she hadn't shied back at the last moment, the thick rawhide would have taken out her eyes. As it was, she jerked hard on the reins and Blue Moon reared. She barely had him collected again when the starting bell clanged, catching them both flat-footed.

The race was off, and all Jessalyn saw was a cloud of dust.

It seemed to take them forever just to catch up with the pack. She hung back after that, although her nerves and muscles screamed with the temptation to forge ahead. It was so hard to let others pass her, to look at the flying tails of the leaders and not urge Blue Moon too early into his breakaway speed.

She made her eyes go soft and wide, opening them to all around her. Bleeding bands of rainbow colors flashed by. The air rushed past her ears in a gentle roar, like a winter sea. Pounding hooves thrummed in her blood. She tasted dust and grass and excitement.

An opening appeared at the rails, and she decided to take it. Blue Moon sprang forward with a powerful thrust of his hindquarters, anticipating her signal by half a second. They closed on the narrow space at the same time as the piebald gelding.

The two horses brushed, and the piebald's jockey shot her a glance. He thrust his knee upward, catching under her thigh, and flinging her out of the saddle.

She lost both stirrups and saved herself from falling only by snatching at Blue Moon's thick mane. She clung, dangling sideways, as the ground rushed past her eyes at incredible speed. It was like trying to sit on top of a greasy pole; she felt as if she were hanging on by her eyebrows. At last she managed to stab one foot back into a stirrup and haul herself upright again. It was, she thought with a shock of silent laughter, the most death-defying acrobatic feat she had ever performed.

Somehow, even with her flailing on his back, Blue Moon had still kept neck and neck with the piebald. The jockey, catching her out the corner of his eye, turned his head. Jessalyn saw his whip come up. She flung her arm around as if she were taking a wild swing with a cricket bat, and her fist caught him hard on the neck. Then all she saw were the soles of his boots.

Riderless, the piebald slowed, and Blue Moon took his place at the rails. Jessalyn cast a swift glance backward. The other jockey was rolling out of harm's way beneath the rails, bellowing curses.

They were nearing the home straight now, and the spectators began to gallop onto the course, crowding the field into the rails. Jessalyn kept her gaze straight ahead between Blue Moon's cropped ears. She held the reins lightly, giving the bay his head, her thighs and calves squeezing gently, her arms making smooth scrubbing motions in the air. Blue Moon's long, fluid stride tore at the turf, every ripple of muscle in his big body seeming to find an echo within herself.

They broke free from the pack with a quarter of a mile of flat green grass to cover and the dark chestnut favorite a furlong in front of them.

The smell of the race was in Blue Moon's nostrils; it thrummed through his blood. He smelled victory, and he went after it, straining, reaching, striving with every beat of his great heart. They bore down upon the winning post, and Jessalyn knew suddenly that they weren't going to make it. Blue Moon ran as if his legs bore wings, but it was not enough. She'd left it until too late.

Merlin's jockey heard them coming and craned a look back over his shoulder. His eyes grew wide to see them so close. He flailed madly at his horse's withers with his whip, as if beating at a carpet, a frenzy of flapping elbows. Merlin's ears went back, and he shied just as Blue Moon stretched out his neck, striding past the finishing post . . .

And winning by a nose.

It wasn't until they'd slowed to a walk that the great waves of sound hit her, though it must have been going on all along. Cheers rolled and lapped over her, buffeting her; shrill whistles pierced her ears. Blue Moon stopped flatfooted, his sweat-foamed sides heaving. Jessalyn leaned over his neck, pressing her cheek into his wet hide, her heart swelling with love for him, and pride in his stamina and courage. "You were magnificent," she crooned. He was truly rare and special, a blue moon.

Horses and men surged around them, plucking at her sleeves, slapping her on the back, shouting questions in her face. The Sarn't Major pushed his way through the crowd. "Give way, damn ye," he shouted. "Give way."

Jessalyn slid out of the saddle, and the Sarn't Major stood in front of her, blocking her from the pressing crowd. "Not 'alf bad," the crusty old trainer said. And then to Jessalyn's utter shock he bussed her on the cheek. A choking feeling clogged her throat, something between joy and exhaustion, so that she couldn't speak.

Suddenly her legs went so weak and wobbly she would have slithered to the ground like a collapsed balloon if the Sarn't Major hadn't caught her beneath the elbow. "Don't ye go turning back into a vaporish female yet," he groused at her as he fumbled with the girth buckles. "Ye've got to weigh in."

It was on her way to the scales that she saw him. Her dark angel. He stood beside a red-and-white-striped ale tent, a leather jack clutched in one fist. Their gazes clashed and held. There was no doubt that he knew her, but then hadn't he once said that he would know her anywhere?

He tipped his hat at her, but he didn't smile. He tossed what ale was left in the jack into the dirt and after, turning on his heel, pushed his way through the sharpers at the hazard tables, walking fast with his long, hitching stride.

After Jessalyn had been weighed back in, and the man had put another tick beside the Letty name on the slate, she borrowed a coat from one of the other jockeys to cover her bright scarlet and black taffeta shirt so that she could slip unnoticed through the crowd. She hurried past all the tents and booths, with their greasy smells and their flapping flags, until she was almost running by the time she reached the royal pavilion. She wished she could have seen Gram's face when she and Blue Moon had flashed past the winning post, but she would see it now.

She mounted the steps to the upper balcony two at a time. But at the top she paused to take something out of the small slash pocket in her taffeta jockey shirt. She had pawned a garnet necklace, the only piece of jewelry she had of her mother's, to buy it. She thought of it now as her good-luck charm. She had carried it with her on that wild ride and it had brought her down the home straight a winner. It had made winners of them all.

Lady Letty sat in a ribbonback chair before the balcony railing. She looked straight ahead, out over the rolling downs, a scene she must have shared a hundred times in the years gone by with her baronet.

For a moment Jessalyn stood behind her. She saw the white rails that marked the home straight, and she heard again the thunder of a thousand cheers. Tears welled in her eyes—from pride in herself and Blue Moon and from the special joy of at last having a dream come true. She laid her hand on Lady Letty's shoulder and swung around to kneel beside her chair. "We've done it, Gram. We've won the Derby."

Lady Letty sat stiff, unmoving, not speaking.

Jessalyn knelt beside her while the bell rang announcing the next race and a fight between two gentlemen broke out in the seats below her. While the sun melted the last of the mist so that the downs seemed suddenly to be bathed with a brilliant light and the breeze came up again, bringing with it the smell of horses and the turf. And the sweet, hot taste of winning.

"Oh, Gram . . ." she whispered. And closed the old woman's lifeless fingers around a mother-of-pearl snuffbox.

24

The mulberry brocade curtains were snapped open with such cheerful force their rods rattled.

McCady Trelawny lifted his face off his desk and looked at the world through blurred eyes. The bright sunlight streaming through the window stabbed into his head like an awl. "Bloody hell," he groaned.

He looked daggers at the cruel fiend who was masquerading as his manservant. Duncan regarded him out of solemn golden brown eyes. A nun in a brothel couldn't have looked more innocent. "I thought ye rang, yer nibs."

McCady swallowed. His mouth tasted as if a rat had crawled in it to die. There was a toddy glass sitting beside his elbow with a swallow of brandy left in it. He used it to wash the foul taste from his mouth and get his blood to flowing.

"It lacks a half hour before ten, sir."

"What of it?" the earl snarled. He thought about pouring himself more brandy, but some fool had left it sitting beside the chair before the ash-filled fire grate. He squinted at the cut-crystal decanter in the far, far distance. Some fool had also drunk it empty.

"Ten o'clock, sir," Duncan repeated. He was busy trying to see how loudly he could plump pillows and collect the pieces of clothing that some fool had left strewn about the room. "Ten o'clock is when Mr. Tiltwell and Miss Letty are getting buckled."

"And I say again: What of it?"

McCady wanted to plant his fist in his valet's babbling mouth, but it would have required a considerable expenditure of energy to do it. Besides, the impact of the blow could easily ricochet up his arm and do serious damage to his throbbing head.

Since the bloody curtains were open, he decided to get up and look out the bloody window and see what the bloody hell kind of bloody day it was. Red and brown chimney pots poked into a putty sky, their cowls spinning slowly in the still air. Traffic and people bustled on the street below, as if they all had somewhere to go and something important to do once they got there.

In the distance he could hear church bells.

From almost anywhere in London, he thought, one could see the great dome and twin spires of St. Paul's Cathedral rising above the roofs and chimney pots. St. Paul's, where she would become Mrs. Tiltwell. He glanced at the clock. In twenty minutes.

He supposed she and Clarey would make their home in London. If he was careful, he need never see her. They would not be sharing the same friends or the same interests. Clarey would drag her to all those routs and balls and assemblies at Almack's and make a pinch-mouthed boring and bored matron of her in five years. She would fade in London, like a plucked primrose. To him she ought forever to be a wild child of barren moors and rocky beaches.

It was odd, he thought, how one person could make such a difference in another's life. Once his world had been etched in grays. Then one summer day he had met a girl with hair the color of a sunrise, a freckled nose, and a wide, laughing mouth, and for a time his world had become colored with joy fire.

He pictured himself going back to the beach at Crookneck Cove and living that moment all over again. Only this time he would have a fortune and a dream to lay at her feet. A dream to keep the shining light in her eyes as he took her to his bed. And a fortune to keep her there, in his bed, after the hunger had died.

Or perhaps . . . or perhaps a miracle would have happened and the hunger would never have died.

"It may nae be my place to say so, sir," Duncan said as he put a glass into his lordship's hand. "But something havey-cavey's going on. I would've wagered my hope of heaven that it was yer ugly phiz Miss Letty loved."

"You sentimental cabbagehead. She's marrying him for his money."

At least that was what she had said. Only he didn't believe her. But believing the alternative was even worse: that she was marrying Tiltwell because she loved the man more than she loved. . . . Damn her! What made her so bloody different from all the other women in the world? He hadn't wanted to feel this way about her. He didn't think it was *possible* to feel this way. It was nothing more than an itch between the legs and a fire in the blood. His mocking words echoed back at him: *I take the girl to bed, and it's gone by morning.* Yet if that was true, then why was losing her hurting so badly? The pain of losing her seemed to have settled into his chest, gone soul-deep, until it had become a part of his every breath, every heartbeat.

"She's marrying him for his money," McCady repeated, emphatically. But it didn't ease that bloody ache in his chest.

Duncan heaved an enormous sigh. "That's as may be—"

"That is *precisely* how it is." McCady took a big gulp from the glass in his hand, thinking it was brandy, and nearly choked on the bitter tar-water that went down his throat. "Bloody *hell!*"

Duncan clicked his tongue over the condition of the fern that sat on the plant stand beside the window. "This puir thing's not long for this world," he said, lifting one curling

brown frond. "If I dinna know better, I would think someone has deliberately been pouring poison down its throat
every morn. D'ye remember, sir, that time in bluidy Spain,
when we had to get across that bridge, and there were over
fifty Frenchies holding it, and only the five of us? Do ye
remember what ye told us on that day?"

McCady shot him such a hard glare that his eyeballs
ached from it. "No, I do not remember, and what is more, I
don't give a devil's damn."

"Ye said: 'Let's just take the bluidy thing and put the
bastards out of their misery.'"

McCady stared at the manservant, but he wasn't really
seeing him. He was looking into his own future, and all he
could see was a terrible, wrenching loneliness. It grew so
quiet in the room he thought he could hear his heart beat.
He saw a woman with wild red hair, lying on a bed; he saw
Clarence Tiltwell plunging his hard sex between those
long, long legs, sucking her taut brown nipples, plundering
that laughing mouth with his tongue.

"Duncan . . ."

Duncan lifted one perfect blond brow. "Aye, yer nibs?"

"Have my highflyer brought around."

Duncan glanced up at the gilt mantel clock. "Aye, sir.
But if ye dinna mind my saying so, sir, ye've cut it a bit
fine."

"Bloody hell!"

Even perched high as he was on the seat of his phaeton,
McCady couldn't see around the enormous country wagon
filled with bales of straw that blocked The Strand. They
were wedged into a jam of hackneys, dogcarts, landaus, and
gigs. Ahead of him he could hear shouts and curses, a bray-
ing donkey, and the bleat of a brass horn. And in the far
distance, the crashing cymbals and rolling drums of the
daily parade of Horse Guards as they marched from their
barracks to Hyde Park. Marched as they did every morning
at ten o'clock.

He jumped down from the phaeton and started running.

He slammed into a boy who had chosen that moment to duck into the street with a shovel and bucket to collect dung. He picked the boy up, dusted him off, and started running again.

He rounded the corner into Temple Bar and collided with a man adorned head to toe with the buttons he was hawking. He looked back to apologize and almost tripped over a street sweeper's broom. He banked and caromed his way down the crowded street like a billiard ball run amok.

He cut through an alley that smelled of soapsuds and nearly garroted himself on a clothesline that was strung between two doorknobs. An enormous pair of female unmentionables somehow wound up wrapped around his head like a turban. He peeled them off and sent them whipping through the air, to knock the wig off a passing barrister.

He ran up Ludgate Hill, blowing like a sperm whale. The cathedral loomed before him, with its twin towers and great white dome. He thought he would make it in time, and then the fourteen-foot pendulum of the great bell begin to toll.

He jumped a bollard, and pain speared up his crippled leg. He sprinted up the stone steps and banged through the doors. He paused for a moment to catch his breath and allow his eyes to adjust to the sudden dimness. She was there, at the other end of the nave, by the iron and wooden choir, standing before an archbishop of the Church of England. She was there, and Clarence Tiltwell had taken her hand to place his ring on her finger.

"Jessalyn!" McCady shouted, his voice bouncing off the frescoed ceiling. He ran down the nave, past marble columns and saintly statues and gaping mouths. "Jessalyn!"

She and Clarey both whirled, their faces stiff with shock. "How dare you . . ." the groom began, and ended up stepping into McCady's swinging fist. And then, because he knew how good it would feel to do it, McCady rammed a knee hard in Clarence Tiltwell's groin.

The breath whooshed out of Clarence like a boiling tea-kettle, and he sank to his knees, cradling himself.

McCady turned to Jessalyn. She looked as if she had been the one to take a fist in the jaw. All the color had drained from her face, leaving her eyes looking flat and glittering, like beaten silver. He stared at her as if she were the only woman on earth, ignoring the archbishop, who was bleating like a hen whistle, "I say, I say, I say, you can't do this."

"You're coming with me," McCady said, softly so as not to frighten her.

"No!" she whispered on a sharp expulsion of breath. But he grabbed her wrist anyway and hauled her with him back down the nave.

"Stop him!"

Until now the few wedding guests had been too shocked to interfere, but at the archbishop's command several of the gentlemen started forward.

Tall wrought iron candlesticks, with three flaming branches, were bolted to the end of each pew. With a strength he hadn't known he possessed, McCady wrenched one free and threw it like a fiery javelin at the legs of his pursuers.

And then he was running again and dragging Jessalyn after him.

He had her wrist in a tight grip, but still, she could have pulled free of him. That she did not gave him hope. As they pelted through the streets, it occurred to him that he was going to need his phaeton, and he had left it abandoned behind a hay wagon in the middle of The Strand. To his relief he saw that a beadle had drawn the carriage to one side of the street and was holding the horses' heads, a look of outrage purpling his pie-round face.

"Sir!" the beadle expostulated. "You cannot leave this vehicle here."

"You are quite right," McCady said, flinging Jessalyn like a sack of hops up onto the high seat. "If you would kindly remove yourself from my path, I shall remove myself from yours."

It wasn't until they reached the relative calm of Regent's Park that he was able to look at her. Her hair flowed over her shoulders and bare arms, a living fire, held in place by a wreath of tiny white flowers. Her wedding dress was elegant, but of a pale somber gray as befitted her mourning state. Her face was as gray as the watered silk of her gown, and her lips were bloodless.

"Jessalyn?"

Slowly she turned her head, and he looked into a pair of stormy eyes.

"Damn you, McCady Trelawny," she said. "You have ruined everything."

"Perhaps ye might likes t' adjourn now to one o' the nice wedding chambers we gots upstairs," Mr. Hargraves said, producing a smile that was missing a few teeth.

The man was used to nervous grooms and brides, for he was one of the professional witnesses who performed Gretna Green's clandestine marriages. Mr. Hargraves witnessed marriages out of his taproom when he wasn't standing behind his bar of brassbound barrels, serving up wets to the local tipplers.

McCady took his wife's elbow and led her around watermarked wooden tables and benches toward the stairs. She caught her foot on an uneven flagstone and lurched into him. Immediately she stiffened and pulled away. She was unsteady on her feet, but then he, too, still felt the jolt and sway, like the pitch of the sea, that came from spending hours in a carriage.

They had not exchanged more than a half dozen words in the days and nights it had taken them to travel here from London. Before they had left the outskirts of town, he stopped long enough to hock his sword to pay for their food and the changes of horses along the way. He also bought straw for her feet and wrapped her in blankets like a human sausage.

It was while he was gently tucking the wool close beneath her chin that she spoke to him the one and only time. "I suppose you are dragging me off somewhere to ravish me," she said.

"By all means I intend to ravish you." He tried on a smile as he stroked her cheek with the back of his curled hand. "After I have married you."

She said nothing then, merely looked at him out of immense gray eyes that sent a piercing stab of fear into his chest. If she truly loved Tiltwell, then she would never forgive what he had done.

They rode in silence, except for the clink and rattle of the traces, the rumble of the wheels, the ring of the horses' hooves on the hard road. He couldn't get her to eat when they stopped at the coaching inns, though she drank a glass of purl once, standing before a fire in the inn's yard.

He couldn't get his fill of looking at her. There was so much he wanted to say, things he knew he should say, explanations for what he had done. But he couldn't begin to find the words. He doubted he could adequately explain it all to himself. He knew that he had taken her only because he could no longer bear his life without her.

So the milestones clicked by in silence as they drove through grass golden with celandines and dandelions, past farmers' fields squared and planted into a myriad of greens and yellows, like a piece of stamp work. The roads were dry at first, and they threw out a fog of dust that settled on the hedgerows, turning them white. But then it started to rain. He was aware of every breath she took, but she wouldn't look at him.

When she fell asleep, almost tumbling out of the high-perch phaeton, he stopped for a few hours' rest. He didn't dare leave her alone, so he sat in a chair beside the meager peat fire, while she lay fully clothed on top of the truckle bed. They were right above the taproom, and the floor shook with shouts and drunken laughter. She didn't sleep. She lay there, still and silent in the dark, and he could feel her big, haunted gray eyes watching him.

When at last they got to Gretna Green, he paid the witness well to ignore a negative response to the all-important question of whether she was there of her own free will. But it hadn't been necessary. The single word hadn't been loud, but it had been an unmistakable "yes." Too late he realized he had only his signet ring to place on her left hand. Once it was on, she had to curl her fingers to keep it from falling off.

"What God has joins t'gether," the witness had finally said, "let no man puts asunder." And she was his.

He could have wished for a more elegant bridal chamber. The room was furnished with a tester bed with faded green hangings, a small clothespress, and a muted Turkey carpet. The pink grogram curtains at the window contributed the only note of cheeriness to the room.

She went immediately to the window as soon as they had crossed the threshold, keeping her back to him. He doubted she had much to look at. It was a dark, weeping day. Aside from being the place for clandestine marriages, Gretna Green wasn't known for its points of scenic interest. A few stone cottages, a small grove of firs, a little wooden bridge over the river.

He coaxed a reluctant blaze from the smoking fire, then used a paper spill to light the candles in the iron sconces. A pair of plaster figurines, a shepherd and his shepherdess, sat atop the mantel, and he stared at them for a long time, as if they could speak and tell him how he was going to get his wife into his bed if she didn't want to be there.

He joined her at the window, standing at her back, close enough to touch her, though he did not do so. He stared at the top of her bent head. He wanted to press his lips to the center part, looking white and vulnerable in the fire of her hair, but he didn't do that either. Instead he tried several sentences out in his mind before he settled on the most direct one. But when he went to speak, he discovered that his lungs must have forgotten how to work.

He sucked in a deep, hitching breath. "Jessalyn . . . I would very much like to make love to you."

She fingered the lace trim on the curtain. "I didn't think it necessary for a husband to ask permission before he takes his wife."

"I don't want to *take* you . . . I want you willing."

"Willing!" She spun around so fast he took a step back. "And so you abducted me from the altar just as I was about to be married to another man? You wanted me, and you took me without even bothering to ask how *I* felt about it." She slammed a fist at her chest so hard the white floral wreath slipped over her forehead. She pulled it off, staring at it with those haunted gray eyes, and he thought surely that he was damned. She shuddered as she drew in a great, sobbing breath. "Oh, blast you, McCady, you don't know what you have *done.*"

Her face was the white of a fresh snowfall, dusted with gold flakes. Her hair, dark with damp, was like the last leaves of autumn. He saw himself reflected in the clear tidal pools of her eyes. Her beauty made him ache. He was going to start begging soon. He was going to be down on his knees soon and begging her to let him lay his head on her breasts, to lie between her legs, to taste of her mouth.

"I couldn't let him have you, Jessalyn," he said, his throat raw. "I know that I am worthless, a degenerate Trelawny buried in debts. But you're all I've ever wanted out of this life, the only thing I will ever need. Without you I have no reason to live." He held his hands up to her, spreading them in supplication, and they shook as if he had an ague. "I have no pride left. You have it all."

Her head cocked to one side, and her wide mouth trembled. But her voice was thick with feeling, and her words lit up his dark soul. "You silly goose," she said.

And she went into his arms.

He smelled the rain in her hair, and then he was tasting the rain on her lips. And then he was smothering her mouth in a delicious tongue-sucking kiss.

He had wanted to make love to her slowly, to savor her like fine aged wine. But his need was too great. She owned him, did this scrawny carrottop with her rusty laugh and her wide, wet mouth; she owned him body and soul. And he wanted something back from her, even if it was only the hot, exploding pleasure of spilling his seed inside her, long and deep.

He thrust her away from him. "Get undressed," he said, his voice rough because he wanted her so damn badly. "Now."

She stared at him for several heartbeats, her eyes solemn with that deep emotion that he could never plumb and that had always frightened him. Then she turned and lifted her hair off her neck so that he could unhook her bodice. She lowered her head, and his gaze was caught by the white nape of her neck. He kissed the small, protruding bone and felt her silken skin ripple beneath his lips.

His fingers worked at the hooks. "I hate this dress," he said, his breath rustling the tiny wisps of hair that fanned her neck. "You wore it for him."

"No." The word was soft as a sigh. "Not for him, Mc-Cady. I simply wore it, that is all."

The dress pooled around her feet in a whisper of gray silk. His hands clasped her slender waist, and he turned her to face him. She wouldn't look at him. Her fingers became entangled in the ribbons of her shift. It was all tucks and frills and lace, and she had put it on for Tiltwell, not for him, so he hated it as well. He shoved her hands roughly aside, and hooking his fingers into the lacy yoke neck, he ripped it down the middle.

Her breasts spilled free, and he caught them in his hands. A harsh groan tore from her throat. She shuddered violently and fell against him, and he gathered her into his arms and carried her to the bed.

He fell with her across it, rolling her onto her back, pinning her down with his weight. Her eyes stared up at him, two molten silver pools, and he saw within them his surrender. And his triumph.

"You are mine," he said. "My wife."

Her hair spilled over the pillow like a pool of canary wine. He buried his face in it, and her scent filled him, made him sigh. "Primroses," he said. "You always smell of primroses."

He shifted his hips, trying to ease the agony between his legs. He had never felt so enormous, so hard. He was going to have to take her now. He couldn't bear it. Later there would be time to taste the silken skin on the backs of her knees, to run his tongue along the underside of her breast and take her nipple between her teeth, to trace the smooth curve of her bottom with his lips. Later.

His fingers struggled with the drawstring of her drawers. "Damn this thing."

"Don't rip it, McCady."

"No . . . Hell! No, I've got it." He tugged, and she lifted her hips so that he could get rid of the offending garment. He left her stockings on because he thought she looked deliciously wanton that way—gloriously naked except for those thin bits of silk covering her coltish legs and the frilly white garters tied around her slender thighs. He spread her legs wide with his knees and then knelt between them.

He looked down at her, and with reverence and a strange sense of possession, he cupped her fiery mound. He slid a finger inside her, and God, but she was so hot and dripping wet. For him, she was hot and wet for him. Something squeezed his chest and brought the sting of tears to his eyes. It wasn't lust, or only lust. But he didn't want to understand it, so he thrust the thought of it away.

He straightened enough to unbutton his breeches and pushed them down over his hips. His sex sprang free, but he felt no relief. He was hard and aching, and when her hand closed around his thick length, he nearly shouted. She squeezed and pulled, forcing him to grow harder, thicker, and his breath hissed out his tight throat in a shattering groan.

He stilled her hand. "Do you want it now, Jessalyn?"

"Yessss." Her eyes were almost black. Her full mouth wet and parted.

"That's good, that's good. 'Cause now is when you're going to get it."

He braced himself on his outstretched arms so that he could watch her face as he took her. He rubbed the smooth, round tip of himself between the hot, slick lips of her sex, relishing the tiny whimpering noises she was making in the back of her arched throat and the way the white skin of her inner thighs rippled like a wind-licked lake.

He eased into her, stretching her, filling her. Her silk-clad legs wrapped around his hips, sucking him deep, and his breath left him on a keening moan. She throbbed around him, gripping him with the wet, hot mouth of her sex. He lifted his buttocks, almost pulling out of her, then drove into her again and again, stroking her clenching tightness. Again and again, until he was plunging wildly and she was bucking her hips so that with each frenzied thrust he seemed to spear her deeper. A powerful explosion was building within him, like a steam boiler stoked to bursting, and when it came, he knew it was going to kill him, to shatter him into so many pieces he would never be able to put himself back together again. *Not yet, please . . . oh, God, not yet. Not yet, not yet, not yet . . .*

His head fell back, his lips pulling away from his clenched teeth in a rictus of pleasure and pain. She was turning him inside out, utterly destroying him, and he didn't care. She was heaven and hell and everything in between.

And she was his.

25

The sun beat down on her straw-bonneted head, and what little breeze there was smelled tartly of brine and seaweed.

Jessalyn Trelawny walked along a beach of sand that was soft and dry, like crushed sugar. She paused to turn over a piece of driftwood with her foot. Stringy seaweed had caught on one end of it, looking like a hank of witch's hair. She started to bend over, to pick it up, but then she let it be.

She'd seen a man on top of the bluff. His tall figure stood silhouetted a moment against a mist-washed horizon the color of fresh cream. He began the climb down the cliff path, and she smiled. *Walk with me on the beach this morning,* he'd said, and she had seen his intent in the heavy, slightly drowsy look that stole into his eyes and the tautness of his face. They had almost wound up doing it then and there, on the table among the coffee cups and toast racks.

Always there was this wanting between them. Dear life, such wanting. They wanted with a hunger as fierce and devastating as a Cornish gale. The kind of gale that blows roofs off cottages and tears up the hedges. The kind of gale that whips through a place and changes forever the lives of those caught in its path. They were helpless before the storm that gripped them.

She shielded her eyes from the glare of the sun. He had reached the bottom of the path and was pausing to remove his hat and wipe his brow. Sunlight glinted off golden hair. Jessalyn's breath caught in her throat.

An oyster catcher swooped over her head with a loud cry, before banking toward the cliff in a flash of black wings. Clarence Tiltwell stopped before her, and she was shocked at what she saw. Shadows lay like soot smudges beneath his eyes, and his mouth looked bleak. A fading bruise discolored his jaw. For a moment she pitied him, the boy that he was, the friend that he had once been.

His gaze searched her face, and she had to turn away from the raw pain that glittered in his eyes. "Jessalyn, has he hurt you?"

She shook her head. "No. No, of course not. Clarence, why did you come? Can't you please just leave us alone?"

His head rocked back a little as if she had struck him. "I can't. I love you too much. I never wanted to hurt you or anger you. I only wanted to make you my wife."

"Oh, Clarence . . ." It was odd, but in spite of what he had tried to do to her, of what he was doing to McCady, she still ached for him. "It's too late."

"It is *not* too late. I can arrange for an annulment. You can say he forced you. All London saw him carry you off."

McCady was coming toward them down the beach, his hitching stride leaving marks in the sand. Her heart swelled with love for him. Her whole body tightened at the memory of his touch. "He would never let me go," Jessalyn said. "I don't want to go. I love him."

Clarence had seen the change come over her face, and his back stiffened. But he didn't turn around. "He will only bring you misery. He's going to prison, Jessalyn. I can make sure of it. What will you do when—"

"I will take rooms near Fleet Street and visit him every day," she said. She knew that McCady could hear her now. She wanted him to hear her. "I will take in piecework; I will paste cigar boxes together; I will sell watercress bunches in Covent Garden. I will do whatever is necessary to live until we can be together again."

Clarence took a step toward her, a baffled, panicky look in his eyes. He gripped her arm as if he would drag her away. "Jessalyn—"

"She is Lady Caerhays to you, Tiltwell. And you will take your hand off her." McCady slipped a possessive arm around her waist and drew her against him. Fear for him, for what would happen made Jessalyn dizzy. She thought she could actually feel her heart slamming in slow, painful strokes against her breast. She cast an imploring look at Clarence, but his gaze was riveted on McCady, and it was black with rage and hate.

"You bastard," he said.

A slow smile curled the earl's mouth. "Actually, I'm not. *My* parents were married . . . cousin."

Faint tremors shook Clarence's lanky frame. His face had blanched a sickly gray, the color of old wax. "You once made me swear to be good to her, yet you were the one who carried her off and married her over an anvil in a hovel."

"It was a taproom actually."

"Don't you care what you have done to her? You have utterly and completely ruined her."

"The act of a blackguard, I agree. But then I've never claimed to be otherwise. And she is not complaining." He looked at her with drowsy, heavy-lidded eyes, but his arm was squeezing her so tightly the breath was pushed from her lungs. "Are you, Jessa?"

"McCady, don't taunt him, please. It isn't right—"

"She's afraid," Clarence said, and he forced a high-pitched laugh. "Aren't you, my dear? You're afraid I'll tell him about our little agreement."

"Clarence, don't—"

McCady's voice cut across hers. "What agreement?"

"I was to give her your promissory notes on our wedding night. But there wasn't a wedding night, so I still have them. And you have ten days to come up with ten thousand pounds, because after that I'm sticking the bailiffs on you." His hands fisted, and he spoke between tightly held lips. "You have her now, Caerhays, but I shall have her in the end. It is only a matter of time." He spun around on his heel and strode away from them so fast the tails of his coat slapped at his leg and his boots kicked up tiny sprays of sand.

McCady's furious gaze slammed into her like a blow to her chest. "Was he telling the truth?"

"McCady . . ."

His rough hands wrapped around her arms, and he shook her, hard. *"Was he?"*

"I will do anything for you."

He let her go so abruptly she stumbled in the thick sand. "So I see," he said, and there was that sneer in his voice that could be so cruel and cutting. "Including *selling* yourself like some Covent Garden doxy."

"Yes!" She spit the word at him, going up on her toes and leaning into him. "If that is what it took to save you from prison. Is that so terrible?"

"Yes, dammit!" he spit back at her. The sunbursts in his eyes flared with fury and frustration, and something else: a shocking bewilderment, as if she, not he, were the mystery.

She stretched up farther on her toes, going nose to nose with him. "I love you!" she shouted. "I would do anything for you. Why in bloody hell does that make you so angry?"

"I don't know!" he shouted back at her.

He swung away from her and starting walking.

"Where are you going?" she cried after him.

He didn't stop; he didn't even pause. She picked up her skirts and ran after him, wobbling in the heavy sand. "Damn you, McCady, you aren't walking away from me!" She slammed hard into his back, driving him to his knees and knocking her hat off her head. Its wide satin ribbon pulled tight against her throat. She wrenched it off and sent it soaring and tumbling into the marram grass and rocks.

He rolled, pulling her over on top of him. "What the hell—"

"I'll not let you leave!" She thumped his chest with her balled-up fist. "You aren't leaving me again, do you hear me, McCady?" She gripped his hair and slammed her mouth down on his, and it was like setting a torch to black powder. Their mouths clung, possessed, devoured, and when it ended, it was as if a fierce and violent storm had passed through them, leaving them shaken.

Her breath blew against the skin of his neck in harsh gasps. "Never again," she said. She could feel his heart pounding against her chest. "You're not leaving me ever again."

He sucked in a big breath and expelled it in a bigger sigh. "I'm not leaving you, woman. I'm going to Penzance. I was going tomorrow anyway to put the finishing touches on the locomotive. The bloody trials will still happen whether I'm in prison or . . . or not . . . dammit!" His sex stirred against her belly. It was thick and hard, and she thought she could feel the heat of it through her clothes and his. She rubbed against him in bold, sensuous circles, and heard his breath catch. "Ah, *God.* Even angry with you, there is this craven, aching need in me—" He cut himself off, and his hands closed around her shoulders to push her off him.

She pressed down hard against him, as if she could fuse their two bodies into one. She ran her tongue across his sullen lower lip. "I will do anything for you, McCady," she said into his open mouth. "Anything. Except stop loving you."

His fingers speared through her hair, pulling her head down for the breath space needed for their lips to connect. His kiss, which began rough and punishing, turned soft and seducing. His mouth moved over hers, parting her lips and inviting himself in. He moaned into her open mouth . . .

And tore his mouth from hers, pulling his head back. She stared, breathless, at the harsh beauty of his face, but the shadows had consumed the suns in his eyes. "Damn you," he said. "Damn you, for being able to do this to me." He pushed her off him and rolled in one swift, graceful movement to his feet.

And he was gone.

She lay on the sand until the throbbing in her lips subsided. A wide smile broke over her face, and she spread her arms, embracing the world. *He loves me,* she thought. *He* does *love me.* Only the silly goose didn't know how to say it yet.

She shielded her eyes from the harsh glare. The sun was hot; she'd be left with a hundred blasted freckles for McCady to try to lick off. She pushed to her feet, dusting the sand from her skirts.

Nearby a rock thrust out straight and flat from the sand like a shelf, and Jessalyn went to sit upon it. She unbuttoned her gray kid boots and tugged them off, then untied her garters and peeled down her stockings. She dug her bare feet into the wet sand. It flowed between her toes, cool and slick, stirring her like a lover's touch. His touch. She looked out to sea, at a sun-bleached sky where wisps of memories played, like shadow puppets on a wall.

She smiled again as she thought of that long-ago summer, when the morning breeze had touched her cheeks with fleecy softness, and the sea had seemed to pound against the rocks in time with the wild beating of her heart. When every day the sky had stretched above her head, wide and empty and of so intense a blue the soul could not bear it. When she had loved a man with all of her heart and asked for nothing.

But that he love her back.

The mouth of the blast furnace yawned open, filled with glowing coals that cast an eerie red light throughout the cavernous building. The locomotive sat on a strip of track nearby, the burning embers reflecting in its brightly polished copper box, so that it seemed it had a bellyful of fire.

With its steeply inclined cylinders, it looked crouched and waiting. It looked fast.

The earl of Caerhays leaned against a worktable, deep within the shadows cast by a huge pair of bellows. His booted feet were crossed at the ankles; a lock of mussed hair fell over his forehead. He was in shirtsleeves rolled up to his elbows, revealing muscular arms that gleamed with sweat. He smelled of spent steam and grease.

His manservant, Duncan, had a splotch of green paint on his square chin, directly below the faint dimple. Both men nursed leather jacks filled with smuggled French brandy. They had been working, but now they were celebrating.

Duncan held a dripping paintbrush poised in the air, then drew a slashing cross through the big green *T* on the boiler. He leaned back on his heels and squinted one-eyed at his masterpiece.

"*Comet.* 'Tis a proper name, sir. Very fitting."

A muscle bunched in the earl's beard-shadowed cheek. "It was her ladyship's suggestion."

A dull ache settled over his chest. He missed her. She should be here with him, dammit. He had been going to bring her with him, but she had made him so bloody angry. And every time he thought about it, he got angry all over again, and the devil of it was he didn't know *why.* He only knew he wanted to lash out at something—her, Tiltwell, himself. But then the fury would pass and he'd be left feeling empty. And wanting her.

He thrust the thought of her from his head and took another walk around his locomotive. The boiler had been clothed with sheets of felt, covered by tightly stretched canvas that had been stitched by a Mousehole sailmaker and painted a primrose yellow. At Duncan's suggestion they had also painted the wheels a bright grass green. Every bolt and nut and rivet had been lovingly fashioned by hand. It was unlike anything the world had ever seen.

The special copper tubing, designed for a multitubular boiler, which he'd ordered from a manufacturer in Birmingham, had been installed. It was the innovation he'd first thought of six years ago, when he'd been trying to invent a horseless carriage, that day he'd been knocked senseless by a scrawny carrottop with a laughing mouth. The result was now here before him: a boiler much lighter and powerful, made for an engine that would carry passengers and freight on rails across the land.

He hooked his hip back on the edge of the worktable. Duncan joined him, pushing a pile of spanners and bolts aside, leaning back, laying his palms flat on the old scarred wood, and hefting his butt up so that he was sitting on the tabletop, legs dangling over the side. The two men drank in silent harmony for a while; then the earl said, "She is a beauty, is she not, Duncan?" He felt an odd sort of warmth in his chest that he supposed was pleasure at what he'd built. "Sleek and powerful and efficient. Pity I'll likely never know how she goes."

"Aweel. Ye tipped the dice, and ye bubbled up snake eyes, and there 'tis." Duncan punctuated this observation by taking a swig of brandy.

A faint smile pulled at the earl's hard mouth. "How profoundly and succinctly put. I gambled and lost. No sense weeping and wailing and beating one's breast over it. You're a level-headed man, Duncan."

Duncan grinned. "Thank ye kindly."

The earl frowned. "Unlike a certain female of my acquaintance, you don't allow your emotions to get in the way of your common sense. It's a pity, when one thinks about it, that we couldn't be married to each other."

Duncan's eyes popped open so wide his eyebrows all but disappeared.

The earl made a calming motion with his jack, slopping brandy onto his boots. "I didn't mean it that way, man. The point I was making—trying to make—is that the shackles of matrimony would be easier for one to bear if the one one was married to, the individual, so to speak, in an abstract way, as it were, was a man."

Duncan, who had been following the earl's jack as it waved through the air, had to blink a few times before· he could speak. "I see yer point . . . I think."

"Of course, you see my point. That is because *you* are a man." He thumped Duncan on the shoulder with his finger. "If, for instance, I had preserved your sixteen-year-old virtue at considerable cost to my physical self, not to mention my peace of mind, *and,* I might further add, all the while *you*"—he thumped Duncan's shoulder again—"were cavorting around the countryside, possessed with a laugh that could make a man's blood run hot and lips created to do things to a man only the devil could have invented. . . ." He paused for breath and a hearty swallow of brandy. "Why, the more I think on it, I was a bloody saint. But did she thank me for it? Ha!"

Duncan responded with a solemn shake of his head. "I would ae thanked ye for it. I would ae been so grateful, I would ae kissed . . . uh, I would ae thanked ye. Sir."

"Of course, you would have thanked me. Polite thing to do. And if I had then saved you from a fate worse than death—"

"What's worse than death?"

"Marriage to Tiltwell."

Duncan shuddered dramatically. "I wouldna at all think ill of ye for such chivalrous behavior."

"Of course, you wouldn't. You're a man. Just as a man would not seize upon such a cabbageheaded, cork-brained, bird-witted notion to give himself in marriage to a toplofty, niggardly bastard, merely to rescue the one he lov—cares for from debtor's prison."

Duncan helped himself to more brandy. He cradled the jack between his spread knees and stared into the shimmering golden liquid, a solemn, thoughtful look on his face. "Have you told her ladyship that you love her, sir?"

The earl glared at him. "That is just the sort of question a woman would ask. I fear we would not suit after all."

Duncan shrugged his big shoulders. "My heart is promised anyway. To Miss Poole. Only she willna have me. I'm not good enough for her. I'm too handsome."

Helped along by the brandy, McCady gave this statement careful consideration. "I have just come to a profound conclusion, Duncan. Women are incomprehensible. There is nothing for it. We are going to have to go home."

Duncan had a bit of trouble following the leaps in his lordship's logic. He settled for making a practical observation. "Can't. 'Tis dark out, and we're drunk."

The earl stood up. The world listed slightly. He sat back down. "Tomorrow will be soon enough." He tipped the lip of the brandy bottle over Duncan's jack, filling it to the brim. "In the meantime, you'll be needing to build up your strength, man, for the ordeal ahead of you. Because once we are home, you will drag Miss Poole by the hair up to Gretna Green and you will marry her whether she will have you or not."

"I will, sir?"

"It worked for me, didn't it? Sort of worked. Will work, dammit, once Jessalyn accepts the fact that she belongs to me and that if anyone needs rescuing around here, it's supposed to be her. By me. It's not the woman's place to do the rescuing. A man would know that."

"I still think it would help matters along if ye was t' tell her ladyship that ye love her. Sir."

"You look to your own affairs, Duncan."

Duncan belched. "Aye, sir."

Black Charlie sat hunched like a massive spider in a corner beneath the arcade at Tattersalls Repository. Neat rows of stacked coins of various denominations were arranged on the table in front of her. She was settling last week's bets.

"Morning, Charlie," Lady Caerhays said from beneath the big floppy brim of a stableboy's hat.

The leg flashed a mouthful of brown teeth and clay pipe. "'Ere now! 'Tis Miss Jessalyn. I hardly recognized ye in them togs. I don't owe ye any blunt, does I? I thought we was all settled up."

"Oh, we are, we are. I'm just here because, well, I'm having a dispersal sale."

Black Charlie's bristly brows disappeared into a grimy mobcap. "Are ye now? Guess ye don't have the 'eart for any more racin' now that yer granny's passed on, eh? Ye'll get a pretty penny fer the lot, ye will. Especially that Blue Moon of yours—he's a prime un. A tiptop goer and no mistake."

Jessalyn's smile felt a bit wobbly. "That he is. A tiptop goer . . ." A sudden rush of tears filled her eyes, and she had to blink hard and look away.

A dandy in green-striped trousers and a purple coat with brass buttons the size of eggs came sauntering up just then, wanting to lay a pony on the favorite in next week's Rowley Mile, and so Jessalyn drifted away. The auction yard at Tattersalls was always busiest on Monday mornings, for that was when the horses passed under the hammer and the legs settled last week's bets.

No woman, except for Black Charlie, of course, dared set a dainty foot within the yard at Tattersalls; that was why Jessalyn had once again donned her masculine disguise, this time as a stableboy in a felt hat, whipcord breeches, and an old black wool postman's jacket. As a special touch, she'd knotted a red kerchief around her neck. She must be getting good at strutting and spitting, she thought, for she passed unnoticed among the crush of sporting men.

Coachmen swaggered about, spitting through the holes in their teeth and brandishing their whips. Pinks and swells and tulips of the *ton* paraded before the white temple in the middle of the yard, showing off the cut of their riding coats and the shine on their boots. And the copers, those knowing horse dealers, consulted their notes and eyed the stock in the boxes, sizing up just how high they intended to bid and no higher.

Jessalyn spotted the Sarn't Major, pacing before the

horse boxes, guarding his darlings, frightening away anyone who looked to be a potential bidder with his fierce scowls and growls. He scowled at Jessalyn and turned his back on her.

The Sarn't Major wasn't speaking to her. When she'd told him what she intended to do, she'd thought he was going to cry. "M'lady'll will be turnin' over in her grave when I tells her about this," he'd said, and in the end Jessalyn had been the one to shed the tears.

Blue Moon poked his dark red head out his box, and again Jessalyn's eyes filled. She used one end of the red kerchief to dab at her nose. Dear life, she was turning into a regular watering pot. A hammer rapped loudly on wood, and Jessalyn's heart squeezed up into her chest. For the bang of the auctioneer's gavel signaled the beginning of the day's sales. Saddle horses, coach horses, and hunters all passed under the hammer. And then it came turn for the racehorses.

The Sarn't Major walked the first of their lot—a five-year-old filly called AnnaBell—up and down the arcade so that the bidders could get a good look at her. The diffused green light filtering through the windows in the roof made the filly's immaculately groomed black coat shine like ebony. She went fast, for seven hundred pounds.

The next two, both proven studs, went for more. Jessalyn totaled the winning bids up in her head. Thus far they had made twenty-nine hundred pounds. Added to what was left of her Derby winnings, she already had a third of the sum she needed.

And now it was Blue Moon's turn.

The Sarn't Major led the big bay out of his box, and Jessalyn stepped forward, taking the reins from the trainer's hands. Tears were running down the seams of his craggy cheeks, and his black eyes were swollen and red-rimmed. His bull's head sank deep into his hunched shoulders, and he turned away from her.

The auctioneer stood behind a wooden rostrum at one end of the arcade. Jessalyn started at the opposite end and walked toward him. Her legs were shaking so badly she almost stumbled. But Blue Moon seemed to know that he was now famous, for he pranced and tossed his head and lifted his bobbed tail high.

"Now, gentleman," began the auctioneer, "if I might beg of you your attention. You have before you Blue Moon, out of Tulip and Catch-Me-if-You-Can. Three years old, he is, winner of this year's Epsom Derby by a nose while carrying the Letty colors. Young and strong, he is, with lots of races left in him and prime stud material. Can I say a two thousand? Two thousand pounds is the bid, gentlemen. Can I say two and five? Two and five, I'm bid. Can I say three? A Derby winner, gentlemen. Can I say three and five? Three and five I am bid. . . ."

Jessalyn craned her neck trying to see who was leading the bidding. He was an older gentleman, with a shock of white hair and a monocle fastened tight to one eye. She thought he looked kind. She hoped he was the sort of person who wouldn't forget to give his horse a dram of canary wine after the hard gallops.

"Against you, sir. At five thousand." The auctioneer pointed to the man with the monocle. The man raised his glove.

"Five and five then. Thank you, sir. And may I say six then? Six it is to you, sir . . . No, sir? Are we done at six? Six is the bid. Going at six thousand pounds." He banged the rostrum with his hammer, and Blue Moon was sold.

A natty groom ran up to her and took the big bay's halter.

Jessalyn buried her face in Blue Moon's glossy neck, clinging to him until the groom gave a gentle tug. "I'll take care of 'im, lad," the boy said. "Coddle 'im like a nestling, I will. Don't ye worrit none."

Jessalyn bit her lip and nodded, releasing her hold on Blue Moon's neck and stepping back. Tears filmed her last sight of him as the groom led him off to his new owner, the gentleman with the white hair and monocle and kindly face, and just like that he was gone.

And Jessalyn was still short two hundred pounds.

26

Becka Poole didn't know what to think. Her mind was in a whirligig over all these comings and goings, her body near death's door with exhaustion and spasms of the nerves.

First, Miss Jessalyn had been all set to wed Mr. Tiltwell, and Becka was that pleased. Because what with milady's sad passing, poor Miss Jessalyn had been left alone and broken-hearted.

But *then*, on what was to have been the happy day, she'd been abducted by the devil earl, stolen right out of the church she'd been, heaven preserve her. Carried off to barbarous Scotland and ravished she had been, and Becka got all shivery just thinking about it. Then he'd up and brought her back with him to Cornwall, had the mad earl, and Becka had been sent for from London Town, where she'd been left alone with all the crocodiles and sphinxes, a prey to hillas and God knew what else. By ship she'd gone, and her belly hadn't been the same since. So bilious had she been that she'd had to feed off biscuits and soda water for days after, leaving her so weak she could barely lift a spoon to her mouth.

Yet no sooner had Becka been safe in Cornwall—or as safe as a body could be, what with that Mr. Duncan astaring at her all the time with lustful eyes—than off they'd gone again, back to London Town. Becka supposed she couldn't blame Miss Jessalyn for running away, what with the way the devil earl had been keeping her in his bed-chamber day and night, ravishing her again and again. Becka got all shivery just thinking about it. And so back to London they had come, by mail coach this time, and her dairy-air still bore bruises black as tar pitch. But her bones were what had suffered the worse—rattled and battered, they felt, as if they'd been taken out her body and used for cricket bats.

Nor had she been allowed a moment's peace to recover a bit of her strength, because yesterday Miss Jessalyn had went and sold Blue Moon. Becka would have thought there was nothing ever going to part the young miss from that horse, she loved him so. It had fair broken her heart to do it, too. She'd cried all of last night, she had, keeping Becka awake, so's she'd had to drag herself from bed this morning with a gouty pain in her head.

Not Miss Jessalyn, though. Up bright and early *she'd* been, and off she'd gone again. And now this afternoon here she was back again, with a smile fair to splitting her face and clutching a piece of paper in her hand.

"I've done it, Becka!" Miss Jessalyn said, laughing and crying both at the same time and whirling around on her toes, fit to make a body dizzy just to look at her.

Becka touched her hagstone and prayed to St. Genny. She was beginning to fear that marriage to the mad devil earl was turning Miss Jessalyn mad along with him, the way a dollop of buttermilk in cream turns it sour. "Ee done what, miss?" she asked warily.

"He'll not go to prison now! Oh, he'll be furious with me when he hears about what I've done, and then he'll sulk for a bit, because he is a stubborn, arrogant Trelawny to his very bones. But he'll forgive me soon enough. All I'll have to do is . . ." She trailed off as a pretty blush suffused her cheeks. "Well, when you marry Duncan, you'll understand what I mean."

"I told ee, I bain't marryin' Mr. Duncan. Not never, and—"

A fearsome pounding rattled the front door, and Becka shrieked, clutching at her throat. Miss Jessalyn ran into the hall, and Becka followed, sure she was going to have a heart stroke, and wouldn't Mr. Duncan be sorry then, when she was dead and laid out in her coffin.

"Jessalyn! Open the bloody door or I will kick it in!"

Becka gripped the brass hat rack for support, certain that she would faint any minute now. "Oooh, God's me life."

Miss Jessalyn stared at the door as if it were about to leap off its hinges and bite her. "It's Caerhays," she said, as if this were a great surprise.

Becka looked at her mistress as if she'd gone daft, as indeed, she must have. She nodded her head slowly. "Ais, miss, 'tes his lordship a'right. He sounds multitudinous angry."

Miss Jessalyn lifted her chin high in the air. "I am not receiving him," she said loud enough to be heard on the other side of the polished black oak panels.

"You bloody well will receive me, wife," his lordship said, loud enough to be heard back again. "You'll receive every bloody inch of me."

Becka clutched at her pounding heart. "Ooh, me life an' body. He means to ravish ee. Again. He's a scavenger, he is. A ravenous scavenger."

Miss Jessalyn turned her back on the door. "Becka, you will wait until I have retired to my room, and then you will admit his lordship. You will escort him into the parlor and explain to him that I am not at home to him."

"Ooh, but I've come all over queer of a sudden, Miss Jessalyn. With collywobbles in me belly and dreadful heart pulpy-taties fit to perspire me . . ." Becka squeezed her eyes shut and tried to faint. But though she felt all weak and fluttery, blessed darkness wouldn't come. She opened her eyes. Miss Jessalyn had already disappeared up the stairs. "Oooh, St. Genny preserve me."

"Miss Poole, ye'll be opening this door now."

It wasn't the earl's voice this time, it was Mr. Duncan's, and Becka didn't like the tone of it. Where was *he* getting off giving her orders? She didn't work for him, nor was she his wife either, so he had no *right*, and she wasn't ever going to *be* his wife, so—

"Becka!" Duncan roared.

Becka's hands were shaking like a leaf in a gale as she unbolted the door. She curtsied to the earl, too frightened to look up into his devil's face. "Afternoon, milor'. Funny that you're thinking to come round callin' today, when Miss Jessalyn, she be out—"

The earl brushed past her without so much as a by-your-leave and went pounding up the stairs, off to do his ravishing. Mr. Duncan's broad shoulders filled the doorway, and there was an odd look in his eyes as if he, too, had ravishing on his mind.

Becka's chin shot up, though she was careful as always to keep her hair pulled across her scarred cheek. "Ee can just keep yer distance, Mr. Duncan."

"And ye can just get yer bonnet and gloves and a warm cloak to wrap up in. Because ye're coming with me."

"Ee be absconding me!" Becka cried, backing up and clutching at her bosom so tightly a button popped.

Duncan threw back his head and let loose a hearty whoop of laughter. "Aye, lass. I'm *absconding* ye. We're getting married."

"I've told ee and told ee, I bain't never goin' to marry ee."

"And I say you are. Willing or not, ye're going to be my wife, ye're going to sleep in my bed, and ye're going to bluidy well like it!"

Becka bit her lip and ducked her head. Then she flung it back up again and yanked the hair out of her face. "Will ee look at me?"

Duncan took a step toward her. "I'm seeing ye."

"Nay, ye're not. Look at me!"

He took another step, bringing himself right up against her, and God's life, he was so *big*. "I see the scar," he said, his voice a gentle purr. "And if the man as put it there were nae dead already, I'd kill him for ye." He cupped the pretty side of her face in his big hand and turned it so that the scar was bared to the merciless light coming in the open door. He bent his head and kissed it. "There, now. 'Tis gone."

"But . . ." Becka touched her cheek, feeling the rough, ugly welt.

"'Tis gone. When I look at ye, my love, I see the face of heaven, and she is beautiful."

McCady broke the flimsy lock with one blow of his booted foot. The door slammed against the wall, rattling a pair of Egyptian funeral urns on the mantel.

Jessalyn was sitting before a dressing table in a massive chair that had clawed feet and a roaring lion's head carved into the back of it. She was applying powder to her face with a hare's foot, and she looked back at him, cool and remote, from the mirror. He gripped the door and slammed it shut behind him, and the urns rocked.

"I do not recall hearing you knock," she said. "Nor do I recall giving you permission to enter."

"I don't need bloody permission." He advanced on her, and she jumped up so fast the heavy lion chair teetered. Whirling, she backed toward a wall papered with a tangle of vines and lotus flowers. Her hand fluttered to her throat, and her eyes were two enormous silver saucers taking up the whole of her face. She was afraid of his anger—good. She deserved to be afraid since he'd been frightened half out his mind ever since he'd come home and found her gone.

He bracketed her to the wall with his hands and pressed his pelvis against her stomach, grinding it against her. He was hot and hard for her, and he wanted her to know it.

He brought his face so close to hers he could see the

black centers of her eyes widen to swallow nearly all of the gray. "Have you been to Tiltwell?" he said though his teeth.

Her breasts pushed up against his chest as she drew in a breath. Her throat worked, barely getting the word out. "Yes."

"Did he touch you?" He wrapped his hand around her throat. Her pulse beat wildly against his palm. Her skin was the softest thing he'd ever felt. Her mouth was wet and trembling and slightly parted, as if she'd just been kissed—or were about to be kissed. "Did you allow him to touch you, Jessa?"

"No!"

He didn't know if she told the truth, and he didn't care. He wanted only one thing from her right then, and he was going to begin with the taste of her mouth.

He spanned her jaw with his long, hard fingers. He forced her lips to open beneath his, and he filled her mouth with his tongue. She whimpered first in outrage and then in surrender. She wrapped one arm around his back and tangled her fingers in his hair. She sucked on his tongue, pulling it deeper.

He swept his thumbs back and forth over nipples that were budding against the soft stuff of her dress. Her hands gripped and bunched the taut muscles of his back. They made love with their mouths, sucking, tonguing, rubbing kiss upon kiss against each other's lips. Her roaming fingers found the top button of his buckskins, and she popped it free. He shuddered as the back of her hand brushed across his lower belly. He undid the rest of the buttons himself, pushing his throbbing sex into her hands.

She gripped him roughly, stroking him almost to the edge of pain, and if he didn't get inside her soon, it was going to be too bloody late.

He bunched her skirt up around her waist and grasped a handful of soft linen drawers.

She tore her mouth from his, panting. "McCady, please don't rip—"

The thin material made a satisfying tearing sound as it parted beneath his fist. He pushed a finger inside her, and she gasped, arching against him. She was very wet and very hot.

He stoked her with his finger until he had her humming and vibrating and building up steam like a fired locomotive. Cupping the silky underside of her bottom with both hands, he lifted her and slowly sheathed himself. She cried out, arching and throwing back her head so violently it banged against the wall. He pressed his open mouth against the wildly beating pulse in her throat and pushed himself deeper.

He gripped her hips to hold her still so that he could grind and thrust into her, and she was biting his shoulder and her nails were clawing at his back, and he let the pressure build and build and build to an explosion that was fierce and scalding . . .

And not enough.

Her head fell onto his shoulder, and she sagged against him, as the last shudders washed over them. But already he was kissing her again. Already he was quickening and stirring inside her again. His fingers grasped her head, spilling pins and hair down over his hand and wrist, and it felt like liquid silk.

He pulled her head up. "Were you lying about him?" She licked her lips; he licked them after her. "You didn't let him touch you?"

Her eyes were wet and glazed with passion, like glass. "He didn't touch me," she said into his open mouth.

He made a small movement to lodge himself deeper. "Never again will I come home to find you gone."

"I can explain—"

"Later. You'll explain later. Right now I want to get only one thing fixed firmly in your aggravating head. I shall never come home again to find you gone. Nor will you ever spend another night out of my bed without my permission. And since I intend to spend *all* of my nights in *my* bed," he said, punctuating the key words with little thrusts of his hips, "it is highly unlikely that permission will ever be forthcoming. Do we have an understanding, Lady Caerhays?"

"Yes, my lor—"

His mouth seized hers in a deep kiss that filled him with the taste of her, but it was not enough. It was never enough. He moved in slow, rhythmic strokes, and she was gripping him, squeezing him, pulling him to the edge, and it was still not enough. He pumped his hips, and her head thumped against the wall.

"McCady . . . the bed," she gasped out between panting moans. "Why . . . can't we . . . do this . . . on the bed?"

"Yes, yes. The bed." His hands spanned her waist, and she grasped his hips with her strong thighs. He tried to carry her in this fashion over to the bed.

The bed was a monstrosity of black curtains embroidered with gold hieroglyphics and a bedstead supported by enormous crocodile feet. He stumbled over a webbed claw, and they fell onto the bed in a tangle of legs and arms and laughter.

He rolled to his side, pushing himself up on his elbow to look at her. Her hair was a summer sunrise, all rust and burgundy red with a few vivid streaks of fiery orange. Her mouth looked pillaged and ravished, and as he watched, it fell open and curled up on the ends, and a rusty, squeaky noise spilled out of her throat. He caught her laughter with his mouth, and it filled him with fire.

His hands went looking for her breasts, and he pulled back from her, cursing. "Why does there always seem to be all these bloody clothes between us?" His impatient fingers slipped beneath the prim high neck of her dress.

"McCady, don't rip—"

"Then take it off."

Clothes went flying, hers and his both. When he gathered her back into his arms, she was wondrously and gloriously naked at last.

She had large nipples, rosy brown like hazel nuts. He laved each in turn, then drew one deep into his mouth. He loved the feel of it, hard and puckering against his tongue, and he loved the sounds she made—the little trembling sighs and incoherent pleas.

He traced an imaginary path with his lips and tongue across her rib cage and down her belly until he found the edge of her crinkly, curly hair. Her thighs were around his shoulders, gripping him, trembling. She was burning him alive.

He spread her legs wide and buried his face in the fire. She smelled of him, as if he had marked her with his scent like a wild animal. He plunged his tongue into her, sucking, licking. He scraped her tiny nub of pleasure with his teeth, pulling on it gently with his lips. Her thighs opened wider still, and she grasped the sides of his head with her hands, writhing and whimpering and coming hot and wet into his mouth.

He waited for her tremors to fade, savoring the hot taste of her; then he rose above her, to enter her. But she pressed her palm against his chest, stopping him. "Lie down on your back."

He rolled over, and she straddled him. She gathered up her hair, lowering her head, and then she let it slowly fall, over his chest. It slithered and coiled across his sweating skin, filling his senses with the smell of primroses, and he was sure that never before had he known such pure, piercing pleasure.

She took one of his nipples in her mouth, nipping it, and a ragged groan tore from his throat. Her lips went lower, tracing sex patterns over his shuddering belly, and lower still, her tongue licking at the edge of his dark, tightly coiled hair. And then he died as she grazed the length of his hard and trembling sex with her teeth, lightly, lightly, before she opened her mouth wide and took him into her.

She sucked in her cheeks, drawing her lips along his hard length, again and again, until he could bear no more. He tangled his fist in her hair and drew her up and then slowly lowered her down on top of him until he was buried so deep he was sure he must be touching her heart.

She rose and sank down, riding his length, harder and faster until she was plunging wildly, and he was chanting her name, "Jessa, Jessa, Jessa," and her head fell back and her mouth opened wide on a silent scream of pleasure as they climaxed together.

A long time later, when he could breathe again, he settled her down within the crook of his arm, and his eyes slowly focused on his surroundings. He took in the hieroglyphic bed-curtains, the jungle wallpaper, and what looked like a sphinx crouching next to the fireplace and serving no apparent purpose except to fix him with an enigmatic stare.

"How the devil can anyone sleep in this room?" he said.

Her laughter, wild and lusty, shimmered through the air, wrapping around them and drawing laughter from him in turn. She nuzzled his neck with her nose and chin, tugging at his gold earring with her teeth. "Did you really think I had left you for Clarence?"

His gave her a typically arrogant Trelawny look, although she didn't know he was doing it because she couldn't see. "Of course, I didn't think such an idiotic thing. I thought you had gotten a maggoty notion into your head to sell yourself to him for an afternoon of delight in exchange for those damn promissory notes. And don't look like that. You said you would do anything for me." He pulled her head up so that he could look into her face. "So what did you do?"

She pulled out of his embrace, got up, and went to the dressing table, where she retrieved a weighty-looking document from beneath a jar of face powder and a hare's foot, and he enjoyed the sight of her hair swaying back and forth, caressing her naked hips. She came back to him and gave him the document.

It was a statement in a clerk's trained hand, attesting that the yearly interest on all his promissory notes had been paid in full. The signature was Tiltwell's, although it looked a little shaky. A very official-looking seal had been affixed to the end of it.

He looked up into solemn gray eyes. "What did you do?"

A deep emotion pulled at her face, and she looked away. "I sold Blue Moon."

"Ah, hell, Jessalyn . . ." McCady's belly caved in with a feeling so wrenching tears burned his eyes. He wanted to weep the way a child weeps, loudly and harshly and beating his fists on the floor. He wanted to do everything over and do it right this time. He wanted to give her the world, but she had already given the world to him.

He stood up and cupped her face with his hands, using his thumbs to collect the tears she didn't know she was shedding. He drew in a deep breath, trying to find a way to speak around the clot of emotion in his throat. "That horse was the most important thing in the world to you."

Her lips trembled into a watery smile. "*You* are the most important thing in the world to me."

He gathered her into him and pressed her head into the curve of his neck. "I sold the others, too, along with Blue Moon," she said, the words muffled. He could feel her tears, warm and wet against his throat. He swallowed hard around the thick lump, but it still didn't go away. "Only it wasn't quite enough," she went on, her breath gentle on his skin. "What I got for them wasn't enough. S-so I had to s-sell Gram's snuffboxes, too."

"Ah, Jesus . . ."

He held her for a time in silence; then she snuffled a little sob into his throat. "You aren't angry with me?"

He squeezed her shoulders. "Only angry with myself." He pulled her head back so that she could look at him and see that he spoke the truth. "Someday, sweetling, I swear I shall find a way to make it up to you."

She looked up at him out of great, solemn eyes. "Such a

thing can never be made up, McCady. But then it doesn't have to be, nor should it be. Not when it was done willingly, from the heart."

He stared at her, stunned by her wisdom and the purity of her soul. His chest tightened with that strange mixture of wonder, fear, and joy that came over him so often now whenever he looked at her or touched her. Or even thought of her.

She shivered, and he frowned at her. "For Christ's sake, Jessa, you're freezing," he said roughly. "Put something on."

She pushed her lips out in a parody of a pout that made him want to kiss her senseless. "I don't know why I should bother," she said. "You'll only rip it off."

Yet she went to the clothespress, and he watched her, savoring the sight of her naked body until she covered it with an Oriental-style silk wrapper. He pulled on his buckskins, not bothering to fasten them, and stretched out on the monstrosity of a bed. He waited for her to come back to him.

She sat beside him, a secret little smile playing about her mouth.

"I've always hated it when you do that," he said.

"Do what?"

"Smile at me as if you know something that I don't know."

Her smile widened, filling her face. "I was thinking that I love you very much McCady Trelawny."

He stroked the bare white flesh of her arm, unable to look at her. "Jessalyn, I . . ."

"Yes?"

"Nothing."

She withdrew from him, going to the window. He searched for words that would bring her back, but words had always been his downfall with her because they never came easily, and they were always the wrong ones. Freckles of rain pelted the panes, casting speckled shadows on her face, like a gull's egg. It had grown cool in the room.

A look of surprise crossed her face, and she pressed her nose to the glass. "McCady? Your Duncan is driving away with with my Becka in your phaeton."

"Nothing to concern yourself with, Lady Caerhays. They're only eloping. Some of the most respectable folk have been known to do it."

She spun around, and her laughter, rich and rusty, filled the room, until she caught it back with her hand. "That handsome devil—he said he would talk her around to it!"

"I'll wager it was more a case of seducing her into it," he said, smiling because she was laughing again. "That is the only method you women respond to with any degree of proven success."

"Oh, is it indeed?"

"Indeed." He patted the bed. "Come here and let me prove it you."

She came quickly and willingly. Slipping his hands beneath the silk wrapper, he began the slow, delicious process of bringing two satiated bodies back to arousal.

Her fingers tangled in the hair that spilled out the open flap in his buckskins, and he discovered that he was not so slow after all. "McCady? Duncan will never be able to make it back from Gretna Green in time for the trials."

"Not . . ." He lost his breath somewhere and had to start again. "Not unless he sprouts wings and flies."

"Then who will go along with you to drive your locomotive?"

And then he thought of one small gift that he could give her, and he smiled. "You will, Lady Caerhays."

27

The letters *COMET* had been scripted with dripping green paint onto the locomotive's bright yellow boiler. The *O* sagged at the top, like a boiled egg with one end bitten off it, and the *T* lay at a drunken angle, nearly on its side. It was crossed by a long, sweeping slash, which might have been a comet's tail, although somehow Jessalyn doubted such had been the artist's intent.

Her contemplative gaze went from the lopsided lettering to the bent head and broad shoulders of her husband, who was on one knee, oiling the hub of a bright green wheel. "McCady, what addlepated fool painted—"

"I didn't do it," he said, quickly. Too quickly. He cast her a sheepish look as he straightened. "It was some other addlepated fool."

Jessalyn sucked in her lower lip to catch a laugh. "Dear life. Whoever he was, he must have been frightfully foxed at the time."

Her husband pursed his lips, blowing his breath out in a soft whistle while he took a rag out of his pocket and polished imaginary streaks and thumb prints off the *Comet*'s copper firebox. He was trying to look innocent, and being a Trelawny, he was failing miserably at it.

More laughter bubbled up in Jessalyn's chest, and she

barely restrained herself from whirling around on her toes and letting it out all spill out of her from pure joy. It was a glorious day. Thin clouds wreathed the sun, bathing the countryside in pale marzipan colors. The air felt smooth as milk against her skin. It also battered her ears.

They said that more than ten thousand people were lining the tracks along the twenty-mile course of the trials. The air was a din of coach horns, pie hawkers, neighing horses, and screaming babies. The starting point for the trials was right across from the Crooked Staff Inn, which had already sold out of gin and was fast depleting its stock of ale. Many of its customers were the navvies, those rough and tough men who had dug out the cuttings and the tunnels and laid the tracks for McCady's railway. And when they weren't digging and drinking, they liked to wrestle.

A match that had been going on for quite some time was suddenly decided by the winner's bodily picking up the loser and throwing him overhanded like a cricket ball at a stack of ale barrels. The winner turned, dusting off his hands at a job well done, and Jessalyn was astonished to see this behemoth was a woman.

She was further astonished to discover the behemoth making a beeline right at her. She backed up a step; the behemoth kept coming. She backed up another step. She was just about to pick up her skirts and run when the behemoth smiled.

"You be his woman?" the behemoth bellowed out of her deep chest, and Jessalyn was nearly knocked off her feet by the powerful odor of raw onions.

She smothered a sneeze with the back of her hand and tried to breathe through her mouth. "Whose woman?"

"Why, his nibs's, o' course. The earl what built this tramway."

Jessalyn wondered if the behemoth meant to wrestle her for the right to ravish McCady's body. She would do a lot of things for that man, she decided, but a woman must learn

to draw the line somewhere. She pointed to the *Comet*.
"He's over there."

"Aye. He's a right un, is his nibs." The woman took a big
yellow onion out of her pocket and bit into it like an apple.
She was dressed like a navvy in corduroy trousers, stout
boots, and a brightly colored scarf knotted around her neck.
She had muscles to rival Duncan's. "Many was the time he
swung a pick right 'longside the rest of us, building this
tramway. Not too proud to dirty his 'ands and lift a tot or
two o' gin with the likes of us." She eyed Jessalyn up and
down, her nose quivering. It was big and hooked like a
lamplighter's pole. "You be his woman or not?"

"I suppose I am. We're married. Actually."

"Not married long, I'll wager. I seen the way he been
lookin' at you." The navvy woman threw back her head and
hooted like a coach horn. "Cor! Ye're pretty enough, I'll
grant ye that." She reached out and gripped Jessalyn's arm,
squeezing hard. "But ye'll be needing t' put some flesh on
yer bones, if ye expect t' be keeping up with his nibs. He
told me oncet that he were going to build a railway from
one end o' this isle t' other. Fancy that."

Jessalyn smiled with pride. "But he will. From one end
of England to the other."

"That he will, cor! That he will." The woman turned
onion-watery eyes onto Jessalyn. "I have little uns t' feed,
but maybe afterward ye might want to lift a tot or two with
me. The stories I could tell ye about that man of yours.
He's a hell-born babe, but with a soft heart underneath for
all that. Aye, a soft heart underneath," she said, hooting
again as she lumbered off.

Left alone for a moment, Jessalyn smoothed down the
bodice of her wine-colored merino riding habit. She wet
her palms with her tongue and ran them along the sides of
her hair, smoothing back any stray strands. She looked
down, saw dust on the toes of her half boots. Quickly she
pulled a handkerchief out of her sleeve and brushed them
off. Dear life. Why did she always wind up looking like a

ragamuffin? All these people here today. They all would be watching her when she stood up by his side on the *Comet,* and she wanted to do him proud.

She felt someone's gaze on her, and she looked up into the dark, piercing eyes of her hell-born babe. She blushed to have him catch her fussing, yet she could not help asking, "How do I look?"

His gaze roamed the length of her, up, down, then up again, and a drowsy heat came into his eyes. "All I can say is that when I get you alone tonight, you had better be out of it fast. Or I won't be answerable for its condition come morning."

"McCady, honestly. If you persist in ripping off my clothes, I'll soon be reducing to wearing nothing but rags."

He flashed an unrepentant grin and had opened his mouth to say something more, when one of the government officials who was running the trials hailed him and drew him aside to sign a document festooned with ribbons and seals.

Nervous excitement made Jessalyn fidgety. At least an hour yet remained to be endured before it would be the *Comet*'s turn to run the trial. Each locomotive started separately, at times staggered a half hour apart. The engine to cover the twenty miles in the least amount of time would win, and winning meant a contract from Parliament to supply the engines for all of England's railways for ten years to come. Winning meant untold wealth and a dream come true.

But as Gram had so often said, "You mustn't jump the fence, gel, before you trot out the stable door." So Jessalyn strolled past the other locomotives to size up their competition. One, painted an apple red and with blue wheels, seemed twice as big as the *Comet.*

She joined her husband who was squatting on his haunches on the *Comet*'s footplate and scowling into the empty interior of the firebox. "That *Falcon* looks awfully big and powerful, McCady. Do you think we can beat her?"

He flung a glance down the tracks at the other locomotive. "She's too big. See, she's so heavy she has to be mounted on six wheels to carry her load. She'll never make it up that long grade outside Exeter. No, the one we have to worry about is the *Essex Lightning.*"

He nodded with his chin at a sleek-looking iron horse painted orange with black trim. "She's fast," McCady was saying. "But her weakness is in the positioning of her boiler. The way they've got it lying on its side like that makes it inaccessible in the event of a breakdown. But she is fast, curse her."

"We're faster," Jessalyn said emphatically, for she did not doubt it.

McCady flashed her a stunning smile as he jumped off the footplate. She looked up into his beloved dark angel's face. Today the shadows had been banished from his eyes, allowing the golden sunbursts to come shining through. She had never seen him so joyous.

Love for him filled her heart, squeezing her chest. She had to say it, even at the risk of seeing the shadows creep back in and swallow the suns. "I love you, McCady Trelawny."

"Jessa . . ." His hands fell on her shoulders, gripping them so tightly she felt a sting of pain. His throat worked, as if he were having a hard time pushing out the words. "Jessalyn, I . . ."

"What?"

"I . . ." There was a harsh tautness to his face now. His gaze jerked away from her to the *Essex Lightning.* The muscles along his jaw bunched.

"McCady, what's the matter?"

"I . . . There's someone I need to talk to." He crushed her against his chest, kissed her on the mouth in that fierce, rough way of his, and strode away from her so fast he was almost running.

She watched him until he had disappeared among the navvies drinking and wrestling in the Crooked Staff's yard.

She would never completely understand him. She supposed that was what made him so exciting to be with. And
the thought of spending the rest of her life with her exciting
hell-born babe was so wonderful that her face broke into a
wide smile as she went in search of the navvy woman to lift
a tot or two. And to hear more stories about how McCady
Trelawny's railway had got built.

Clarence Tiltwell's thin mouth curved into a faint sneer
as he watched the red and blue locomotive huff and puff its
lumbering way down the track toward Exeter. The *Falcon.*
What a silly, fanciful name. As if that that clattering,
thumping monstrosity could ever hope to emulate the
sweeping, soaring flight of the noble hawk.

The next entrant had started to fire up its boiler, and
steam rose white in the still air with a whistling sigh. It was
odd, Clarence thought, but there seemed to be a tingle in
the air, like a hot summer's day after a lightning storm. A
part of him couldn't help being caught up in the excitement, the way he had been caught up that summer when
he and McCady had built the locomotive to run on his
father's tramway. He remembered those long afternoons in
the Penzance ironworks, McCady putting the engine together and he mostly watching. And listening as McCady
talked and spun dreams in the air. He had wanted to believe in those dreams, yet he had not wanted to believe.
And in the end he had been glad of McCady's failure.

Today the *Falcon* carried sandbags packed into the carts
that were hitched one after the other behind her like a
cranberry string. But suddenly Clarence could picture the
way it would be if the carts were filled with coal and bales
of hay. And carriages hooked up, too, carriages with wheels
made to go on rails, all filled with people. He could see it
just the way McCady had described it that summer, and a
bittersweet ache filled his chest. He wanted to go back and
live again those afternoons in the ironworks, with the blast
furnace making the sweat pour off their chests, and the

hammers battering their ears. And McCady talking and spinning dreams and flashing that devil-be-damned smile.

Those afternoons before Jessalyn had come between them.

He knew she was here today, and his gaze sought her out, although he would not go to her yet. That was for later, when she would need him, need his comforting arms, his soothing words. For now he only wanted to look.

She was easy to find, a tall woman with hair the color of autumn leaves. She was no different, and somehow that surprised him. He would have thought that it would show on her face—all those nights in a Trelawny's bed. Yet she was the same girl, a girl with too-bright hair and a too-wide mouth and a leggy way of moving that always reminded him of an unbroken colt. The same Jessalyn whom he had kissed before the Midsummer's Eve bonfire six years ago.

As he watched her, a vivid look came over her face, and her whole body seemed to shimmer with breathless excitement. For a moment Clarence thought that she had seen him, that the wide, laughing smile was for him. He actually started toward her. But then McCady Trelawny came out the swinging door of the Crooked Staff, sauntering toward her.

She hurried to meet him at a little tripping run. He said something that made her laugh, and the joyous, raucous sound of it rose like whistling steam into the air. McCady slid a possessive arm around her waist and pulled her against him, and Jessalyn stood at his side, smiling, as if she belonged there.

A man with shaggy hair and pock-mottled skin sat with his back pressed against a high stone hedge. He was gnawing on a hunk of bread and cheese and swilling it down with a pail of ale. On the ground next to him were a burning candle in a dish and an opened canister of fulminating powder. From time to time he peered through a crack in the hedge and looked down the gently sloped gully toward the mouth of a tunnel newly hewn through a hillside of yellow granite.

Jacky Stout finished his dinner, mopping the sweat off his face with a filthy rag that left behind smears of black powder. His gaze dropped down to the spalling hammer in his lap, then quickly jerked away. He couldn't look at the hammer anymore without feeling a bit queasy in his innards.

God, the boy had screamed.

Squawked like a chicken right before its throat is cut. But the sound the hammer had made was even worse—a horrible scrunching sound, like stepping on one of those big black beetles that live down in the mines. Blood had spurted everywhere, and the bones had pierced through the bruised flesh, jagged and white. Jacky was sobbing as loudly as the boy when he had raised the hammer high again.

He hadn't told the guv'nor that part, though. That he hadn't been able to bring the hammer down a second time. That he'd done only the one hand.

This was why it was important that he do this job right. He had planted enough black powder in the railbed to make a bang loud enough to rattle the pewter in the kitchens all the way up in London Town. Enough powder to blow a hundred loco-whatsits into nails and kindling.

A chill roached up Jacky's spine, and he whipped around, peering into the copse of trees behind him. A pair of jackdaws sat on a tree branch, cawing at each other. A rabbit bounded off into the gorse, its white tail flying. Jacky rubbed his ripe nose and shrugged. He was hearing things only because his nerves were on edge. This was private land, patrolled by dogs and guards to keep the curious away, needed especially today what with all the crowds drawn to watch the trials of the loco-whatsits. No, there was no need to worry about anyone sneaking up on ol' Jacky Stout unawares. The guv'nor owned this land; that was why Jacky Stout was here, good and alone, with a burning candle and enough black powder to make one bleedin' hell of a bang.

The guv'nor had said the loco-whatsit would be coming through the tunnel at about four o'clock. Jacky pulled a gold-plated repeater's watch out of his coat pocket. The guv'nor had given it to him, a little token of appreciation for taking care of the boy's hands . . . hand. Jacky cast another look at the spalling hammer and shivered. He squinted at the black numerals on the watch face. He hadn't dared tell the guv'nor that he didn't know how to tell time.

He heard it first, a huffing sound like a teakettle simmering on a trivet over a hot fire. Steam billowed out the mouth of the tunnel in thick white puffs. Swearing, Jacky flung the hammer out of his lap, snatched up the candle dish, and climbed, clawing and scrambling, over the hedge. A fire-breathing iron monster on wheels came hurtling out the tunnel, a red and blue monster.

"Bleedin' Christ!" Jacky exclaimed. Red and blue!

He skidded to a halt, the sweat streaming down his face, his chest heaving. Red and blue, bleedin' hell! The loco-whatsit he wanted was supposed to be yellow and green.

As he trudged back to his lookout behind the hedge, Jacky Stout went over the guv'nor's instructions one more time. The moment the green and yellow loco-whatsit came out of the tunnel, he was to light the fuse. He had already marked off the 450 paces from the mouth of tunnel and set the charge in the rock bed that supported the rails. He'd done it just the way he'd set that charge down in Wheal Patience. He had drilled a hole in the rock with a steel borer and dropped a case of black powder in the hole. He'd pushed an iron nail into the powder and packed clay around it. Then he'd pulled out the nail, leaving a thin hole in the clay. Through this he had threaded a hollow reed filled with fulminating powder for the fuse.

"You see the nose of her coming out of the tunnel, you light the fuse," the guv'nor had said, and he had drawn a lot of scriggly lines on a piece of paper and babbled nonsense about loco-whatsits traveling at such and such a speed and taking such and such amount of time to go such and such a distance. Jacky hadn't understood a word of it, and he didn't have to. He knew what he had to know: powder at 450 paces from the mouth of the tunnel; set the fuse when the green and yellow loco-whatsit came out.

But no one had warned him how bleedin' difficult it was going to be to see colors when the bleedin' thing was coming out a black hole into bright sunlight and wreathed in steam and smoke.

The muscles of McCady's arms bunched and strained as he slung a shovelful of coal into the firebox. Sweat stung his eyes. A whiff of primroses drifted past his nose.

He flung the hair out of his face with a toss of his head as he swung around and thrust the shovel blade into the pile of coal. But his gaze was on the tall, slender girl in a wine-colored riding habit. A yellow straw bonnet covered hair the color of a sunrise at sea, but enough sunshine had found its way beneath the wide brim to tint her cheeks a gold-flecked pink. She looked delectable.

With him on the footplate and her standing on the ground, the top of her head came to the middle of his chest. She leaned forward, as if to speak to him, and slid her hand inside the gaping, unbuttoned neck of his shirt. Soft fingers slid over his sweat-slick flesh, pulling gently on his chest hair and lightly scraping across one nipple. A quick, sensual, secret caress that no one had seen, and that sent an immediate fire to his groin hotter than anything he had going in the belly of the *Comet*.

"The carrier pigeons have just come in with the *Essex Lightning*'s time," she said, shouting a little to be heard over the hissing, simmering boiler. "Seventy-two minutes."

Dammit, that's fast. McCady thought. He grunted as he hefted another shovelful of coal. According to the rules, each entrant had to start with the water in his boiler cold and no fuel inside the firebox. Every minute it was now taking him to build up a head of steam was already being counted against his time. The boiler hissed and sucked. Seventy-two minutes. Bloody hell. He wanted to win so badly he could taste the wanting in his mouth, rusty and salty, like blood. He wanted to do it for her.

He had the fire stoked good and hot now. He thrust the shovel straight up into the coal pile and looked down at his wife. His whole body stilled as a feeling that was piercing and sweet shot through him. She was a rare woman, his Jessalyn. He knew that he was nothing without her. Yet because of her, he had the moon and the stars within his grasp.

Jessalyn, his wife, put her fists on her hips and threw back her head to lance his heart with her wide, shining smile. "I should like to come along with you, Lord Caerhays."

He leaned over, offered her his hand, and pulled her up onto the footplate beside him. He thought of that first loco-motive ride that long-ago summer: the way she had kept brushing against him, breathing on his neck as she asked her questions in that excited little-girl way, and the purity and innocence about her, the laughing joy. He had wanted her then as he had wanted nothing else in his life before. He still wanted her in that same way.

Now, just as he had done that summer, he put his hands around her slender waist and lifted her into the tender, where she would ride with the coal baskets and water butt. "This one isn't to going explode now, is it?" she teased, and he knew that her thoughts moved along with his, in tandem with memories. Memories that now tasted only sweet.

He leaned over and kissed her mouth, soft and gentle. "We're going to win this, Jessalyn."

She looked at him with eyes that were gray and endur-ing, like the cliffs of Cornwall. "Make her go fast, McCady. Neck or nothing."

Flashing her a devil-be-damned smile, he turned around

and depressed the pedal, while deftly working the two
small valve handles in proper unison until the engine began
to move, scorching, as always, the backs of his knuckles on
the firebox. Valves and cranks and spindles all began to
move so fast he would have lost a finger or two if he hadn't
done this a thousand times before.

The locomotive clanked and rattled and coughed as it
chugged into motion, slowly at first; then it began to pick
up speed. Spent steam puffed into the air, carried back to
them by the breeze, dampening their faces and smelling of
coal soot. They left the Crooked Staff behind them, but
crowds of people lined the tracks, cheering and whistling,
beating on drums and blowing on horns. Jessalyn laughed
and waved and called out to an enormous woman wearing
trousers, who tossed what looked like a big yellow onion
into her lap.

It all turned into a blur of color and noise, though, as the
Comet started to fly. The first part of the course was on a
downhill slope, and soon they were singing along the rails.
Well, perhaps *singing* was not quite the word. Even with
the spring suspension he'd invented, the *Comet* moved
with a rollicking up-and-down thrust, like a galloping
hunter. He would have to work on that, McCady thought.
He wanted her rocking like a baby in a cradle.

The wind pulled at his hair and whipped at his shirtsleeves. He could feel the throbbing power of the engine
vibrating through the soles in his boots, the pulsating
throb-thump, throb-thump that always seemed to him to be
mimicking the heartbeat of life. A thatched cottage was
there, out the corner of his eye, and then gone in the time it
took to blink. Running along the rails through a deep cutting in the earth, then out across an open field stubbled
with newly cut hay. Over a three-arched wooden viaduct,
looking down into a brambly gill and a trickle of silver
water. Ahead of them a hole in the face of a hill, like a
wide-open mouth, yawning bigger and bigger, like the maw
of a cannon.

I built this, McCady thought, with a sudden rush of pride. *A Trelawny has actually built something.* Something that would last.

They plunged into the tunnel, and the sudden, dense blackness after the bright light was startling. At first McCady could see nothing, and the noise of the engine sounded louder than the inside of a thunderstorm. Then his eyes picked out the glow leaking around the door of the firebox and sparks shooting out of the smokestack. The black world filled with smoke and steam and the rebounding echoes of his wife's lusty laughter.

They burst out of the darkness into sunshine. He blinked back a rush of tears that came from the suddenness of the bright light. And the sight of his darling Jessalyn with her head thrown back, still laughing.

And suddenly, in that moment, he believed. He believed that the shining light would never die in her eyes, that the passion they shared would last forever. Even if he failed today, even if he faced poverty and disgrace, he would never lose her. Always she would be his Jessalyn, his wife. He believed this, was as certain of it as he was certain of his next breath. He believed that they would have children and grow old together, living dreams and disappointments, tragedy and joy. But together, always together.

They had the rest of their lives.

Green and yellow. Jacky Stout scrambled over the hedge and ran down the incline, leaping in and out between the cover of the rocks, like a bounding hare. He paused behind the trunk of a lone hawthorn, then dashed to the railbed. Green and yellow, green and yellow—

Bleedin' hell.

Dashing like that had nearly put out his candle. He took his hat off and gently flapped the brim at the smoking wick until it flickered into a flame. He put the flame to the reed fuse. It caught with a spit and a hiss.

After whipping around, he ran at a crouch, making for

the hedge. He leaped over it and slid to the ground, his shoulders pressing against the stones, his legs thrust straight out, his big belly and chest heaving and huffing.

He peered through the crack. There it was, green and yellow, and about in line with the hawthorn tree. Four hundred and fifty paces. He started to laugh. Any second now, any second and bang. Green and yellow, green and yellow . . . Bang! Green and . . .

Something behind him. A scrape of leather on rock. His skin prickled all over as if he'd just brushed up against a wasp's nest, and he whirled, shading his eyes with his hands against the glare of the sun. He saw the black, blunted end of the spalling hammer. . . .

And then he saw nothing.

Clarence's stomach churned. He took out his watch, glanced at the time, then stuffed it back into his pocket. The *Comet* would just be hitting the tunnel right about now.

"He's a right un, is his nibs."

Clarence looked up into the hooked-nose face of the biggest woman he had ever seen in his life. At least he thought it was a woman, although her sex was open to some debate. Clarence pulled out his handkerchief and held it up to his nose. The woman reeked of onions.

"A hell-born babe, but with a soft heart underneath for all that."

Clarence drew in a careful breath through his handkerchief before he took his nose out. "I beg your pardon?"

"His nibs. Caerhays. A navvy now, he knows his woman can swing a pick good as any man. But fancy a gentleman thinkin' such a thing—cor! 'Tis rare for a nob to honor his woman like his nibs's just done, bringing her along with him to run his iron horse as if she 'twere his equal. A soft heart underneath for all that, eh?"

All the blood seemed to rush from Clarence's head, and for a moment he swayed dizzily. He gripped the woman's iron-hard forearm. "Are you telling me Lady Caerhays is on the *Comet?*"

"Ais. Right 'longside up there with him, as if she 'twere his equal. And a right pretty picture she made, too. Lookin' like a queen."

"But he couldn't have. He *couldn't* have."

The woman opened her mouth . . .

And the world exploded into a great, coughing roar.

28

He'd killed her. Oh, God, he had killed her.

Clarence Tiltwell sat in the fading light of late afternoon, behind a scarred and ink-spotted desk in his room at the Crooked Staff Inn. His eyes burned with unshed tears, and sobs kept welling in his throat. He'd open his mouth, trying to let them out, but they wouldn't come. Over and over he'd do that, open his mouth and gulp at the air, like a drowning man.

He stood up, heavy and stiff, as if his legs had turned to stone. He went to his portmanteau and took out the ivory inlaid case of French flintlock dueling pistols he always carried when traveling. A man couldn't be too careful, he thought, as he lifted one of the deadly weapons from its slot in the velvet-lined case. Not too careful, oh, no, not with highwaymen and footpads allowed to roam loose around the countryside and do their murderous deeds.

He rubbed his thumb over the pistol's engraved silver mounts. It was of a hunting scene, a man on horseback following the pack, tallyhoing as he jumped a fence. Clarence always felt a pang in his chest when he looked at the scene, for it made him think of his father. Not Tiltwell, of course. Henry had always hated hunting. No, his *father* . . . Caerhays.

He brought the pistol and its case back to the desk with him and lit the candles in the pewter branch to see better what he was doing. He stroked the smooth, cool barrel. He turned the wooden stock over in his hand and pointed the pistol at his face.

Once, when he was a boy, he had gone swimming off Crookneck Cove, and for a few horrifying moments he had been caught in the current. That day he had felt a terror as black as the bowels of hell, a terror made all the more horrible by his utter helplessness in the face of it. He had wanted to explain how it was all a mistake, that he hadn't really meant to go swimming, that he would never, ever do it again, that forever and ever he would always be a good boy if only this once, this one time, he would be spared the punishment he deserved. But the current hadn't cared about little Clarence Tiltwell. The current would have drowned him in spite of all his pleas and promises.

He thought of Jessalyn, of how he had killed her, and it was like that, as if the current had gotten him.

He closed his mouth around the muzzle.

It tasted bitter, of burned sulfur and cold metal, of death. He took the barrel out of his mouth and licked his lips, swallowed. He slowly set the pistol onto the blotter in front of him and wiped his sweating, shaking hands on his doeskin pantaloons.

He didn't know someone had come into the room until he heard the door click shut.

"Ullo, guv'nor."

His head flung up, and he stumbled to his feet. The boy Topper stepped into the light cast by the candle branch. Clarence felt his jaw sag open in shock, for the boy seemed more wraith than human. His eyes wild in a pale and skeletal face. His lips pulled tight against his teeth as if he was holding back a laugh. Or a scream.

Clarence's gaze jerked down to the boy's hands. One was wrapped in bloodstained splints and bandages, the fingers splayed and clawed like a falcon's talons. The other was thin and white, and very whole, and gripping the handle of a spalling hammer. The hammer's poll shone black and wet in the flickering light.

Topper held up his mangled hand, and Clarence's teeth sank into his lower lip, trapping back a whimper. "He did for me, your bullyboy," Topper said.

"But you—you didn't obey orders?" Clarence whined, his voice rising in the end as if in a question, as if Topper was being unreasonable not to understand that if one didn't obey orders, one was punished for it.

Topper hefted the spalling hammer as if he was about to throw it, and Clarence flinched. "Aye, well Stout did for me, so I did for him. I smashed his bleedin' head in. Now I've come to do for you."

Clarence snatched up the pistol and pointed it at the boy's chest. "I'll shoot."

Topper looked from Clarence's face to the pistol and back to his face. He seemed a little surprised but not frightened. He thought a moment, and then his mouth pulled into a smile so tight it didn't even reveal the gap in his front teeth. He shrugged his bony shoulders. "So, if not today, guv'nor, then I'll do for you tomorrow. I can wait. I've nothing better t' do, eh? Can't ride the bleeding 'orses no more, can I?"

"They'll hang you on a six-shilling gibbet, boy," Clarence said. At least he thought he said it. He felt his lips move, but he couldn't hear for the blood roaring in his ears.

Topper shrugged again. "It don't make no nevermind what's done to me. I've got the sooty warts. You heard of the sooty warts, guv'nor? The climbing boy's sickness? I'd just as soon hang tomorrow as watch me privates rot off and take a year adyin'.

"Nay, I likes it better this way," Topper said, and he stroked his own cheek with the poll of the hammer. He did it gently, like a lover's touch. "Think on this, guv'nor. I'll be out there somewheres, ready to do for you whenever the notion takes me. Tomorrow, mebbe, eh? Or the day after.

Then again, mebbe not. Ye see, I ain't got nothin' to lose, and when a bloke's got nothin' to lose, he don't care what 'appens. 'Cept fer revenge. But even revenge is cold comfort when ye're in yer grave, so it's best to draw it out real good whilst ye're alive, eh? Like it's a pleasure just lookin' at ye right now and seein' ye sweat."

Clarence licked his dry lips, and the gun in his hand trembled slightly. A part of him was contemptuous of the boy's lack of will. Another part of him wanted to sob with relief, and the bowel-loosening residue of fear. And a whole different part of him didn't care about any of it. She was dead. What did it matter, what did any of it matter, when she was dead?

Topper had to stuff the handle of the hammer through his belt in order to lift the door latch with his one good hand. He paused at the threshold, turning, and this time the smile parted his lips, revealing the missing teeth. He looked young then, like a schoolboy all set to play some prank while the master was gone from the lecture room. "Oh, by the way, guv'nor. Did ye hear the news? His lordship, the earl o' Caerhays—he came home a winner. Won it 'ands down, he did."

"*What?*" Clarence felt his heart stop. Then start up again in harsh, pounding strokes that sounded like a cannon volley going off inside his head. "But the explosion . . ."

Topper cackled a laugh. "Well, that was a surprise, that explosion. Blew a good twenty feet out o' them shiny new rails. Lucky fer his lordship he'd just gone steamin' past that bit when the bleedin' thing blew." The laughter remained on Topper's face, but his eyes dimmed, turned crafty and hard, and Clarence thought this was far worse than the madness of before. "Mebbe the iron horse was faster than you figured, guv'nor. Or mebbe your bullyboy counted his paces wrong. He always was a stupid un, was Stout. Big an' mean, but stupid."

Clarence stared at the door, watching it swing shut, hearing the latch fall into place again, but he wasn't really aware of any of this. There was this great flapping sound inside his head, as if a thousand crows were flying off at once. She lived, lived, lived. She was alive! And then, on the heels of this stunning joy, came incredible terror.

If she lived, then so did Caerhays.

He sat back behind the desk and picked up the pistol. He turned the chair around so that he could look out the window. A group of men were playing skittles in the alley between the inn and the stables. Some navvies seemed to be having a drinking contest, passing jugs around and slapping one another on the back. An old woman pushed a cart among them, and Clarence smelled roasting chestnuts on the breeze that came through the open crack in the sash. The sun was hugging the tops of the hills, turning the cornfields a burned red, the color of her hair. And glazing the iron rails of McCady's dream, turning it into a ribbon of fire. He would know, Clarence thought, he would know who was responsible for that explosion.

And he would come hotfoot here to kill him.

The sun fell behind the hills and it began to grow dark. The yard below had quieted, except for a barking dog and scullery maid drawing water from the well. And the occasional bellow of laughter coming from the open windows of the taproom below.

Clarence watched the hack come trotting along the new rails from the direction of Exeter, watched the man turn into the yard of the Crooked Staff, watched him dismount, tossing the reins and a coin at the stableboy, watched him disappear beneath the thatched eaves that sheltered the entrance to the inn.

Clarence picked up the pistol and turned the chair to face the door.

Bootheels rapped on the bare wooden floor of the hall. Clarence watched the latch depress and turn. He gripped the smooth, oily stock of pistol so tightly his fingers hurt. The door swung slowly open.

He looked into his cousin's face, his *brother's* face, and pulled the trigger.

The pistol's cock swung forward, and sparks flashed as the flint scraped the frizzen. Clarence's hand jerked, and his eyes squeezed shut in anticipation of the bang and recoil.

And nothing happened.

McCady kept coming right at him, and for a moment darkness dimmed Clarence's eyes, and he wondered if he would faint. He flinched when McCady took the gun from his hand.

His cousin looked the gun over with the critical eye of a soldier and tsked, shaking his head, admonishing Clarence as if he were a raw recruit. "Clarey, Clarey . . . Damp powder. Rust in the barrel. I'm surprised the bloody thing didn't misfire and blow your hand off."

"I swear I didn't know about her," Clarence grated out of a throat raw with fear. "I didn't know you'd taken her up with you on the *Comet.* I swear it, Mack. I swear, I didn't know. I wouldn't have seen her hurt for the world. Not the world."

McCady cocked a brow at him, but he said nothing. He hooked the leg of a wainscot chair, pulling it around so that he could sit down on the other side of the desk. Clarence watched, mesmerized, as his cousin's slender, steam-blistered hands pulled the ramrod from the pistol's recess and extracted the unfired ball and powder from the barrel.

"Mack . . ." *This is like the current at Crookneck Cove,* Clarence thought. *You explain and explain, and it doesn't do any good.* "I would never hurt Jessalyn. I love her."

"You remember, Jacky Stout, Clarey?" McCady said, and Clarence's chest tightened with renewed fear, squeezing all the breath from his lungs.

McCady took a small swatch of oiled linen from the pistol case and used the ramrod to thrust it up and down the barrel. "You and I did a bit of smuggling with him once— that time someone peached on us to the gaugers." He brushed away the burned gunpowder off the priming pan. He looked up, pinning Clarence with his fierce dark gaze. "Someone bashed poor old Jacky Stout's head in this afternoon. He lived for a while, though. Long enough to talk."

Suddenly his hand shot out, gripping Clarence by the throat. He came up out of his chair, jerking Clarence to his feet. He brought their faces so close together that Clarence could feel the heat of McCady's breath and see strange, glowing lights in his cousin's dark eyes, like tiny, flaring fires. They were the eyes of the man who had slashed and slashed with his sword until the bodies of the enemy piled up around him, and the taste in Clarence's mouth was that of the gun barrel, cold and bitter, and of death.

McCady's lips pulled back over his teeth. "You burned down her house, you bloody bastard. You had her horses nobbled, and you crimped her races. You *hurt* her."

"I only wanted her to marry me. I would have been good to her. I could have made her happy."

McCady opened his fist and let Clarence fall. Clarence's rump hit the edge of the chair, and he had to grip the desk to keep from falling. "You will resign your seat in Parliament," McCady said.

Clarence licked his lips. His mouth was so parched he couldn't swallow. "You have no proof. No real proof."

"I don't need proof. I have influence." McCady took the powder flask from the pistol case and primed the pan. "You understand influence, Clarey, how it works? I know your patron, Lord Arbrury. Close we are, Lord Arbrury and I. Bosom bows." He tapped more of the black powder down the barrel and compressed it with the ramrod. "His only son and I fought on the Peninsula together, and he has this quaint notion that I once saved the boy's life. A nasty word in his ear about you from me, and you could run for cowherd in the poorest borough in Wales and lose." He wrapped a small linen patch around a lead ball and rammed it down on top of the powder.

He looked up again, and Clarence saw no mercy in his

eyes. "When I am through with you and your reputation, Clarey, my man, there won't be a club or residence in all of London that won't be denying you the door. No more invitations to Lord So-and-So's rout. No more house parties at the duke of So-and-So's Somerset estate. I am going to take away everything you have ever wanted in this life, Clarey, and then leave you alive to live without it."

It was too much for Clarence; he couldn't take it all in. He knew it was terrible, this punishment that McCady was promising him, but he could focus on only one horror right now. "Please don't tell Jessalyn what I did. Please, don't tell her."

"She already knows. She knows it all. And she never wants to see you again, Clarey. Ever."

A great hollowness pressed down on Clarence's chest. He looked out the window. The dog had stopped barking; the scullery maid was gone. He felt empty inside, a vast emptiness like a great barren desert. He really had lost her, for good. Forever. He wondered how he was going to stand it. "But I love her," he said.

He saw McCady move out the corner of his eye, and he turned his head.

The pistol came up until it was pointing between Clarence's eyes. The muzzle seemed enormous, the maw of hell. And McCady's words seemed to come shooting out of the bore, killing him. "She is *mine*, Tiltwell. Learn to live with it."

McCady's finger tightened on the trigger.

To Clarence's bitter shame he felt himself begin to tremble like an old man with the ague. Hot tears filled his eyes and started splattering onto his cheeks. He squeezed his lids shut and waited, waited . . . and made a spastic little jerk when he heard the click of the falling door latch. He opened his eyes; McCady had gone. He looked down. The gun sat on the blotter in front of him. Loaded and ready to fire.

McCady paused at the top of the stairs, his hand resting

lightly on the newel-post. He waited a few moments, waited for the sound of a shot, but it didn't come. And that, he thought, answered one question at least.

A Trelawny would have pulled the trigger.

It took him awhile to find her, and in those moments an irrational panic squeezed his chest that he might never find her again.

He had seen Clarey's face when the man had at last comprehended that Jessalyn was lost to him forever. McCady understood well that kind of hell. He had to find her now and reassure himself that she was still his.

He came upon her standing on top of a small rise a few hundred yards down the road, past the navvies' turf huts and flickering campfires. He could barely see her in the deepening twilight. She stood with her feet spread apart, her hands loose at her sides, and she was looking down into the cutting below, where the iron rails lay like a great seam across the freshly scarred earth. His boot disturbed a stone. She turned, and her face broke into a dazzling smile that stopped his heart.

He wanted her.

He wanted her with a fierce hunger that made him tremble, as if he had not had a woman in years. But it was *she* he wanted. Not just any woman, not the most beautiful woman in the world. He wanted her, with her raucous, lusty laugh and her sunbeam smile, with her long legs and bony knees. He wanted to hear the little breath-catching sighs she made when he entered her and feel her hair sliding across his naked belly. He wanted Jessalyn, his Jessa. And what made his happiness complete, what made him want to whoop and shout and laugh aloud, was that he knew, he *knew* she wanted him in just the same way.

He thought that he should say all these things to her, that it was important she understand, but he couldn't find the words. They piled up in his throat and got stuck there, so instead he crushed her against him and spoke with his kiss. A kiss that quickly turned so raw and hot that he had to break away.

"McCady!" she gasped, straightening her straw hat, which he had knocked askew. Her bosom trembled with her panting breaths, and she licked her lips. He wanted to kiss her again, but there was something he had to tell her first.

"Jessa—"

"I'm glad you've come, for I've been thinking," she said, her voice bright with excitement and happiness. She slipped her hand into his and turned so that they looked together down the rock and gorse-tufted hillside. "What do you see?"

He shook his head. He had eyes only for her. "I don't know; it's rather dark. Rocks and grass, some trees." She emitted a soft snort of exasperation, and he laughed. "All right, I see a railway. My railway."

Her grip tightened on his hand, and she brought it up to cradle against her breasts. He looked at her face, at the sharp curve of a cheekbone, at the full swell of her lips. Awe filled his heart at the thought that she was his, awe and a sweet ache.

"Don't you understand?" she said, her face vivid. "Even if they had managed to stop you, they could not have stopped *it*, the idea of it. You had gone too far, taken the idea too far. This"—her hand flashed in the darkness—"this is going to change the world. It is the future."

She turned her face, and her gaze captured his, pure and deep, like a hidden spring. "And this is our future." Slowly she moved his hand down her body until it was pressing low against her belly. She gave a sudden, gurgling laugh and leaned into him to rub her cheek against his chest, still clutching his hand. "We're going to have a baby, McCady."

The breath eased out of him in a great sigh, and tears of piercing joy stung his eyes. "God."

Her laughter, rusty and squeaking like a old pump handle, filled the night. "Well, yes, He did have something to do with it. But so did you, my love."

My love.

She had never called him that before. A warmth, a sweet and gentle warmth, enveloped him. He wanted her to know something, he had to tell her that . . . He tried for the words, but his tongue felt stiff as old leather. "Jessa, I . . ."

She looked up at him, smiling, expectant, and dammit, he couldn't get his throat to work. She cupped his cheek with her soft hand. "Silly goose. Are those flowers that you're crushing in your fist for me?"

He had spotted them growing along the top of a hedge while he'd been searching for her and on impulse he'd picked them. They were primroses of the pale yellow color that always made him think of her and of that long-ago summer. He handed them to her now, feeling slightly foolish.

And then he felt inordinately pleased with himself when her mouth broke into a wide smile of pure delight. She buried her face in the starred yellow blossoms, breathing in their scent. She lifted her head, and he thought she would smile again when her face quickened with excitement and she pointed toward the village behind him. "Oh, look, McCady! Look at the moon."

It rose over the tops of the distant trees, a great golden ball in the deep velvet purple of late twilight. Like a ripe, juicy peach ready to be plucked out of the sky.

She breathed a soft sigh and leaned into him, her head falling on his shoulder. "Is it a blue moon, do you think?"

"I don't know," he said, his throat full. To him it didn't matter. Since that night he'd made her his wife, all his moons had been blue. Rare and special and filled with . . .

"Jessalyn, I . . ." God, why were the words so hard to say? He lived for her. She was his hope of paradise and in a way his glimpse of hell. The hell that he would suffer should he ever lose her. And this he understood at last was . . .

"Love. I love you, Jessalyn."

Author's Note

McCady Trelawny is, alas, only a figment of my imagination, although it is certainly within the realm of historical possibility that he *could* have lived to invent his steam-powered locomotive and to build his railway.

In 1804 a Cornishman by the name of Richard Trevithick made the first steam locomotive to run on rails, and as early as 1801 Parliament had already passed an act establishing the principle of a public railway. But as with any radical innovation, there was considerable skepticism that a steam-powered engine could ever replace the stagecoach and horse, and investors were hard to come by. The first public railway in England, which ran from Manchester to Liverpool, did not in fact exist until 1830. In the fall of 1829 the Raintree Trials were held on a portion of that line to determine who would win the right to supply the locomotives for the railway. A steam locomotive called *The Rocket* won the trials. It was designed by George Stephenson and his son Robert Stephenson, who became instant millionaires from the profits of their invention. Within only ten years after the Raintree Trials, railways were crisscrossing the island of Britain and steam-powered locomotives had indeed changed the world.